Remaining in Provincetown

Provincetown

A Novel

By S. N. Cook

An imprint of Truro Works
2981 Solomons Island Road
Edgewater, MD 21037

Designed by Sarita Design
Type set in Sabon

Cook, S. N.
Remaining in Provincetown
ISBN-10: 0615773427
SBN-13: 978-0615773421 (Truro Works)

Provincetown is like a Latin lover.
You know he's cheating on you
But you keep coming back for more.

—an old proverb

Acknowledgements

Without the support and encouragement of family, friends, and colleagues, who read various versions, this novel would not have been completed. Thank you for your help, (you know who you are), because an author never works completely in a vacuum.

Part of the thrill for me of being a writer are those moments when I am able to successfully crystallize ideas into words on a page. The other thrill is when someone else reads those words and lets me know they were enjoyed. Thus I ask that if you like this book, please tell your friends to read it too. You can also visit my website, www.remainingin-provincetown.com and leave your comments.

Remaining in Provincetown is a work of fiction, set in approximately 1990. While the names of some of the places and organizations are real, they are being used fictiously. Names, characters, and incidents are the product of my own imagination and any resemblance to actual persons, living or dead, events, or locales is entirely coincidental.

—S.N. Cook

Remaining in Provincetown

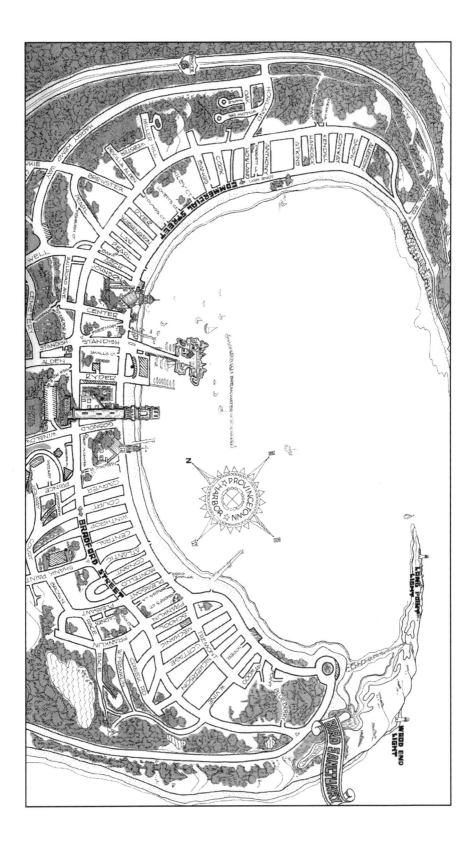

Prologue

Sonny Carreiro gently leafed through the stack of antique postcards inside the small metal box. Considering their age and value, they belonged in separate plastic sleeves. But what had the old gent sitting there said?...something about finding them stashed in the attic and wanting to sell them to someone who "appreciated them." Did that mean the man expected to get a lot of money?

"Joseph Holland told me you collect postcards," he had told Sonny on the phone. "I have a few very old ones of Provincetown you might be interested in."

Joe Holland was an amateur flea marketer who had a booth at the Wellfleet drive-in during the summer months, selling used books and old bottles. A while back he'd sold Sonny a few cards found inside an old book. Probably Joe put ideas in this old fellow's head about high prices being paid for antique postcards and told him about Sonny Carreiro, who owned lots of real estate plus an insurance agency, making Carreiro a very wealthy man.

Sonny did not want to pay list price for the cards. He'd only pay the "dealer's" price or less. Good businessmen made money when they *bought* something, not when they sold it.

Sonny began talking as he laid each card on the table, one by one. Silence made him uncomfortable and he didn't like the sensation of being watched as he picked up and examined each card. Besides, Sonny had always liked hearing the sound of his own voice. "Back in the days when I had an antiques business, I'd travel part of the winter," he told the old man. "I'd go to lots of different places...North Carolina, Maryland, Florida...places that are warmer than here. Sometimes we'd do a mall show. Oh, I didn't like mall shows, and my wife, Sarah, hated them even more. Long hours, ten in the morning until ten at night, and that awful Muzak would be playing all day long. Monotonous!"

"I used to work for the railroad," the old man said while leaning back in his seat. "We worked real long hours."

Sonny Carreiro cleared his throat and continued his story. "No real serious customers...but the buying was good. Everyone wanted to sell you something, and many people didn't know what they had. So we did the shows to buy."

The old fellow interrupted. "Ever see that antiques show on television...the one where they tell you how much your antiques are worth? It's really fascinating."

"Sometimes I watch it," Sonny replied. "But you realize they only select a few choice items to film out of all the stuff brought in there...."

"Anyway, as I was saying, silver was high then, silver and gold. We were paying scrap prices plus a little more if it looked like something good. A young woman came to our booth with a bracelet to sell. Sarah felt sorry for her. Even though the bracelet was unmarked and the clasp was broken, she wrote her a check for the value of the bracelet as if it was fourteen-carat gold.

"I was angry. 'Why did you do that?' I asked her. 'You overpaid for that piece...by as much as fifty percent!'

"Well, not more than five minutes went by and the young woman was back. She handed us the check and wanted her bracelet, insisting that we hadn't paid her enough. I was happy. I handed her the bracelet while taking the check, and I ripped it up right in front of her.

"Ten minutes later, she was back again. 'I've changed my mind. I would like to sell you my bracelet.' You see, her boyfriend had told her that another dealer was paying more for gold than we were...only it turned out they were paying less. 'Sorry. You had your chance,' we told her. She stormed away in tears, angry at us and angry at her boyfriend. Greedy. She was just plain greedy, so she got nothing."

It was a good story, one of those Sonny liked to tell when he was in the throes of a negotiation. It had the obvious message: If you keep wanting more than your fair share, often you end up with nothing at all. It applied to all kinds of things, like stocks, real estate, antiques, even personal relationships.

He turned to face the old man, expecting some kind of reaction. The man smiled and nodded his head. "It's amazing what they sell at those malls nowadays."

Sonny was a bit perturbed that he'd gotten no direct response to his storytelling. He studied the old man's face, trying to speculate as to whether he was going senile. Senility could be an advantage or a disadvantage.

Now…what was this fellow's name? Sonny struggled to remember. It had been a long day and he was terrible with names. That's why as a salesman he had resorted to calling customers "Sport" and "Buddy." Faces he remembered, but names….

He watched the man's hands as he attempted to lift one of the old postcards off his dining room table without bending a corner. They had a slight tremble. Was it nervousness or old age? Perhaps it was Parkinson's disease. Sonny had noticed a slight shake to the head when the fellow had first let him in the door…. What was his name? Something formal sounding. Thomas. William. Frederick…that was it! Frederick Marsh. Marsh managed to pick up a postcard from the table. He tried to keep his hands from trembling as he made an attempt to read what was written on the back. It had been a long time ago, when the cost of sending a postcard had been a mere penny, just one cent, and the picture on the front was a pretty one. It showed Provincetown back in the old days when the streets were dirt, and instead of a sidewalk you walked along a wooden boardwalk.

Frederick Marsh figured ten dollars for a rare card in mint condition wasn't too much to ask. He'd heard Sonny Carreiro was an avid collector, somewhat of a fanatic about wanting to own an example of every Provincetown postcard ever made. But he'd also heard that Carreiro was a sharp businessman, shrewd and tough. He had twenty-two cards to sell and wanted two hundred and twenty dollars in cash…but perhaps he should ask for more. Didn't dealers always offer less than you want?

The man standing in front of him was handsome and well dressed. He looked about forty years old. What Frederick wouldn't give to be forty again, young and spry, able to clearly hear and see. It was always so embarrassing to ask people to speak louder, and hearing aids had all that background noise.

Even though Frederick's eyes were partially covered with cataracts, he could see Sonny had a sparkling vibrancy about him and seemed the kind of young man who could tell a good story. Too bad he couldn't hear everything Sonny had been mumbling about...something about buying gold in a mall. Carreiro...the name was Portuguese, and this young fellow had the dark hair and golden-olive skin to go with the ethnicity. Not that all Portuguese were olive skinned, but didn't the old Yankees used to call them niggers? Most of the old families, the original ones like Marsh's own, had moved out of Provincetown to other towns further Up Cape. The Portuguese had taken over most of the Lower Cape businesses. Now the Portuguese were being pushed out by the gay crowd. Whiffentafts. That's what his late wife called those gay blokes...a bunch of whiffentafts.

Sonny pulled a roll of twenty-dollar bills out of his right pocket and laid five on the table. "I'll give you one hundred dollars cash for the lot, Mr. Marsh."

"Gee, son, I don't know," replied Frederick while scratching his head. "Joseph Holland told me postcards like these usually sell for ten and fifteen dollars apiece."

"Maybe people mark them that high, but they don't actually sell them at those prices. A dealer needs to make money. Auction houses take twenty percent and there's a record of the transaction. I'm offering you cash, right here and now," Sonny said in a strong, persuasive tone of voice.

"How about two hundred dollars. I really think they're worth that much," said Frederick, trying to speak as firmly as he could. "And if you can't pay a decent price... it's not as though they're taking up room in my house."

"One hundred and fifty dollars. That's my final offer, and it's really too much. But I'm willing to pay it because there's one card that I don't currently have in my collection."

"And which one is that?" asked Frederick, curious to know.

"Oh, the one of the town crier with the long, stringy mustache. I haven't seen him before," Sonny said offhandedly. "Besides, you realize I'll probably be donating the whole collection to a museum or historical society, so these cards will be going to a good home."

"Okay, okay," Frederick replied, suddenly growing weary of the whole bargaining business. Probably there was something good to watch on TV, although he'd already missed most of the evening news programs. After all, the postcards had cost him nothing. Whatever he got, he got. It was only money.

Sonny counted out two more twenty-dollar bills and pulled a ten-dollar bill from his left pocket.

"I guess you don't want a receipt," Frederick said, relieved the whole transaction was over and done with.

Sonny smiled and shook his head. "That won't be necessary."

The half a dozen postcards of the Race Point Life Saving Station, those were the cards Sonny was really interested in. They were hard to find and easily worth fifteen to twenty dollars apiece. The ones he already had could always be traded or sold to other collectors.

Sonny chuckled to himself as he backed his black Bimmer out of Frederick Marsh's narrow driveway. He couldn't wait to get home and compare these cards with what was already in his collection.

He fiddled with the radio knob, trying to find a good station, but gave up and instead inserted a CD with one of his favorites, Pachelbel's "Canon in D." Although he generally listened to jazz, this was a baroque music moment…he was feeling the rush of having just completed a favorable deal.

If only there was someone to share it with. Even if she hadn't left, Sarah just wasn't into postcards. But Stephanie, his younger daughter, liked them. A lump formed in his throat. Soon. Soon. He would be seeing them all very soon: Sarah, Cassie, and Stephanie. His eyes began to well with tears so he reached for his sunglasses, even though it was now dusk.

No one was going to see him this time of the evening, he told himself. You don't need sunglasses. Just keep driving and you'll be home soon. Everything was going to be okay. In a few days, they would once again be together as a family.

He pulled into his driveway, lined on each side with a white picket fence. The *Cape Cod Times* was lying on the front walkway. Why couldn't the paper boy throw it by the side kitchen door like he had asked?

Wearily, Sonny got out of his car and walked towards the front of his home to retrieve the newspaper. Suddenly his whole mood had changed from elation to depression. In an attempt to bring back his previous high spirits, he pulled the packet of postcards out of his inside jacket pocket and examined the one on top as he walked. It was a card with a beach scene, postmarked 1913. Two women in old-fashioned bathing suits were standing ankle-deep in the waves. Scribbled across the back in black ink was: "Dear Jack, I wanted to tell you...."

Bang. A loud sound rang through his ears and reverberated through the back of his skull. The sharp burning that began in the back of his head then moved forward and into his right eye. Dizziness began to overtake him as felt the urge to close his eyes and start to dream. Perhaps it would be a happy dream, one in which he would see his wife and the girls.

Sonny Carreiro hit the ground with a thud and lost consciousness.

1

Early Sunday Evening

Roz Silva Fidgeted in front of her computer screen. Her fingers moved skillfully as she began to type on the plastic keyboard, but her body was swaying back and forth in her chair. She could type without looking at the letters beneath her fingers, allowing her to focus on the screen that was to contain this week's editorial. But there was one problem: she had no idea what to write about. So far, all that appeared in front of her was the subheading "Editorial" and the headline "Our Say."

Who should she bash? What should she criticize? Nothing particularly scandalous was happening in town this week, a rare exception. No town official had been charged with shirking on the job or accepting bribes. No one was resigning. No one important had died. No issue about individuals' rights had been raised. The opposing interests of the gay and straight residents of this small town on the tip of Cape Cod, which Roz called home, had not catalyzed into any political issue that was particularly newsworthy.

The lead story read, "Gilligan announces candidacy: First-time run for Board of Selectmen." She could write something pretty spicy about Sean Gilligan, one of the S&M guys and successful owner of a dance bar in town called the Cowboy Club. He'd probably been charged once or twice for contributing to the delinquency of a minor before moving to town eleven years earlier. But did any of the charges stick?

She'd see Sean around town with his young "houseboys," the young boys who worked in gay guesthouses changing beds, doing laundry, and cleaning in exchange for room, board, and a small salary. Where did his houseboys sleep? What exchange of services did he require? Did he tie them up? Wear a mask? These were all suppositions. Her suppositions. Her prejudices. Roz had no tolerance for those into leather restraints, whips, chains...people who got off on inflicting pain.

"Beau Costa charged with bank fraud." That newspaper sold a lot of copies. Circulation probably increased that week by at least ten percent. "Business partner accuses Costa of lying on financial statements submitted to bank."

Yes, Beau Costa, a prominent businessman and Provincetown native, had been accused of falsifying financial statements. No matter that Beau was never indicted and was subsequently cleared of any charges. No matter that the accusations were the result of a soured business deal. That was not Roz's concern. She merely published what Sonny Carreiro claimed took place. And the fact that he had filed charges with the attorney general and written a seething letter to the president of Provincetown Savings Bank made the story real.

It also happened to be a coincidental fact that she, the powerful and quite attractive Roz, short for Rosalyn, had been rejected by Beau two years earlier. She had never forgiven him. Well, she had put him in his place. And now she had a better lover, much better and more powerful: the town manager.

It was her relationship with John Murphy, the new town manager, that made her hold back on immediately casting aspersions on Sean Gilligan as a candidate for selectman. It was better to wait and see who was running against him, then narrow down the field. John probably had his opinion on who he'd prefer taking his orders from, and to her, his confidante, he would make his opinions perfectly clear. The selectmen set town policy, and the town manager was their employee. But the town manager had a certain power, on a day-to-day basis, over the issues he chose to more thoroughly investigate and bring up to the board. It was a strange form of government because no one person was in charge and the selectmen were always bickering amongst themselves. But hey, this was Provincetown, a community of strong-minded, individualistic nonconformists.

Political viewpoints that might be considered liberal or moderate in other communities were considered conservative here. Being part of a traditional, nuclear family was the exception, not the rule. In some extreme circles of the gay community, straights were referred to as breeders. But who were the real breeders when there were so many variations in between, like single mothers, single fathers, some who had become gay or bisexual, as well as gay couples who had adopted children? Not to mention the variety of group relationships: ménage à trois arrangements between three men, three women, two women and one man, two men and one woman. So there were families, just different kinds of families.

And there was the variety of professions: restaurateurs, innkeepers, artists, poets, trash collectors, contractors, plumbers, electricians, chambermaids, real estate agents, marine biologists, teachers…and, yes, a few lobstermen and fishermen keeping alive a shrinking commercial fishing industry. There were plenty of whale-watching vessels, as well as the complement of charter fishing boats and sightseeing boats. Whatever their disagreements, members of the Provincetown community were united in their love of the sea and sand dunes, along with the winding, narrow streets and nineteenth-century architecture that dominated this small New England town.

The shrill ring of the telephone brought Roz's mind back into focus. She grabbed for the receiver, knowing full well who was calling.

"Roz?" asked the deep, resonant voice.

"Yes, John," she answered.

"Liz is off to a special PTA meeting at the school and I told her I had some work to do at the office to get ready for the Board of Selectmen's meeting tomorrow night. Is the coast clear at your house?"

"No, actually it isn't. Sally is home working on a term paper. You'll have to come by my office."

"Okay, I'll be there in twenty minutes."

"See you soon then," she responded.

Making love in her office to a married man…that was pretty racy. But it had all begun innocently enough. When John Murphy had first arrived in town, Roz had interviewed him for the newspaper herself, eager to scoop the Up Cape dailies. She liked him immediately. Roz liked to rely on first impressions.

Although he was not obviously flirting with her, there was something about the way his eyes met hers as they talked that she found intriguing. Later on, his face kept popping up in her mind. Maybe he was thinking about her, too. He had an open, pleasant face and a clean-cut appearance. Roz began to wonder what John was like in bed.

Aware that his wife and two children, who were still living in West-field, Connecticut, would be joining him in Provincetown at the end of spring term, she began to speculate on how happily married he really was. He had told his wife that he didn't want to move them in the middle of the school year, but maybe that had been an excuse for him to take some time out for himself.

When Roz wasn't engaged in something specific, John's face, with those big brown eyes, kept drifting into her mind. It was an infatuation, a crush. Yet she couldn't help herself. She started finding reasons to call him, like to get his opinion on stories and editorial pieces that she or a staff member might be working on. They'd meet for coffee or lunch. Just an innocent friendship, Roz would tell herself. Perfectly normal. Just two professional people with a lot in common. We're both lonely and just enjoying each other's company.

Then one Friday evening after work, they met for a drink. A live band was playing.

"Would you like to dance?" John had asked her.

"Why not?" Roz had answered.

As they stepped out onto the dance floor, all the reasons for "why not" became plainly obvious. Their eyes locked into each other's gaze, and they couldn't stop smiling because they were having so much fun. So it seemed perfectly harmless when he took her arm, swung her around, and ended the dance with a hug and a kiss. They were just friends, weren't they?

But electricity was passing between them, a spark that had ignited and had taken on a life of its own, and then both she and John lost all sense of reason. They went back that night to his apartment, made wild, passionate love, and told each other it would never happen again. But it did.

John walked quickly, first to town hall to turn on the light in his office so that if anyone asked what he had been doing on that particular evening, he had been working. The *Provincetown Observer* was located only a few short blocks away. Briefcase in hand, he hoped few people were on the street, and he tried to walk with an air of authority to give the impression he was going somewhere on business, not to a clandestine meeting with his mistress. Mistress...that was a strange word. But what was he to call this woman he had fallen in love with while still loving his wife?

He was well aware that, according to society's standards, he was doing something wrong: committing adultery. But it felt so good, how could it be wrong? He was still a good husband and father. In no way did he feel he was neglecting his wife. They had an amicable relationship and still occasionally made love. They talked about the day-to-day running of the household, the kids, his work. But now he had something more. A freshness had entered his life, an excitement that made him feel twenty-two instead of forty-two. As long as he could keep his extramarital relationship a secret, all would be fine.

Bruno Marchessi chuckled to himself as he saw John Murphy walking down the street with his briefcase, a serious look on his face, trying to appear self-absorbed. Everyone familiar with town politics knew what was going on: John Murphy was having an affair with Roz Silva. Hell, maybe his wife didn't know, but probably because she didn't want to know. It had to be the case; otherwise, Roz would have been tearing him to bits in her editorials like she did with anyone else who was active in the political scene.

Not that he blamed Roz for sleeping with the guy. He was a good-looking, intelligent individual. A little over six feet in height, nice and tall, the way Bruno liked his men. If John had been twenty-five years younger and gay, Bruno would be pursuing him, too. After all, life had been tough for Roz and you take your pleasure where you can. Three years earlier, her husband had dropped dead of a heart attack. With two teenage girls to raise, she had been forced to shoulder the responsibility of publishing the town's only newspaper and continuing to turn a profit.

The summer months were easy. With so many flourishing restaurants, motels, guesthouses, B&Bs, and retail stores, everyone bought ads. But after the fall months were over and the weather grew cold, the town gradually became empty and many businesses could not afford to pay their bills. If the summer accounts were still not paid up, they were difficult to collect on. It took organization and planning to keep a newspaper going. Reducing the number of pages and lowering winter advertising rates was not enough. Revenue from the summer needed to support the paper during the lean months.

The same applied to most of Provincetown's businesses. Bruno needed to generate the majority of income from his guesthouse during the summer. Yes, there were visitors in the spring and fall, even over the Christmas holidays. But January, February, and March were bleak, and many residents headed to Florida or other warm places during these months.

Now that it was early spring, the reservations were starting to come in. Bruno was pleased. It looked like it was going to be a good season. There was only one problem: his septic system was old, and it was only a matter of time before the system would completely fail.

Provincetown had no central sewer system. Every home, motel, apartment building, store, and restaurant had its own septic system. And, according to Massachusetts state law, it had to be a Title V septic system if any expansion or new construction was to be done. If an existing system failed, it needed to be upgraded to Title V or the building would eventually be closed down. The problem with Title V was you needed land. Many of the lots in Provincetown were small, and oftentimes if they were located on the waterside there was no room for a proper system. Or if one could be built, it was very expensive. A simple Title V might cost ten thousand dollars for installation and landscaping. An expensive one, for a guesthouse or restaurant, might cost anywhere from thirty to fifty thousand dollars. Bruno didn't have that kind of money, so he kept nursing his old system along.

It meant he had to drive Up Cape to Orleans to have the guesthouse laundry done professionally…and pouring Aidox, an enzyme that eats up solids in the system, into the septic tank each month to help keep the water level low. You weren't supposed to pour any chemicals into your septic system, but everybody did it. At the end of last summer, Bruno had paid a couple of guys from Wellfleet to come at six in the morning and shovel out some of the sludge from the sides while they pumped out the cesspool. He had gotten their names from Charlie Mackin, his handyman.

"Don't you dare tell anyone where you got them from," cautioned Charlie. "This is strictly between you and me. Do you understand?"

"Don't worry," Bruno assured him. "I won't tell a soul."

Bruno had waited until his neighbor, Aida Clementine, left town on her annual post-Labor Day weekend trip to Bar Harbor, Maine, with her friend to celebrate the end of summer season. He didn't want Aida snooping around because she would almost certainly call the Board of Health, as she'd done in August two years ago when his system had overflowed. Did Aida call him so he could immediately contact the cesspool pumper? No! Instead, she called the Health Department.

"Four strikes and you're out, and then we'll have to shut you down," they explained. "If you pump more than four times during the year, your system has failed. And under no circumstances are you to let the system get to the point where it overflows. You're creating a health hazard!"

In order to build a new system, Bruno needed money, lots of money, which he didn't have. Right now the guesthouse was generating enough income so that he could comfortably pay the mortgage and have just enough to live on and take a few vacations. Whether the bank would lend him more money was questionable, and at commercial lending rates the money just wasn't worth it. He might as well give up his dream and sell the building, if he could even find a buyer.

"Bruno," hailed Frank Chambers. "Care to join me for a cup of coffee or are you on the way to a meeting?"

Bruno was a member of the Art Commission, the Parking Needs Study Committee, and on the board of the Provincetown Library, but tonight there were no meetings. "Sure. Why not?" he responded. "I just completed some heavy-duty bookkeeping and I decided to go out for a walk to clear my head. You know, get some fresh air. So how's your love life? Any new men on the horizon? Say, isn't the restaurant supposed to be open this evening?"

Frank ignored the first question and then raised his eyebrows and flipped the palms of his hands up towards the sky, gesturing there were certain circumstances over which he had no control. "Unfortunately, I'm without a waiter and a prep chef. Both sick. So I thought it would be best to just shut down. Everything should be back to normal by the end of the week. Otherwise, I'll have to bring in some substitutes."

Frank Chambers had opened his restaurant, Indigo Inn, two years earlier on the west end of town in a small building where many previous restaurants had failed. But his was quite successful. He kept his menu small, to cut down on overhead costs, but changed it from week to week. In a short time, he had developed a reputation for innovative, creative cuisine. His menu read like an international cookbook: hot gazpacho bean soup, orzo and black bean salad with cilantro, mahi-mahi with fresh pineapple salsa and lime, couscous with Mediterranean meatballs, and pan-fried soft-shell crabs flown in from Maryland's Chesapeake Bay with homemade tartar sauce. And his desserts were notorious for being delicious and unusual. Bruno loved his lemon-rhubarb pie, while many people swore by his Mexican mocha cake, filled with a coffee-flavored custard and covered with rich chocolate frosting.

Bruno was half tempted to suggest that they take a walk back to Frank's restaurant so he could have a piece of lemon-rhubarb pie with his coffee, if there was any left over from the previous evening. He could almost smell the flaky, buttery crust and the tangy fruit filling just thinking about it. But he knew Frank wanted a change of scenery, plus restaurateurs were notorious for wanting to spy on their competitors. If they had an evening off, did any of them settle down into a quiet meal at home? No, they went out to dinner at someone else's restaurant.

"How about a walk up to Mitzi's," Frank suggested. "I need the exercise. I've been eating too much of my own good cooking."

Bruno smiled. "That's fine."

Mitzi's was a small coffee shop specializing in various kinds of coffee concoctions: cappuccino, espresso, and café au lait, along with good muffins, scones, and cookies. They didn't serve pie, but their cookies were pretty good, especially the granola almond chocolate chip ones.

The two friends walking down the street made for an interesting contrast. Frank…tall, angular, fair skinned, and just approaching middle age; Bruno…swarthy, robust, and well ensconced in what he liked to call "the productive years." Bruno's salt-and-pepper hair fell into close-cropped, tight curls, and the lower part of his face was covered with a thick, impeccably groomed mustache and beard. Frank was clean-shaven with pale gray eyes and a slender, slightly upturned nose covered with a light sprinkling of freckles. Bruno's eyes were dark brown and his nose large and broad.

"Otherwise," said Frank, "until today, things at the restaurant have been going along just fine for early spring. I need to see how many of the old wait staff are coming back and I need a new assistant chef. I can pretty much manage the kitchen by myself right now so it's just a skeleton staff running the place."

Mitzi's was located on the east end of town, about a fifteen-minute walk from the center. Behind it, on the waterside of Commercial Street, was a string of condominium units, soaking up the bay view. What Mitzi's offered, besides good coffee and snacks, was a view of the street. A half a dozen small tables were located on the small patio in the front. In warm weather, one could sit out and watch the parade of locals and tourists walking, bicycling, and driving by.

Mitzi's was out of granola almond chocolate chip cookies. Bruno had to settle for a walnut-raisin-carrot muffin with cream cheese icing.

"I'll have a tall skinny cappuccino," requested Frank.

"Hey, have you gotten a call yet from my friends, Bud and Charles?" he asked Bruno. "They're coming out for a visit over the Fourth of July and I just don't have the room to put them up at my place, so I recommended they call you."

"No, I haven't heard from them yet but I appreciate the recommendation. Actually, they might have called today and I didn't pick up the message.... What a pleasure to get out after focusing on my tax returns," Bruno spoke aloud to his friend.

"You don't do them yourself?" Frank asked incredulously.

"No, but I have to make sure I've got all the information and the receipts in order. The one beauty of owning a guesthouse and living there is that almost everything is deductible. I serve breakfast, so I can deduct groceries. Who knows whether I'm eating breakfast or whether I use part of the breakfast supplies for my lunch? Heat, electricity, and landscaping are all innkeeping expenses. A small percentage isn't deducted because it's considered for my personal use, but everything else counts. I have to keep track of my expenditures, organize receipts... you know how it is."

"The great fun for me," said Frank, "is I can deduct trips to go visit food suppliers, wineries, and the like. All my trips Up Cape and to Boston are a deduction, because as far as the IRS is concerned I'm buying supplies. Have you ever been audited?"

"No, thank goodness," replied Bruno. "That's why I use a CPA, so they can check that everything looks somewhat in line. And they know what will raise a red flag."

The walls of Mitzi's were paneled with faded barn board. On top of the panels hung watercolors of the woods, town, sea, and sand dunes painted by local artists. The furnishings consisted of a mismatched assortment of acquisitions from various yard sales and auctions. Most of the tables were heavily varnished wood, while the chairs had all been painted bright primary colors. Looking into the room, it appeared that some of the chairs were slightly crooked, and the tables didn't all sit flat on the floor. Since the town rested on a spit of sand, most of the buildings had a slight slant. Inside houses and apartments, this could be compensated for by putting small pieces of wood under pieces of furniture or installing floors that slanted slightly in the opposite direction.

This evening, to his delight, Bruno was sitting in a fairly comfortable chair that fully supported his back and weight. Many of the chairs at Mitzi's he found to be uncomfortable. They are not designed for people with some "meat on their bones," he would say to himself. A man who enjoyed good food, Bruno had some extra weight around his middle, which he considered to be okay. "It's not good to be too thin," he would tell his friends. "What happens if you get sick?" Of course, in the back of his mind he was thinking about HIV and several of his friends who, in the past several years, he'd seen wasting away. Extra weight was good, even though now they had better drugs to counteract the virus's effects. Not that he wanted to think about AIDS.

Bruno leaned back to savor the muffin he had just bitten into and took a sip of his coffee. He preferred the house brand, black. None of this fancy cream and flavored stuff for him with names like Misty Irish Cream and Hazelnut Supreme.

The phone rang behind the counter and Bruno could then hear Mitzi talking, in her deep, brassy voice, to the person on the other end of the line. He wondered who would be calling Mitzi at this time of the evening. It was getting near closing time, so it probably wasn't a customer calling to place a take-out order. Did Mitzi have any kind of social life? She wasn't very attractive, but who knew what some of these dykes were into. They certainly did not pride themselves on their looks.

Pushing fifty, Mitzi came to work each day in an oversized white T-shirt and dark, baggy pants. Over her clothes she donned a large, white bib apron, which she double tied around her waist as protection from inevitable flour dustings, grease, and coffee stains. Her salt-and-pepper hair was clipped short, and her face was pale and pasty from years of working indoors for long hours.

"What? I don't believe it!" Mitzi said to the person on the other end of the line. "Are you sure?"

Bruno strained his ears to try and listen to the conversation. All he could hear were little bits and pieces.

"Here in Provincetown...whoa!" Mitzi plopped herself down on the tall stool she kept for herself behind the counter, and with the back of her hand attempted to wipe the perspiration off her brow. Suddenly she was feeling both hot and damp. "When did it happen?...Do they know who did it?..."

Although he couldn't quite make out what she was talking about, Bruno had a feeling it was something important. As soon as Mitzi hung up, he was going to ask her who she was talking to, even if it might give her the impression he was being nosy.

Bruno didn't have to be nosy. Mitzi was anxious to share the news and get someone else's reaction. After taking a few moments to collect her thoughts, Mitzi ambled her large frame over to Frank and Bruno's table, pulled up a chair, and sat down. The place was now empty except for the three of them sitting around a table in the center of the room.

"Sonny Carreiro has been killed," she told them in a hushed tone, as though the murderer might just be lurking outside the door, trying to eavesdrop on their conversation. "Shot in the head, right in front of his home. My friend Francine just called me. She heard the call on her twelve-band radio. So far it doesn't sound as if there are any witnesses."

"Well, we all know who had the motive and who hated his guts," Frank piped in. "Beau Costa. After those criminal charges and the bad publicity in the newspaper, he probably lost his marbles and went out and bought a gun."

"I don't think so," interrupted Bruno. "Beau just doesn't strike me as the murdering type. He just got married and is settling back into town after his honeymoon. Do you think he's going to suddenly up and commit a murder? I don't think a few trumped-up charges from an ex business partner would cause him to go berserk."

"Bruno, didn't you used to play tennis with Sonny?" Frank asked.

"I did last summer, early in the morning up at the high school," Bruno replied. "I know a lot of people didn't like him. but he really wasn't a bad guy."

"Talk to him much lately?"

"Oh, occasionally I'd run into him on the street. But Sonny was much more of a user than a friend."

"A user?" Mitzi asked. "Say again."

"It's a term I like to use to describe people that use people. If Sonny was talking to me, it was because he wanted to find out some information. How's the guesthouse business? How I thought people were going to vote on a certain issue at the town meeting. Could he sell me some more insurance or did I know anyone in town who wanted to buy life insurance? I wouldn't exactly call him a real friend, but he was a decent tennis player...." Bruno shook his head, letting the knowledge he would never again be playing tennis with Sonny sink in. He felt a chill go up his spine.

There was a moment of silence before any of the three felt the urge to speak. "You never know when your number is up," said Frank.

"All I know," said Mitzi, "is this is the first murder committed in Provincetown in about twenty years. Until they find out who did it, I'm locking my door day and night, and I'm not so likely to go out at night alone."

"Would you like us to walk you home tonight?" Bruno teased.

"That wouldn't be such a bad idea," responded Mitzi.

Roz and John heard the news over the twelve-band radio as they were basking in the afterglow of their lovemaking. They had been "doing it" on the old, brown leather couch in Roz's office.

"I knew I kept this couch for something other than taking catnaps," Roz had told him jokingly the first time they had used her office to make love. Luckily, she had installed an inside bolt on the main office door so that none of her staff could come in to work at night without checking in with her first. Besides, this time of year, the newspaper was still fairly small. But now she had a big story.

"I've got to call Elliot and put him on the story," she told John. Elliot was her main reporter and always covered the crime beat. "Plus,

I think I should go over to Sonny's house myself and see if the police have any leads. What do you think? Did Beau do it?"

"He's the likely suspect with a motive, but we don't know what else Sonny was into. How long ago did he and his wife separate? Maybe it wasn't a soured business deal; maybe it's just a case of a revengeful ex-spouse or lover."

2

Later Sunday Evening

L IZ MURPHY PRESSED HER HANDS against her aching forehead as she walked out of the PTA meeting. All that talk about coming up with some kind of anti-bias curriculum in the school and who was qualified to teach sex education to the students...it had all been downright irritating. She knew, of course, the pressure from her fingers pushing against her temples wouldn't really relieve the throbbing in her head, but the feeling of her hands against her forehead was comforting.

If only she had been able to speak her mind. These people had no idea. Let *them* move to Westport, Connecticut, for a while, or some other mainstream community where the majority of the population was straight and held "normal" jobs. One small, very vocal group of parents had gotten it into their brains that the Provincetown school system needed to develop a special program for teaching children tolerance of different lifestyles. Liz believed in being tolerant of everyone. Live and let live. But the school had more pressing problems to deal with, like drugs, discipline, and teaching competent writing and math skills.

Evidently, in this seasonal, small-town community, people had too much time on their hands during the winter months. They were all still living on unemployment checks. As soon as the summer season preparations kicked in, she knew attendance at these meetings would diminish.

Anti-bias? Provincetown was about acceptance of everyone. There wasn't much of a black or Hispanic population, but there were a variety of religious and political beliefs, as well as sexual orientations. Children absorbed what they needed to absorb. As long as everyone in the school was treated fairly, Liz did not think it was the school board's role to introduce this totally unnecessary program. But she couldn't say anything outright. She was, after all, Mrs. John Murphy, the town manager's wife. Her opinion would be considered his opinion.

She couldn't make John vulnerable to other people's criticisms, like what had happened in Westport. As a board member of the Community Development Coalition Project, she had supported the Sanco building project, which would have provided low-income housing, in addition to a mid-price-range condominium complex and a shopping center.

The criticisms at zoning hearings had to do with traffic congestion and environmental impact on land and wildlife. But the whispered murmurs in the background were about "niggers," "spics," and other "undesirables." People cared about the poor when they didn't live nextdoor. "Not In My Neighborhood" was written on placards and signs. "Not In My Backyard"...NIMBY...is what all the protests were all about.

John had tried to remain neutral regarding the project, but Westport's power brokers felt uncomfortable with his political orientation. The selectmen started finding fault with his work and began asking for more reports and his attendance at more committee meetings, piling on more and more work. Seeing the handwriting on the wall, he started looking for another job.

Provincetown...it was a beautiful place, views of the bay every time you took a walk down the street. But real estate was expensive, not the bargain she had anticipated when moving to this somewhat isolated town at the end of Cape Cod. Part of it had to do with the lack of central sewage. The new Title V systems were expensive, and that drove up the prices.

Truro, the neighboring township, was a much better value. But John felt that, because of his job, they must live in Provincetown. They were still looking for a place to buy, living in an apartment while waiting for a bargain to come on the market. Liz was secretly glad they were waiting. If this job didn't pan out, they could easily move.

No wonder she had a headache.

Just down the hill and a few blocks away, John Murphy was saying his good-byes to his mistress. He looked at his watch. If he left now, he thought to himself, he might be able to get home before Liz returned from her meeting.

"I think you ought to ask for some police protection," John advised Roz as he kissed her before leaving the newspaper office. "If Beau Costa is the murderer and he's still at large, he may be coming after you next. That wasn't exactly favorable press coverage you gave him a few months back."

Roz smiled. "I'm flattered you worry about me. I'll be okay. Somehow I don't think it was Beau, but I'd love to figure out who did it because I can plaster it all over my front page," she said with a laugh. "But for the time being I've got plenty of material to print, so I'll just see how the story unfolds."

She stuffed a legal pad and a small tape recorder into her briefcase in case she was able to interview the police or any witnesses. Her destination was what the locals called Snob Hill, a small subdivision on the east end of town off Harry Kemp Way where some luxury housing had been built several years earlier. Sonny Carreiro's house was a brick and wood colonial. The backyard had a swimming pool. She pictured the house as she drove the few blocks from the center of town down Bradford Street towards Snob Hill. Imagine that! A swimming pool, as if anyone needed one here with the bay, ocean, and many freshwater ponds. The murderer could have drowned Sonny in the swimming pool. That would have been a classic. Then she could write a hokey headline, such as: "Sonny Carreiro found drowned in a pool of death."

Roz felt no grief, just shock. She had never liked Sonny. He was an arrogant sonofabitch who always wanted to do everything his way, which is why he and Beau had a falling out. Sonny had inherited his business, a successful insurance agency, and had expanded his wealth by investing in real estate. That's what everyone who wanted to make money did: they bought and developed real estate.

She parked her old Chevy sedan at the foot of the street. Once a shiny red-maroon, the car's color had faded to a dull red-brown. Rust was appearing on the body, behind the wheels, and on the bottom of the rear doors. But it still ran pretty well, getting her to where she needed to go in a pinch.

"Roz, this is a crime scene. The place is blocked off. I can't let you get any closer," Jean Cook, one of the officers on the scene, told her as she walked towards Sonny's house. Yellow plastic streamers cordoned off the Carreiro home from the sidewalk. She could see a few drops of blood on the pavement where he fell, as well as a silhouette of tape where his body had been. For one brief moment, Roz tried to imagine Sonny Carreiro's body lying there. A few yards away, it was now inside one of those black plastic body bags and lying on a stretcher inside one of the Provincetown Rescue Squad ambulances. Just yesterday, Roz had seen him at the post office when she was picking up her mail. He had been smiling about something and very much alive. This evening, he was a corpse.

She tried to focus on hearing the radios transmitting information from the patrol cars and the words the various officers were speaking into their walkie-talkies. It just sounded like a lot of static. Instead, she began looking around at all the bystanders.

"Elliot," she called out. She recognized the tall, lanky frame of her star reporter in the distance interviewing someone. It looked like Gil Hanover, one of the neighbors.

"Thank you for your help," Elliot was saying to Gil as Roz approached. Gil was the retired president of Cape Cod Savings and Loan, which had been bought out by Massachusetts First National. He spent most of his days playing golf in favorable weather, and bridge or poker with his cronies when forced indoors. Every December, Gil and his wife, Margaret, headed to Florida, returning each spring in time for Easter. So here he was, back in Provincetown.

"How's it going, Gil?" Roz asked while shaking Gil's heavily wrinkled hand. Rumor had it that he received a fat retirement check every month. But he wasn't particularly active with any of the town's local charities, just the Catholic church where he regularly attended mass.

"Terrible shame," he said, shaking his head. "I just had a nice conversation with him this morning. He was going to visit his kids in Virginia and then take a trip to Bermuda." That's where Sarah Carreiro had moved to: Virginia. "Sarah has some fancy job working with computers, and she and the girls have been living with her mother. What a mess! Now those kids have no father...not that they were going to once

Sarah left town. Young people nowadays just don't know the meaning of commitment."

"So, did you see anything?" Roz asked.

"See anything? No. But I heard a gunshot. Thought it came from the TV set. I was watching a good program about crime on our streets. I thought the shot was part of a chase scene, but then I heard screeching tires and a dog barking. By the time I got up and looked out the window, the car was gone. I didn't walk outside...too dangerous. I dialed 911 and reported what I heard to the police."

"They're the ones who discovered the body," Elliot interjected. It was an easy getaway for the murderer. Route 6 is so close by."

"Maybe the killer is long gone," Roz theorized. "And maybe he's still here in town. Any clues?"

"The police are saying nothing," Elliot replied. "If they have any information, they don't want to give it out and risk jeopardizing their investigation. But I think we can safely conclude they currently have no suspects. Lots of theories but no suspects."

"Maybe we should offer a reward for information. That would get our readers excited. What do you think, Elliot?"

"It'll probably flood the newspaper phone lines, and we don't have much of a staff right now for fielding calls. But we'd probably get some juicy stories...."

Elliot was one of the few straight bachelors in town. Thirty years old, he was too young for Roz. Besides, he liked younger women. His bevy of girlfriends had ranged from slender, serious brunettes to vivacious redheads and voluptuous blondes. They all had one thing in common: firm, young bodies. At age forty-five, there was no way Roz could compete. It was a bad idea to get too close to your employees, anyway.

Roz admired Elliot from afar...his tightly muscled, tall frame and shock of almost-black hair, which constantly fell into his eyes. And he was a good reporter. Took his job seriously. As for the women in his life, he never seemed to let them get too close. Roz's relationship with Elliot was strictly professional, and she liked it that way. In many respects, she knew much more about him than the bimbos who fell in and out of his life did.

"Any other neighbors hear or see anything?" she asked Elliot, once Gil had started making his way up the flagstone path that led to the house nextdoor to Sonny's. It was another brick and wood combination but without the swimming pool, and was surrounded by a low, white picket fence.

Elliot watched as Gil walked with a slow limp, the by-product of age and arthritis. He turned back to face Roz. "You notice how these houses just don't look like they belong in Provincetown? They're too new...and ordinary."

Roz smiled. "I know what you mean. Perhaps if they were painted purple, mauve, or yellow, and there were some wind chimes, driftwood sculptures, and a boat or bathtub filled with dirt and flowers, they might fit in."

"Perhaps. The town keeps getting filled with more and more de-signer-type condos. It won't be long before the old beach shacks and cottages will be in the minority and places with wall-to-wall carpeting, dishwashers, and air conditioning will be the norm."

"Air conditioning! Who needs air conditioning around here when we've got the sea breeze?"

"I can tell you haven't lately been speculating in real estate, Roz. These city wimps who come here on weekends think they need air conditioning. All the new condos have it.... To get back to your original question about witnesses, I don't think anyone else heard or saw anything, although the police will certainly question everyone on this street."

"Call Sarah Carreiro in the morning and get her reaction," Roz told Elliot. "The police will have notified her by then, don't you think?"

"I'll check on it," Elliot replied. "After all, I'd hate to be the one to break the news: your husband has been murdered."

"Husband or ex-husband?"

"They're separated, not divorced."

"That means she might be getting a fat life insurance policy. Why did she split?"

"Rumor has it that Sarah couldn't stand living here. And Sonny certainly wasn't going to leave, what with all the deals and investments he had his hands on. So, according to Sonny's sister, Jo, they had a parting of the ways."

"What does Jo know about Sonny's business?"

"I'm sure she knows plenty, but what she'll tell me is another story."

"Well, see what you can find out."

Annie Tinker nervously looked at her watch. Her husband, Beau Costa, was talking on the telephone. She had to think about what she was going to say when the police came and asked questions. Should she just say that Beau had been home all evening? It's not that she thought he had anything to do with Sonny's murder...that slime bag! He deserved what he got! No, not really. His death was too fast. He should have suffered, writhed and pleaded for mercy, confessed his crimes, asked for forgiveness. Annie imagined herself standing over him, looking him straight in the eye and asking him, "How can you be so greedy and selfish?"

But if Beau didn't have a tight alibi, he would be open to public scrutiny and considered a suspect. Where had he gone earlier in the evening? She didn't dare ask. She had to trust him. He needed her to trust him.

They'd been through enough legal hassles with their real estate, what with Sonny, the bank, the newspaper. And now they were being audited by the IRS. When was it going to stop? Talk about stress on a marriage!

When Annie glanced over at Beau and he smiled at her with his blue eyes, that smile made all the stress go away for a moment. It wasn't that he was handsome. His teeth were slightly crooked, his hair was thinning and starting to turn gray, but he had an enchanting smile and a great voice. Annie liked voices and would never have dated a man who didn't have a nice-sounding voice...deep, rich, and resonant. At night, talking in the dark under the covers, or during the day on the telephone, you didn't see a face but you heard his enchanting voice.

Beau began to speak. "That was Roger. He's friends with John Rose on the police force. It was just one shot. The killer presumably got away in his or her car because the neighbor heard screeching tires. Most likely they'll be coming around in the morning to ask us a few questions." He looked at Annie meaningfully with his eyes and asked, "So what are you going to tell them?"

"We were home last night," she responded. "We took a walk to look at the stars. It was a beautiful, clear night. We read the newspaper, talked, had some tea, and went to bed. Then we made love. Should I tell them how we made love?"

"I don't think that's necessary," he replied with a smile.

Sometimes Annie wondered if she had made the right decision by leaving Garrett and marrying Beau. The romance that blossomed between them had been innocent enough, like something out of a Jane Austen novel...based on subtle glances, fragments of conversations, and growing slowly over the course of a year before anything tangible had taken place.

Both had been serving on the Auction Committee of the Provincetown Fine Arts Work Center, helping to plan the annual fundraiser. Beau, of course, was representing the local business community. Annie, a sculptor, had been the recipient of a Fine Arts Work Center fellowship years earlier. Choosing to remain in Provincetown after her grant expired, she became a member of the board and volunteered as much time as she could to help the Center remain a positive sphere of influence, particularly in the winter months when boredom and isolation set in. She helped raise money and organize readings, exhibitions, and workshops for community members.

Her boyfriend, Garrett, was a highly respected carpenter who specialized in interior finish work: building custom cabinets, countertops, and unusual pieces of furniture. His work was exhibited in galleries Up Cape, in Orleans and Osterville, as well as in Boston. He'd moved to the Lower Cape from Philadelphia several years earlier and had established a small, loyal following of clients.

Annie and Garrett had lived together for five years, and everything was going along fairly well. They did have their ups and downs. Sometimes Garrett got annoyed, because he was neat and orderly by nature and she was such a slob. "Can't you put your clothes in the hamper?" he would complain. "Why do you have to just drop them on the floor?"

Annie, on the other hand, grew disgusted with his erratic work schedule. Some weeks, he would get up at five in the morning to leave for a job and she wouldn't see him until nine in the evening. And within an hour, he'd fall asleep, exhausted, in front of the TV right after finishing the overcooked dinner she would reheat in the microwave.

"If you'd simply give me a call and let me know when to expect you, I'd be able to cook things right," she'd say. "It would be nice if we could at least sit down and eat dinner together." But Garrett couldn't be bothered.

Despite the typical issues that most couples, married or unmarried, seemed to have, the two had some great times together. They enjoyed fishing, working with their hands, and creating a beautiful home and garden.

There must be something missing, Annie had thought to herself when she tried to examine why she kept thinking about Beau Costa after they first met. Why else would she have developed such an obsession with him? Beau's face would loom in her mind and she couldn't help looking forward to the boring meetings just so she could hear to the sound of his voice. When they broke down into subcommittees and she found herself working with Beau on soliciting donations while others worked on the catalogue, publicity, catering, and setup, she'd been secretly delighted. Did he feel the same way about her, she wondered?

Annie was always careful not to be too attentive...to appear busy, talking to other people, and, if necessary, to look preoccupied because it would be embarrassing if Beau knew she harbored a crush and he didn't feel the same way. That's what it was, wasn't it? The words of one particular song played over and over again in her head: *"I've got a crush on you, sweetie pie...cause I have got a crush, baby, on you."*

Then her mother died. Annie returned to Columbus, Ohio, for the funeral, missing several meetings and falling behind on Auction Committee work. Beau picked up the slack.

Garrett had done his best to be supportive but couldn't understand her grief. She'd felt empty inside, and sometimes the slightest little thing would cause her to break into tears.

That's what had happened. She had started crying one afternoon, sitting with Beau in Mitzi's Coffee Shop, talking about whether they should lump some of the items together that had very little value or possibly save them for another time without hurting anyone's feelings.

"We could wrap them up and give them away as door prizes, or sell tickets to buy chances for a mystery gift," she had suggested. "My mom was doing an auction for her church...." Annie found herself unable to finish the sentence. The tears started flowing down her cheeks.

Beau took her hand in his. The warmth of his hand felt good and comforting, and he squeezed her hand tightly as if to say, "You know

I'm here for you. All you have to do is ask." He pulled a handkerchief out of his pocket and tenderly wiped away her tears.

It was then that she knew the attraction she held for him was mutual, and the love affair began. They'd only met in secret a few times before she felt compelled to tell Garrett. It would have been easy to keep him in the dark, but everyone else in town either knew or suspected that something was going on, or was about to go on, between her and Beau.

The others on the Auction Committee did seem to notice the glances that passed between the two of them, and the way he helped her with her coat and opened the door for her as they left the meetings. That was one of the nice things about Beau...he was old-fashioned in his gallantry. He would always walk her home or walk her to her car.

Garrett moved to a house in Truro. Annie would have let him keep the apartment. It was all her fault. And it wasn't that she stopped loving him; she just loved someone else more, which to most people made no logical sense. So she didn't try to explain, and Garrett just wanted out.

"I trusted you," he'd kept repeating. She felt awful, but the thought of giving up Beau because of her guilt felt even worse.

It wasn't until later, a year later when she and Beau had gotten married, that she began to realize there were things about Beau she didn't particularly like. The way he did business...he had no ethics regarding what was right and just, and he based his decisions on the degree of profit, *his* profit. If the building materials were slightly inferior, but not enough to cause a problem, and the profit margin was higher, he'd buy the inferior materials. If he could wiggle out of a deal because he'd found a better one, even after giving his word, he'd wiggle out.

Some of the slightly shady things he did she could understand. Why pay Social Security taxes and withholding on all your workers if some preferred cash? Why always bother to get a building permit and go through a bunch of rigmarole with the town if you could get someone to do the work on weekends when none of the neighbors were around?

But where do you draw the line? When do you decide which rules are worth following and which ones suit Beau? In Beau's world, it seemed that it was okay if it suited Beau.

Maybe she should have suspected something about his self-centeredness based on the way he talked incessantly when they were making love.

"Doesn't this feel good? Isn't this what you like...?" She was usually too enraptured to respond, so he would keep talking and providing her answers: "Yes, it feels so good. Oh, I know what you like."

Initially, it was a big turn-on. He was so different from Garrett, who had been silent and intense. But lately, the talking had become annoying. "Isn't this the most beautiful penis you've ever seen? You're such a lucky woman. I'm such a lucky man. You've got the most beautiful...."

Oh, if sometimes he could just keep quiet for a change.

Inside the office of the *Provincetown Observer*, Elliot and Roz set to work making fresh coffee. While Elliot rinsed out the glass carafe and filled it with water from the water cooler, Roz ground up some new beans in the coffee grinder in the small office kitchen. The two had returned for a late-night brainstorming session.

"I like this coffee. The other was just too intense," Roz told Elliot.

"Where'd you get it? At the new discount warehouse in Hyannis?"

"Absolutely. That's where I'm buying all our office supplies these days. You just can't beat the prices."

"They're going to be driving all the smaller stores out of business."

"Yes, eventually that is probably what's going to happen. There'll still be the specialty shops with unique goods and services, but those stores in the middle are going to get pushed out. As the business consumer, or consumer in general, what can I do but buy what I need at the lowest price?"

"I don't know, Roz. Maybe they're just taking us down the primrose path. Once they wipe out the competition, they can always raise their prices."

"I guess that's a risk I'll have to take. After all, this is a supply-and-demand economy. If they become too expensive, another store will open, with lower prices, to steal away their customers. I'm lucky I have the time to drive up to Hyannis to shop. Otherwise, I'd be stuck with paying the high prices here in town."

"Hey, when you're located at the end of the line, so to speak, that's the price you have to pay for a little isolation. It may be more expensive to live here, but we enjoy more beauty and solitude."

"Oh, there are some things here you can save on," Roz told Elliot with a smile. "You certainly don't need to spend much money on clothing. No one here ever dresses up, and when they do it's usually in secondhand glitz and glamour from a thrift shop." Roz looked down at her faded jeans and tennis shoes. It was hard to remember the last time she'd worn a suit and stockings. She hated stockings because that meant she'd have to shave her legs.

"Well, let's get back to the issues at hand," Elliot suggested. He sat down at his desk and reached into his file drawer to pull out his notes from the story he'd written about Beau Costa on the basis of his interviews with Sonny Carreiro. "And I quote: 'Intentionally overstating the value of property and securities to qualify for bank loans,' unquote. That was Sonny's big beef with Beau," Elliot said sarcastically.

"Not exactly a capital crime," responded Roz. "What about overstating how much he was spending on his construction costs?"

"He'd still have to pay back what he borrowed on the construction loans."

"Sonny also said something about Beau buying a lot of his property under the table."

"You mean paying partially in cash so the full value of the transaction wasn't reported?"

"That's what I'm talking about. But he could never provide any hard evidence. It was just suppositions."

"But where did he supposedly get the cash in the first place? Previous real estate transactions...or drugs?"

More than one successful businessperson in town was a drug dealer. Occasionally, someone got busted. The large dealers remained untouched. They drove their Mercedes, bought their expensive houses, and took lavish vacations in Europe and the Caribbean. No one close enough to the situation was going to turn them in. And the rest of town could only suspect.

"Didn't Sonny collect a lot of insurance on a fire a few years back?" Elliot queried.

"He certainly did," replied Roz. "In fact, he collected on two fires. The first one was before you came to town...and it was a big deal, a complex of six retail stores, only three of which were rented. Rumor was that the bank was going to call the note. And then, mysteriously, that winter there was a fire, a big fire. A man was killed...a drunk who lived on the street, camping out under the wharf and living in abandoned buildings. Rusty Ogel. He'd evidently broken into the back shop and was living there. They said he started the fire, just trying to keep warm."

"Did this Rusty fellow have any friends or relatives?" asked Elliot. "Someone who might blame Sonny for the fire and be out for revenge?"

"As I recall, no one knew too much about him. He was a loner. And even though that fire seemed to have gotten Sonny out of a financial pickle, no one was able to prove arson. It looks like you're going to be spending a little bit of time going through the town's tax records. See how much property Sonny owns, or owned in the past...and Beau, too. Then check out the Barnstable County Courthouse records and find how much he paid on the books."

"Why is it that I get all the fun jobs? You do realize that everything he's owned hasn't necessarily been in his name."

"This is a small town. If anything is owned by a trust or corporation and you don't know who the shareholders or trustees are, you can look it up. It'll be useful information for us to have in the future. Maybe this summer we can get some eager-to-please intern to type it all into a database so that anytime we want to know who the players are, the information will be right there."

"What about the second fire?" Elliot asked.

"That was just a little grease fire in one of Sonny's rental units that got out of hand. As I recall, the flames from a frying pan leaped up and spread to the kitchen curtains. One wall got pretty charred, and there was a lot of smoke damage. He blamed it on the tenants. Next thing you knew, the kitchen was completely remodeled and he was converting the building into condominiums. The man sure knew how to turn misfortune into money."

"So it seems. Any ideas about how to pursue a possible drug connection?"

"We'll have to tread lightly on this one. Perhaps Sonny's sister, Jo, will talk to me. I suppose she'll be busy with the funeral arrangements, so it wouldn't be too cool to ask her to lunch."

Elliot smiled. "Isn't that Sarah's responsibility?"

"Theoretically, yes. But since she flew the coop, Jo is bound to take over. I bet by the time Sarah gets to town, most of the arrangements will have been taken care of."

3

Early Monday Morning

FRANK CHAMBERS TOOK INVENTORY of the supplies on hand in his kitchen. He had plenty of flour and sugar for baking. An adequate amount of butter was in the freezer. So there was certainly everything he needed for baking the muffins, he thought to himself.

Jo…Jo Carreiro Landon…had called him about catering the gathering after the funeral services at Saint Peter's.

"We'll be going back to my home," she had told him on the phone. "I don't think it would be appropriate to invite guests back to Sonny's house, considering the circumstances…," she stated in a hushed tone.

Jo Landon had a large home. Her husband, Bill, ran the Carreiro Insurance business while Sonny pursued his real estate schemes. Taking early retirement from the Navy, Bill was a steady, even-tempered man. Slightly overweight, with wire-framed spectacles and a receding hairline, he usually wore dark, formal suits to his office…one of the few suit wearers in Provincetown. Occasionally, he donned a pair of khaki pants and a polo shirt. "People want to buy insurance from a man with a professional image," he'd constantly say to Jo.

Jo didn't care. Bill was a fine husband. He was predictable and reliable, someone she could count on, and best of all he let her run things the way she wanted. It was her family's business, even if people thought it all belonged to Sonny.

Their home was in the new subdivision at the end of town, over-
looking the dunes, marshlands, and, in the far distance, the meeting of
the ocean and the bay. Their neighbors were mostly wealthy out-of-
towners, and Jo loved to show off her view and material possessions
to her acquaintances and friends.

"It will be a morning mass," she had explained. "The burial should
be over by eleven thirty or twelve. Let's just serve sort of a light brunch:
muffins, a nice fruit salad, some sandwiches. What do you think?"

Frank's initial reaction was that it all sounded pretty boring, although he could make even the most mundane menu turn exotic. The
muffins could be squash, pumpkin, and carrot with plenty of plump
raisins, brown sugar, and crunchy nuts. The fruit salad could contain
mandarin oranges, yogurt, pineapple, and sprinkled with almonds on
top. And he could always caricature those women's club teas with a
shrimp salad, tuna fish, and cream cheese and olive loaf. That would
be kind of fun.

He'd need some help getting everything quickly transported and set
up at the Landons' home. He had plenty of platters for arranging the
various food selections.

Frank picked up the phone and dialed the Landons' phone number,
which he'd jotted down on the memo pad with the list of food items
Jo had requested.

"Hi, Jo. This is Frank again…from the Indigo Inn. Sorry to bother
you, but do you want to use your own dishes or should I bring plates
or paper goods?" he asked as soon as he heard Jo's slightly nasal voice
on the other end of the line.

Jo thought long and hard for a moment. It would be fun to show
off her new set of Wedgwood, but she only had place settings for twelve
guests. Even if she combined it with her mother's Haviland Limoges,
it still might not be enough. And there was always the risk of break-
age. People can be pretty emotional after funerals, jittery hands and
sometimes crying.

Why wasn't *she* almost on the verge of tears? Because she was
practical. Think about the present, Jo always told herself. Don't worry
about the past. Sonny was dead and there was nothing she could do
about it.

She would miss him, but not for the reasons a sister might normally
miss a brother. Sonny had been as annoying as a buzzing black housefly

in the kitchen. You try to kill it with a fly swatter but it keeps getting away, and after a while you learn to reconcile yourself to the noise.

Now there would be silence. No longer would she have to worry about hearing from someone else about his wild escapades. No longer would she be required to stick up for him in social conversations. "Blood is thicker than water," their mother would say. "Never say anything negative about your family to others. Look out for each other."

Jo never liked her brother. He had always been mean to her when they were growing up, making fun of her glasses, borrowing money and never paying it back, criticizing her friends. She always felt he was laughing at her conservatism. Yes, he lived the fast and easy life: the fancy sports car, the late nights of drinking and snorting lines of cocaine, the trips to Boston to buy his designer clothes. But people seemed to like him, with his easy smile and his generosity. He never paid his bills on time, unless he received a discount, but he always gave lavish gifts and picked up restaurant tabs. That was Sonny.

So who did the police suspect? The likely person with a motive was Beau, who hated his guts. Maybe Beau's wife, Annie, was a suspect. No, most people would figure her as too sweet and naive to do something like that. Maybe the police thought he was in debt and the killer was a loan shark, or perhaps his estranged wife, Sarah, had a motive....

"Well," said Frank on the other end of the phone line, "what do you think?"

Jo jolted herself back to the question at hand: which dishes? "Much as I dislike paper plates, I really expect a large crowd...thirty-five to forty-five. So I think that's what we'll have to use. It's not summertime. People don't have that much going on so they'll come by the house to eat, reminisce, and drink my liquor," she said with a laugh. "I'll go Up Cape tomorrow or Wednesday and pick some up."

Sarah's plane would be arriving in a couple hours, so Jo needed to tidy up the guest rooms, put fresh sheets on the beds, and vacuum away any possible dust. The new cleaning girl had done the house a few days earlier, so it didn't look bad. But she hadn't bothered with the guest rooms. And Jo hadn't anticipated she'd be having company.

Sarah was bringing her mother to help mind the children, although, as far as Jo was concerned, at ages ten and twelve they were past the age where they needed minding. Sarah probably wanted her mother there for moral support; otherwise, she'll be completely outnumbered by the

Carreiro clan, all whispering about her behind her back, saying that maybe if she hadn't moved to Virginia things would have been different...Sonny wouldn't have been murdered. Who knows? One couldn't think of what might have been, Jo mused to herself.

But now Sarah has everything, including lots of money from several life insurance policies, Jo thought enviously, and no ex-husband to deal with. This will certainly simplify her life.

"Come by early on Thursday morning," Jo suggested to Frank. "If we've already left for the church, the key will be under the mat."

"Sounds good," Frank replied.

Inside he felt a little hurt because the thought had evidently not occurred to Jo that he might like to attend Sonny's funeral. It's probably because I'm gay, Frank thought to himself, and she thinks I'm less of a person so it doesn't even enter her mind that maybe I'd like to pay my respects to his family and attend the services.

It wasn't like they had been close friends, but Sonny was a regular at the restaurant. Almost everyone in town would be there, and it would be fun to see what they all were wearing and who sits with whom. Most of the mourners, however, he'd see back at the house, Frank rationalized. If he got everything set up, maybe he could slip away and go to the church anyway.

What would the priest say about Sonny Carreiro? Probably something generic about his being a good husband and father, because Catholics were so uncreative. In Frank's mind, Catholics did everything by the book...except for the Jesuits, who were the intellectuals and the thinkers. At Saint Peter's of the Apostle, the funerals he had attended in the past sounded as though they were being read out of a textbook and the deceased person's name was merely inserted in all the right places. If you were someone who liked pomp and ceremony, but wanted something a little more innovative, you went to the Episcopal church. In the East End was Saint Mary's of the Harbor, a small, waterside church with a gated garden in front. Its size and location provided a lot of intimacy. Frank had attended some interesting services there.

Frank himself was a member of the Unitarian Universalist Meeting House, which had a grand building modeled after a church in England by Christopher Wren, complete with the original heavy oak pews and whale-oil chandeliers. He liked the sermons, all the social outreach programs, and especially liked going with his friends. Yet he also found it interesting to check out the rest of the local religious community.

With only a few days' notice, Frank questioned whether he had time to place an order with Lamborni, the produce wholesaler. He seemed to recall that the A&P was running a special on strawberries and grapes, both good for garnishes. He reached for his denim jacket, hung up behind the back door of the kitchen, and checked the pockets for his car keys. Luckily, they were still there. Frank had a habit of misplacing his keys, so he tried to keep track of them by leaving them inside a pocket. Sometimes it was a question of which pocket, in the event he changed jackets or pants, but at least it limited the search exclusively to clothing.

Shopping at the A&P in the off season was always enjoyable because you ran into so many people you knew who you might want to chat with. The post office and grocery store were two central hubs in Frank Chambers' life. He lived alone with his cat, Dolly. During the winter months, meetings, church, trips to check his post office box, and shopping at the A&P were sometimes his only contact with other people.

Of course, who was the first person he saw in the produce section but that bitch, Roz Silva, pushing her chrome shopping cart and then stopping to examine a bunch of green grapes for brown spots.

"Hello, Frank," she greeted him. "Looking forward to the Easter break to kick off the tourist season?"

"But of course," he glibly replied. "We'll be ready with plenty of new and exciting menu selections. Come by for dinner one night, if you dare." His voice had a slightly taunting edge to it, but what he didn't dare say was something that might overtly offend "Miss Publisher and Editor."

Roz had the only paper in town, and people read what she wrote. So when her food critic had made some comments about the Indigo Inn's limited menu choices and steep prices in one of the previous summer's columns, Frank had felt the pinch. He was certain it had hurt business. Not so much from the locals and regular summer clientele, who knew what he had to offer, but business from first-time tourists who might have the money to spend on a memorable meal. He had pulled his ad from the paper for a few weeks, but it was silly to cut off your nose to spite your face so he'd reluctantly put it back in.

"Maybe you'd like to offer some special coupon or discount," the paper's ad rep had suggested when Frank called in to have an ad run again. "Perhaps you should put a little something in the advertisement to coax them inside your door," the rep had advised, as if he was desperate for customers...which maybe he was. The season was short; he needed to do business while the tourists were on the Cape and spending money.

Frank had thought long and hard about what kind of ad he should run. Ha! He'd show those fools at the *Provincetown Observer* a thing or two. He included in his advertisement a quote from a favorable review published in the *Cape Cod Recorder*:

"You would be well advised to take refuge from the worries and cares of traveling by paying a visit to the Indigo Inn, a charming Provincetown restaurant. The chef and proprietor takes great pains to explain his innovative and creative menu, which changes every week, to his guests while providing them with excellent service from a well-trained waitstaff."

I'm paying for the space and there's nothing they can do about it, Frank had reasoned to himself. The ad worked, and business increased by twenty percent. Of course, it helped that he had bought a quarter of a page rather than his usual two columns in four-square-inches format.

Roz tried to smile, knowing full well that Frank didn't really like her. Why should he? She had run a critical review of his restaurant even though the "in crowd" in town loved it. But nothing was perfect, not even everything cooked by Frank Chambers. And not everyone who visited Provincetown wanted to pay twenty-five dollars or more for a dinner. Some people just wanted basic food choices, like meat and potatoes or chicken and rice, rather than everything being exotic. Folks with families or a large group of friends might simply want a larger menu to choose from. So Roz had agreed with her food critic, a journalism major from Boston University, that the Indigo Inn was: *"For the sophisticated palate with a fat wallet."* It wasn't entirely negative, but it wasn't entirely positive either. Nothing in the world is black and white. There are many shades of gray.

Shades of gray...that was an expression Gene liked to use. Not a day that went by that Roz didn't think about Gene, her late husband. Three years had passed. Well-meaning friends and acquaintances had told her that once she got through the first year, things would get easier and the pain and grief would start to fade. But they were wrong. The grief and pain were just as powerful some moments of every single day as they had been the first month after Gene's death. The grieving moments, however, had become further apart to make space for other things, such as mooning over John Murphy and laying out the newspaper.

This was one of those moments. Continuing with her grocery shopping, Roz began thinking nostalgically about how every morning over coffee the two of them would sit and discuss their plans for the day. Gene was an early riser, up at six a.m and out for a jog and to pick up the morning dailies. He'd do a little bookkeeping and then at nine was ready for a short break. If the weather was nice, they'd sit on the front porch or in the garden. Sometimes, if it was low tide and they weren't too pressed for time, they'd walk the few blocks over to the beach and bring a thermos of coffee with them.

Gene loved to talk about the responsibility of the press and the ideology behind good journalism. Roz was more practical. She wanted to sell more papers so they could pay the bills. Together, the two loved to talk. It was Roz who always wanted to pick up controversial issues that got people excited because it meant increased newspaper sales. Gene didn't mind controversy, but he always wanted to be certain about the facts. "Put yourself in the other person's shoes," he'd tell her. "Try to think like they think. What are the motivating factors?"

How she missed having someone to discuss all these issues with. What would Gene think of Sonny's murder? What would he think of this larger, remodeled A&P? Sure, her news editor, Elliot, was sharp, young, and fun. But Elliot was not Gene. As for Roz discussing her business with John Murphy, she felt it was inappropriate and would appear as a sign of weakness. She ran things herself, as she had promised Gene she would do if anything happened to him. John had the town and all of its offices and employees to take care of. He didn't burden her with his problems, so why should she burden him with hers?

She felt some regret that Frank Chambers thought she was "out to get him." It was nothing personal. It was just business. She knew he worked hard and was confident in the choices he'd selected for his restaurant's format. But different people had different tastes.

Roz smiled to herself and pushed her grocery cart towards the meat department. Her younger daughter, Sally, had asked her to cook up some "plain, regular hamburgers." Sally was a good kid, studied hard and was a member of the National Honor Society. This weekend, they were having a car wash to raise money.

Glancing up the cereal aisle she noticed Annie Tinker, Beau's wife. Annie looked disgustingly beautiful even with no makeup, Roz grumbled to herself. Her long, shiny auburn hair was pulled back into a pony tail this morning and her pale, white and rose complexion had a glow from within. Their eyes met, forcing each to smile and say hello.

"It must be a terrible shock for Beau," Roz found herself saying to Annie. "He worked so closely with Sonny."

"His being shot down like that in front of his own home has to be a shock to everyone," Annie responded, choosing her words carefully.

"Have any ideas about who might have committed the crime?" Roz asked.

"That really is more of a matter for the police. Sonny was not exactly the most popular person...." Annie moved her cart forward, clearly indicating it was time to end the conversation.

Roz steered her cart towards the bread department. Well, of course, why should Annie want to talk to her? She hadn't exactly given favorable newspaper coverage to Beau. But Annie was the kind of person who seemed to always be nice to everyone and didn't appear to hold a grudge. No wonder her name was always suggested for appointments to town committees....

This was not turning out to be a very good morning, and Roz felt a wave of sadness welling up inside her. She didn't have many friends. Who did? It was time to head over to the checkout line, and then to the newspaper office.

4

Mid Monday Morning

S ARAH CARREIRO ARRANGED and rearranged her legs, thinking to herself how uncomfortable small planes were. Sitting next to her, intently staring out the window, was her younger daughter, Stephanie. This time of year, Provincetown Air only used the six-passenger puddle jumpers, the ticket agent had explained when Sarah was hurriedly buying their tickets. "Just not enough passengers traveling from Boston to Provincetown so early in the spring."

First they had to catch a seven a.m. flight out of Washington, D.C., and then wait two hours in Boston for their connecting flight. Stephanie and Cassie didn't seem any worse for wear. They'd seldom flown on an airplane, so they thought the trip was exciting.

"Wow! Look how small this plane is!" Cassie had half shouted as they boarded for the last leg of their journey.

"Are you sure this tiny plane is safe, dear?" Sarah's mother had inquired as she gingerly climbed up the ladder steps of the aircraft.

Sarah didn't mind the limited number of seats, but she wasn't thrilled with the lack of leg room. When you had long legs like hers, cramped spaces just weren't comfortable.

Sonny had loved her long legs. That's what he said attracted him to her. "Long legs and beautiful eyes," he told her. "That's what I look for in a woman."

"And a tight pussy," he'd whisper conspiratorially in her ear after he'd downed a few drinks…martinis. Sonny loved martinis, vodka martinis, extra dry with just a drop of vermouth and three jumbo olives.

After she had given birth to Stephanie, he literally stood over the doctor, who was putting in the stitches after her episiotomy, and instructed him, "Make sure you stitch her up tight, nice and tight."

Sarah had wondered whether he was joking or was actually serious. Even though they'd been married for fifteen years, it was hard to tell when Sonny was joking or being serious. Maybe his murder was just another one of his jokes, another scam. "April Fool's!" he would shout when she stepped off the airplane. But it wasn't yet April. It was the nineteenth of March, tomorrow was the first day of spring. In exactly one month, Sonny would have turned forty-nine. A lump welled up in Sarah's throat, but she found it impossible to cry. It all seemed surreal, like she was living in a dream.

"Mommy, Mommy! Look! There's the tip of the Cape. We're almost there," Stephanie yelled in her ear.

Sarah looked over Stephanie's shoulder and through the window down at the sparkling bay and curved spit of sand. There was no better way, in her opinion, to see the tip of Cape Cod than from a small airplane. The sun's rays danced on the surface of the water and she could see the broad expanse of sand dunes, the scrub pines, and the Province Land Visitors Center. Luckily, the weather was good…sunshine, not rain. Maybe she'd have the chance to walk the Snail's Road Trail across the dunes, if her mom would keep an eye on the kids.

"Will we have to look inside the coffin?" Cassie asked from the seat behind.

"I told you I asked for a closed casket…Mom, what have you been telling her?" Sarah sternly asked her mother, Emma.

"I merely suggested that maybe she'd like to say good-bye to her father," Emma Green stated indignantly. "In my day, everyone in the family came and paid their respects to the dead in person, not to a wooden box."

"Well, we're not living in your day," Sarah retorted. "And I believe that viewing the dead is a matter of choice. Besides, I don't think Sonny would have wanted an open casket. He wouldn't have wanted to be macabre."

Macabre…now, that was a good word. What did it mean? Morbid. Gruesome. Connected with death. At Vassar, Sarah had been an English major, but that couldn't get her a job. She'd started working towards her MBA at Northeastern because she wanted to be in Boston, and with their work/study program she could help pay the tuition.

Boston…that's where she'd met Sonny, at a bar in the North End. He was so handsome with his dark brown-almost-black eyes, which seemed to contain a glint of mischief, and his deep olive tan. "Care to dance?" he asked her in a nasal-sounding tone, which she assumed to be a Boston accent. He had seemed so self-assured, so calm and relaxed, not like most of the young men she'd dated. Of course, it helped that he was considerably older…a man, not a boy.

And when the band started playing an old jitterbug tune, boy, could he swing! He knew all the moves, leading her into a turn and then a cuddle-up and then a spin. "Learned it from Mrs. Emory, an old dance instructor my fraternity at Boston College hired. That lady was great. She taught us all kinds of stuff. Plus, it was a perfect excuse to bring some girls into the frat house…as our dance partners; then get real cozy and whisper sweet nothings in their ear. You know what I mean, jelly bean?" Up close, Sarah could smell the liquor on his breath, but she'd been too intrigued to push him away when he put his arm around her.

"Would you like to get high?" he whispered.

It had been a few months since Sarah had smoked any dope, not since she'd moved from Poughkeepsie to Boston. It wasn't something she made a big effort to find. If it came her way, she'd take a few tokes. But she'd only bought the stuff a few times. It was nice in certain situations, particularly at parties where she felt insecure. It made the world appear friendlier. It took the rough edges off whatever she was looking at and everything seemed to flow together. She called marijuana her "rose-colored glasses"…after a few drags, her fears didn't seem so serious, so important. And if the dope was good, Sarah felt like she was literally floating high above everyone else.

But sometimes the effects hadn't been so positive. Sometimes it seemed as if she could read other people's thoughts, and she didn't like what they were thinking. They wanted something from her, particularly the men who would drag her back to their room to make out and then try to push her back onto their waterbed. Sometimes it was beautiful and everything flowed, but other times she would push them away and leave, saying, "I just don't feel like it. We're just not in sync."

Sonny had some really good shit, powerful, and in a few moments Sarah had felt a high-acceleration rush, followed by a send-off into another realm of reality. Around her she could still see the apartment he'd "borrowed" from a friend who was traveling in Europe. Very modern furniture with bright colors and clean lines, probably purchased from one of those Scandinavian import places, she figured.

In the bedroom was a queen-size platform bed with navy blue sheets and a white and blue comforter. Cube-shaped, white Formica tables with blue ceramic lamps flanked each side of the bed. Sarah hated dark-colored sheets, but nothing was ever perfect. And when she closed her eyes and just laid back on the bed while Sonny devoured her with his hands and then his tongue until she burst into orgasm, the color of the sheets didn't matter.

"You feel so good," he said as he entered her. Sonny was wearing a condom, and Sarah didn't even have to ask. He was gallant enough, even back in those days, to do some things right.

"Well, you didn't bring much luggage," Jo observed, once Sarah and the others were inside the small terminal building at Provincetown's airport. Sarah never liked Jo, her sister-in-law. Too pushy. But Sarah didn't have a choice...she couldn't bear the thought of going back to the old house. Too many memories. It was easier to stay in Jo's gracious surroundings than to camp out in a motel room and risk pissing everyone off.

"We try to travel light," she replied. "Jo, you've met my mother before...Emma Green."

Jo smiled. "Yes, of course. Did you have a nice flight, Mrs. Green?"

"Please, dear, call me Emma." Soon it will all be over, Emma was thinking, and these horrible Carreiros and this disgusting town will be out of our lives. Once Sonny is buried and the estate is settled, why, there'll be nothing to tie Sarah or the girls to this place. "It's so nice to see you again," Emma said aloud.

Jo looked at the stately lady, who appeared to be in her early six-ties, and admired her dark gray suit, wondering how much it cost. It looked like a designer label. Jo wished she had more opportunities to wear really nice clothes. Maybe they could squeeze in a trip to New York after this funeral business is done with, she thought to herself... *if* she could convince Bill to take some time off. The two of them could get away, see some shows, and she could dress up for a change.

Sarah looked over at her mother and then at her sister-in-law. There was only about a ten-year age difference. But whereas her mother had accepted the role of the stately senior citizen, Jo, in her late fifties, still wanted to be thought of as middle-aged. Dressed in navy blue linen pants, a crisp tailored blouse, and a cardigan, Jo had kept her figure trim. Her short hair was skillfully colored to allow a few strands of gray, while the majority was a warm brown with highlights of gold. Her skin, however, had the weathered look of years in the sun: gardening, sailing, playing golf. No amount of makeup could completely cover the leathery patches of lines around her eyes and mouth, nor the small, brown age spots.

Emma Green's salt-and-pepper hair was pulled back into a low bun. She couldn't be bothered with makeup, just moisturizer and a little pink lipstick. A real lady did not paint her face, she'd always told her daughter.

"Where did you park your car, Aunt Jo?" asked Cassie, who was impatient to get to her aunt and uncle's house so she could get something to eat. They must have something she could snack on...or she could always go into town, if she had her bicycle.

"Mom, do you think we could go over to the house so Stephanie and I can get our bicycles?"

"Not now," Sarah answered. "Maybe later. Are you hungry?" she asked, knowing that her twelve-year-old always seemed to be hungry these days. It must be another growth spurt, she reasoned. The death of her father certainly had not in any way destroyed Cassie's appetite.

"I think I have some hot dogs in the freezer and some linquicia," offered Jo. "I know how much you girls like linquicia, and I'm sure you can't buy any down in Virginia, can you?"

Linquicia...that was something Sarah herself had missed. Hot-and-spicy Portuguese sausage, which was drier and firmer in texture than other types of sausage, except maybe kielbasa. But Sarah didn't like kielbasa. Too bland and fatty.

"You'd be surprised what you can buy in the gourmet food stores nowadays: andouille, chorizo, and sometimes linquicia. But the linquicia they make is not the same as what you buy up here, and it's so expensive," replied Sarah.

You could find good linquicia in any area that had a large Portuguese community, primarily in New England. Portuguese bread and linquicia were the two food items Sarah missed the most after moving from the Cape. She thought back to the first time she'd tasted Portuguese bread, fifteen years earlier. "I'm taking you on a picnic," Sonny had told her, "but first we're going on a long drive."

It had been two weeks since that night Sarah had met him at the North End bar. A week later, he'd taken her out to dinner. Another week went by and they'd gone out dancing. Then, the following morning, Sonny had told her to pack a few things. "We're going to be gone overnight," he said secretively. "It's a surprise. But don't worry…you'll be back in time for your classes Monday morning."

Sarah was not worried about her classes. She was intrigued. Who *was* this handsome man with plenty of style and charm and money? His name was Sonny Carreiro. He owned an insurance agency and a real estate agency. He lived in Provincetown, and during the winter he played in Boston.

Spring was just arriving in New England. The wind was damp and chilly by the sea, but the sun was shining. The first thing Sarah had noticed as they drove along the highway in North Truro, which ran parallel to the bay, was the salty smell of the water. Sonny had rolled down the car windows of his two-door, red Camaro. Then he said, "Take a deep breath, Baby, and inhale. Doesn't it smell good?"

They stopped at the Portuguese bakery for a loaf of bread and next at a deli/liquor store for wine and cheese and fruit. Sonny had a large blanket in his trunk and a thirty-five-millimeter camera. He snapped pictures of her sitting on the beach, toasting him with wine drunk from a plastic tumbler.

"You aren't too cold, are you?" he asked. They were sitting at Race Point Beach and the wind was strong, creating large waves that crashed forcefully against the shore. Sarah, bundled up in a turtleneck, sweater, and sweatshirt, smiled and said she was fine…because she didn't want to complain. What a glorious place, she thought to herself. She couldn't wait to see his apartment.

In Provincetown, Sonny lived in a small cottage on Brewster Street. Certainly different from the Boston apartment, it was cluttered with all sorts of knick-knacks and the walls were covered with paintings. "I've been collecting art since I was a teenager," Sonny explained. "Most of the work is by students. We've had a number of art schools here in town over the years. There was Hawthorne, and then Manso, Candell, Henry Henche…and now we have the Fine Arts Work Center, as well as classes at the Provincetown Art Association and Museum and Castle Hill Center for the Arts in Truro. New ones keep popping up all the time. Some of these student artists just might become famous. You never know."

There certainly was a dichotomy of style between fanciful collages, sweet, realistic watercolors, and bold, abstract oils. In the corner was still life of red roses in a vase in front of a window, looking out onto the sea. She noticed the signature was "S. Carreiro."

"Is this your work?" Sarah had asked.

"Well, yes," Sonny answered. She detected a slight blush in his cheeks. "I took a few classes. But I decided I prefer doing photos. It's more my style, instant gratification. Talking about instant gratification…." He pulled her towards him and pushed his hands up inside her sweater. "I wanted to do this on the beach, but it was just a little too chilly," he said before kissing her neck.

At the same time Sarah, her mother, and the girls were loading their few pieces of luggage into the trunk of Jo's Lincoln Continental, Bruno Marchessi was sitting at his dining room table folding letters, a tall stack of them. This year, he had again decided to send letters to everyone on his mailing list, informing them about reduced spring and fall rates, special weekend packages, and all the wonderful, new upgrades in his guesthouse. It was boring work. The letter looked pretty good; he'd chosen green ink on tan paper. The colored ink was a little more expensive, but he thought it worth the extra price.

Inside the envelope, he also placed his usual three-fold brochure, "Welcome to the Willows Guest House," appropriately named because a large willow tree graced the front garden. A small graphic of the building and tree, done by a local artist, was positioned beneath the heading and the statement, printed in italic letters: *"Enjoy our hospitality all four seasons of the year. Comfortable bedrooms furnished with antiques, along with delicious breakfasts and afternoon tea and cocktails, are included in this wonderful setting just steps away from the Provincetown nightlife, shops, gourmet restaurants, and beach."*

Three hundred letters, all requiring a first-class postage stamp...this was going to cost a pretty penny, Bruno thought to himself. He had considered a bulk-mailing permit, but it looked so tacky. A first-class stamp looked nicer, and each envelope was addressed by hand. He wished to imbue a certain elegance and style in his correspondence. Maybe he should have used scented paper, scented with bayberries or cranberries, to make them think of Cape Cod, he chuckled to himself.

The fraud in his advertising was using the universal "our." The Willows Guest House was a sole proprietorship. He had never had a business partner and had never sustained a real long-lasting romantic relationship beyond a few months.

Bruno was a loner, always toying with the idea of settling down with one special someone but perfectly content to enjoy life by himself. Besides, there was the thrill of the chase. Someone new, young, and exciting might be waiting right around the corner. Young...Bruno was fifty years old and he lusted for boys no older than twenty.

These young boys had a certain innocence, a sweetness...and, try as he could, he just found them to be the only males he was really attracted to. Women were boring. Men his own age were okay as friends, but.... Bruno knew his sexual tastes were socially unacceptable. Even within the gay community, at the very least this was considered a weakness because it made one so vulnerable to being taken advantage of by young gigolos.

"Do they have to be so young?" Sonny Carreiro would harp at Bruno on the tennis court between sets. Sonny would sometimes drop by at six thirty in the morning to give him a ride, and he always had a shocked look on his face when he saw a young boy sitting in the kitchen drinking coffee and wearing Bruno's bathrobe. They played early, before the courts got crowded, providing time for Bruno to get back and start serving breakfast to his paying guests.

"There must be some attractive, youthful men who keep themselves in shape, and more like around the age of thirty, that you could date," Sonny would tease.

"Oh, and are you offering yourself?" Bruno would retort.

"Honey, I'm already spoken for. And, besides, I'm way too old. Past forty. How you flatter me."

"I'm just having fun with you."

Bruno thought of Sonny, standing in his white tennis shorts and white knit shirt, the dark tan, the almost-black hair, a good-looking guy…not Bruno's type, but attractive by most anyone's standards. Medium build, medium height, even features. And he was an aggressive tennis player. Too young to die.

Funny, Bruno thought, that even after it was obvious there'd been a rift between Sonny and Sarah, Sonny had refused to acknowledge they were having problems. She'd packed up her stuff, the kids' stuff, and they'd moved out at the end of last summer. Sonny continued playing tennis until mid October. During those several weeks, Bruno had been afraid to mention her name.

5

Late Monday Morning

B Y THE TIME SHE GOT HOME with the groceries, Roz felt a slight wetness oozing into her panties. Once again, her period was a few days early...and she'd forgotten to pick up tampons. She really needed to take a quick shower, anyway, before changing her underwear.

If she really believed in all this hocus-pocus stuff about the power of women's cycles, Roz thought to herself, then she'd just entered her time of power and strength. What is the rationale? We're all part of the cycle of birth, life, and death. A woman's menstrual blood is a visible reminder of the power a woman has to give birth to the earth. It's supposed to be a time for meditation and visions. But Roz didn't feel particularly powerful this morning...she was tired and needed another cup of coffee, even though she'd be really late getting to work.

Elliot was already there, along with Fran Harrington, the advertising sales rep, and Sky Johnson, who wrote features and the astrology column. Tina, the receptionist/advertising assistant, and Lee, the copy editor, had either taken an early lunch or were on a coffee break. "Fran and I were just talking about the advertisement for the reward money we're going to run this week," Elliot informed Roz as she walked towards his desk to see what he and Fran were hovered over. They had sketched out a square with a fancy border, and inside was written: "$_____ REWARD FOR INFORMATION LEADING TO THE

CAPTURE OF THE MURDERER OR MURDERERS OF SONNY
CARREIRO." The cash reward amount had been left blank.

"How about five hundred dollars," suggested Roz.

"Are you crazy?" Elliot said. "How about five *thousand* dollars!
Five hundred is nothing."

"Fifteen hundred, then. It's all I've got available."

Fran looked at Roz with disbelief. What a tight-ass bitch, she thought
to herself. She's willing to gamble when other people's reputations are
at stake, but when it comes to herself she plays it safe.

"But think of all the possible stories we'll get out of this," Elliot
said in a wailing tone of voice.

"Listen, Elliot," said Roz. "Fifteen hundred dollars is a lot of money
to most people in this town. Besides, we might have to pay out the
reward money more than once. What if several people come forward
with useful information?"

"But you don't have to pay them anything unless the information
leads to whoever killed Sonny," Fran interjected.

Roz studied Fran's face for a moment, noticing she was wearing
bright red lipstick and a red bead in her eyebrow ring, which clashed
with her short, carrot-red hair. Then she glanced at her ears to see if
she had red earrings on, as well. No, just numerous gold studs and
rings climbing up the side of each earlobe. Ouch, thought Roz. All
those piercings must have hurt...but, evidently, Fran needed to show
the world that she was tough. Young, smart, and an excellent graphic
designer who had switched over to sales to make more money, Fran
had recently celebrated her thirtieth birthday with yet another set of
holes in her ears....

Roz had no desire to piss off either Fran or Elliot. If they only
knew...just because she's the boss and writes the paychecks did not
mean she was made of money.

"Listen." said Roz. "We can always increase the reward amount,
but it would be pretty tacky to lower it. Don't you agree?"

Fran and Elliot both nodded their heads in assent.

"So let's start with a reward of fifteen hundred. If that doesn't bring
much of a response, we can always raise the ante, so to speak."

Fran walked back to her desk and began making a list of potential
Up Cape businesses she could approach to place ads in the coming
weeks, those that might be intrigued by the murder story they were

going to run. Let's see...there were the alarm companies, of course, since people would be worried about security. Real estate, insurance, mortgage companies...they've always been good for buying ads this time of year....

Elliot looked over at Sky, who was furiously typing something on her computer while talking on the phone. He considered her something of a dingbat. Well, anyone who'd believe in astrology...that spoke for itself. And the way she always started out her articles with something cute, some stupid catch line, it was nothing but simplistic dribble.

He remembered one of her recent pieces: "At Mary Sue Brown's house, they never have to worry about mice because the Browns own ten cats." Catching mice had nothing to do with why the Browns own all those cats, he thought to himself. They were adopted because they had no home, because Mary Sue aspired to be a veterinarian and she can't stand to see any animal in pain. The slug line sounded cute, it sounded glib, but it wasn't the real story. Someday, Elliot was either going to own his own newspaper and make sure his reporters wrote "real stories," or he was going to write for a paper that got to the heart of things.

So why did Roz keep Sky? Probably because she was reliable, predictable, unlikely to quit...and had no high career aspirations with the paper. A sharp person like Fran, however, would move on to something else in a year or two, depending on where her romantic life took her. Elliot surmised that the main thing keeping her around was her girlfriend, Shauna, a vice president at Cape and Islands Bank and Mortgage. But if that relationship were to crumble, Elliot thought it likely that Fran would move back to Manhattan or another bustling metropolis. Sky was here because her husband, Bud, owned a charter fishing boat. She wasn't likely to leave Provincetown any time soon.

Roz headed to the inner sanctum of her office and looked at the clutter of papers on her desk. Should she organize her desk now or wait until later?

There was always a good argument for the desk-cleaning routine...a nice, clean, organized desk provided a nice, clean slate for diving into the tasks at hand. On the other hand, the chore could take all morning. Each piece of paper had to be read. There were those individuals who ascribed to the motto that if you touch it, you immediately deal with it...respond to it, file it, or throw it away. But Roz was not one of those people.

She needed to go through and read and think about the stuff on her desk. And since she generally couldn't afford the time it took to keep her desk clear, the piles of papers grew higher and higher. She tried to keep them somewhat organized by where they were placed, but ultimately many slips of this or that accidentally ended up in the trash. If only she could keep things better organized, she would tell herself, she probably wouldn't have to waste so much time looking for things. It would help to be more ruthless about throwing things away, she'd often think when looking down at the large waste bin beside her desk. Roz's mother always called it a circular file. "Throw this in the circular file," she'd constantly harp while reclining in her easy chair.

A teacher, she had done much of her work, like lesson plans and grading papers, on the living room coffee table. And there were always far too many papers, forms, and such to feel sentimental about keeping copies of her star students' compositions.

A good twenty pounds overweight, Roz's mother had needed to put her feet up at the end of the day. She huffed and puffed when she climbed up and down the stairs. Roz swore to herself that she would never let herself get fat when she grew older, so she adopted a strict exercize regimen and stayed away from snacks and desserts. It worked. At five foot seven, she'd maintained her high school weight of one hundred twenty-eight pounds. If there was only a way to stop the wrinkles and the gray hairs, Roz would sigh when looking in the mirror of her compact, powdering her nose.

At age forty-five, she could maybe pass for thirty-eight, but not much younger, even with her trim figure. She could cover the gray hairs with dye, and use creams and makeup to camouflage the wrinkles. But the bigger issue was *knowledge*...her face revealed too much knowledge to hide the fact that Roz Silva had reached middle age.

Not that she wanted to flatter herself by thinking that she was "oh, so wise." But she'd certainly been through a lot, with raising two children, helping develop a business, running a newspaper, losing her husband.... Roz felt old but longingly wished to still be young. Maybe that was the attraction to John Murphy. He made her feel young.

Beau Costa...now, this was a man who had made her feel old. No wonder he had married Annie, who couldn't be more than thirty-two.

Oh, she'd tried to spark his interest, even going so far as to invite him to dinner. What an embarrassment that had been. He had canceled at the last minute, and Roz had forced herself to pretend it was no big deal.

"Sorry," he said when he called. "I completely forgot a meeting at the Fine Arts Work Center, and I chair one of the committees. I just can't miss it. It's my fault for not checking my appointment book. Can you forgive me?"

"Oh, don't worry about it. It was just a family dinner, nothing special."

Now, that was a lie if ever there was one. Roz had prepared her version of beef Stroganoff, with big, juicy mushrooms, Vidalia onions, and sirloin tips over white rice.

"Who's coming to dinner?" Sally had asked. "Must be someone special. As soon as we're done eating, do you want me to say I have a lot of homework and quickly run upstairs? Or maybe I should go study at a friend's house. Then I'd really be out of your hair."

The canceled dinner had heralded the end to a series of encounters between herself and Beau. After being a recluse the first six months after Gene's death, Roz gradually allowed herself to consider romantic prospects when she attended social gatherings. If anything, it was a good mental distraction. And she soon began to set her sights on Beau. She would try to sit next to him at large parties, like at the Chamber of Commerce Christmas bash and the Year-Rounders Dinner, and it seemed that he liked her. They would have an amiable conversation, with a little bit of flirting, and one time they even danced together. But the relationship went no further. Roz had been persistent...there were just so few eligible straight bachelors around. But she certainly was not going to be so blunt as to say, "Would you like to come home and sleep with me?" though that's exactly what she was thinking.

Roz reasoned that she must not be very important to Beau or he would have canceled his meeting. At the very least, he could have re-scheduled, asked her out to dinner another time. But no, it was obvious she meant very little to him, just a casual acquaintance. And it made her angry. *Hell hath no fury like a woman scorned.*

It wasn't nice what she did, making him look bad in the newspaper. But it was fun. Plus she had the satisfaction of knowing he must have started thinking about her a great deal, even if it wasn't in a positive light.

The chirpy ring of the telephone brought Roz back to the present. If only that phone didn't sound like a robotic bird, she thought to herself.

"Roz?"

She relaxed at hearing the familiar sound of John's voice. "Yes?"

"You sleep okay?"

"I slept like a rock. I was so tired. Elliot and I were up late at the office brainstorming."

"Oh."

"How about yourself?"

"I was tossing and turning. The thought of someone just taking matters into their own hands and taking someone's life...maybe someone we know. It's going to give the town a lot of unfavorable publicity."

"Locally yes, but it means nothing in the total scheme of things. You've lived in big cities. Murders happen all the time, lots of murders. Some are never solved. Whole classrooms of children get gunned down by snipers. People just accept that life is dangerous."

"Coming to the Selectmen's meeting tonight?" John asked.

"I'll see how I feel," Roz replied. I know there'll be a lot of action, what with prospective candidates trying to stir up some trouble and a report about wastewater management. Elliot will be there. I may well be burned out by the end of the day."

"Any ideas on the murderer or motive?"

"Well, lots of ideas, but nothing concrete yet. Sweetheart, I hate to cut you off, but let's talk later because I was late getting to the office and I really need to focus on getting something done. Okay?...I love you," she whispered.

"And I, too," John whispered back.

Inside he felt empty. What was he doing having an affair with this woman who focused so hard on her work and herself? Didn't she know he called her because he was worried for her safety? There was a murderer out there, and maybe Roz was next on his list.

John Murphy needed to feel wanted. That's why he had gone into public service...government management, city planning. He liked all the phone calls, the attention, everyone calling out his name and greeting him as he walked down the street. He liked being someone important. He liked being the man in charge.

Roz sat down at her desk, deciding to forget about the mess right now. She had one day left to write her editorial. What aspect of the murder could she focus on? Safety? Confidence in the police force? The social responsibility of anyone with clues to come forward? All were good topics that would tie in with the reward money. She could also write about the importance of everyone in town banding together... yes. And there was the obvious eulogy about how the town would miss Sonny Carreiro.

Then again, will they? She could fuse together the concepts of losing of Sonny Carreiro and the importance of finding the person responsible for his death. That would be good. She brought up the editorial file on her computer screen and started typing.

"Hello? Mrs. Carreiro? Sorry. This is Sky Johnson from the *Provincetown Observer*. Is Mrs. Carreiro in? I'm writing the obituary on Sonny...I didn't know if she has something written up or would like to give me some information over the phone." Sky hated making these kinds of phone calls. It was always so awkward. Often, family or friends delivered their own statement to the newspaper, along with a photograph, to make certain nothing was left out. Then all she had to do was rewrite the material and try to fill in the blanks. Elliot had said he'd split the work on Sonny Carreiro with her, the reporting, because he was going to do an article on the community's reaction to the murder. Of course, he was looking for clues, as if someone would actually reveal whether they had a secret vendetta against Sonny Carreiro or knew someone who had.

"Sure, I'll wait," Sky said. The voice on the other end of the phone had been Sonny's sister, Jo Landon...Sarah Carreiro's sister-in-law. Elliot had told Sky he was certain that was where Mrs. Carreiro would be staying, instead of back at her former home where there were "too many memories." What kinds of memories? Had Sonny been abusive? Was he secretly a wife beater?

Sky's father had been that way. He used to hit her mother with a belt, saying, "You need this to teach you a lesson." She would hear her mother crying in the bedroom. Sky was six years old. Her brother was eight. Then one morning, Sky's mother had quickly packed their clothes in a laundry bag. Instead of dropping them off at school, she kept driving, all the way to Pennsylvania to Aunt Helen's house. Sky never saw her father again. Two weeks after they left, he put a gun to his head. He died instantly. One bullet to the temple. Who had written *his* obituary, Sky wondered.

"Yes? Mrs. Carreiro? Okay...Sarah. I appreciate your taking the time to talk with me. My sincere condolences on your loss.... We have some information in our files: graduated from Provincetown High School, bachelor's degree from Boston College, Carreiro Insurance and Real Estate Agency...okay, the two are separate corporations, not to be portrayed as one, got it. Special degrees in insurance, Life Underwriters Association, LUTCF fellow, licensed insurance broker, member of the Provincetown Chamber of Commerce, member of the Cape Cod Chamber of Commerce, former member of the Planning Board, former trustee of the Provincetown Library...was a current member of the Wastewater Advisory Commission, member of the Provincetown Art Association and Museum, Friends of the Heritage Museum, Blessing of the Fleet Celebration Committee, parishoner at Saint Peter's Church, member of the Lions Club...was currently involved in several condominium conversions. Your daughters' full names and ages?... Day and time of the services?... If I have any further questions, may I call you?... Thank you so much for your help."

Sky felt a huge sense of relief when she put down the phone. Her armpits and crotch felt slightly damp and sticky, but the hard part was over with. The writing part was more like a puzzle to put together, challenging but rewarding when complete. Civic leader? Local businessman? How should she portray him? Oh, she forgot to ask about a photograph. Did they have a decent file photo? She certainly didn't want to pick up the phone and call Sarah again.

"Okay, Sky...what do you have?" Elliot asked, leaning over her shoulder. He smelled like a combination of shampoo and little too much aftershave. Sky tried to narrow her nostrils to avoid inhaling his scent. A futile exercise. Elliot had a way of making her feel uncomfortable. Was it that he was too assertive or was it that he always acted so superior, as if he knew more than she did? He'll burn out quickly, she thought to herself, if he keeps on putting so much of his heart and soul into this job. Roz will just chew him up and spit him out. He was here late last night, working, and that's why he came in late this morning, hair still wet, fresh out of the shower. How much was he paid? Barely above minimum wage, most likely, when you added up the hours he put in.

"The usual," Sky replied. "A lot of community service, et cetera. Oh...but here's something interesting. Sarah seemed to make a big deal about the insurance agency and the real estate agency being separate entities."

"Well, Sonny's brother-in-law, Bill Landon, works at the insurance office...and Beau Costa was his real estate partner. So, of course they're two separate entities," Elliot said.

"But didn't he also do some sales and rentals?"

"Well, yes, he did some of that. Being an agent, he probably got inside leads on what was being bought and sold ahead of everyone else. But how did he make the bulk of his money...and does that have anything to do with why someone would want him dead?

Sarah went back to the blue guest room and closed the door. It was just like Jo to decorate her bedrooms in totally matching colors. Where did she find all this stuff? The wallpaper border, sheets, curtains, even the waste bin, all had the same design; and the silk flowers in the basket on the bureau were also the same exact shade of blue. Did Jo hire a designer to put this together or did she do it herself? Whoever's idea it was, Sarah thought it was pretty tacky. The room was so mundane and boring.

It *was* nice to have new things, everything clean and fresh, which was why this was such a pleasant house to visit. With two children and her job, Sarah had found it impossible to keep up with the housework. Whenever she looked closely at her own carpet, she saw crumbs. And when she looked in the corners, she saw dust balls. So she tried not to look too closely. But besides cleanliness, there also needed to be personality; a house needed to present a point of view.

That's what Fran had always said. "I see you in this house, Sarah," she'd remarked the first time she visited. It was a Christmas party. "It's got your warmth and style, your point of view."

Should she give Fran a call? Surely Fran knew she was in town, back for Sonny's funeral, but couldn't call her at Jo's house.... Well, why not? She could at least call to offer her condolences, as a friend. After all, Fran was a friend.

Fran had probably been sitting just a few desks away when that reporter called. What was her name? Sky...the one who wrote the weekly astrology predictions: "Someone new will enter your life. Expect the strange and unexpected. Try new avenues of pleasure." Hadn't Sky written something like that the very week she and Fran had "done it"... had become lovers?

Fran, so pretty and so smart, had wanted her. Sarah had wanted Fran for Sonny.

"What do you want for your birthday?" she'd asked Sonny two years ago.

"Another woman. You, me, and another woman. Wouldn't that be a kick?"

"Are you serious?" she'd demanded to know.

"Maybe yes and maybe no," he answered, twinkle in his eye. "Surprise me, sweetheart....whatever you decide to get me is fine. Surprise me."

Who could she ask? What woman did she know who would be interested and willing? And what woman, if any, Sarah wondered, did she find attractive enough to want to make love to? She only had a few women friends, mostly mothers with children the same age as hers. She couldn't ask any of *them*. Besides, most of these women seemed pretty conservative when it came to sex.

Sonny was always telling her about women he was attracted to, like the teller at the bank and the school secretary, none seeming to have much intelligence. Sarah liked a woman with intelligence, someone she could relate to and with whom she would feel simpatico. Then she met Fran at Sonny's office when she paid a visit to sell advertising. Sarah liked her immediately. So did Sonny.

"Pretty wild, the red hair, don't you think?" Sonny had commented. "I wouldn't like the color on most women, but on *her*.... What do you think? Pretty spicy?"

It had been at the Blessing of the Fleet and they were on the same boat, *Captiva*. While the men were busy getting drunk, Sarah and Fran had plenty of time to chat and get to know each other a bit.

"Save the food and drink for when we get out close to the point," Captain Charlie yelled. "We haven't even been blessed yet by the bishop and you fellows are already busy passing the bottle."

The line of boats had been long that year, all decked out with banners and flags, one with a Christmas tree still tied to its mast for good luck. They had formed a regatta to circle around within the harbor following the town parade, which had set out from Saint Peter's, joined by Scottish bagpipes and a high school marching brass band, waiting for the bishop to bless them with holy water. Earlier that morning, the girls had competed in the relay races at Motta Field and Cassie had won a blue ribbon in the potato sack race. And then Cassie had gone with her friend Martha's family on their boat, a small runabout, while Stephanie had joined them on the *Captiva*.

After swimming at Long Point and eating lobster salad sandwiches and brownies, Stephanie had fallen asleep in Sarah's lap. When her weight became unbearable, Sarah had gently moved her onto a pile of life preservers and covered her over with a towel.

"Too much sun?" Fran had asked.

"Too much of a good time. She was up at six this morning all excited about the races, the parade, the ride on the big boat...," Sarah answered.

"Sometimes I wish I had children. They must be a lot of fun...and so rewarding to see them grow and learn."

"Well, Fran, it's not too late. You still have time."

"I don't think so," Fran replied. "I'm just not the domestic type. I like my freedom."

As the two were downing their third or fourth glass of wine, out of the blue Fran had asked, "Ever make love to a woman?"

"Not yet," Sarah answered boldly, then going on about about Sonny's birthday and her plans to surprise him.

"Are you sure?" Fran wanted to know. "No jealousy? No bad feelings?"

"Oh, I love Sonny too much to get jealous," assured Sarah.

"Well...I wasn't worried about *you*," Fran said with a smile. "I was worried about Sonny."

The comment had given Sarah goose bumps. She remembered feeling the nipples underneath her T-shirt grow erect and that all-too-familiar sensation between her legs when she became sexually excited. Was it the way Fran was looking at her, sort of the way men did when they wanted to get into her pants, that had gotten her all fired up? Or was it the idea of doing something taboo?

"Mom?" Sarah snapped out of it and saw that Cassie was standing outside her room. "Can't we go get our bikes today and at least get some of our stuff from the house? I feel so cooped up here. Please?"

Overhearing this, Emma Green told her granddaughter, "Cassie, show your mother a little consideration. She has enough on her mind without worrying about your bicycles. She's still in shock."

"Jo, dear, may I borrow your car so I can get the girls settled down?" Emma called to Jo, who was sitting in the living room and working on the daily *Boston Globe* crossword puzzle.

"Oh, let me check the time," Jo replied, somewhat annoyed that Emma had broken her concentration. A four letter word that begins with "L"...a diving, fish-eating waterfowl, she pondered, speaking softly to herself. The answer was on the tip of her tongue.

Jo glanced at her wristwatch...this was the one without actual numerals. A little hard to read but oh, so stylish, and *real* gold, not gold filled. It was almost two o'clock. "Dear me! We've got to get over to the funeral home and finalize the coffin selection, and then Sarah and I need to talk to Father O'Malley. I suppose I could drop you and the girls off at the other house on the way, if you insist."

From the time they'd arrived, Jo had been hearing the two girls going on about how they wanted to get over to their old house, about how they were considering walking, only it was a few miles away. But she'd ignored them. It was more important to Jo that she be able to just enjoy her afternoon cup of coffee and redo her makeup and nails than be chauffeuring her nieces about. Nice kids, but they could wait. She needed time to relax and pull herself together. There was so much to think about.

"If you're not available to pick us up when we're done, we can always call a taxi," Emma said.

"But Grandma, we're going to bicycle home," Stephanie said.

"That's awfully dangerous. Do you have helmets?"

"Of course." Stephanie rolled her eyes, thinking that grown-ups, especially old people, were always such worry warts.

"Listen," Jo said, addressing Emma, "You can always call up Bill at the office. I'll give you his phone number, He can pick you up."

Why hadn't she thought of Bill earlier to do some driving around? He preferred keeping to himself, but how could he not be involved? After all, he did manage the Carreiro Insurance Agency. And it *was* called Carreiro, not Landon.

"Sarah?" she called as she walked to the blue guest room and rapped on the door. No answer. Jo opened the door ever so slightly. Coming from inside the bathroom was the sound of Sarah quietly crying.

6

Late Monday Afternoon

LIZ MURPHY CONSIDERED whether or not she should bake something nice to take over to the Carreiro/Landon household. Isn't that what you did? Drop by with some sort of covered dish, a cake, some homemade cookies...?

She knew Sonny Carreiro only as a passing acquaintance; but his brother-in-law, Bill Landon, had written up their car and renter's insurance policies. She'd actually been sitting in Sonny's private office at the time because Susan Stafford, the Associate Agent, was meeting with someone in Bill's office.

"We'll just step right in here and use Sonny's office," Bill had said while gesturing her into the large room at the end of the hall. "I'm sure Sonny won't mind. He's rarely here anyway," he'd added with a nervous laugh.

Liz had been surprised by the furnishings: large, comfortable, leather-covered chairs, an antique walnut partner's desk with a double green-shaded Emeralite lamp, and dark gray walls displaying nice oil paintings. The artwork was not characteristic of the typical nautical prints you usually saw in commercial offices.

"Sonny has quite an art collection," she had commented.

"Oh, yes," replied Bill. "He loves collecting paintings. I think it makes him feel important, patronizing all those 'starving artists.' And we have a lot of them around here, you know. Artwork is for sale all over the place. Most of it I don't much care for. Too strange. I like pictures of things I can recognize.... Now, this John Whorf..." he'd said, pointing to a watercolor of sailboats in the harbor, "...it's a nice picture. But the Motherwell silkscreen over there," continued Bill, gesturing towards an abstract that combined two vivid colors, "I can't even tell whether it's hung in the right direction."

"Have you lived here long?" she had asked, wondering how someone as traditional as Bill Landon could coexist with the usual bohemian types who largely populated the town.

"I met my wife, Jo...let's think a minute...about twenty years ago on a Caribbean cruise. Can you believe it? A regular 'love boat.' Well, we began courting and she brought me here shortly thereafter. In the Navy, I lived in various places...Norfolk, San Diego, Annapolis. Always by the sea. I like the water. I was just getting started in the insurance business down in New Bern, North Carolina, but moved up here instead. How about yourself? Where do you originally hail from?"

"The Midwest. Columbus, Ohio," Liz had answered. She really didn't like talking about herself. She thought of a way to quickly change the subject. "Can you explain to me how this no-fault auto coverage works in Massachusetts?"

Jo Landon had sat next to Liz at the Nautilus Club luncheon at the Holiday Inn. She'd been as nosy as him; so many annoying questions. "How do your children like our school? Found a house yet? Which church do you belong to?"

When Liz had finally finished what was on her plate and excused herself to go to the ladies' room, she'd gotten involved in talking with someone else on her way back to the table.

"Here's an empty seat. Why don't you have a seat and chat with us?" Peggy Noonan had suggested. Peggy's husband was retired from the police force, and she served on the board of the Provincetown Library. "It's okay if we mix around a little," she'd said before introducing her to a lady who ran the Seashell Guest Cottages along with her husband.

So many senior citizens, Liz had thought to herself...but younger women didn't have time for these clubs, of course. She supposed they all meant well, but enough was enough. That was the problem when you moved to a new place, people asking so many questions. It was probably better than being ignored, though.

As far as taking food to the Landons' house, maybe one of those ladies would come in handy now, Liz thought. She could call someone and ask their opinion, someone close to Jo. Who could that be? Maybe one of Jo's bridge or golfing partners would know whether it would be appropriate. Didn't Jo play golf with Hattie Sherman, one of the managers at the bank? Perhaps she could call Hattie.

It was so difficult living in a small town...Liz felt as if everyone was watching her. She didn't want to make a mistake. If only she had a job or something that kept her so busy she wouldn't have the time to ruminate over these things.

John had said if the kids were set up with summer jobs or some kind of camp program, she could take a seasonal job once Memorial Day weekend rolled around. But what kind of job? Restaurant, motel, gift shop jobs...they weren't exactly what she had in mind. Sooner or later, a teaching position would open up. That's what Liz really wanted to do, go back to teaching. In the meantime, she should really be working towards her master's degree. Boston wasn't too far and so many colleges were there. Surely there was some way she could accomplish her goal.

⁜──☵──⁜

Jo Landon drove her car slowly as she rattled on about the police investigation and funeral arrangements to Sarah. "I visited Mother early this morning and broke the news. I don't know whether she fully understood, poor thing. It might be too upsetting for her to attend the funeral."

When the children had been in the car, she was reluctant to speak about Sonny's death. Now that she had dropped Emma and the girls off at the other house, Jo felt she could talk freely.

"Well, she *is* your mother," Sarah said diplomatically. "Do what you think is best."

What would be best, Jo thought to herself, was for Mary Rose Carreiro to stay right where she was, where she could do no harm, where Jo wouldn't have to deal with her...in the Cape End Manor.

She could still hear her mother's voice. "Sonny! Sonny! What did they do to my Sonny? How could you let this happen, Josephine, to your little brother. God will punish them. They say what goes around comes around. You remember my words. You better go to church and pray!" she had shrieked in that high-pitched voice.

Weighing scarcely ninety pounds, the nursing home attendants kept Mary Rose's white hair tied back in a severe bun. The prominent Roman nose looked more and more like a bird's beak each time Jo visited. Where did her mother get so much energy to rant and rave? Though partially paralyzed on one side of her body from a stroke, words certainly came easily enough when she had something harsh to say.

"*Tenho vinte anos. Preciso de aqua.* My throat is dry...did you walk the dog this morning? He needs to be walked."

"You don't have a dog, Mother. You're in the Manor."

"I know. But the dog still needs walking...I know where I am!"

"Lucky died ten years ago."

"Oh, yes. I just forgot. The mind does that sometimes. He was a nice dog, wasn't he? *Gusto cachorros.* I like beagles. They're good hunting dogs.... So tell me, did *she* come back?"

"She? Who, Mother?"

"You know, his wife...what's her name? Sarah...that good for nothing!"

"Sarah's flying in later, a little before noon," Jo had said. "For the funeral."

"It's all her fault. She never should have left. This never would have happened. Of all the women in the world, he had to pick 'Miss Fancy,' an overeducated Jew. I knew she'd be trouble the moment I laid eyes on her. *Esta mau.*"

Jo turned her head a few times to quickly check out Sarah's profile. She didn't look particularly Jewish. Actually, Sarah was only half Jewish. Her mother was a Presbyterian. Who knew what their beliefs were? But the point was, *they weren't Catholic.*

Sarah felt Jo's glances. It was bad enough to deal with Sonny's death, but his family...they made her feel uncomfortable. They did and said all the right things on the surface, but she knew they didn't fully accept her. She was Sonny's wife...that was the only connection. Now that Sonny was dead, the bonds between them would surely become frayed.

It didn't matter what sort of memorial service Sarah wanted. The Carreiro side of the family was having the funeral mass at Saint Peter's. No one had bothered to ask her how she felt about it. How could she make waves about the whole thing, Sarah thought to herself, especially since she had been the one to leave.

In a way, it was nice to be passive. Let them rush about and make the arrangements. Later on, she could gather Sonny's real friends together for the kind of memorial service he would have wanted. But for now, she needed time to herself to think things over.

The dinner hour was always a good time to make an appearance, thought Roz...well, it really wasn't the dinner hour yet. It was cocktail hour. People in mourning must be drinking plenty of cocktails. So the diplomatic thing to do was to take them a bottle of Chivas Regal scotch, a hefty chunk of sharp Vermont cheddar cheese, and an assortment of gourmet crackers, all tastefully arranged in a basket with a nice card... from Rosalyn Silva and staff of the *Provincetown Observer*.

If they didn't feel like having company, she could unobtrusively leave the basket. But the seeds of goodwill would be planted. Sooner or later, she'd have a chat with Jo Landon, at the very least, and possibly with Sarah Carreiro, as well.

She tapped hesitantly on the clear-varnished oak door with the oval glass inset. Through the glass, she could see the green and apricot, oriental-style runner on the stairway leading up to the second floor and the colonial, candle-style chandelier hanging from the ceiling. Jo does have good taste, Roz thought to herself, but it seems much too formal for Provincetown.

"Roz, my dear," Jo greeted her with a warm smile. "What a nice surprise that you dropped by."

"I don't mean to intrude. I just wanted to bring a little something to let you know you're in my thoughts. If I can help in any way...."

"Well, do come in. We're just sitting down with drinks after a long day of dealing with the arrangements. You know what I mean," she whispered conspiratorially. "You've been through all this."

Jo took hold of the basket, peered in at the bottle of Chivas, and smiled. "We're out in the family room."

Roz followed Jo through the formal living room, down the hall, and into the massive great room, beyond which was a deck that looked out over the expanse of marshlands and tidal flats at the flat end of the arm-shaped peninsula that was Cape Cod.

Dusk had begun to set in and the room's lighting was already fairly dim. Roz could make out the faces of Sarah, Bill Landon, the older daughter, Cassie, and someone else...Liz Murphy.

"Liz was kind enough to bring us a big pan of her homemade lasagna. She assured me she'd made a second one for herself, John, and their children...what were their names?"

"Erin and Michael," Liz said in a soft, timid voice.

"Yes, of course...pretty names, Erin and Michael. I'm sure you two have met...Bill, how about getting Roz a drink."

Yes, I could definitely use a drink, thought Roz with relief, a big stiff drink. If she'd only known Liz was going to be here.... Oh well. It was always a good idea to assess one's competition. Roz had been introduced to Liz before. But she'd made a point of avoiding her, maybe because she was afraid if she spent any real time with Liz, somehow Liz would begin to sense that, hey, this lady is fucking my husband. But how would she know unless somebody told her...then again, maybe she really didn't *want* to know.

Roz could not dispute that Liz was attractive. Reddish-blonde hair, even features...perhaps a little faded, and noticeable crow's feet, if you got a good look at her complexion...plus a little extra weight around the middle. Certainly not overweight, but somewhat out of shape, one of those women who probably never bothered to get back their figure after bearing children. Roz knew the type...women who felt justified in having a bit of "middle-aged spread," as they referred to it. Midriff bulge, flabby buttocks, broad hips. Being mothers justified letting themselves go.

Well, I have news for you, honey, Roz thought to herself. When you don't take care of your body, men's eyes will wander. You have to stay lean and mean...it's a cruel world out there.

Liz looked up at Roz from her seat and smiled. Maybe she should have stood to say hello, but the gin and tonic had gone straight to her head. She hadn't meant to stay. She'd only intended to bring the lasagna and express her condolences, but it seemed rude to refuse when asked to join them for cocktails.

John had mentioned it would be good for Liz to get out and socialize more. "You need to make some friends. You won't meet anyone if you stay at home...and you know I'm tied up a lot with those damn meetings."

Roz Silva didn't seem a likely prospect for a friendship. Too intimidating and walked with an air of self-assurance that gave the impression she owned the room, and everyone in it, when she entered.

Her nice, trim figure was infuriating to Liz, who felt compelled every few months to go on a diet. Olive skin and dark, wavy hair...Roz had strong features, with expressive eyebrows, thick, dark lashes, and a slightly aquiline nose. Definitely striking, but not necessarily beautiful by everyone's standards. You needed a taste for the exotic.

How old could she be, Liz wondered. Must be at least in her early forties based on her children's ages. Liz had heard one was already in college. But she looked like she was in her thirties...and that was reason enough not to like her. Liz had to admit, however, that Roz *was* very personable and charming.

"So, Liz...at last we get a chance to chat," said Roz. "Have you gotten all settled in?"

"Pretty much. We're still looking around for a house."

"A few new listings came in yesterday," interjected Bill Landon from the other side of the room, seated next to Sarah and Cassie on the overstuffed floral sofa. "There's a nice house on Bradford Street in the West End and another on Bangs Street."

"Well, you certainly don't want to live on Bradford Street," Jo exclaimed. "Too much traffic."

"Nonsense. There are plenty of nice houses on Bradford, and traffic's only an issue in July and August," responded Bill.

"Cassie, why don't you check on Grandma...see if she's woken up from her nap and wants to join us down here," Sarah said to her daughter. "Then see what your sister, Stephanie, is up to."

"Probably watching television," Cassie answered.

"Well, why don't you go watch it with her. This is getting to be a grown-up conversation."

"Okay. I get the message." Cassie made a slight grimace and took heavy steps out of the room and up the stairs. She did think the conversation had been pretty boring, but maybe they'd start talking about who could have murdered her father. A lump welled up inside her throat and tears were forming in her eyes. She quickly headed for the bathroom so Stephanie wouldn't see her crying.

"So…how old is Cassie?" asked Roz.

"She's twelve going on twenty-two," Sarah replied.

"You don't mind that I've been handling the real estate side of the business, do you?" Bill asked, turning towards Sarah. "When you feel like it, we'll have to sit down and talk about what you'd like to do about that operation."

"Do you have your real estate license, Bill?" inquired Roz. "I thought you were the insurance man. And are those two businesses merged?"

"Carreiro Insurance is a family corporation. Carreiro Real Estate was owned and operated by Sonny. And yes, I do have my Massachusetts real estate license. If I happened to assist in a sale or rental transaction, Sonny paid me a commission."

"So who actually owns the majority of shares of Carreiro Insurance?" asked Roz.

"My mother, Mary Rose Carreiro, of course," Jo interjected, tersely adding, "I think we've now had enough talk about our personal business, Roz. What's going on at the newspaper? Have you hired any interesting columnists for the summer season?"

"A young man from Emerson College is coming and will be writing the music and entertainment reviews. I'm still looking for an art critic, even though the galleries would probably like me to simply print the news releases they provide, along with plenty of photographs."

"But I know you won't do that," responded Jo, "especially if the photos are pornographic…like that show last summer at the Unicorn Gallery. Pretty repulsive, all those close-ups of female genitalia. Those damn lesbians are starting to think they own the town and can get away with everything…holding hands in public, kissing. Gay men are so much more discreet."

"Not necessarily," Sarah replied after taking a sip from her Bloody Mary. "It depends on which gay men you're talking about."

"Well," said Liz, "when I first arrived in town last summer, I seem to recall several young men walking around downtown wearing nothing but tiny leather bikinis. They were definitely advertising something."

Everyone in the room nervously laughed. It was easier to bash someone else than talk about themselves.

"So you aren't going to the Selectmen's meeting tonight, Roz?" Jo pointedly asked.

"Well, it's been a long day...and it *is* Elliot's beat," Roz answered.

"You keep him awfully busy, don't you?" continued Jo.

"He enjoys it. We're all pretty fired up at the newspaper about possibly unearthing clues that will help us find out who killed Sonny. I mean, we can't just rely on the police investigation."

"Yes, you're probably right, Roz," said Sarah wearily from the couch. "What kind of experience does the Provincetown Police Department have in solving murders? Probably not much."

The conversation was conveniently turning back to the subject of Sonny's murderer, and Roz was not going to let the opportunity pass without finding out some more pertinent information.

"So tell me, Sarah...being an insurance agent, of course Sonny had a life insurance policy to provide for you and the children. Did he also have other policies to protect his loans?" Roz inquired.

"I believe he had what's called a buy/sell policy with Beau Costa," Bill Landon abruptly offered before Sarah had time to answer. "If one partner dies, it theoretically provides the other partner with enough money to buy out the other half so they don't have to get involved with the heirs of their partner's estate. I think the policy is for half a million dollars. I can look it up in the files for you."

"Well, Sarah, it sounds like you are going to be quite a wealthy widow," remarked Jo.

"Maybe I don't want to sell out to Beau," Sarah responded indignantly.

"I don't think you have a choice," Bill informed her. "If they took out the policy, which works both ways, they have a buy/sell agreement on file."

"I seem to recall another life insurance policy on Sonny, a key man policy," said Sarah.

"Yes, and I have one on myself, as well," said Bill. "That's for the insurance agency, to enable us to invest in another managerial employee."

"How much is that policy for?" Roz asked eagerly.

"Two hundred and fifty thousand dollars," answered Bill.

"Which goes to Mary Rose...indirectly, of course," piped up Liz from her seat. Perhaps the others had forgotten she was in the room, as they'd been so preoccupied with money and insurance policies. Liz figured she should say something.

"Mary Rose?" Roz repeated the elder Mrs. Carreiro's name.

"Well, yes," said Liz. "Didn't I hear Jo say that Mary Rose owns the majority of shares of the Carreiro Insurance Agency?"

"I guess you're right," Roz said, appreciating that Liz had been paying attention to the fine points of tracing who got what money as a result of Sonny's death. Of course, just because Mary Rose *owned* the majority of shares didn't mean she *controlled* the majority of shares. And wasn't she at the Cape End Manor? With now only one living child, Josephine Carreiro Landon, as well as two grandchildren, who controlled her finances?

"But," said Liz, now thinking outloud," who has the bigger policy? Beau stood to gain a lot from Sonny's death."

Sarah shook her head. "I've spent a lot of time with Beau. He used to be a fixture at our house before he took up with Annie. Sonny and Beau had their differences, and I don't think they were on speaking terms for the past several months, but Beau a murderer? I just don't think so."

"How can you be business partners and not be on speaking terms?" Liz wondered.

"Oh, you'd be surprised!" chuckled Roz. "In a small town like this, there are feuds aplenty. There are brothers who don't talk to one another who run competing businesses. There are ex-wives and ex-husbands, children who refuse to talk to their parents. They all communicate through their lawyers. We have plenty of lawyers."

"Well, I guess I shouldn't discourage my son, Michael, when he talks about going to law school. Sounds like it continues to be a growing profession," Liz said with a sarcastic tone to her voice.

"How old is he?" asked Sarah.

"Fourteen, two years older than Cassie. And on that note, I really should be getting home. John is off to the Selectmen's meeting and I need to check up on the kids. Jo, Bill, thank you so much for inviting me into your beautiful home. I wish we could have met under more pleasant circumstances, Sarah. Nice to see you again, Roz."

Liz got up and straightened out her vest, which had gotten crumpled up in the back from sitting all this time. She'd worn it to camouflage the fact that her pants were a little tight in the front. Hopefully, it did the trick.

"Let me see you to the door," offered Jo while getting up from her chair. It felt good to stretch her legs.

"Oh, that's not really necessary."

"No bother," said Jo, who wanted to make certain Liz followed the right path out. She didn't want her to end up in the kitchen and see the pile of dishes that needed washing. It was always so embarrassing when people saw messes they weren't supposed to see.

"So, how did you come to write that big front-page story about Beau being accused of bank fraud?" Sarah asked Roz as soon as Liz and Jo had left the room.

The question caught Roz by surprise because she was busy observing Liz leave and wondering whether anyone in the room knew about her affair with John. It seemed as though Jo had given her a significant look when making the introductions after Roz arrived...maybe it was just in her imagination.

She quickly collected her thoughts. "A file of papers was dropped off at the office with all the information. We called up the various people involved to verify the facts and then went with the story.... Don't give me that look, Sarah. I'm running a business. I need headlines. I need to sell newspapers." Roz took another sip of her vodka and tonic and sat back in her chair, fully expecting to be lambasted with a lecture from Sarah on responsible journalism.

But Sarah was too tired, too weary, to deliver a lecture on anything. It had been a long day, one that now seemed more and more like a dream. She just wanted to go upstairs, lie down on her bed, or any bed, and go to sleep. And when she woke up, maybe things will have changed and Sonny would still be alive.

Jo returned to the great room and announced, "I think it's about time we put some real food in our stomachs. I'm going to start heating up that lasagna. Care to join us, Roz?" Jo knew she had to make the gesture; otherwise, she wouldn't be a good hostess. But she really hoped Roz would decline the invitation.

"That's very kind of you, but I do still have one child at home who needs checking on...although she doesn't think of herself as one."

"What year is Sally in?"

"She's a junior, so we need to start thinking about colleges."

"Plenty of scholarship money here."

"Absolutely. Anyway, I'll be casting off now. Thanks again," Roz said while rising and getting the kinks out of her legs.

Once again, Jo led her guest towards the front door. "Liz seems to be such a lovely person," Jo commented to Roz as they walked into the hallway.

Roz entertained the fleeting thought: Wouldn't it be wonderful if the chandelier above them fell down and banged Jo on the head so she would shut up? And what a busybody. She must know something about her affair with John because usually Jo never says anything positive about anybody.

"Oh, yes. She seems very nice," Roz echoed. "Let me know if there's anything I can do to help."

"Thank you, dear," replied Jo as she closed the door, immediately asking herself sarcastically why she would ever ask Roz for any sort of help…unless she wanted to read about it in the newspaper. But she can be useful….

7

Early Monday Evening

AT THIS TIME OF YEAR, the restaurant was closed Mondays through Thursdays. So with Dolly purring in his lap, Frank was enjoying just being in his apartment and spending some leisure time flipping through copies of *Bon Appetit* and *Southern Gourmet* magazines. There was an intriguing recipe for red peppers stuffed with a combination of chicken, scallions, capers, anchovies, garlic, and oregano. But it required a lot of work. First, the chicken needed to be marinated and the peppers roasted and peeled. The next step entailed sautéing the chicken and then pulverizing it into a paste, along with the other ingredients, in a food processor. Finally, the peppers were stuffed with the paste and baked in the oven with sliced potatoes and tomatoes.

He could first try making just a small batch. If it became a big hit, he could prepare the paste and roast the peppers in advance. Still, there was a thirty-minute gap between putting the dish in the oven and serving it at the table. Twenty minutes' cooking time was better because it allowed for some leeway, but thirty minutes was doable.

At the Indigo Inn, his dishes were all prepared to order. It might be forty-five minutes between drinks and the main course, if the guests ordered soup or appetizers. Appetizers were important. The profit margin was high. Prices for a few ounces of marinated sea bass, a half-dozen pieces of lobster-stuffed ravioli in pesto sauce, or a small skewer of marinated Thai chicken with peanut sauce and grilled vegetables ranged between six and twelve dollars. Soups were even better; those consisting primarily of vegetables cost him just pennies a cup to make.

But it was the easy things you just marinated and threw on the grill that Frank liked best. Part of dining out was the description and presentation of what you were offering. The sauces and garnishes decorating the plate were what created a special look. He thought about some of his favorite garnishes: thinly sliced yellow squash with a mound of diced red pepper, topped by a sprig of fresh dill; and green zucchini that was put through a shredder and made to look like thin pieces of spaghetti, next to a salsa of red tomatoes and purple onions. If you made it sound special and look special, people felt special eating it.

Maybe he should write a cookbook, his own cookbook, Frank pondered, and sell it at the restaurant. That could be a great idea. How much would it cost to print? He could keep it simple, one color, and maybe put a black-and-white photograph on the cover. What type of investment were we talking about? Frank became excited just thinking about the prospect...*The Frank Chambers Cookbook*, or *A Visit to Frank Chambers' Kitchen, Recipes from the Indigo Inn, The Indigo Inn Cookbook*....

Including some advertising from local guesthouses, bars, shops would offset some of the printing costs. Hey, why not a magazine? It could be a cooking magazine. No, that wouldn't sell. It has to have a local slant. It could be *Provincetown Vacation Magazine*, with local recipes, tips on shopping, where to find the beaches, things like that. And, of course, his ad rates would be lower than "you know who's".... Wow, that would really piss her off, chuckled Frank.

"What do you think, Dolly?" he asked his cat. "Do you think we ought to start publishing our own magazine?"

Frank excitedly started pushing the buttons on his telephone. "Bruno...are you busy? I have this idea...."

Cheap advertising, or cheaper advertising, was something Bruno Marchessi always liked to hear about. You didn't get paying guests exclusively from word of mouth.

"You realize that you need money to start a magazine, Frank, lots of money. If it was so easy, don't you think someone would have challenged the *Provincetown Observer*'s monopoly a long time ago? And there are some other summer magazines around...the *Lower Cape Guide, Provincetown Entertainer*...."

"Yes, I know. But they're not *really* local. They're just spin-offs of magazines printed Up Cape that they try to localize for other areas on the Cape. Mine would be different."

"Well, I suppose if you started talking to all the real estate agencies, they might be interested, especially Polly Smithfield. She hates Roz's guts and has lots of money to invest after all the dough she made from that subdivision in Truro. Also Sean Gilligan over at the Cowboy Club. He finally got his liquor license back after being suspended a few months ago...and he certainly didn't like the newspaper coverage. He might front you some money or at least take out a full-page ad. The real estate agents, clubs, restaurants...those are your most likely potential backers, and they'd also be your biggest advertisers."

"See, Bruno...I knew you'd have some good ideas," said Frank. "Okay, I'll get in touch with Polly tomorrow. In the meantime, don't tell a soul. If I go ahead with this, I want it to take Roz Silva by surprise."

"Well, I don't see how you're going to keep it a secret," replied Bruno. "As soon as you start trying to drum up advertising, people are going to start talking."

"True. Anyway, first I need to put together a prototype and write some articles, plus design a snappy-looking cover. Once the concept is in place, of course the word will spread. I just don't want Roz to steal any of my ideas."

"What do you think she's going to do? Start her own magazine?"

"Well, she could, you know. All she has to do is make it an insert in her newspaper, and also distribute it separately. Don't think she wouldn't try if she thinks I'm stealing too much of her advertising dollars."

"Okay. You made your point. Keep me posted, and put me down for a quarter-page ad if this gets off the ground."

"Thank you, Bruno. Hey, how would you like to write an article about the ins and outs of running a guesthouse? I won't be able to pay you but I'd print your ad for free. Think of all the PR you'd get from writing about your own guesthouse. Perhaps you could include some attractive pictures of you and your guests."

"I do have some pictures you could use. I'm not much of a writer... but I could give it a try."

"Great," Frank replied. "Talk to you tomorrow."

Frank lifted Dolly off his lap and went into the kitchen to fix himself a smoothie, something he always liked before going to bed. Depending on the time of year, he tried different fruit combinations, but he always included yogurt, honey, and protein powder. Tonight, he poured into the blender some Florida strawberries…and a banana, for the potassium, he said to himself. From the inside shelf of the refrigerator door he pulled out a half-dozen bottles of herbal capsules: echinacea, goldenrod, milk thistle, garlic, valerian, and St. John's wort. A pound of prevention is worth an ounce of cure, Frank believed. Yes, he had tested positive for the HIV virus, but so far his blood count was good and he didn't feel a need to begin taking those expensive protease inhibitor medications that often came with unpleasant side effects.

He tried to put the thought of death out of his mind. It wasn't really death he was worried about; it was the thought of a slow, debilitating illness. No wonder more than one person he knew had intentionally taken their own life after learning they were HIV-positive. Oh, it wasn't necessarily a case of taking a gun and blowing their brains out. Larry Bronstein, the antique furniture dealer, had gotten drunk and ran his car into a tree. And there was Ted, the popular bartender, who had gotten mangled up in the rotor blades of a powerboat while water-skiing. Both had technically died from "accidents," but Frank knew better… they'd intentionally caused these accidents.

It was scary, like waiting around for a time bomb to finally explode. It might take a year. It might take ten. For now, Frank was not about to let himself get depressed. He was going to do his best to take care of himself and try to enjoy life. He was going to think positively and try to make some positive changes in the world.

By starting a magazine, maybe he could make a difference. It would definitely have an impact on the monopoly and control that Roz Silva relished. When the magazine came out, it would hit her like a ton of bricks.

The vodka tonic had gone straight to Roz's head. Perhaps it was fatigue. Maybe it was the tension of being around Liz Murphy, plus dealing with all the members of the Carreiro family. She drove home slowly, careful to keep her eyes focused on the road.

Pulling into the narrow driveway of her ramshackle, gray-shingled house on Pearl Street, Roz could see that most of the lights inside were on, meaning Sally was home. She'd probably already managed to fix herself some dinner. It was pushing seven o'clock.

Roz lamented the fact that she needed a driveway. It had taken away some of the space she'd wanted for a garden. Paved with bleached white oyster and clam shells, it now took up half the front yard. The car door made its familiar noise, a cross between a whine and a creak, when she opened it. It only took a few short steps to be standing on the flagstone path to the front door. Her house sat on a small lot, like most others in Provincetown. As it was nearly impossible to find street parking during the summer months, Gene had decided there was no choice but to put in a driveway...and now he wasn't around to use it.

Summer tourists were always parking in the lot at the *Observer*, so Roz would constantly be calling Santos Towing Service to haul the cars away. "PARKING FOR EMPLOYEES AND ADVERTISERS OF *THE PROVINCETOWN OBSERVER*. ALL OTHERS WILL BE TOWED TO SANTOS PARKING GARAGE AT THE OWNER'S EXPENSE." It was amazing how many people ignored signs.

The lights inside the house may have been on, but the ones outside certainly weren't. Teenagers couldn't be bothered to think about such things. Roz gingerly made her way up the wooden steps and onto the front porch. She managed to get her key into the lock. No key was necessary; the door was unlocked.

"Sally, I told you to lock the door behind you when you come in," Roz called to her daughter, who was sitting at the kitchen table with an open math book in front of her."

"Sorry, Mom. I'll try to remember. I've got a big math test tomorrow, pre-calculus. I don't have time to talk."

"I wasn't trying to have a chat. I was just interested in some security precautions, with a young girl alone in the house."

"I don't think you have to worry, Mom. Maybe if I was a young guy, *then* you'd have a reason to be concerned...."

"Ha ha ha," responded Roz. "I know it was some time ago, but there was that man who went around in a raincoat, wearing nothing underneath, who raped over a dozen young girls and women before being caught. There are plenty of weirdos in this world. Besides, Sally, we now have a murderer on the loose. Or have you forgotten?"

"Right, the Sonny Carreiro murder. Everyone at school says Beau Costa did it or hired someone to do it."

"Well, if that's the case, why haven't the police arrested him yet?"

"They're probably still gathering evidence."

Roz shrugged her shoulders in exasperation. There was no reasoning with Sally, who thought she knew everything. Maybe she did. Maybe she was right. The possibility of owning the entire Seascape Development Company might be enough of an incentive for Beau to commit murder.

Roz walked out of the kitchen and back into the front hallway to check the mail. It was neatly stacked on the small Victorian side table to the left of the door. At least Sally had done something right…she'd actually retrieved the mail and brought it inside. Probably just checking to see if anything was for her. Lately, Sally had gotten more mail than Roz some days, mostly college brochures. That's what happens when your name is on all those lists after taking the SATs, Roz told herself.

Amidst the junk mail and bills was one handwritten envelope, addressed to Roz, with no postage stamp. She ripped it open.

"Can't Stop Thinking About You" was the sentiment on the front of the commercial card. Handwritten inside was, "I'll miss you tonight. Take care of yourself.

Love, John."

How sweet, Roz thought, feeling the tears welling up in her eyes. A little risky, though, because it meant John had actually driven or walked over to her house during the day and placed the card in her mailbox. Did any of the neighbors see him?

Perhaps she should do the same. Send him a card. Write him a love poem. Suppose his wife happened to find it?

The feeling was more than a little strange, having just seen Liz and then coming home and finding a love note from John. Despite her criticisms, she liked Liz. But Roz *needed* John and wasn't willing to give him up.

She returned to the kitchen to look for something to eat. The card had been carefully placed inside the back zip section of her purse, to be put in some secret hiding place later. Or she could just throw it away. It wasn't wise to keep incriminating evidence around, but it might be nice to read it again when she found herself feeling lonely. Roz liked to save nice letters people had written to her. So few people took the time these days to write anything, especially in longhand.

A whole box of letters and condolence cards, sent when Gene died, was stored away in her memory trunk...the same trunk that held a few special things from their marriage she had wanted to save: one of Gene's signature Hawaiian shirts, their wedding invitation, one of Gene's ties, his journal, love letters they'd written while courting, ticket stubs from vacations taken together, her wedding dress.... She rarely looked inside the trunk anymore. It made her too sad. Besides, isn't that why she packed the items away, so they'd be out of sight? They were special things she'd saved to look at later, years later...or maybe never again.

Wasn't she really saving those things for her daughters? They'll probably end up throwing everything away, although maybe one of them would use the wedding dress, Roz thought to herself cynically.

Some orange cheddar cheese and a package of corn tortillas in the refrigerator got Roz's attention. Quesadillas might be nice, she thought.

"What did you have for dinner, Sally?"

"A peanut butter and jelly sandwich and some chips."

"Doesn't sound very healthy to me."

"It was easy, and peanut butter has plenty of protein. Are you going to cook something?"

"Maybe. I was thinking of doing up some quesadillas."

"Well, if you're going to fry them on the stove, could you make a few for me? In the microwave, they're not as good."

"They're really healthier in the microwave, no grease. But corn tortillas need the oil. If I only had the flour ones, you'd be out of luck," Roz told her daughter with a smile.

She finally took off her jacket and swung it over the back of a chair. It was too much trouble now to take it over to the closet. She would hang it up later, if she remembered.

"Busy at the paper, Mom?"

"Very busy. With all the stories about Sonny's murder, and gearing up for the summer season with more advertisers, things are hopping. Perhaps you'd like to come in and help out this weekend. We always need help with filing...."

"You know I don't like working for you. We have a track meet on Saturday, anyway."

"Oh, sorry. I forgot," Roz said while pouring enough olive oil to cover the bottom of a medium-size, cast-iron frying pan.

"Don't worry about it, Mom. I don't need you to be there. Besides, it's up in Harwich."

"Your sister never seemed to mind working in the office."

"Well, Andrea is Andrea and I'm me...she's not coming back here this summer to work for you, is she?"

"No. I think that work-study program in England is a great opportunity for her." The oil was starting to sizzle, so Roz placed the tortillas in the hot oil and waited for them to bubble up from the heat below.

"I'm sure if she didn't get that, she'd get something else. Mom, nobody likes working for their parents. It just took Andrea a while to figure it out."

"Well, *thank you, Sally!*" Roz replied, grabbing the hunk of cheese and aggressively pushing it against a metal grater to create a shredded mound.

"Hey, it's the truth. I'd rather be selling T-shirts or scooping ice cream than working at the newspaper. I know you think it would be more educational, but it's not. Just a bunch of filing and no way for me to meet anybody very interesting."

"You might just find there are plenty of interesting people to meet, and maybe I'd even let you write a news story," said Roz as she flipped the tortillas, topping them with a handful of grated cheese, and folding one half of each over the other half like you would an omelet.

"Yeah, and maybe you'd edit it or totally rewrite it. Plus, people would be saying I only got the job because I'm your daughter."

"And it would be the truth. But that doesn't mean you don't have talent."

"Thanks a lot, but I'll follow my own path. I might be able to get a job this summer teaching windsurfing! Wouldn't that be awesome?"

"I'm sure it would. But just remember to wear lots and lots of sunscreen, and a life vest."

"Mom, I'm not a baby."

"I know you're not, but you are *my* baby...my youngest," replied Roz as she slid two of the finished quesadillas onto a plate and handed it to Sally. It was hard to believe...it seemed like only yesterday that

Sally was just a toddler, waddling around in diapers. And now she was almost an adult, talking back to her mother. But Sally still preferred that her mother do the cooking.

Elliot pored over the volumes of bound and archived old newspapers. He could have gone over to the library and perused them on microfilm, but the feel of newsprint in his hands was so much more real. A picture was beginning to develop in his mind, a picture of a growing real estate enterprise that began with one small apartment building nearly twenty years earlier. In the beginning, it had been Sonny and his father. Upon his father's death, the building had become Sonny's...in reality, Sonny's *and* the bank's.

Sonny had then used the equity to buy more, specifically another apartment building as well as a downtown storefront that he developed and turned into a complex of shops, six to be exact. A few were down below in basements; the others were located along an attractively landscaped corridor of cobblestones and planters. He named it Cranberry Square and painted the shingled buildings a cranberry red.

That was in the days when Provincetown still had a town crier. Sonny paid the town crier extra money to ring his bell at the entrance to Cranberry Square and announce special promotions and talk about the wares being sold by the merchants who had rented the various shops. The Selectmen and Chamber of Commerce both objected, and the town crier almost lost his job. Eventually, there was no more official town crier, just an honorary town crier.

We should have one again, Elliot thought to himself. He recalled all the pictures of town criers he'd seen in an exhibit of old postcards at the Heritage Museum. There are all kinds of other characters around here dressed up in costume...hawking time-shares at condominiums, handing out flyers announcing tea dances and female impersonation shows. True, town criers were usually old men with white hair, evoking memories of pilgrim days, but advertising nothing other than the town in general and calling out the time of day and when the tide was high.

These days, it would cost a lot of money to pay someone to walk around in breeches and buckled shoes, getting their picture taken with tourists. The town wouldn't want to foot the bill, nor would the Chamber of Commerce or gay-oriented Business Guild.

Most businesses here weren't interested in attracting history buffs and families. They wanted a fast return on their money. They were looking to sell expensive dinners, drinks, and merchandise. The fact was, people without children had more disposable income: no school tuitions, braces, summer camp, clothes, babysitters, piano lessons. Single people spent their money on vacations. They ate at expensive restaurants, stayed at nice hotels, went to shows, and bought expensive souvenirs like clothes, jewelry, antiques, artwork, and home furnishings. The marketplace developed and the successful survived.

Cranberry Square was not an instant success. It seemed to have run into some problems. About the time the project was completed, the cost of gasoline went up and the dollar was strong on the foreign exchange. Tourism went down. For more than one summer season, people were instead vacationing abroad and New Englanders weren't taking their usual weekend trips out to the tip of Cape Cod.

In what was typically peak season, business took a nosedive, and the hardest hit were those not located directly on the street. Merchants weren't paying their rent. Some had even packed up their goods and skipped town in the middle of the night to avoid their financial responsibilities. The bank was probably about to foreclose on Cranberry Square the winter after it was built, but something lucky happened. There was a fire.

Fires were not uncommon in Provincetown. At various times in its history there had been arsonists, usually troubled youths who got their kicks from setting fires to closed-up, isolated buildings during the quiet winter months.

But this fire was different. It took place downtown. And someone had lost their life, a bum sleeping inside one of the buildings in the complex. The theory was that he had made a small fire to keep warm. The temperature was twenty degrees Fahrenheit, but five degrees with the wind-chill factor, and the heat had been shut off and the pipes drained. But the fire had gotten out of control, spreading quickly due to a strong wind that night.

Almost everything had been destroyed. Most of the frame structures were burned to the ground, including a large antique shop owned by Sonny that was filled to the brim with merchandise. But whereas oftentimes the buildings that had previously been destroyed by fires had minimal insurance coverage, or not quite enough to cover all the costs of rebuilding, Cranberry Square had been well covered. After all, its owner was an insurance agent.

Elliot's stomach growled angrily. He had eaten nothing since lunchtime and it was now fifteen past seven. The other staff had left a couple hours earlier, but Elliot had been absorbed in what he was learning. That's what he liked about writing; it was the absorption. In the several other jobs Elliot had tried, his mind would wander. He'd spent one summer on a building site as a carpenter's helper and another fighting forest fires with his cousin out in California. Those had been fun summers, out in the open air, hanging out with the "real men." But after getting the hang of what you needed to do, like drive a nail in straight or build a firewall, the work became monotonous...boring, with a capital B.

Newspaper writing had not occurred to him until his senior year at Amherst. He decided to give it a try because he'd grown so tired of the fraternity parties and all those cutesy girls from Smith and Mt. Holyoke, some pretending to be lipstick lesbians. So where had it gotten him but to this quaint little town, at the end of a peninsula and surrounded on three sides by the ocean, to which he'd arrived by boat. And populated by a lot of *real* lesbians.

He and his friends, Rick and Mike, had gone on a sailing adventure up the coast of Maine to Swan's Island, located just south of Mt. Desert Island and Acadia National Park, where Rick was determined to attend a two-day folk festival. It was a beautiful island with several churches, houses, a library, school, museum, bakery, and general store. But no bars; the island was dry. Not much in the way of real restaurants, just a few take-out joints with ice cream, sandwiches, lobster rolls, and fried clams.

Elliot had been hoping to scam on some chicks. Several weeks on a boat with two other guys had him craving some female companionship. But where do you meet them? Elliot didn't much go for the naturalistic, folksy types, who seemed to go out of their way to look dowdy...loose clothes, frizzy hair. He liked women who were attractive, strikingly attractive. Early on, he had learned that many men were scared of women who were too attractive. He wasn't.

On Swan's Island, he had met one woman, Julie, hanging around outside Odd fellows Hall after the first night of the folk festival and invited her back to the boat for a few beers. She kept bringing up Provincetown, which Elliott had never visited, although he had been to other towns on the Cape during his college years. "Too far a drive," his buddies had said. "Besides, just a lot of gay people and freaks, and very expensive," they had added. She had talked about walking across the sand dunes and picking beach plums and making jelly as a child when she lived there. Julie's parents had divorced when she was ten, and her mother had moved up to Portland, Maine, and her father out to Santa Fe, New Mexico. She wanted to go back and see if it was still the way she remembered.

"We could sail there, if you like," he had suggested. What was one more person aboard the boat? He was so horny and just wanted to get in her pants. She was pretty...long, dark hair, arched eyebrows, long lashes, plus a graceful figure. Not much in the way of breasts, but no one was perfect.

So that was how Elliot first got to Provincetown. It was because of Julie. She left after a few weeks, once she'd rehashed all the memories. But Elliot had seen an ad in the local newspaper: "Reporter Wanted." It was a full-time job; and since it was after Labor Day, rents were cheap.

He remembered thinking at the time that it might be fun and maybe he should give it a try. His parents had been shocked because they were hoping he'd enter law school. But Elliot had convinced them he needed some time out in the world to gain some experience. "Then I can make an intelligent decision about what I truly want to do," he'd said. By now almost seven years had gone by, and Elliot was still trying to figure it out.

For a young, straight man in this town, it had turned out to be such a great life because there were a lot of foxy women around as well as a lot of intelligent, interesting people. Some were kind of strange and eccentric, but what an opportunity it had been to meet artists, writers, musicians, scientists, and entrepreneurs of all kinds.

The living was cheap, and Roz was not such a bad woman to work for. Also, Gene had been really nice and Elliot had felt an obligation to stick around after his death to do what he could to ensure the newspaper continued to run smoothly. Many people had quit, like rats leaving a sinking ship, because they were certain Roz was going to sell. They were wrong...Roz was a fighter.

The hunger pains were becoming unbearable. Elliot really needed something to eat before heading over to the Selectmen's meeting, and it was getting late. Instead of going to a restaurant, he decided to just go home and grab a quick sandwich.

Eating out in Provincetown all the time could get to be expensive, but Elliot didn't especially like to cook and it also took too much time. What was in his refrigerator for making a sandwich? The easiest thing would probably be simple peanut butter and jelly. Besides, it was hard to keep much else around because the refrigerator had been acting up lately and wasn't keeping things cold. He needed to talk to his landlady, Mrs. Medeiros, again about buying a new one.

The problem with senior citizens was they seemed to think everything was still almost new. "I just bought it a few years ago," she had told him the last time he'd complained about it. A few years to seniors was like ten or more years to everyone else. But she was always nice to him and he'd been lucky to find his little year-round cottage...even though his newspaper connections helped him land it. Elliot had literally waited until someone died, the previous tenant, and this was after spending two months networking and scouring the classified ads for a place to live.

To keep her happy, Elliot cut the grass cut during the summer. Mrs. Medeiros had rarely raised his rent, but it wasn't easy getting her to make improvements. Perhaps he should just offer to buy a refrigerator himself. That was a novel idea. He could always take it with him if he decided to leave.

8

Later Monday Evening

DINNER HAD BEEN DELICIOUS. Shauna liked to cook, which was one reason Fran had moved in with her. "They say the way to a man's heart is through his stomach," Fran mused to herself, "and some women's hearts can be reached the same way."

"Great dinner, Shauna. What did you say this chicken dish is called?" Fran asked.

"It's just chicken with rice, an old recipe I got out of *The Alice B. Toklas Cookbook*, no less," Shauna replied. It's my mother's book... she probably bought it before she knew anything about Alice B. Toklas and Gertrude Stein being lesbians."

"I thought Alice's specialty was brownies."

"Oh yes, the brownies," Shauna giggled. "Sorry to say, we're clean out of dope today. Did you want me to check and see if Lisa or Bob are getting anything good in?"

"I don't know. It's getting so expensive. It's cheaper now to do a little coke."

"Whatever you'd like."

That was the thing about Shauna. She was always so agreeable. Sometimes Fran liked a woman who talked back. She didn't always want to be making the decisions. She liked some give-and-take.

Fran started clearing the table to do the dishes while Shauna put away leftovers. The kitchen was warm from the heat of the oven. Shauna's short, honey-colored hair clung to her head.

"You ought to think about getting a perm," Fran suggested as she scraped their plates into the garbage can. "It would give your hair a little more body."

"Well, I don't want one of those silly, curly-type perms. I need to look professional. Working in a bank is a lot different from working for a newspaper. But maybe a body perm...."

Fran looked over at the way Shauna's hair framed her face and imagined her all dressed for work in one of her tailored suits. A little more fullness to her hair would only add to the professional image. Fran, on the other hand, didn't need a professional image. She could be as outrageous as she wanted.

One day, maybe she could live off the money she made from her periodic graphic design work. She'd been getting quite a few clients off the web. In the meantime, her job at the *Observer* wasn't so bad. You just needed to be aggressive...and Fran knew how to be aggressive. That's how you got what you wanted in this world. It was all there for the taking. You just had to go for it.

"Any more leads uncovered at the paper on the Carreiro murder?" Shauna asked.

"Nothing concrete. Elliot's hard at work researching this and that. Me, I'm selling advertising. Hell, I'm selling a lot of advertising because I've got everyone convinced our circulation is going to increase by at least twenty-five percent."

"How are you going to do that? There aren't that many people here this time of year, you know."

"We're going to the towns Up Cape, up beyond Truro and Wellfleet...Eastham, Orleans.... With a headline screaming, "Murder in Provincetown: Exclusive Story," people will buy. They're all so morbid, you know. Why else do those bored housewives buy the *National Enquirer* and all those other stupid magazines? They want to read all the gory details."

"You don't think the newspapers Up Cape are going to be running the same kind of stories?"

"Yes, but they don't have the information we do. A detailed history about Sonny, beginning with his childhood, neighbors' reactions, an interview with the chief of police...."

"So, Fran...how many shots and what kind of gun?"

"One shot, probably a pistol. But it's only been about twenty-four hours. The county coroner's report hasn't been released, and the police don't want to give out information that might 'interfere with their investigation,' quote-unquote."

"You're so silly," Shauna said, running her hands through Fran's thick, short, dyed-orange hair, causing it to stand on end. "I'm going to sit down, put my feet up, and see if there's anything good on the boob tube."

"As soon as I finish these dishes, I'll join you," Fran said, giving Shauna a pinch on her bottom as she turned to walk into the other room.

Fran thought to herself they really should be sitting out on the deck and enjoying the view. In another two months, they'd be having to move, and that will be a drag. Not that living in a cottage in the Truro woods was all that bad, if you liked rustic. But Fran was a city girl. Although by fall, if all went well, Shauna was planning to buy a house. So if she was still with Shauna then, she'd have a nicer place to live.

Still with Shauna, Fran kept repeating in her head while moving the sponge in a circular motion over a plate, producing an array of white soap suds. She was such an ingrate. Why couldn't she just happily settle down? Easy...she didn't need to.

Commitments were hard. Caring was hard. Hell, Fran couldn't even bring herself to call Sarah. She really should call, write her a note, something.... She really had loved Sarah, in her own way. Loved her, but not totally *in love* with her. Wrecked her marriage, didn't she? But that was bound to happen. There were seeds of despair. They just needed to grow.

Sonny...well, Sonny had put Sarah inside a hothouse, and Sarah just wasn't a hothouse plant. She needed to be outside. If he had just let her move beyond the barriers he'd built, maybe things would have been different.

Fran rinsed the dishes. Everything was now fresh and clean, ready to be used again. Tomorrow was another day, and maybe then she would feel like making a call. But not now. She dried her hands.

"Shauna," she called to her girlfriend, "I'm going to make some coffee. Let's spike it with brandy and go sit out on the deck under the stars and listen to the water. It's high tide. When it gets too chilly, we can come inside, make a fire, get naked, and make love."

"Sounds good," replied Shauna. "Anything you say."

Annie lay down to next to Beau in their queen-sized, cherry, four-poster bed. It was too early to actually go to sleep, just ten o'clock. Beau was reading a news magazine and Annie was reading a book about women's health issues. But she wasn't really reading. She was thinking.

First there was the question about attending Sonny's funeral on Thursday. Annie didn't want to go, but Beau had told her in no uncertain terms that she had an obligation to attend.

"We were in business together. Sure, everybody knows we weren't getting along. But sooner or later, you have to bury the hatchet," he'd explained to her earlier in the day. "What's the big deal? It's just a funeral mass. We don't have to stop by the Landons' house afterwards. We just need to pay our respects."

"Couldn't I just stay home and you say I'm not feeling well? Most women would do that…you know, develop a cold or sore throat, some stomach virus, and not even discuss it with their husbands. They'd just say, 'Dear, I just can't seem to get out of bed. You run along without me.' Don't you remember how Sarah supposedly had a bad cold the day of our Christmas party, when we announced our engagement, and Sonny came by himself? Do you think she was really sick? No, I just think she didn't want to come."

"Is that what this is all about? Are you trying to insult Sarah? Or is it that you just can't stand funerals?"

"Maybe a little of both," Annie retorted. "Maybe I am angry at Sarah because she didn't stop Sonny from making those absurd charges and plastering your name all over the newspaper."

Beau shook his head. "I think Sarah was already on her way out the door. Sonny was hurt and angry. One way he took his anger out was on me."

How could Annie suspect any wrongdoing on Beau's part when he said things like that? She looked at him and smiled, sliding her body towards him to get closer, until she was able to wrap her arms around him. He returned the embrace, squeezing her close. "It's going to be okay, Annie. It's going to be okay."

Annie just wanted to hold the embrace as long as possible. It felt so good being held in Beau's arms and knowing that he was taking care of everything; that she had no immediate responsibilities. But Beau had other things in mind.

His arms began stroking her back and his mouth began to nuzzle her neck, following one kiss with another.

"Let's get this thing off," Beau said while attempting to lift Annie's blue flannel nightgown over her head. "Why do you always have to wear such heavy things to bed?" he complained.

Because it feels warm and cozy, Annie thought to herself. "Because you keep the heat turned down so low at night," she replied.

"I'm just trying to save money. Besides, I sleep better when it's a little cold. All I need is my warm winter blanket. Have I told you you're my warm winter blanket?" Beau asked with a big grin.

"Yes, many times," said Annie. "You've told me many times."

God, she is so beautiful, Beau thought to himself. So stunningly beautiful. And she's mine, my wife. He felt an immediate urgency to be inside her, to possess her, as quickly as possible. Foreplay could wait.

Liz was still awake when John came home. It was late, close to midnight. Perhaps she had dozed a bit, but Liz couldn't seem to fall into a solid, deep sleep. Too much spinning around in her brain. She kept thinking about the Landon/Carreiro family, so much unhappiness. It wasn't just the murder. There was more...perhaps the emphasis on money. They had lots of money and all those insurance policies.

How much insurance did she and John have? Maybe a hundred thousand each? Financial advice columnists claimed it was a rip-off. They advised buying term insurance and putting the rest of your savings in mutual funds or the stock market. Liz had insisted on buying a whole life policy for John. "Suppose you get sick," she had told him.

"What if we can't renew the term insurance? Then you have no life insurance."

"I have a benefits package at work," he had replied.

This was true for now. As long as John was gainfully employed as town manager, he had two hundred fifty thousand dollars' worth of term life insurance. But people lost their jobs all the time. Liz thought about an old friend, whose husband had been a sales manager at one of the up-and-coming computer companies, making a big salary. But then he'd been laid off and didn't bother with COBRA benefits. In the meantime, he'd been diagnosed with pancreatic cancer that progressed quickly. He had no life insurance when he died at age forty-six.

"How was the meeting?" Liz called out in the dark as soon as she heard John enter the room.

"The usual. A lot of complaints about the cable TV service. Concerns about parking and traffic, not that anyone seems willing to close off any street or build parking lots. Of course, the continuing debate on whether the town should go forward with a central sewage system.... What are you doing still awake?" John asked as he took off his clothes, hanging some in the closet and tossing others into a pile on the floor, depending on whether they were clean or dirty.

"I just couldn't sleep. I paid a visit to the Landon household late this afternoon, brought them some lasagna. Sarah Carreiro and her girls are staying there. Her mother, too, but she was taking a nap so I didn't meet her. They were all drowning their sorrows in booze...and then Roz Silva, the newspaper lady, showed up with more booze and was sniffing around for information."

John nervously cleared his throat at the idea of Roz and Liz in the same room. "Did she learn anything?" he asked while pulling a nightshirt over his head.

"She learned Sonny had several fat insurance policies. Beau probably had the most to gain...five hundred thousand to buy Sonny's share if he died. And I wonder how much that condominium project they've been working on is really going to be worth?"

"Well, the way real estate prices have been rising the past few months, probably close to a million."

"So there's the gain, right there. When are they going to arrest him?"

"You don't just arrest someone on motive alone. There has to be some kind of evidence. Besides, I hear he has an alibi," John said, climbing into bed. "He was with his wife that evening."

"She could be lying," Liz said, putting her hands under John's nightshirt. Perhaps if they made love she'd be able to sleep.

John put his hands on Liz's breasts. They were much larger and softer than Roz's, which were small and firm. You might even say Liz's breasts were flabby. But it would be mean to tell her that…after all, they *had* nursed both of their children. And Liz had been a good mother. She'd also been a good wife.

He kissed her mouth gently and conjured up the image of a beautiful movie star, someone in their twenties with large, succulent breasts. As Liz stroked him, he could feel himself getting an erection. Now he was in business. It was getting to be difficult, making love to Liz, because he only wanted Roz. But he had his obligations as a husband.

9

Tuesday Morning

BRUNO WOKE UP with a sense of urgency. Not only was he eager to get out of bed and empty his bladder, he was eager to start writing that magazine article for Frank. As he stood up, after getting out of bed, he looked down and admired his large, engorged, plum-and-olive colored penis, bragging to himself that the old boy was still looking good. It was a misconception that men woke up with erections just because their bladders were full, he'd read in a magazine. Morning erections were caused by hormones, and he had plenty of those.

His dreams hadn't even been particularly sexual. He'd been dreaming about the magazine article he was going to write and the phone ringing off the hook with reservations for his guesthouse. In fact, that was what woke him up, the sound of a ringing telephone. Bruno's phone hadn't really been ringing; it was only in his dream. That was the funny thing about dreams. They seemed so real while you were having them.

After relieving himself, he took a look at his watch. It was only seven o'clock. The day was young and there was no reason to immediately get dressed. He walked back to his room and threw on his soft velour robe over his silk pajamas, slid his feet into his sheepskin slippers, and went downstairs to brew some coffee.

As usual, the *Boston Globe* was outside the front door. A proper day began with reading the newspaper. Two sections were Bruno's favorites:

"Style" and "Business." The front page was sometimes interesting…and, yes, it was a necessary evil to check the long-range weather forecast. But he mainly wanted to keep abreast of the latest trends in fashion, books, movies, and personalities. He wanted to know how and where people were spending their money. Sometimes he would pretend to buy a particular stock based on what was written in the newspaper, and then for weeks on end he'd check the daily stock quotes to see if it went up or down. If he had any extra money, indeed he would have gambled on some stocks. But he was well aware he had nothing extra to spend. Sometimes he let the boys with whom he had spent the night believe he was a player, only because they would watch him check the morning stock market prices and truly believe he was an investor. Bruno figured, let people believe what they want. After all, their perception of how successful you were was based solely on appearance, Bruno mused to himself.

Besides, at Bruno's age, how could a middle-aged man hit up on younger guys unless they thought you were rich. Young guys didn't date old guys for kicks. They dated them for security. Not that Bruno had any real security to offer. He *could* offer food, a place to live…but nothing ever lasted or got to that point.

It didn't matter to Bruno. He kept busy. He maintained a beautiful house and garden. He was a good host to his guests. Bruno did what he wanted…*much* better than a lot of men who were stuck in their boring jobs, married to boring women, chasing around a bunch of brats they never really wanted, perhaps fantasizing about how life could be so much better. *This* was Bruno's life, and it was okay.

But it would be fun to have a little more, he thought, like some power. Writing for this new magazine, people would be calling him and asking him to write about *them*. They'd be wanting the free publicity, positive reviews, favorable coverage. And they'd get it…all those deserving people who Roz Silva always seemed to neglect. In his mind, Bruno had suddenly elevated himself to being Frank Chambers' business partner.

Bruno heated up a cinnamon bun he'd taken from the freezer while the coffee made its burping noises and dripped into the glass pot. He really should start drinking tea in the morning, he told himself, remembering Doc Brown saying that too much caffeine was liable to irritate his prostate. Lately, sometimes coffee gave Bruno stomach cramps…but it tasted so good. Part of the price of getting older, he lamented, recalling the days he could drink three cups of coffee on an empty stomach, no problem. Perhaps some scrambled eggs were in order, scrambled eggs and linquicia. Then again, there would be pans to wash, and that would only take time away from writing. He settled on a bowl of granola and strawberries with low-fat milk.

As he sat down with his breakfast at the dining room table, Bruno's eyes focused in on all the letters that were waiting to be taken to the post office. The long cardboard boxes, designed for holding envelopes, were now filled with neatly stacked letters, all arranged by zip code. He made a mental note to go to the post office probably during the early part of the day. He didn't like clutter, and the boxes were cluttering the floor. His guesthouse needed to be kept tidy at all times.

Each room in the Willows Guest House was decorated according to a color and a theme. There was the turquoise-blue room, filled with kitschy items from the fifties; the red room, resembling a Victorian brothel; the yellow room, with sweet, cottage-style furniture, hand-painted by renowned Cape Cod artist/decorator Peter Hunt; and the white room, with fishnet curtains and mosquito netting hung around the double bed. The red room was the most popular.

Bruno's bedroom, located on the first floor, was tastefully done up in various shades of brown, the centerpiece being a Victorian Renaissance Revival walnut bed adorned with panels of burled fruitwood. Scattered at the head of the bed were pillows covered with an antique paisley fabric in the same warm brown, red, and orange tones. On the floor was a handsome, brown Bokhara oriental carpet incorporating a subtle geometric design.

Bruno mostly liked to collect large things: furniture, prints, paintings, pottery, textiles. He had a particular fascination with mirrors because they made a room look so much larger. So, of course, also in the front sitting room was a large mirror over the fireplace, besides a vertical mirror in the entryway. Each guest room had at least one large mirror, and a couple had two. He figured his guests liked the additional mirrors so they could watch themselves make love, perhaps with secret lovers they never had time for in the off-season.

How many of his guests led straight, "normal" lives most of the year? How many had to pretend they were someone other than who they really were? For some summer visitors, Provincetown was their opportunity to let down the facade, take off their masks...or, ironic as the case may be, to put on a new mask. After all, if they were visiting during Carnival Week, they were dressing up in masks or makeup and costumes. It was the thrill of assuming a different role. It was the freedom to hold hands and kiss in public. And if you wanted to live amidst that freedom all year long, you stayed.

Bruno had stayed. He had once been a summer visitor. He'd also been a schoolteacher, and his penchant for young boys had gotten him into trouble. That was a long time ago, when Bruno had been a young man himself and once engaged to a beautiful Italian-American girl chosen by his parents.

Marta...her name was Marta. Wine-colored lips and warm, olive skin, with long, dark, wavy hair, and full hips and breasts. If only those hips had been narrow and the breasts small and flat, he might have been satisfied. He could have pretended she was a young boy. He could have pretended that when he entered deep inside her tight virginal hole that he was deep inside another place. Bruno had really tried. And he'd almost succeeded. But then he'd visited Cape Cod with a fellow teacher, Chip, who taught math.

"You've never been out to the Cape?" Chip had asked incredulously. "You've lived in Boston all your life and never been to Cape Cod?"

"If I want to go to the beach, I go to the South Shore," Bruno had replied offhandedly. "And I hear the Cape is expensive and full of weirdos."

But he had secretly wondered what types of weirdos were there. Were they anything like him? Because the way Bruno acted around others and the things he would say to appear "normal" were nothing like what he felt inside. Did other men hold the same interest in what their friends were wearing? Did they notice a particularly handsome male face, stately gait, or the bounce and curve of their butt as they walked?

Chip must have known, at least suspected, that Bruno Marchessi, the supposedly straight English teacher, wasn't so straight after all. Inside the mind of the conservative dresser in solid, button-down shirts, dark ties, and tweed sports jackets was a gay man anxious to break out and be free of society's rules for proper behavior.

He had been almost thin in those days, just a little extra around the middle. Love handles, he liked to call them. Like Chip...Chip had love handles, too.

Chip had seduced Bruno when they visited Provincetown. He had taught him all about oral sex. No...it hadn't actually been in Provincetown. It had been in the room of a cheap motel on Route 6A in North Truro. But they had just spent the better part of the evening in Provincetown, eating a lobster dinner, hitting all the bars...many of them gay bars.

Suddenly it didn't seem so strange to find men attractive. It was the norm here, far from the North End of Boston. Geographically, the distance wasn't that far. But emotionally, he had traveled light-years.

Bruno had broken off the engagement at age thirty-two after trying for another year to make things right. But he knew it wasn't going to work, so he let her go. Last he heard, Marta had five kids and her husband owned a string of bakeries. Bruno continued to teach and lead a supposedly normal life...except now he was visiting gay bars on weekends and spending vacations at places like Fire Island, Key West, and San Francisco.

He continued to live with his parents so he could save the money to follow his dream: own a country inn. Did they suspect he was different from his two brothers? If so, they never said anything. Perhaps they'd hoped that one day, if he chose not to marry, he would become a priest.

Then he started getting less careful. "Never play in your own backyard," a friend used to say. But Bruno forgot to heed that practical advice. He let himself become infatuated with one of his students, who was obviously infatuated with him. At age forty-four, he was caught having an affair with a seventeen-year-old boy. Luckily, he taught at a private school and it was all kept "hush hush," very quiet. No story ran in the newspapers, only a lot of whispers and an early retirement.

The whispers were enough. He never went home. Well, hardly ever, just on holidays: Mother's Day, Christmas, Thanksgiving...and for his father's funeral.

It was difficult playing the role of a "normal" man, once Bruno had finally let himself go. What was "normal," anyway? It was some kind of "average," the average everyone expected you to be. No wonder he never so much as glanced at the "Sports" section in the newspaper.

It was something he didn't *want* to read. For so many years, he had forced himself to read it and become familiar with every type of sport and team, because men were *supposed* to be interested in sports.

Now, if he had a cleaning or painting project and needed newspaper to protect the floor or table, he'd grab the "Sports" section first. Who cared whether the Boston Red Sox were going to play in the World Series? It was a waste of time.

Bruno wondered what was in the newspaper today, so he quickly surveyed the headlines. Once again, there was a feature story on the problems plaguing Boston's public schools. Once again, there was a story about homeless people. The President and Congress were squabbling over some bill. In the "Real Estate" section was a story about enlarging your attic. Now, *that* was a story Bruno found interesting. Maybe one day he could make another guest room or two up in the attic. The problem was, no more rooms unless he upgraded his septic system. "God damn town," he thought to himself. "They won't let you do anything around here unless it costs a lot of money."

He headed to the kitchen, grabbed a pad of lined paper, sat back down at the dining room table, and started writing.

The copy deadlines were only a few hours away, Roz was thinking as she attempted to wake up, throwing back the covers and the sheets. However, there was more to put in the paper, items written in the dead of the night by Elliot pertaining to the murder story she would need to add. Well, she would just have to pay the printers extra if deadlines were not met and things had to be rushed. Money…if only she had more money.

First she needed to go to the bank to renegotiate the mortgage, ask for more time to pay it. A ridiculous thought. The bank wasn't going to give her more time. They charged interest and penalties. That's how they made their money.

Feeling sufficiently chilled, Roz got up out of bed and looked at herself in the mirror. Her hair was borderline dirty. Did she have time to jump in the shower? When she ran her hands through her locks, they stuck together in sections. If she washed it, her hair would be nice and fluffy. It would make her feel better. She needed to feel good. A shower it would be. It would also give her a little more time to decide what to wear because she wanted to look a little more businesslike. Perhaps she would wear her long denim skirt with a blazer.

The bathroom was old, like everything else in the house. The tiles needed to be regrouted. They looked slightly gray in color. She also noticed that the caulking around the bathtub was starting to peel. A little scrubbing with a toothbrush and some cleanser might help, she thought to herself as the warm water beat down against her back. But who has time to do it? Tonight she should at least clean the bathtub, or get Sally to do it. Not that Sally would do any kind of decent job. Kids don't know how to clean. Roz figured she'd be better off just doing it herself.

After lathering her hair three times to make certain it was perfectly clean, and leaving on the conditioner for two minutes even though the instructions on the bottle said one minute was sufficient, Roz was convinced her hair was completely done. She stepped out of the shower, grabbed a towel from the hook on the inside of the bathroom door, and started to dry off.

The phone was ringing. "God damn it. I forgot to bring in my slippers!" she cursed to herself while running to answer the phone in her bedroom. She hated the feeling of wet feet on the floor. Besides, any wetness would cause dirt and sand to stick. When was the last time she'd had a chance to sweep or vacuum?

"Roz?" It was Elliot.

"Yes. What's up?"

"They've called in the state police for assistance and they're bringing in Beau for questioning. Maybe they'll make an arrest. Should I put a hold on the paper?"

"That's a hard decision. My gut feeling is no. Just proceed as usual. I've got to stop by the bank. I'll have my cell phone with me. If anything new breaks, give me a call and I'll reconsider."

Roz started pulling her clothes out of the closet. Where is that skirt? There are so many things jammed in here, she told herself. She really should take a load of stuff down to the thrift shop.

In her mind, she was thinking, oh Beau...did you shoot your business partner, Sonny, for a quarter of a million dollars, soon to be worth half a million? Am I such a poor judge of character that once I was even attracted to you because of that nice smile? It *would* make a great story, though....

"Aha," she said aloud, at last finding the skirt and unsnapping it from the hooks holding it in place on the hanger. "There you are. I've got you."

A pretty bra with lace, her striped, button-down oxford shirt, some high socks, her comfortable crepe-soled Rockports, and she was all set. John likes this outfit, Roz thought to herself, seeming to recall she'd been wearing it the day they'd met.

She hoped it looked businesslike enough for Ernie Martin, the bank president, now deciding to trade her high socks for a pair of navy blue tights, which matched her denim skirt.

The car easily started, a good sign for a Tuesday morning with the copy deadline drawing near. Now everything go smoothly, Roz prayed to the forces of the universe. Please let everything go smoothly today. First she'd go to the bank, then a stop at the post office, and then over to the newspaper. She went over her list of places to go. Roz could only focus on one thing at a time on a day like this. If she thought about it all at once, it was too overwhelming.

The Cape and Islands Savings Bank looked like a bank in any other town and city. All the furniture placed in the customer service area was the generic dark mahogany, pseudo 18th-century style, so typical at financial institutions. The desks were covered with a sheet of glass and the chairs had dark pink upholstered seats that matched the plush pink-and-gray floral pattern of the carpet on the floor. The bank officers wore business suits and the tellers wore skirts or slacks with stockings and pumps. Still, the bank clientele looked odd enough. Waiting in the teller line were two men with shaved heads and nose rings, along with a couple of women wearing jogging clothes and sporting crew cuts, and a gray-haired old lady dressed in a long, heavy coat, a beret on her head, and toting a heavy fabric bag.

Probably doing all her shopping and errands in town this morning, Roz thought. A closer look revealed she was one of Gene's distant cousins, Margarite Cook, from the side of the family Roz didn't like. But she had to smile and say "hello" anyway to be polite.

Gene's father, as well as his father before him, had been born in Provincetown, but not Gene. His uncle had inherited the family hardware store, being the eldest brother, and Gene's father had moved west to Framingham, Massachussets, to become a schoolteacher.

But Gene had always wanted to come back. He and his sister, Jemma, would visit their grandparents for two weeks every August, and he'd fantasize about one day coming to live in the wonderful town with the beach at your doorstep, woods behind the house, and an easy walk to the sand dunes.

At least they had inherited the house, the house on Pearl Street that had been Gene's grandparents' home, which is why Gene had convinced Roz to invest every penny they had in the *Provincetown Observer* when it had come up for sale 15 years earlier.

"It's a wonderful investment and way of life for both of us, plus a legacy for our family," he had told her. What he didn't tell her about were the outdated presses, overvalued real estate, and shoddy book of business filled with bum pay advertisers and companies no longer located on the lower Cape. The *Observer* had operated in a forgiving manner for years, regularly advancing credit to any advertiser willing to sign up for the large, half- and full-page ads. Many accounts, some as much as nine months past due, were allowed to purchase even more advertising for the upcoming season.

"That has to change," Roz had told Gene. "No more credit unless they are up to date on past bills. No credit advanced to new accounts unless they provide several references. Two percent discount for cash up front. Make them sign contracts that include stiff penalties for late payments. Get a commitment for so much advertising each year."

Ten years into their mortgage, they had taken out a new one to pay for an upgraded computer system so operations would be streamlined and labor costs would decrease. But then they needed a new roof, sales were weak, business was poor, and a couple of large accounts skipped town. Never mind...Roz and Gene plugged on, confident that business would once again pick up. And it did. It was booming the year of Gene's heart attack.

Adding insult to injury, Molly Brummell, the new bookkeeper, had embezzled some of their funds. Where did the money go? Up her nose, perhaps? Indeed, Roz soon learned that Molly had been heavily addicted to cocaine. A major party girl, she had skipped town a few months after Gene's death.

Roz had been too obsessed with her personal problems to pay attention to what was going on in the accounting department. She assumed things were taking care of themselves. Or she wanted to assume so, because she was so tired and overwhelmed with her sorrow and the pain of just trying to get through each day without Gene that she didn't want to worry about paying bills. That's why she'd hired a bookkeeper.

Elliot had pointed out the mess. It was Elliot who learned that, although money was being received, it wasn't always being deposited, particularly if it was cash. And no bills were being paid, except for a bunch of commissions for nonexistent sales to a certain ad rep named Ellen, who happened to be Molly's girlfriend.

Molly and Ellen were fired, and Elliot received a fat raise. No one else ever knew about the embezzling because Roz had been too embarrassed and had never pressed criminal charges. But in a backhanded way, the bank had been aware of something because Roz needed to borrow money, put a second mortgage on her home, just to meet her regular payments.

The financial losses brought an end to her grief. Roz was now angry. She was mad and became filled with a fury to get even with the world, or at least the town and those who had betrayed her.

They didn't care about her, she reasoned, so she didn't care about them. It seemed that people liked to kick you when you were down, seize opportunities when you were weak and not able to fight back. Roz had told herself that she was going to publish a profitable newspaper, and to do that she would ferret out the juiciest stories possible, which would result in selling more newspapers.

"Mr. Martin will see you now," said Amanda Miller, one of the bank's vice presidents, whose desk was out in the main lobby. As president, Ernie Martin was the only bank officer with a private office.

Of course, the bank had a loan department, but why deal with an underling when you could talk to the man in charge? The president was the one who ultimately made the final decisions, even though the board reviewed all decisions. But it was Ernie alone, sitting fat and complacent behind his desk, who would decide whether or not Roz got an extension on her previous two months' overdue payments in light of the summer-season revenues that would soon be coming in.

"I've tried," she explained, "to make all my payments on time. I really have. But a few of our ad accounts didn't pay their summer bills and skipped town. You know I'm good for it."

Ernie thoughtfully rubbed his dark, greasy chin. His pants were feeling uncomfortably tight and his shirt collar had too much starch.

Why couldn't Roz Silva manage to make her loan payments consistently on time? With penalties and interest, however, the bank was always making money off the account. The fools...if they took into account all the extra bank fees being paid, they'd be less eager to over-capitalize. But that's why banks always made money. Especially in this case, because there was no way Roz was ever going to let the paper go bankrupt, and there was no likely reason the bank would ever have to foreclose.

He shouldn't have eaten all those donuts for breakfast. Now they were sitting heavy in his stomach and he had the sudden urge to burp. But he couldn't do it here, now...and certainly not in front of Roz Silva. It would appear so unprofessional.

Ernie Martin had been president of the Cape and Islands Savings Bank for seven years. In that time, he'd increased profits by twenty-two percent. Interest paid on passbook accounts and CDs had consistently remained low, while commercial lending rates had continued to climb. "High risk," was their excuse. "Volatile economy."

"I suppose we can come to some sort of arrangement," he told Roz. "I'll write you up a short-term note for six months to pay off this debt and give you a little up-front money for next month's mortgage so you'll be all set."

"But can't you reduce the interest rate? It seems awfully high. If I rewrite a mortgage on my house for a larger amount, the rate would be lower."

"Yes, but you don't have enough equity in your home to cover the amount you borrowed. Besides, there'd be points to pay."

Roz felt powerless. What was she going to argue about? What could she negotiate? Perhaps if she went to a bank Up Cape, they'd offer a lower rate. But those Up Cape banks considered businesses in Provincetown a high risk.

She really needed to get over to the newspaper after quickly checking her post office box. Already she was feeling tired and the day had just begun.

Roz convinced herself that it wasn't so bad…one can only live in the present. She had food and shelter, her children were healthy and doing well, and she could now pay her bills. What more could she want?

Frank Chambers had always admired the granite and marble polished floor of the Provincetown Post Office. The shiny brass fittings on the post office boxes and the broad, wide, white marble counter where the transactions occurred reminded him of post offices you'd find in large cities rather than in a seasonal, small town. Probably built during the town's more prosperous days, towards the end of the 19th century when the whaling and fishing industries were at their peak, Frank thought. He felt for his keys in his pants pocket. Yes, still there. He walked across the hard, shiny floor to his box, P.O. Box 508, to see if there was any mail.

It was the usual: restaurant trade magazines, a renewal form from the Chamber of Commerce, credit card solicitations, and credit card bills. Bills and junk mail, that's all he seemed to get these days, Frank grumbled to himself, also wondering why he never got anything decent, like a real letter.

No one wrote letters anymore. They picked up the phone and talked, sent e-mails, sent faxes. Nothing was tangible, written on paper, these days. And if you did get a letter, it was rarely written in longhand. Frank's friend, Carl, had always written letters…beautiful, heartfelt letters, with jokes and stories and scraps of poetry. But Carl had been dead for over two years now, yet another victim of AIDS.

When would it be *his* turn? When would his identification as carrier change to victim? Frank wasn't sure from whom had he contracted HIV, the virus that causes AIDS. He had no proof, but there were several possibilities…. After all, there was a time when no one knew much about the virus, and then there had been other times when he'd been careless and neglected to wear protection.

Life was a game of Russian Roulette. Maybe you got sick. Maybe you didn't. Maybe you unexpectedly died crossing the street. No one knew what tomorrow was going to bring. So the important thing was to focus on the present, live fully in the moment.

It was an accident, being HIV-positive, one he really couldn't have prevented, especially if he'd contracted the virus early on before anyone knew about prevention. What Frank most hated thinking about was that, in all probability, he had passed it on to somebody else.

So these days, Frank lived a fairly celibate life. His last committed relationship had been with Jake, his former business partner. They'd met working together in Boston at Joe's Table, a restaurant on Boylston Street where Frank was the chef, of course, and Jake was the manager. The two had made a great team. Jake was a whiz at bookkeeping. He could quickly add up a list of numbers in his head, calculate loss and profit margins, and knew when to take advantage of up-front discounts. And Frank would use his imagination to create daily specials from the extra food inventory in the pantry.

"Let's open our own restaurant," Frank had suggested to Jake. "Why let someone else profit from our hard work and expertise?"

"Rents are expensive," warned Jake, "and you need plenty of start-up capital. Do you have any money saved?"

Frank had only a few thousand dollars in his savings account. That was all. He liked nice things. It was hard to save money. Even though he did his shopping at Filene's Basement, he *had* to have quality cookware, fine linens, and fresh flowers on the table. Besides, chefs weren't paid much, especially at a family-style restaurant with a name like Joe's Table.

Then his Aunt Emily had died, leaving him forty thousand dollars, after estate taxes. Frank suddenly had capital, working capital. Perhaps that's when Jake really became more affectionate and suggested they rent a place together, a spacious apartment he'd seen in Brookline.

Jake had been so handsome and had a taut, muscular body that he maintained by lifting weights in the morning and working out at the gym every other afternoon. He'd been a wonderful lover, powerful and commanding when he mounted Frank and entered him. He had seemed to be a wonderful companion and lover, a real take-charge kind of guy. Nothing was too daunting for Jake to take on. "Of course we can do it," he would say. "Anything is possible. You just have to believe."

In retrospect, Frank realized that Jake had just been spouting off trite clichés and that he'd been far too much in love with Jake to see him for what he really was...a smooth confidence man, a glib talker.

But, oh, it had been so wonderful believing that Jake was truly looking after Frank's interests instead of just his own.

They called it F.J.'s Bistro, not excitingly original but they couldn't seem to agree on anything else. They might as well have named it F.J.'s Bar and Grill because most items on the menu were prepared on the grill, cooked over an open fire, and most of the profit was from the bar.

It was at the bar that Frank had figured out where Jake had managed to come up with his share of the start-up money. More than once he'd caught Jake opening the cash register and putting the larger bills in his pocket. "Just a little cash advance," he would reason. "Just a little cash advance."

So it became clear that, at Joe's Table, all the money Jake had saved the owners by being a shrewd manager had never benefited them as a large profit. When business was booming, Jake had pocketed a portion of the cash receipts, and they'd never suspected.

Jake had squeezed even more money from his former employers by setting up a private moneymaking scheme at the bar. "Liquor is quite profitable," he had bragged to Frank one night while running his hand though his bleached blonde hair and devilishly raising his eyebrows. Jake had a way of talking, as if he were preferentially confessing and flirting at the same time. He had made Frank feel as though he were his exclusive confidante, the only one who truly understood him, and this had made Frank feel very special. In reminiscing about Jake, all Frank felt now was: Very special my ass...a very special pigeon!

"Did you know that just a ten dollar bottle of vodka at Joe's Table earned me hundreds of dollars?" Then Jake had said that while he was bartending, he'd pour from his personal bottle of vodka whenever a drink with vodka was ordered and pocket the money. Since he wasn't using up the house inventory, the owners assumed vodka drinks just weren't popular.

"We all know about bartenders...they always steal," Jake had told Frank. So it was usually Jake tending bar, or keeping a close eye on it. Knowing employees' potential for unscrupulous behavior, he trusted no one.

Frank had then started wondering what kind of ethics his boyfriend had and whether Jake's impulsive move to Boston might have been to escape prosecution by an angry employer rather than to experience the charms of a new city.

What was ethically correct as far as the tug-of-war between employer and employee? At what point does "taking advantage" become
"stealing"? There was the fudging of hours, inventory that disappeared,
and then the actual stealing of sales that weren't rung up and went into
the employee's pocket instead.

Frank had always been on salary so there was no fudging with the
time clock, but he did take food. It started with food that was going to
be thrown away: the green tomatoes, mushroom stems, and day-old
bread. But then it had escalated to whatever he needed. He'd rationalized, that since he could always eat his meals at the restaurant, even
breakfast, why not take some home?

Office workers always took paper, pens, and binders. Everyone
knew that. They used the copy machine for their personal business.
Employees felt they were never paid enough or fully appreciated, so
any extra perks they could claim, from ice cream given away to free
drinks for friends, they took.

When you owned the business, however, things were different. Starting a new business like F.J.'s Bistro required a conservative eye for cut-
ting down on as many expenses as possible. Jake knew about sponging
off other people and looking out for himself, but not about efficiently
running an entire business to turn a profit. And in this instance, it was
a profit to be shared with someone else.

Jake's imperfections didn't initially register with Frank. The restaurant was doing well, the bank loan was being paid, and both Frank
and Jake had money to live on. Plus they were the proprietors of their
very own restaurant...restaurateurs. They'd established an image and
were quickly gaining respect amongst the neighboring businesses, the
affluent gay community, and their dining patrons.

Perhaps it was his swelled head, now owning a restaurant. Maybe
he'd grown bored or was looking for someone more powerful or more
handsome. But it had soon become apparent, less than a year after F.J.'s
Bistro opened its doors, that Jake was seeing someone else.

"When were you going to tell me?" Frank had asked, retreating to
their bedroom on Christmas Eve when Jake was two hours late getting
home for dinner. Knowing business would be slow, they had closed the
restaurant for three days. Frank had prepared a small dinner party for
friends. The others arrived on time, but not Jake. It seemed everyone
knew that Jake was seeing someone else, an assistant professor of so-

ciology at MIT named Larry. Everyone knew except Frank, because
he hadn't *wanted* to see and because he was too busy in the restaurant
kitchen working.

Frank didn't know what was worse, the hurt or the embarrassment. The only way out was to sell the business, or at least his share.
So he decided to get back his money and start over again. Lucky for
Jake, Larry had plenty of working capital. Maybe Jake had planned it
that way. From a wealthy Virginia family, Larry was able to put up the
money to return Frank's forty-thousand-dollar investment and cosign
with Jake the restaurant loan. His hard work, sweat equity, Frank
realized, would never be properly reimbursed. He could only stand so
much bickering and fighting. It was easier to walk away.

How many others had Jake slept with while they'd been together?
Most likely, it was Jake who had given Frank HIV. What a bastard!
What a going-away present!

Five years had now passed, and Frank seldom talked about Jake to
anyone. But he thought about him often.

There's the bitch again, Frank said to himself as he looked up
and saw Roz walking towards her post office box, P.O. Box 625, and
wondering why her box just had to be so close to his.

"Good morning, Roz," he said aloud and smiled. How he longed to
tell her about his new magazine, which was going to give her newspaper
a run for its money. Instead, he smugly chuckled to himself.

Roz didn't notice Frank's self-contained glee. She was more interested in seeing whether the mail contained any money. It did…there was
a fifteen-hundred-dollar check from Mason's Hardware and Marine.
That will help, she thought to herself. At least some people paid on
time. With all her concerns about dressing correctly, she hadn't noticed
that the elastic around the waist of her tights was starting to give out.
Now, less than two hours later, they were starting to sag and the crotch
was sinking low, making it difficult to walk. She certainly couldn't hike
them up here and now, but at least she could take the damn things off
soon, at the office.

"Have a good one," she said to Frank as she was leaving. Maybe
he would stop hating her guts one of these days, Roz told herself.

Elliot was in the office, at his computer and editing his cover story one more time. He checked his watch. His noon deadline was just two hours away. The *Observer* was a weekly paper, dated Fridays and distributed to newsstands on Thursday afternoons.

A search warrant had been issued the previous morning, Monday, so the police could search Sonny's home and gather any clues that might point to a likely murder suspect. State Trooper Marc O'Brien, who worked on criminal investigations through the district attorney's office, had been called in to assist local police with the case.

Neighbors, friends, family, and business associates had already been interviewed, but the formal statement released by Cape & Islands District Attorney Robert Wells was that: "We are still gathering evidence and no arrests have been made."

The autopsy was performed by Dr. Hallie Anne Meachum of the Boston Medical Examiner's office. According to spokesperson Sally Huntfield, Sonny Carreiro had died of a gunshot wound to the head, and the death had been ruled a homicide. As if this was something we didn't already know, Elliot mused. Nevertheless, it was important that he include all the facts for those who had not been closely following the story, as well as for future reference.

So what was in the future, as far as the murderer was concerned? What did they have in mind when they pulled the trigger? What were they hoping to gain by ending Sonny's life? These were the questions Elliot hoped to resolve. If he could figure out who Sonny had pissed off the most....

"Hey Roz," he called out, seeing her enter the office. "Come over here for a minute."

Roz walked as quickly as she could while thinking how wonderful it will be to finally get inside her office and take off her damn panty hose. She was determined, however, not to appear impatient. She stared over Elliot's shoulder at the words on his screen. "Looking good, Elliot. Thought of a good headline?" Roz asked.

"I was thinking of another little story. I was thinking that maybe I could flesh out the murderer if I wrote something that made them nervous and put it in the paper."

"Not a good idea," Roz admonished. We have to tread softly here. Labeling people as possible suspects is tricky business and subject to a libel suit. But I see nothing wrong with writing an article that gives the reader some background on Sonny's business dealings and mentions the life insurance policies."

"What life insurance policies?"

"A buy/sell policy for half a million to Beau so he can buy out Sarah, and a quarter-million key man policy that goes to the family insurance agency. Plus, of course, a quarter-million policy for Sarah and the kids."

"So Sarah ends up with the most cash out of the deal."

"Well, Beau doesn't do too badly with a million-dollar piece of real estate. Besides, Sarah has a great alibi. She was in another state."

"She could have hired a hit man."

"Wow, Elliot. You don't trust anyone...."

"No, I just watch too many gangster movies."

"You do realize that money may not be the motivating factor at all," voiced Fran, who had walked over to join the conversation, unnoticed by Roz. "People kill for all kinds of reasons. They kill out of passion. They kill for power, revenge...."

"You seem awfully familiar with the subject of murder. Spent some time thinking about it?" Roz queried.

"I did a research paper for a psychology class," Fran retorted. "It's a very interesting subject."

"Well," said Elliot, "you're welcome to join our team of crackerjack amateur investigators...investigative reporters, that is."

"I don't know, Elliot," replied Fran. "You're starting to act more like an amateur detective, and that could be dangerous. I think we should leave the tough work to the police, so I'll pass."

"Why, Fran!" exclaimed Elliot, noticing she was looking particularly striking this morning in a blue silk shirt and a matching blue silk bandana wrapped around her head. "I didn't know you were such a wuss," he teased.

"I'm not," she smiled. "I just want more time to be out there selling ads."

Roz didn't think much of the blue silk next to Fran's bright orange hair. She'd liked it better when Fran was dying her hair a deep red-burgundy...it went better with the black eyeliner and mascara she likes to wear. Ah, well. To each his own, or her own, as the case may be.

It was time for Roz to get some work done, much as she hated sitting at her desk.

"Elliot," said Roz outloud, "we'll go with the straight news story about Sonny on the front page, and the obituary. On page three, we'll run the piece on community reactions, as well as a story on 'What Happens Next' in the ongoing investigation that makes mention of the insurance polices. When you've finished, proofed the stories, and done a tentative layout, give me a holler and we'll come up with the headlines."

"Fran, is page two ready?" Roz yelled over to Fran, who had returned to her desk.

"Yes, and we're almost done with page four."

"Great!" Roz breathed a sigh of relief. It looked like today they wouldn't be missing any deadlines. Page two always contained a lot of advertising, plus the tide chart and regular gossip column, "News Around Town." People's eyes always focused to the right, so the more-important news was always placed on the odd-numbered pages of the newspaper, and the front and back covers. Much of the ad copy could be tentatively placed in advance, particularly on the even-numbered pages; some always appeared in the same place, so that made things easier. The news releases, horoscopes, and movie and art reviews were set up and laid out by the beginning of each week. The editorial page and letters to the editor were completed on Mondays. It was just the hard news and late-breaking stories that needed to be finished this morning and placed on the appropriate pages. Three o'clock in the afternoon was their final deadline.

Elliot's stomach was growling. Too bad there hadn't been time for a real breakfast this morning, he lamented to himself. He'd only eaten a bowl of cereal and an orange. Plus he'd had three cups of coffee while sitting at his computer and was about ready to go pour himself a fourth before convincing himself it would be better to drink some water instead. Too much coffee...and the only exercise he'd been getting was his walks to and from the coffee maker and men's room. Maybe later, after a good nap, he'd go for a jog along the beach, he thought to himself...if the tide's right.

He took a glance at the page two layout on his way over to the water cooler. Friday's low tide would be at six in the evening, so that meant today's low, approximately two hours earlier, would be at four this afternoon. Perfect! Plenty of beach for running and walking, as long as the weather held out and it didn't get too windy or cold by then.

For now it was back to his desk. But he was tired of sitting. If only he could figure out some way to work standing up. He bent down to touch his toes while keeping his knees straight and then bent at the waist from side to side. Exercise never hurts.

The front-page news story was done so he brought up the obituary to take a final look. Sky had done an adequate job. She certainly had plenty of material to work with and had managed to get a couple quotes. The first was from Bill Landon: "Sonny was an energetic businessman with a vision of a prosperous future for our town. He was a wonderful brother-in-law and business associate." The other quote was from Beau Costa, no less: "Sonny will surely be missed by the community. His death is a great loss."

Elliot jumped up from his chair, walked across the room, and stood quietly behind Sky, who was working away at her desk. It felt good to be up and stretching his legs again. Yelling over to Sky would disturb Fran and Sally, the part-time layout assistant. Besides, sneaking up on Sky was kind of fun. She always seemed so focused while she was working.

"Sky," he whispered in her ear, "how did you manage to get a quote from Beau?"

Sky jerked back her shoulders slightly at the sound of Elliot's voice. So...he's impressed with something she'd done for a change, she thought to herself.

"Actually," she said, "he called me and asked if I was writing the obituary and could he say a few words about Sonny."

"Really...," Elliot stated incredulously. "So he's trying now to get some good press for himself."

"I don't know whether making a statement about someone's death could be called 'good press,' Elliot. He seemed genuinely shaken."

"Perhaps he's remorseful."

"Perhaps he feels badly that he and Sonny never mended their differences. They used to be close friends. If you could just cozy up to

Beau, maybe he'd provide you with some information that might just help you solve who dun it," Sky chided him.

"You know something? You're absolutely right. As soon as we've put this paper to bed, I'll go buy a bottle of good whiskey and I'll go visit Beau and see if we can get drunk together."

"Yeah sure, Elliot. I hear he's not such a bad guy, but I wouldn't want to get him drunk," Sky responded, pretending to believe what Elliot was telling her. "I've heard that he does have a short temper."

Why didn't Elliot ever take her seriously, Sky fumed to herself. She found him to be so annoying sometimes. The problem with these newspaper people, which Sky did not consider herself to be one of, was they always thought they were better than everyone else.

And just because they put something in print did not mean it was true. Roz and Elliot would *never* apologize about having printed things in the past that were possibly misleading. Beau had been depicted as an "enemy," having supposedly committed bank fraud. So Beau was on the "bad list." Since they figured he must hate them, they were going to hate him first.

Elliot had been half serious about the whisky idea. Maybe if the barriers were down, the inhibitions, Beau would talk to him. What Sky didn't know was that, the week before, Elliot had seen Beau and had attempted to bury the hatchet, so to speak. This had been before the murder, of course. But Elliot bore no animosity towards Beau…and he didn't like anyone in town to be really mad at him. It wasn't good for gathering information and it wasn't a comfortable feeling when you walked down the street. Yes, he had written the negative story about Beau and the mortgage application fraud, but he was just using information that was provided. Sonny had filed a lawsuit, and it was news.

It had been last Thursday. Elliot had gone into Adam's Pharmacy for an ice cream cone, and Beau was sitting at the lunch counter drinking a cup of coffee, with rosy cheeks from the cold and wearing a blue wool stocking cap on his head. From the look of his heavy work boots, plaid hunting shirt, insulated vest, and blue jeans, Elliot had theorized he was taking a break from work at his new condo construction site.

He'd greeted Beau with an open-faced smile saying, "Taking a break from work, I see."

"There's no such thing as a break for those of us who work with our hands for a living," Beau fired back at him. "Maybe you pencil pushers have time for breaks, particularly when you let other people do your work for you, feeding you storie and all that."

"Okay, we do rely on tips but we need to check them out before they make a story."

"Check again, cowboy. There's an old saying in the construction trade: 'When a job is too easy, you must not be doing it right.' I don't think you know how to do your job, Elliot," Beau said, stressing the first syllable of Elliot's name. With that, Beau had gotten up, pulled a quarter tip out of his pocket and placed it on the counter, and then had walked to the glass-and-chrome exit door, pushed it open, and headed out onto the street. Elliot was still standing there, waiting to place his order and trying to think of a clever retort, reassuring himself that it was better to say nothing than something stupid.

"I'll have a single cone of cookie dough," he told the waitress.

It would be embarrassing to try and have another talk with Beau, but maybe he would have to try; otherwise, he could always send Sky.

Over at the *Observer*, the main phone line rang. Fran picked it up, pushed a button, and Sky's phone started to ring.

When Sky first picked up the phone, for a moment Elliot imagined that the voice on the other end of the line belonged to Beau, but as soon as he heard her say, "Bud," he knew she was talking to her husband.

"Bud, you know this is the busiest morning of the week."

"I'll let you go," Elliot mouthed to Sky as he walked back to his desk.

He turned and took one more glance at the mousy young woman with the wire-frame spectacles, twisting her shoulder length hair around her fingers as she talked. Maybe she's less threatening to Beau, being somewhat of a space cadet with all that astrology shit. Elliot began to think that maybe he should send her out at the end of the week to do a little interview.

"Sky, I know you said not to call on Tuesday mornings, but I need to drive Up Cape and probably won't be back till late this evening," Bud said, his deep voice booming in her ear. "The toilet's got another crack, so I thought I'd go buy and install a new one before things got too busy, one of those new water-saving models instead of using that dam in the tank. Any color requests?"

"White will do just fine," replied Sky. Did he really need to get her permission to buy a toilet? She agreed they did need one. The less water used with each flush the better, because less water would go through the septic system. Sky and Bud's house actually had a Title V septic system, but it was ten years old and one couldn't be too careful. They didn't have much land so if the system failed, it would cost a lot to install another one. "Just drive carefully," she said. "I love you."

She shouldn't be so critical, Sky told herself. During the off-season months, Bud did a lot of work around their old, dilapidated house, such as mending the roof, replacing old, worn shingles, painting, rebuilding the back deck. The weather was so tough on things. Paint peeled after only two or three years, so most people were resorting to aluminum siding. To hell with historical preservation. One needed to be practical. Shingles were better than clapboard, but they had a tendency to weather and fade, just like everything else.

She was lucky to have a husband who was handy, even though she figured that on his jaunt Up Cape he'd stop and indulge in a few drinks, probably at the Land Ho in Orleans where a bunch of his buddies hung out. That's why she had admonished him to drive carefully. For Bud, there was no such thing as drinking just one beer. He had to down two or three. At home on a Saturday night, he easily consumed a six-pack.

Tonight, maybe she'd go to dinner at Napi's Restaurant with a couple girlfriends. Why not? She deserved to indulge herself. Tuesday was always a hard day at the paper. But this week had been particularly stressful, and it was only half over.

Sky had been foolish enough to think that once Roz was getting laid on a regular basis, she'd let up on hassling everybody and pushing so hard. But nothing seemed to slow her down. There was always this undercurrent, this tension. "Definitely a fire sign, that Roz," Sky whispered to herself with a grin. She remembered that time, on Roz's birthday, she had done her chart: an Aries, the ram, with Leo the lion as her ascendant. Pushy and willful...that was Roz for you.

Back to work, she told herself. She shouldn't let her mind wander. Sky started proofreading Elliot's write-up on this week's Selectmen's meeting. Boring stuff, as far as she was concerned, all this bickering back and forth about the Wastewater Committee report. But she needed to find any misspellings...misspellings and grammatical mistakes. They checked each other's work. It was cheaper than a proofreader, and the computer picked up plenty of errors.

Across the room in the small group of desks, tables, and computers that served as the Advertising Department, Fran was checking to see that ads were placed on or at least near the pages advertisers requested, while her assistant, Betty, was putting the classified and legal ads in place. Today, Fran's work was easy. The harder part of the week was going out and soliciting ads, trying to get businesses to sign contracts and commit to an entire campaign of advertisements in the *Observer*.

"Just a single ad is not going to do it for you," she would tell them. "And the rates are much better when you sign a twelve-week contract. Studies have shown that consumers need to see the name several times before they associate it with the product you sell."

The best advertisers were restaurants, which might publish featured specials or even their entire menu, and the large stores Up Cape that sell home improvement products. Some of the businesses selling gardening supplies or carpeting regularly advertised sales or reduced-priced items and paid additional money for color inserts.

Fran made a lot of phone calls, but she did even more driving, walking, and bicycling. She'd learned her best sales had always been made in person. You needed to press the flesh, look into their eyes, and touch them on the arm or shoulder to get your point across.

Plus you needed to flatter. Flattery was very important. A good strategy was to do a little research first. Fran would try to locate a previous customer of the business she was about to visit. It always made the proprietor blush if you could mention someone by name. "[So and so] _____ told me what a nice _____ [man or woman] you are and how you went out of your way to give them good service." If you made someone sound generous, they often wanted to act generous by ordering large-size ads. Sometimes it worked and sometimes it didn't.

The reverse angle was to make them feel exceedingly cheap if they ordered ads smaller than a quarter of a page. "Are you sure an ad that small is going to be noticed? Don't you want to spend a little more so the copy doesn't get too crowded?"

Another strategy was to tell them their product or business was so superior it deserved being promoted, so more people could find out about it.

The best customers, of course, were those who didn't need prodding. Those were the confident, successful businesspeople who knew you needed to spend money to make money...Sonny Carreiro, for

instance. Only there was no Sonny Carreiro anymore to sell ads to...
he was dead.

The thought of Sonny made a big lump in Fran's throat because she
could see him so clearly in her mind. The dark, sparkling eyes, devilish
smile on his face. The way he had made love was nothing like she'd
imagined. He was positively gentle, gentle and skillful. She had half
expected him to be one of those forceful, plodding types...in and out,
in and out, the thing that made most men so positively boring, with a
capital B. But not Sonny. He liked to titillate and play.

That's how he ran his business, in a playful manner. He liked to
have fun. Perhaps too much fun had killed him. Had he owed someone
too much money? Generally speaking, Sonny had always paid his bills
on time. He liked the discount. Pay in advance and get a two-percent
rate reduction.

"Certainly, you can give me your sales pitch," Sonny had told
her when she had cold-called him one March morning two years earlier. "Why don't you come by at around eleven thirty, before I take
off with my lovely wife for lunch. I'll be ready to take a break from
paperwork."

His office had been very neat. Not like some offices Fran had walked
into, where paperwork was scattered across desktops, tables, even
chairs. Everything in Sonny's office was kept in its place. Soothing,
dark colors had been chosen to complement the antiques and artwork.
There was nothing not to like. But something about him she had found
annoying. Was it the way he seemed to enjoy listening to the sound of
his own voice? Or was it that he acted as though all women should
find him simply irresistible?

Sarah had seemed pretty enamoured with him. But, after all, she
was his wife. How many couples continued to have lunch together
several years into their marriage. Not many...although Fran had heard
of some husbands, even into their fifties and sixties, who went home
every day for lunch, a special lunch prepared by their wives. That was
old school. That was from a previous era when women stayed at home
and cleaned, cooked, sewed, gardened, canned, and preserved. Some
of those skills were becoming a thing of the past. Fran had never even
seen homemade preserves or handmade potholders created for church
fairs until she moved to the Cape.

Fran had been raised in Manhattan, where her father worked as an editor for a publishing house. Which one? They were always being bought out and changing names. It wasn't worth keeping track. He brought home a paycheck. Her mother worked part-time as a librarian for one of the private schools. The rest of the time she stayed home and took care of Emily.

What a pain that had been. Fran loved her older sister but had always resented her. Why did *she* have to be the one with a sister who spent her days in a wheelchair, drooling and being pushed around from place to place? With Emily, you couldn't be angry. You couldn't be mean. And, oh, how Fran longed to be mean some days. You just had to smile. And you had to talk.

"Tell your sister about your day at school," her mother would say. "She'd like to hear what you've been doing." As if Emily could really understand what it was like to sit in one of those desks, pass notes to friends, play hopscotch on the playground blacktop, or be chosen for one of the lead roles in the school play. She would never understand what she was missing, but maybe it was better that way.

"Your sister has severe cerebral palsy," her mother had explained when Fran was about seven years old and asking questions. Her father didn't like to talk about such things. It was probably why he spent such long hours at work.

The tragedy was that the whole thing could have been prevented. Emily had been one of those "at-home births" gone wrong. Her parents had been foolish, naive hippies. No hospital. No doctor. Just a midwife. And by the time they'd realized they were in over their heads, with a detached placenta and other complications, it was too late. They waited six years before trying again, before having another baby. This time, they'd done everything right. Proper medical care. An obstetrician. A hospital birthing room. And they had a healthy, normal baby…Fran.

But her family was not what one would call "a normal family," so Fran had left home as soon as she could. She graduated from high school early, got a job, took courses at City College, and shared a room in a loft with a friend. Living was expensive, and she didn't care about actually getting a college degree.

So one summer, a girlfriend, one of Fran's first lovers, brought her to Provincetown and she decided to stay. After being hired at the *Observer*, Carreiro Insurance Agency had been one of her first large accounts.

"I'll take a quarter-page ad for twelve weeks...by the way, how's old Roz doing?" Sonny had said all in one breath. "Let me look in my files and see if I have a copy of the one we ran a few years back." He had quickly left his office to go to another room, evidently where some of his file cabinets were located.

"Is he always like this?" Fran had asked Sarah, who had arrived and was ready to go out for lunch while she and Sonny had been initially talking. Sarah had entered the room quietly, hung her jacket on the brass standing coat rack in the corner, and taken a seat in the other green, leather-covered chair that clients would sit in while Sonny sat behind his large, impressive desk.

She had looked beautiful, in a subdued sort of way. Very natural... rosy skin with a few stray freckles and shoulder-length, warm brown hair. Definitely younger than Sonny, but how much younger Fran hadn't been sure. She'd already studied the photographs on the bookshelves that pictured Sarah with their two daughters, and another with Sarah, Sonny, and the girls as baby and toddler on a large sailboat.

Sarah had seemed lost in a reverie of thought, so she hadn't fully heard Fran's question. "I'm sorry," Sarah had replied. "What did you ask?"

"Is your husband always so...." Fran suddenly had been at a loss for words. "What I mean to say is, does he always make his decisions so quickly and decisively?"

Sarah smiled, and when she did her whole face had become animated, particularly her eyes...large, golden-brown eyes with thick, dark brown lashes.

If she smiled that way all the time, everyone in the world would fall in love with her, Fran had thought to herself many times. But the truth was, Sarah kept her smiles in reserve. Most times Fran would see her, the expression on Sarah's face was a blank, as if she wasn't really there. Perhaps she wasn't and instead her mind was someplace else.

Damn it, Fran thought to herself. It was Tuesday and she still hadn't called Sarah. Maybe it would just be easier to go by the house. She could stop by with a bouquet of flowers. Or she could send a bouquet of flowers. She could always just pick up the phone and order a bouquet to be delivered. Baby's breath and daffodils, an unlikely combination perhaps, with some birds of paradise mixed in. Something exotic, not funereal.

10

Later Tuesday Morning

Tuesday morning...almost the middle of the week, Annie was thinking while leisurely drinking a second cup of coffee and sorting laundry. This was the day she liked to do household chores, although for a few hours at least she was sure to slip into her studio and do some work. Would it be modeling or casting? Most sculptors nowadays sent their work out to be cast, but Annie liked to do small pieces herself. The act of creating...she liked to practice every day. It was the other things that went along with being an artist that she tried to limit to just a few days a week, the promotion and paperwork. There were always bills to pay, bills to levy, letters to answer, slides and photos to send out, along with news releases and brochures, to various publications and galleries. Customers didn't find *you*. *You* had to find them. And grants weren't given to artists based solely on merit and need. Grants had to be solicited, proposals written.

The picture of an artist happily working away in their studio, free from the cares of the world, that was only the wealthy artists who didn't need to make money and could pay others to handle the other stuff. Those who wanted to make it, be recognized as professionals, labored to promote themselves if they wanted to eat.

"I'll take care of putting food on the table," Beau had told her many times. "You really don't have to worry so hard about how many pieces you sell." But it was a matter of pride and ego. Annie was already a working artist before she had gotten married. She had started to build a reputation, a following, and she wasn't going to give it up.

Two years had gone by since her last one-woman show, she thought to herself while putting her underwear in neat stacks alongside Beau's. And if the Windsor Gallery wasn't going to give her a show in August this season, then maybe she ought to change dealers. Jesse Cronin, who owned the gallery, had suggested having a show in late June along with Katy Healy's artwork.

"Not acceptable," Annie had told Jesse. "I really don't like her work. Those shrill colors and sweet landscape paintings are just not compatible with the artistic message I'm trying to convey."

Annie was usually more tactful, more polite. But when it came to her art, she spoke frankly and freely. "Besides, June isn't exactly the best time for me. Most of my summer collectors don't come out to the Cape until July, and many are only here for the month of August."

"Blessing of the Fleet weekend is a very good time for an opening," Jesse had maintained. "And Katy is one of my best sellers. I don't understand why you don't want to exhibit with her. She likes your work very much."

Annie sincerely doubted how much Katy liked anyone else's work besides her own and that of other members of her family. She was largely trading on her father's reputation. He had been a great painter, original. But her work was very derivative.

Perhaps she should get in touch with the owners of the new gallery opening up in the center of town. They were doing a beautiful job restoring the old building that had been a dry goods store years earlier. They lived in New York, and back in the fall one of the partners had given her his card when they'd met at an Art Association opening reception. Now...where had she stashed it?

The front door of the house slammed and Beau walked in. "Are you feeling better today, my pumpkin?" he asked, kissing her on the forehead. "I forgot my deposit slips for the bank, plus one of the detectives is coming by at eleven to ask me more questions. You don't mind if we talk here, do you?"

Here? The word echoed in Annie's head. Police detectives coming *here*, invading *her* domain? No! For one thing, the house was a mess: laundry all over the dining room table, dirty dishes in the sink, newspapers and unopened mail scattered around the living room....

"The house is kind of a mess," she said aloud.

"Oh, don't worry about it," Beau assured her. "They're coming to talk to me, not to check out your housekeeping."

That's what *he* thinks," thought Annie. She'd seen those detective shows where the lead homicide detective noticed something in some suspect's house while asking a battery of questions, something that turned out to be crucial to solving the case. But didn't she want the case solved? Was there anything she was trying to hide? Just her own world. Just her privacy. Just her home.

Beau had built this house for her. It was theirs. Up on Atkins Mayo Road, a dirt road that ultimately led over to Route 6, it had been the perfect location for a house and studio. Nothing and no one bothered her, except the mosquitoes. They were incessantly buzzing and swarming during the summer months because there was lots of warm, damp earth and swampy patches of land on their lot.

"I bought this lot a few years ago," Beau had explained, "back when Jerry Lester was subdividing his land. There are so few buildable lots left in town that don't cost a fortune, when an opportunity presented itself I thought I better go ahead and buy it and just put it aside."

"This is great!" Annie had told him when she first saw it. "I never even knew this road was here. It's a veritable nature trail...all these tall trees, ferns, wild berries, mushrooms, rabbits, and toads, the kind of place where elves and fairies might just want to live."

Beau had been amused by her observations.

"What are you laughing at?" she had demanded, wanting to know if she had said something foolish.

"Come on. I want to show you something." He had taken her hand on that crisp fall morning and led her up a side trail, past a "No Trespassing" sign, and up to a small blue-and-white stucco structure that resembled something straight out of a fairy tale.

"This is the Mushroom House. When I was a boy, we used to sneak up to this house and watch the fairies who lived here," Beau had said with a laugh. "They were real fairies, if you know what I mean, and they had the most beautiful garden. There were all kinds of tall, exotic flowers in every color of the rainbow. Some days we'd sneak up to take a look and there would be smoke coming out of the chimney. It looked really magical. No one lives here now so it's all overgrown, but in my mind's eye I still remember the way it used to be."

"That's a lovely story," Annie had responded. "Maybe one day we'll build our own "mushroom house" for our children to play in. And in the meantime, maybe you can build me a tall, sturdy studio in the middle of these woods where I can create some magical sculptures."

"I'll do you one better. We'll build a house and a studio and maybe even a parking garage," Beau had boastfully said. She had grabbed his hand tightly in hers, then tighter, as if to say, "I never want to let you go." The two had been so much in love in those days, just a couple years earlier, and she had seen none of her husband's flaws.

Building the house had been fairly quick. Every day, Annie would stop by the site of their future home, where Beau and his crew were working. She'd bring thermoses of hot coffee, sandwiches, some days even hot soup. Anything to keep them from taking a break and going home. When men did leave every so often during their lunch hour, they'd have a few drinks, what Beau called a "liquid lunch," and never came back.

Of course, they did start working at seven thirty in the morning, so keeping at it until three thirty or four in the afternoon meant they'd done a full day's work. More often, though, they would leave somewhere between two thirty and three o'clock. But Beau was lucky just to have a crew. He guaranteed them a certain base pay and kept track of their hours. The project had worked out great for Beau, from a business standpoint, because it kept his crew busy in the off-season, even when most other building projects took place during the spring.

What Annie had not been aware of was that Beau already had house plans and an approved building permit before he'd even asked her to marry him. His plans were to build a house on Atkins Mayo Road when his regular workload slowed, in order to keep his crew busy. It was going to be a spec house, which he could always sell when the market was right. So when his personal life had changed to include Annie, all he had to do was add in some blueprints and permits for the studio.

"This is the kind of house you want, Annie," he had half asked and half told her at the time, "a New England saltbox. And they're the best kind of house for this climate, the most economical, their use of space. We'll try to position it facing south, but there may not be much sunlight in these deep woods."

"That's okay. I don't mind," she had responded. "I like trees."

As a child, Annie had liked pretending she was a wood nymph, playing in the forests outside Ann Arbor, Michigan, where her father had been a college professor. He had died young, at age fifty-two, when Annie was fifteen years old, the youngest of three children. Her mother had held the family together, maintaining the house, putting Annie and her brothers through school, and working part-time as a teacher.

After getting her bachelor's degree from the university, Annie had already begun work on her master's when she got the Provincetown Fine Arts Work Center fellowship and headed east. For the first time, she saw the ocean and a bay. Incredible, she had thought on seeing the force of the open sea, immediately feeling that she never wanted to leave. So she stayed.

"They don't get many sculptors," a fellow recipient had explained, "particularly not many women sculptors. And you've got talent, something unique." Yes, Annie's semi-abstract bronzes of human beings, objects, and nature were striking to those who appreciated them. She liked to use a variety of textures and play with different interpretations of standard forms.

She had chosen sculpture over other art forms because of the opportunity to work in three dimensions. It was not enough to merely observe with the eyes. Annie liked to create something you could touch and feel.

It had been a difficult decision, sculpture or pottery. But the deciding factor was the need for more mass production when working with pottery, which Annie didn't find as appealing. Pieces of pottery were more fragile and breakable when compared to metal. Plus, someone might be willing to pay two hundred dollars for a work of clay, but the same work in bronze could bring two thousand. Even if your pottery creations were pieces of art, it was difficult to charge prices comparable to those of quality art. So you had to sell more to make the same amount of money.

The expense of making cast bronze pieces was greater, but so were the rewards. For Annie, constructing the molds to make the castings and working with molten metal were interesting tasks in themselves. Sometimes she liked to incise added textures to the surface of her metal sculptures while it was still warm and malleable. It was also fun, buffing and polishing a piece of sculpture until it developed a shine.

Still working with clay to make her originals for casting, Annie had a potter's wheel and a small kiln for her own enjoyment. Her mugs, plates, and bowls for household use were her own creations.

"These are so wonderful," Beau had commented when he first held one of her mugs in his hand. "You ought to sell these."

"For the amount of time and labor I put in making them, they'd be too expensive for most people to want," Annie explained. Hand-applied renditions of starfish, shells, fishnet, and seaweed adorned each mug, along with a textured finish of sand. Several different colors of glaze were painted on the inside and outside of each mug, adding another design element.

Her pottery was expensive to make and somewhat fragile. That was how the fight had begun the other evening, the night Sonny had been killed. Beau had put a big chip in one of the plates, being careless.

"These things are too goddamn heavy," he'd complained. "And impractical. Look how easily this thing chipped. Can you fix it or should I just throw it away?"

Annie was almost in tears. "You are such an oaf. I told you to let *me* wash the dishes if you're going to do them in a rush."

"Complain, complain, Miss Prima Donna. I try to help you out and you find fault with everything I do."

"Breaking dishes is not what I call helpful," Annie sarcastically retorted.

"Breaking dishes…. Here, you want to see a broken dish?" shouted Beau as he smashed the chipped plate down on the floor. "Now that's what I call *broken*," he yelled, storming out of the room. She had heard him turn on the engine of his truck and drive off in a fury.

He didn't return until three hours later. Annie was sitting in the family room reading a detective novel when she heard his key turn and open the front door of the house. After cleaning up the broken pieces of pottery and putting away the dishes, she had scrubbed the grimy burners on the stove, trying to work away some of her anger. Men… they always think they're right and everyone else is wrong, she'd complained to herself. Why had she ever gotten married?

She shook her head, decided to fill the kettle with water for tea and paced the floor waiting for it to boil. Of course she knew why she'd gotten married. She was in love and she wanted commitment. She wanted children, a family, but so far the pregnancy part of having children had not happened. Why not?

Her doctor had told her that just the egg and sperm connecting was not enough. "Implantation has to happen. Eight out of nine times a couple has intercourse, the conditions aren't exactly right. Relax and don't just aim for the days you think you're fertile. It will happen in time. It often takes a year for a couple to conceive."

Well, it had been about nine months since Annie stopped using birth control. She was still trying. But when things like this happened, she didn't want to try at all. Beau could go sleep in one of the spare bedrooms, for all she cared. And if they did make love, she doubted the baby would stick. Nothing would grow in the womb of a woman uncertain about being loved. Babies were made from love, from trust. Of course, that didn't explain all the women with unplanned, unwanted pregnancies. All Annie knew was that a baby would not grow in her womb unless she was confident and sure she and Beau had a future together.

"Oh well," Annie said to herself as she poured the hot water into one of her handcrafted mugs and threw in a tea bag. She had selected a "relaxing mixture" of chamomile and mint leaves. She needed to calm her nerves and wait for Beau to return with his standard "I'm so sorry I lost my temper" apology.

When he returned, Beau hadn't bothered to look for her. Instead, he went straight upstairs and into the bathroom to take a shower. Twenty minutes later, wearing a fresh pair of blue jeans and T-shirt, with his hair still wet, he was in the kitchen filling up the washing machine with dirty clothes and starting a load of laundry.

"I don't know why I do these things," he addressed her in a plaintive tone, standing in the doorway between the family room and kitchen. "I love everything you do and make, Annie. I just had one frustrating day and I shouldn't take it out on you. Can you forgive me...please?"

When Beau looked at her that way, with that look in his eyes and the sound of remorse in his voice, she couldn't say no. So she said, "Yes, I guess so."

He walked over, took her hand and pulled her up from her easy chair. "That's my girl." He stroked her hair and her face. "You're the light of my life. I couldn't stand for you to stay mad at me. How about some fresh air? A walk into town, perhaps, or down to the beach?"

"Okay," she had answered. "I'll get on my coat and a sweater. And you should dress more warmly than that. It's getting late and it's nippy out."

It was fun walking late at night. With so many lights off in the houses on the street it was easy to see the stars, especially at the beach. The town was quiet and took on an eerie quality, late at night in early spring. They held hands, like a new couple out on a first date. Walking down Atkins Mayo Road, they used flashlights to see their way. Even during the summer months the road was dark. At the beach, they could hear the quiet lapping of the waves on the shore. The tide was just coming in.

"Watch where you step," Beau warned her. "There's a lot of old wood that washes up this time of year, plus all the seaweed and possible dog poop."

"I'll be careful," she laughed. "Too bad the town won't take it upon itself to have the beaches professionally cleaned."

"It's waterfront owners and responsible citizens who do the job," said Beau. "And the high tide...we can always depend on the high tide to wash most of the debris away."

"So where did you storm off to tonight?" she had asked.

"Oh, I just had to take care of some business." Beau gently pushed back some of Annie's hair, which the wind had blown forward into her face. "Nothing that you have to be concerned about."

Annie was pulled back to the present by a knock on the door. Beau looked at his watch.

"It's only ten forty," he remarked. "Trooper O'Brien must be running a little ahead of schedule today. Did I mention he's a detective from the state police? Our local force felt the need to call in the 'big guns.' It's not like they have much experience here with murder investigations." Beau self-consciously checked to see that his shirt was properly tucked in. "He said he would meet me here at eleven. Ah well...I'll go answer the door."

"Maybe he came early on purpose," said Annie, "trying to catch you off guard."

O'Brien was disappointed that the face greeting him at the door belonged to Mr. Costa. He'd hoped it would be his wife instead. He had thought that if he showed up a little early, perhaps he'd get to spend a little face time with the missus first and ask her a few questions when her hubby wasn't around.

No such luck. On the other side of the door was Beau Costa himself, big as day. He was taller than O'Brien had expected because he'd known some of Beau's cousins, the Costa family that lived in Harwich where O'Brien had grown up. He recalled them being dark-haired, swarthy-skinned, and solidly built....great football players on the high school team. But this side of the family must have married some Irish stock, he reasoned, because Beau Costa was tall and lean with blue eyes and light brown, almost golden hair, streaked with gray. Perhaps, O'Brien jokingly thought, far back in his own family tree Beau could even be related to one of *his* relatives!

"Mr. Costa, I presume," he said, holding out his hand to clasp Beau's callused, paint-covered hand.

"I have to apologize, Officer," Beau said. "Since you're here a bit earlier than expected, I haven't had time to wash up."

"Oh, that's okay. Don't worry about it. If you'd like, I'll just have a seat and you can go ahead and clean up if it's bothering you."

"I just don't like to get too much paint and dirt around the house. My wife works too hard to have to clean up after me."

As Beau walked away, he yelled toward the kitchen, "Annie, do we have any coffee we can offer our guest?"

"I just made a fresh pot," she replied while walking through the living room to the front hallway to greet the officer. "Come on in," she said, punctuating her greeting with a big smile. "Have a seat and I'll bring you some."

"That would be wonderful. Just a dash of milk and one spoonful of sugar."

O'Brien sat down in one of the two large, overstuffed chairs that were covered in an orange-toned, knobby upholstery. Square in shape... quite different from the traditional brocade or beige-toned, plush, ve-lour-covered furniture he was used to sitting in when he visited folks' homes. He'd already downed two cups of coffee earlier in the morning, along with his blueberry muffins and orange juice, plus a cup of tea while interviewing Sonny Carreiro's neighbors, the Hanovers. But he knew it would be impolite if he didn't accept the offer.

Always accept food and drink, except alcohol, his training su-pervisor had advised him during his rookie days. When you accept someone's hospitality, it establishes a bond, a connection. "Delicious," said O'Brien after forcing himself to swallow a large gulp. "What a beautiful mug!"

"I made it myself," Annie replied. "A little personal sideline other than my sculpture."

"That's right. I heard you've got quite a reputation as an artist, for someone as young as yourself." Always lay on the flattery...another technique he'd learned for establishing a bond with possible witnesses. Everyone had something to tell, but first you had to gain their confidence. If they liked you, they were willing to tell you what they knew. The key to getting someone to like you was to make them think you admired them.

"Oh, I'm not *that* young," Annie said with a sly smile, taking a seat on the overstuffed sofa amongst the multitude of tapestry-covered and embroidered pillows, some of which were covered in the same orange fabric as the two angular chairs. "I've been working at my art for over ten years. How about yourself? How long have you been a state trooper?"

"I've been on the force now almost twelve years."

"You must enjoy your work."

"That I do. On the investigative end of things, I meet people of all kinds."

"Met many murderers?"

"I've met a few. What about yourself? Met many murderers?"

Annie laughed nervously. "Not that I'm aware of."

Beau reappeared and took a seat in the other big chair. "So, how are *you* doing with the investigation?" he asked, putting a particular emphasis on the word "you."

"Say, you wouldn't by any chance be related to John and Tony Costa down in Harwich?" O'Brien asked. "We used to play football together."

"They're first cousins of mine, once removed," Beau replied. "Their father, Joseph, is the son of my Uncle Manny, my father's older half brother. My grandfather was married twice. His first wife, Mary, died of cancer at age forty. Then he married Maggie, my grandmother, who died just last year."

"Do you ever see John or Tony at any family reunions?"

"I think I remember meeting them at one of Grandpop's birthday's, but that was quite a few years back. I don't think they get up to Provincetown very often, and I don't spend much time in Harwich."

"They were great football players in high school. Ever play much football?"

Me, not much. I played halfback for a few seasons, but fall of my junior year I tore a cartilage in my knee and that was it. I take it you were an enthusiastic player?"

"That I was. But back to the business at hand. You asked about my investigation...this homicide investigation, pretty unnerving business. It wasn't a robbery, an argument, a random act.... Someone had it in for Mr. Carreiro. You were his business partner. Did he have any enemies?"

"Well, Sonny pissed off a lot of people, but so do I. When you're in the building business and you start making money, some people don't like it and they get jealous."

"Anyone in particular have a vendetta against Sonny? Hear anyone make any kind of threat against him in the past few months?"

Beau looked over at Annie, who was listening intently, to get a sense of where the conversation was heading. He looked once again towards O'Brien, who took note of Beau's change of focus. "It's common knowledge around town," said Beau, "that Sonny and I had been barely speaking to one another recently. Sonny wanted a portion of the condominium complex we're building to include year-round housing, using grant money and a loan program from HUD. That would have meant being landlords for at least ten years. I told him I wanted to build, sell, and move on. He felt it was a good, long-term business investment, cheap money and all, as well as a charitable thing to do for the town.

"Being a landlord is not my thing. We got into a big fight about it. He tried to make it look to the bank as if we wouldn't qualify for a loan without the HUD money. But hey, I've got some equity. But according to Sonny, I overstated my income and investments...ergo, the newspaper story a while back in which I was accused of falsifying income and assets on my loan application.

"The charges against me were dropped. That's the long and short of it. The building project proceeded as we'd originally agreed, without the year-round housing component, but Sonny was kind of disgusted. He was always used to getting his way."

"So he was angry at you. You weren't so angry with him."

"Well, of course I was angry at him. I was fuming, partly because of what had appeared in the newspaper, but then I'd keep reminding myself that what was really tearing Sonny apart was Sarah's having left town. He just wasn't thinking straight. But I still figured, hey, business is business...we needed to finish this project together and then maybe I'd go back to working for myself."

O'Brien had pulled a small pad from his side pocket and was jotting down a few notes. "So, what made Sarah leave? You and Sonny ever discuss it when you were still talking to one another?"

"I don't know for certain. Maybe she just fell out of love.... What did she tell you?"

O'Brien smiled at the question. "She said she needed more space."

"I think she was seeing someone," Annie piped in. "I was just never able to figure out who. There was just this look in her eyes."

"You women know these sorts of things, huh?" O'Brien listened to Annie's observations with a grain of salt. In his mind, women had a tendency to overdramatize, although it was true that most marriage break-ups were due to extramarital affairs. But this was a small town. How come no one knew who she may have been seeing?

"Maybe it was Sonny who was seeing someone else," speculated O'Brien. "Did he play around?"

"Sonny...he liked to flirt a lot," Beau offered, fidgeting a little in his seat. "I don't think he ever cheated on Sarah, but you never know. He claimed to be into group sex. Invited me once to have a three-way with him and Sarah, before I started seeing Annie, but I thought he was joking. That kind of stuff is pretty passé, but there's probably a contingent in town still into it."

"Maybe it was the kinky sex that caused her to bolt," suggested O'Brien. This was getting interesting, he thought to himself. "I wonder if they ever did act any of these fantasies out," he said aloud. Sex and jealousy were always good motivating factors in a murder case. He couldn't ask Sonny about his sex life, but he *could* ask Sarah. However, she might not be very forthcoming. If Sonny liked variety, he may have been seeing another woman, O'Brien reasoned. And if his mistress had become too possessive, too jealous, bam...maybe that was motive for a murder.

"Now, where did you say you were Sunday night?" O'Brien pointed his question towards Beau while taking a sideways glance over at Annie. The woman had the most beautiful shade of auburn-red hair. Her hazel eyes were focused intently on her husband.

"I was with Annie. We had a late dinner, talked, and took a walk around the East End and down to the beach."

"I take it you can verify this?" O'Brien asked Annie.

"Yes," she answered simply.

Having downed most of his coffee, O'Brien had felt the overwhelming need to empty his bladder but had suppressed the urge, not wanting to break the flow of their conversation. The more you talked with informants or witnesses, the more relaxed they became as their fears of being questioned in a homicide investigation subsided. Once they felt they weren't suspects, information started to flow.

Any kind of knowledge about who Sonny Carreiro was and who might have wanted him dead was what O'Brien was seeking. Beau and Annie had been close to the victim. Unfortunately, according to them, over the past few months they had barely been on speaking terms. Was this true? Others in town might possibly be able to either confirm or dispute their story.

"If you don't mind, could I use your facilities?" O'Brien asked.

"No problem at all," replied Beau, who stood up and led the state trooper to the powder room just down the hall from the laundry room.

"That wasn't so painful," Beau remarked on returning to the living room where Annie was still sitting.

"I wouldn't say 'painful,'" Annie told him. "To me, it was more disconcerting. I don't even like thinking about Sonny. I'm sad and angry at the same time. Plus, think of the work I could be getting done if I wasn't sitting around here talking to this guy. Even dead, I find Sonny annoying."

O'Brien took note of the large vase of flowers on the dining room table, sitting amidst piles of folded laundry. Red roses, pink snapdragons, and some feathery, purple flower he didn't know the name of, were framed by asparagus ferns and eucalyptus. "Birthday or anniversary?" he called out when returning to the living room and nodding his head back towards the flowers on the table behind him. The two rooms were divided by a slightly indented wall on each side of the large opening and a change from wood to terra cotta tile floors.

Annie and Beau exchanged looks, which included raised eyebrows and smiles. Beau spoke first. "Annie and I had a little spat so I brought her the flowers."

"They're beautiful…so, how long have you two been married?"

"Seven months," Annie answered. "I didn't know state troopers had an appreciation for flowers."

"Oh, there's a lot about state troopers you probably don't know."

Back at his restaurant, after writing up his menu for the weekend, Frank started making phone calls.

It took a while to reach Polly. Spring being one of the busiest times of year for realtors, with all the upcoming summer rentals, she was either on the other line or with a client.

"Lunch, my dear…are you cooking?" she asked jokingly when he finally got her on the phone.

"We're not generally open yet for lunch this time of year, but I could throw together a salad."

"Salad! Come on, Frank. You know I like fattening foods. I could go for some buttery quiche or some New England clam chowder with lots of cream."

"How about we meet at Sally's Chowder Bowl then. I'd love to cook you lunch, but right now I don't have a full staff or well-stocked kitchen, and I'm very busy."

"Sounds good to me. Twelve thirty then," agreed Polly who didn't even have time to put down the receiver before she was beeped with another call. Five foot four and weighing close to two hundred pounds, she liked to eat and she made no excuses. People could either accept her the way she was or they could go talk to somebody else.

Maybe Frank was ready to buy a building, she wondered. The real estate business was finally picking up after remaining level for several years, and Polly was anxious to make as many sales as she could while interest rates were low.

"Yes, dear, your lease is all set," she told one of her wealthy summer clients calling from New York. "I've gotten you a beautiful two-bedroom unit on the water, with a dishwasher, laundry facilities, large deck, and you can bring your cat. I"ll mail it out today."

Polly put down the phone, twisted a strand of her short, dark brown and gray hair, and thought nervously about the Zigfelders' cat. Last year, it had done a lot of damage, scratched up the arm of a sofa and urinated on the carpeting in one of the bedroom closets. Luckily, it was easy to replace a piece of carpeting inside a closet. Cat pee was one of the most difficult odors to remove. Those people would be better off boarding that spoiled cat at a kennel. They have more money than brains. One of these days, she'd sell them a condo because there won't be any landlords left who'll be willing to rent to them, with that cat, regardless of the large security deposit they'd offer. A thousand-dollar security deposit should cover any potential damages this time, she hoped.

It was more pleasant to think about Frank Chambers and lunch. Her stomach was beginning to grumble. Maybe there were still some apple Danishes left on the tray over by the coffeemaker. Polly always had muffins or Danish for her clients in the morning and a basket of cookies and fruit in the afternoon. How much she ate versus how much was eaten by staff and customers, she didn't keep track. There were two associate agents and a secretary who could skip breakfast or lunch if they needed to. They didn't have the voracious appetite of Polly Smithfield.

She rationalized that it was better to save room for a large bowl of clam chowder and a basket of fried clams and fries than eat something sweet when it was already close to eleven thirty. Maybe Frank *was* ready to buy a building. Or maybe his lease was running out and he needed to find another place, she speculated, trying to picture a good location for the Indigo Inn, preferably one of her listings. Restaurant leases are tough, she lamented to herself, what with so many places closing down due to limited septic systems.

Well, it was fruitless to speculate on what Frank wanted to talk about in private. She'd find out soon enough.

Frank sat at his desk writing a few notes to himself. Should he go for eight, twelve, or sixteen pages? Of course, he needed a real estate section, which would have a featured home of the week, and then there would be a focus piece on a chef, with a number of recipes, a cooking column, theater review, and some kind of column on the environment. Perhaps a fishing or shellfish report. Nature excursions. Maybe something on fashion, for the clothing store ads. After all, this is a magazine, he reassured himself.

"Sean, did I wake you?" Frank had waited as long as possible to dial up the owner of the Cowboy Club, knowing full well that Sean Gilligan was likely to stay up late, into the early morning hours, overseeing the operations of his bar and doing a little partying afterwards. But it was almost noon, so surely he was awake by now.

"Oh, Frank, my man. Nice to hear from you. Hey, you should have been at the show last night. It was fabulous. We had quite a crowd. Lefty Geiger wrote the script, and Charles and Georgie were our star performers. Charles looks great in drag. Have you ever seen him...or, should I say, her? Miss Charlotte, he calls himself. What a wonderful pair of legs, in high heels, and her black-sequined minidress was to die for. Oh, you should have been there."

Frank imagined Sean on the other end of the phone with a cup of black coffee in one hand, a lit cigarette in the other, hands slightly trembling. Yes, he sounded like he was still buzzing...he'd probably taken an upper of some kind. Frank wasn't really up on what they were taking these days, but he knew there were pills for everything.

"Sounds like fun! When's the next performance?" he asked reluctantly, figuring he would have to force himself to go see a few of these shows Sean was so hot about if he wanted Sean's financial backing.

"Eight o'clock every night. You should come by soon, before you go back to opening the restaurant seven days a week. We'll leave you a free pass at the door." Tall and lean with steel-gray hair and a black mustache, Sean Gilligan was in his mid fifties and still trying to act thirtysomething. Not fully dressed, he had slipped on a pair of tight, faded blue jeans and a long-sleeve polo shirt for warmth. His feet remained bare.

"That would be great. Say, Sean, how would you like to see a local magazine in town, something that would compete with the *Observer*?"

"Who started the rumor this time?" Sean asked while looking for an ashtray, shell, just about anything to flick his cigarette ashes into. The place was a mess: a box of half-eaten pizza on the floor, empty beer cans, his leather jacket, a lace tutu. What had he been doing last night, he puzzled to himself. Ah yes, he was with Georgie and Buzz, doing poppers after closing time. They must have then come here. Georgie's tutu...he'd take it back to the club later, before the next show.

"Rumor? This isn't a rumor," Frank replied. "I'm thinking of starting up a magazine, but I need some investors." That was the problem with Sean. He took no one but himself seriously, yet most of the time he was going out of his way to show the world that he wasn't serious, partying all the time.

"Frank, you're a great chef, a *restaurateur*. What do you know about running a magazine?"

"I know what I like and what I don't like about the *Provincetown Observer*. I figure if we keep our costs low and keep it simple, we can do it."

"Who is *we*?"

"Well, I talked to my friend Jeff, the graphic artist, this morning and he's agreed to design the layout and be our art director, and Bruno Marchessi is going to cover guesthouses and lodging." Frank was slightly exaggerating since Bruno only knew about the initial article he was going to write, but it sounded good. "And I'm having lunch today with Polly Smithfield to discuss a section on real estate."

"She in on this?"

"She could be."

"Polly has a pretty good head on her shoulders. How much money is she going to put in?"

"I don't know yet."

"Well, whatever she's willing to invest, put me in for the same," said Sean.

Frank was stunned. Now the pressure was on to get as much money out of Polly as possible. Maybe he could offer her a free weekly dinner at the restaurant to sweeten the deal. The woman did love to eat and everyone liked perks they didn't have to pay taxes on. He needed to think of something quick to throw back at Sean to keep the conversation going. Advertising, of course.

"You'll need to get me a photograph and the information for your ad," Frank told Sean. "Of course, we'll be giving you a full page and maybe a feature story, as well."

"Who's going to write this feature story?" Sean asked suspiciously, certain that Frank couldn't possibly have gotten a writing staff together so quickly.

"Well, did you have any suggestions?" replied Frank, throwing the ball back into Sean's court.

"As a matter of fact, I do. How about a first-person account of putting a show together, written by Lefty, of course. He's a writer. He'd do a good job. And it would give the club plenty of publicity."

"Sounds good to me. Tell him to start working on it. Or would you prefer I call him about it?"

"It would seem more professional if you did. You are the editor-in-chief, I presume...."

"I guess I am," said Frank.

11

Early Tuesday Afternoon

SALLY'S CHOWDER BOWL WAS THE TYPICAL New England restaurant, with heavy maple tables and chairs in the style of what
decorators in the 1950s had considered "colonial." That's when
the tables and chairs had been originally made. Solid, heavy, durable...
they lasted, which is why they had been in more than one restaurant
over the years, from Hyannis to Wellfleet and from Provincetown to
Chatham. When one eating establishment went out of business, they
turned up in another.

Where they had been used before arriving in Provincetown three
years earlier, only the chairs and tables could say. If it had been able
to speak, one chair certainly knew that someone extremely heavy was
now bearing down upon it while leaning their elbow on the top of the
table and intently studying the menu.

"I think I'll have the clam chowder...and what did you say the
special was?" Polly Smithfield asked the middle-aged waitress. She really ought to do something about that hair on her face, Polly thought
to herself while listening to the day's specials. The woman didn't used
to look like that when she was younger and waitressing over at Wine
and Roses, Polly remembered. Maybe she was now on some kind of
steroid treatment or something....

Polly forced a smile. "I think I'll just stick with the fried clam platter. Sliced tomatoes instead of cole slaw, please."

Frank stared down at his paper place mat, which pictured a map of Cape Cod. Pale green and gray on a white background, mats like these were so generic. But maps were good. "Probably we'll have a street map of Provincetown inside," he told Polly, "so people will be able to find their way around town."

"They run a map inside the *Observer*. I want to know what you're going to have that will be different."

"What about a map with the sites of all the houses on the market?" Frank was half joking but it sounded like something that would appeal to a real estate agent.

"That's interesting," Polly perked up, "but probably hard to do. What I'd like to see is a large real estate section. I like your idea about a 'home of the week.' That will give people ideas about how they can make their house look nicer; and when they start thinking like that, they might start thinking about buying a better home...something larger, better location, better view, better long-term value."

"I can't promise the first couple of issues are going to be very large, Polly. We need to start small until we get our bearings."

"You just need more advertisers," she said while noticing Beau and Annie entering the Chowder Bowl's front door.

"Beau!" she called out, not wanting to get up from her chair. "How's it coming?"

What Polly was referring to by "it" was the Seascape Development Company's newest condo project, the one in partnership with Sonny Carreiro, the ownership of which was now in limbo until the insurance policies and estate were settled. Polly didn't care who was the ultimate legal owner or who killed who. What she cared about was getting an exclusive listing.

Beau walked over to Polly and Frank's table, with Annie reluctantly following behind.

"Hey Polly. Hey Frank," he said. "We're taking a little breather with the construction and all, what with the funeral for Sonny the day after tomorrow. Don't worry, Polly. I'll give you first crack at an exclusive, but it will only last three months."

"I can do a lot in three months," Polly responded.

"I'm sure you can, particularly if you spend enough money on advertising. How about running some ads in the *Boston Globe*, get some off-Cape investors out here?"

"How about I advertise in the new publication that's coming out this summer...." She turned to Frank and asked, "What did you say the name was?"

"I didn't mention a name," said Frank. "But I was thinking about *Provincetown Vacation Magazine*."

"Hmmm...I don't like it. Then we'd only be catering to the tourists. We want the locals to read it, as well."

"Then how about *The Provincetown Star*?"

"That sounds like a scandal sheet. I was thinking about something more distinguished like...I've got it! *Province Town Crier*. Get it? Three words. Instead of *Provincetown Crier*, we have *Province Town Crier*, sort of a double entendre."

Beau just stood there, amazed at the what he was hearing. "I had no idea you folks were scheming to start a new paper."

Polly laughed. "It's not a newspaper. It's a magazine. And I'm not starting it...Frank is. He's merely asking me for a little financial support."

Polly turned to Frank. "Isn't that why you invited me to lunch, dear?"

Annie silently observed the interaction. A new magazine, she thought to herself, wondering if they'd have an arts section or whether it was just going to be some gay party rag that focused on who wore what outfit to which tea dance, interviews with the hottest female impersonators, and all that.

"I suppose I could run a small ad for my construction business," Beau was saying. "Perhaps you'd even like to do a story on Annie, sort of 'a step inside a sculptor's studio.'"

He turned around to face his wife standing behind him. "You're having a one-woman show this season, aren't you?"

Annie felt slightly annoyed. One voice inside her head was saying, "What do you know about promoting my artwork?" But another voice told her, "He is your husband. He's only trying to help."

"The question is where the show is going to take place," she answered wryly. "My gallery plans are still up in the air." She was trying to be as vague as possible because she didn't want to offend anyone. Maybe Polly was friends with Jesse Cronin and word would get back to her.

"Still, that's not a bad idea," said Frank, after taking a long sip of water. "We are planning to have an arts section. Although in the beginning, this magazine is going to be pretty small."

"How small is 'small'?" demanded Polly. "You need to make an impact, be noticed the first time you come out."

"Well," said Frank, "I've been looking at other magazines and it really has to do with advertising. If we want this thing to fly, it's got to be fifty percent ads in order to be self-supporting."

"Fifty percent ads!" Polly said incredulously. "That's a lot of advertising."

"Look at any magazine, particularly the free ones for tourists, and they're full of ads. We're going to give ours away free, too, because it will make things easier when it comes to bookkeeping, et cetera, and we can immediately boost up circulation for the advertisers."

"So what you're saying," said Polly, "is that you'll have as many pages of ads as you do of stories and pictures?"

"That's exactly right," replied Frank.

"Then it's obvious to me that you need an advertising salesperson, someone to sell those ads."

"Well, yes. But I can't afford to pay them anything, except maybe a commission."

"You just leave that to me," said Polly.

What Frank wanted to ask, but didn't, was how much money was Polly willing to invest or loan to help get the magazine off the ground. After all, he needed to get back to Sean Gilligan with a figure.

Interrupting Frank's train of thought was the arrival of two steaming containers of chowder, a bowl for Polly and a cup for him. After the waitress had set his down, along with a round soup spoon, a cellophane-wrapped bag of oyster crackers, plus an extra napkin, he took a deep inhale through his nose to smell the aroma of the chowder.

"I think we'd better go take a seat and leave you to your lunch," said Beau. "It's been an interesting conversation." He looked behind him and around the room to see who else was in the restaurant. "The place is starting to fill up," he said with a grin.

Although some faces were familiar, he saw no one he needed to worry about having overheard their conversation, until his eyes landed on John Murphy having lunch with his wife, Liz, in the far corner booth. Now, *that* was switch, seeing him with his wife, since Beau recalled more than once seeing him at places with Roz. But maybe that was before Liz and the two kids had come to town. They seemed wrapped up in their own conversation, so maybe John hadn't paid any attention to the talk going on in the center of the restaurant. On the other hand, if there was something he had overheard, he was sure to tell Roz. Should he warn Polly and Frank? No, that was their problem. He had other things to think about.

John Murphy took another bite of his fried-fish sandwich. The lettuce was crisp. the bread toasted, and the flounder fresh and flaky. Liz wasn't as enamoured with her clam roll. Too greasy, and she didn't like all these stomachs. She should have ordered clam strips, but John had said they weren't local. Were any of the fried clams you got around here local? They were probably all pre-breaded and frozen from somewhere off-Cape. But Liz knew better than to argue when John thought he was an authority on something; let him have his say. She had been in the mood for fried clams and ordered what he'd suggested. At least the cole slaw and coffee were good.

"So what did you want to talk to me about?" John asked. He had gotten a call that morning at the office from Liz.

"Are you free for lunch? There's something we need to talk about," she had told him in a serious tone.

But when they met at the restaurant, she seemed more interested in talking to him about the blue curtains she was going to make for the living room and how she planned to put several rosebushes and a trellis in front of the shed. "It was nice last night," she'd then whispered in his ear. Was she trying to rekindle the romance in their marriage? Probably feeling insecure, new town and all, which made John feel somewhat like a heel but he tried to put the thought out of his mind.

"I'm worried about Michael," said Liz.

"What about Michael?"

"Have you seen his grades lately?"

"He always does well in school," John replied, taking a few french fries and dipping them into catsup. "Is there a problem?"

"Well," Liz said glumly, "he got a D on his Spanish test and a C on the government exam. That's why we're talking *here*...I didn't want Michael or Erin to overhear us and I think we need to present a united front. He's almost in high school now and these grades will start to count!"

"So what seems to be the problem? The classes are certainly small enough. Didn't you tell me there are only twelve kids in his Spanish class?"

"The problem is, he's hanging out with the wrong crowd."

"And what's that supposed to mean?"

"Exactly what it sounds like. He's hanging out with a bunch of loser kids who are probably drinking and smoking dope in their spare time instead of studying. I think you, as a father, need to spend more time with him, and I think together we need to talk about the dangers of alcohol and drugs," she said in a voice just slightly above a whisper. "Do you really need to spend so much time at night at the office?"

"Are you sure about this? I mean, are you sure about the drugs and alcohol thing? I'd hate to accuse him of something he's not guilty of." John shook his head in disbelief. Just when he thought things were going along fairly smoothly, something had to come along and bite him in the ass. Although he was right in assuming that Liz didn't seem to feel he was lacking as a husband, Michael was perhaps finding him lacking as a father...and this was something he needed to fix.

What could they do together? In the fall, a lot of fathers took their sons deer hunting. But this was spring. Maybe they could go fishing. He could rent a small skiff and they could go out for the day, this Saturday perhaps.

And what about sports? He should have insisted Michael go out for lacrosse or baseball. They must have some sort of team...but now the season was halfway over. Maybe he could still run track. Even if he just went to the practices and didn't run in the meets, it would keep him out of trouble. They'd have to talk about it. He'd have to offer him some kind of bribe, an incentive to be the good kid again.

"So how did you find out about these bad kids?" John asked.

"I talk to the other mothers. Plus, when I picked him up a few nights ago at his new friend Scott's house, the place was pretty appalling, disheveled on the outside and inside. No parents home. I didn't see any books opened, so I didn't believe they'd really been studying. And Michael even criticized me for going inside: 'I told you to honk the horn. Why did you park the car and come in?' It was as if he had something to hide."

"Why didn't you talk to me about this before? You could have mentioned it last night."

"I was hoping it was just a passing phase…you know, like the time he was friends with that miserable Tull kid, who was such a 'big mouth.' Thank goodness Michael outgrew him after a month. And I've read that when you start interfering too much, your kids will resent you for it. They have to learn how to make their own choices. But this morning, I was taking some dirty laundry out of his room and about to dump his trash can when I noticed those test papers in the trash! That was the last straw. If he was serious about his work, he would have taken them to his teachers and learned what he did wrong. I think we have a serious problem on our hands, John. What are we going to do about it?"

"First off, we're going to ground him; and second, we'll meet with his teachers and put some more structure in his activities."

"That's what I was hoping you'd say."

John took another bite of his sandwich, thinking to himself again that nothing was ever easy. And just when you thought things were going along on an even keel, something came along to shake things up.

Matters at the town hall were pretty much under control. The usual bickering about the reports from the engineers and the Wastewater Advisory Commission had simmered down to a low drone, while the Selectmen seemed generally pleased with the way the nursing home, which they called The Manor, was being run. Perhaps one day the town would decide to have perimeter parking and a recreational marina… one day, but not any time soon. Not being an elected official, John felt no urgent desire to get anything done under his "administration." His job was to run things smoothly and keep everyone happy, particularly the Board of Selectmen, which had hired him.

Probably part of the reason the petty squabbles had subsided a bit for the past day and a half had something to do with Sonny's murder. Those who generally chose not to think about death had been reminded of it and the arbitrary way it could strike at any time without warning. Everyone, whether or not they personally knew Sonny, whether they liked him or hated him, was curious. Who had pulled the trigger? Why? Was the murderer planning to kill anyone else? Maybe he or she was a madman, or madwoman, and the killing was arbitrary. Maybe they or someone close to them would be next.

Seldom was the town united about anything, except when tragedy struck. A major fire, an accidental drowning, the loss of a fishing boat in a storm were all past events that had pulled the town together. But this unity was always temporary. Within just days or a few weeks, the threads of unity became unraveled and the town once again began to pull apart into individual concerns and factions. The same would probably happen after the shock of Sonny's death had died down and the murderer was apprehended.

"So, Liz," John found himself saying, "is anything else bothering you? Is Erin doing okay?"

"She seems to be doing fine. Luckily, she hasn't quite entered adolescence yet. But our respite isn't going to last too long, I fear. Girls these days! At age ten, she's already talking about shaving her legs and asking when I'm going to allow her to start wearing makeup."

"Doesn't she know that women around here don't shave their legs?"

"Ha ha! Very funny," Liz replied. "Some of the women do. Although some also have a half a dozen holes in each ear, along with a few in their nostrils and one or two tattoos.... How long were you planning for us to stay here?"

"Let's evaluate a year at a time. Nowhere is it going to be perfect. Professionally, I have a good opportunity here, and in theory the school system is supposed to be good. We'll just have to see how it works out."

Leaving the restaurant after finishing lunch and John had paid the bill, Liz noticed a few familiar faces: Beau and Annie, who she'd met a month or two ago at the Year-Rounder's dinner, and that fat, obnoxious-looking real estate agent, Polly Smithfield, clicking her glass of beer together with restaurant owner Frank Chambers' iced-tea glass. Polly was laughing in a way that sounded like a grunting pig. Probably celebrating some business deal, Liz surmised. Maybe she sold him a building. Perhaps the Indigo Inn was going to move. This was how rumors started....

But he didn't ask me how *I* feel, Liz lamented to herself. He's concerned that the kids are doing okay and about advancing his career, but what about me? Men! They're so self-centered.

John took his time walking back to town hall. He didn't want to get cramps from not giving his stomach enough sedentary time to digest his food. He took deep breaths and tried to feel thankful that the news wasn't worse.

So Michael was having some school problems. *That* could be fixed. But Liz seemed to be having some doubts about being in Provincetown… and maybe she should. Provincetown wasn't doing a whole lot for her marriage, what with him seeing Roz and all. But she didn't know about that, or didn't seem to know about it. And she didn't seem to be finding fault with *him*, just the environment.

Liz just needed another cause besides the PTA and a few friends. Maybe he should encourage her to get a good job, which would mean her going back to school for a time. It would also mean he'd be more responsible for the kids and have less time for himself. But if they were involved in activities, sports practice and all, it might not be so bad.

Stop seeing Roz? John asked the question of himself. Why should he? She's what was making his life so great right now. And let's face it…all men do it, see other women on the side. We say we'll be faithful to one another and "til death do us part," but it gets boring after a while. Everyone needs a little spice every ten or fifteen years. It's commonplace and accepted in Europe. Americans are such oafs because we want to pretend everything is going to be perfect and nothing is going to change. But then we sneak around on the side trying to maintain a facade that everything is still the way it was.

But if he had to choose…Liz or Roz? How could he know? Divorces are a messy business. Would Roz even want to be married to him? She seems happy the way things are right now, maintaining her own separate life and independence.

John approached the benches in front of town hall, locally referred to as "the meat rack." Not many people were sitting out on this nice, brisk, sunny afternoon. Of course, there were several senior citizens: an elderly lady wearing a full-length coat, hat, and gloves; an old man, missing several teeth and wearing a battered khaki army jacket with his fly partially unzipped; and two women in their mid sixties wearing jogging suits and warm-up jackets. With their protruding bellies and wide asses, they looked as if they had never gone jogging or running in their lives. But there they sat, jabbering away to one another about sports celebrities.

And then there were a couple of tourists, one with a camera hung around his neck, and the other, evidently his wife, who was avidly studying some tourist guide while sipping her coffee out of a covered styrofoam cup while he stared blankly ahead. Dressed stylishly in matching blue ski parkas, John theorized that they must be visiting from a more southerly state like Virginia or California where they weren't used to the spring New England chill.

During the summer months, these same benches were packed. In the center of the square were often street performers playing guitars, accordions, violins, drums, or performing magic tricks for fickle tourist audiences in the hopes that they might put a few bills or coins in their hat. Hot, tired families rested their feet and licked on ice cream cones while single visitors "on the make" sat, watched, and waited to see what the town had to offer. Young and old, rich and poor, attractive and homely, you could see all different types of people sitting on these benches. They sat to watch the town...and townsfolk walking by watched them.

After the bars closed, that's when things got really lively, and that's how "the meat rack" earned its name. If you hadn't found a pick-up at the bars and you were looking for one, you could go sit at the meat rack. You could also sit on the steps in front of the post office or in front of Spiritus, the pizza joint, perhaps chewing on a slice of cheese pizza to quell a case of the munchies. But in front of town hall was *the* original place, and right at the center of things. Besides, if the various other gathering spots got too crowded, the police could insist you clear the steps and move on. But no one could make you leave your seat on the benches...the meat rack.

Late at night, particularly during the touristy summer season, invariably those at the meat rack were horny gays. But, as usual, at noontime in the middle of the week in late March, the occupants of these benches today were anything but.

John wondered if he should use the front or side entrance. The side entrance was the one that employees used since it was closer to where they parked their cars. The front entrance was grander, with its heavy, brass-handled double doors. Either way, you had to climb a substantial set of stairs, because the actual first floor was well above ground, what many would almost call the second story.

Squeaky, dark wood floors were what John walked on as he went into the town hall building using the side entrance and walked past the bulletin board with posted notices of all the various board and committee meetings and hearings. It was an old, grand building. The topmost floor held the auditorium, complete with a balcony that could be reached by not one, but two sets of stairs. Town meetings were held in the auditorium, in addition to concerts, shows, and dance performances, whenever the Selectmen saw fit to rent it out. In earlier days, the police station was located on the ground level, but now they had their own building on Shank Painter Road.

Offices, meeting rooms, files, paper, and computers filled the main floor of the old, clapboard, white-painted building, which was expensive to heat and maintain. At one time, there had evidently been a suggestion, made by one of the many groups of planners hired to study and make recommendations on how to deal with the town's growth, of building a new town hall in another location. The report had underlined the importance of parking availability and recommended demolishing the old building so the site could be turned into a park. That suggestion had gone nowhere. Provincetowners had many different ideas about a lot of different things, but most were attached to the old town hall and it being a focal point of the town.

Liz Murphy walked back home, setting out from Sally's Chowder Bowl in the opposite direction. It was a long walk to Cook Street, but she needed the exercise. Besides, walking gave her time to think.

Something was wrong. Liz could feel it. John had said all the right things regarding Michael. Yes, Michael temporarily needed to be grounded and the two of them needed to sit down with his teachers, and so forth. But it had sounded almost hollow. It was as if John's mind was elsewhere. Maybe he was too preoccupied with town politics.

If only she had someone else to talk to. She wanted to cry. Maybe it was simply that time of the month when her hormone levels started running a little high and she was more emotional about things. No... she was in the middle of her cycle, not towards the end.

She needed to do something, Liz told herself, some kind of diversion, because maybe she was just taking this town too seriously. Maybe a good book. The library was coming up on her left. Perhaps this time it was open. Often Liz was up and about early, before the library had opened its doors, or taking a stroll after dinner. Evening hours at the Provincetown Library, other than during summer, were limited.

Shaded under two large trees, in summer the library was another good location for street performers. It was set back from the street on the corner of Freeman and Commercial, across the street from Land's End Marine, the town's major hardware, appliance, housewares, and toy store. If you couldn't find something at Land's End, chances are you needed to drive Up Cape to one of the larger towns.

Another white-painted clapboard building, the library was an odd mixture of old and new. Inside there was carpeting, glass, and plenty of computer terminals that had replaced the now antiquated Dewey Decimal System.

"Years ago, when I was a child," Hattie Sherman, who worked at the bank, had told Liz when she asked her about the library at the Nautilus Club luncheon, "we had just one librarian, Mrs. Mayfelter. She was very old with dyed red hair and lots of rouge on her cheeks, and she would always lick her thumb every time she turned the pages of a book to find the pocketed card to check it out. She sat there behind the desk every day with her grown daughter, Belinda, sitting behind her. Belinda must have been forty-some-odd years old, but she was dressed like a girl of sixteen, in a fancy dress, big straw hat with flowers... and, yes, always a pair of gloves. I remember those gloves and the red lipstick she wore.

"Whenever I think of the library, I think of Mrs. Mayfelter. I seldom go in there these days. It's easier to just go and buy a paperback to read. I like those romance novels. The library doesn't have a great selection and I always have to worry about when the books have to be returned. But if you like more serious kinds of stuff, maybe you'll find some books there you'll like. Talk to Peggy Noonan. She's a member of the Board of Trustees, you know."

Liz looked at the wooden sign with the posted hours. Yes, it was open. She walked up the steps and entered into a world of hushed quiet. The librarian was sitting in a booth of sorts to her left, behind a sliding window of glass.

"I need a library card," she told her.

"Are you a resident?" the librarian asked.

She sat at her desk alone, a middle-aged woman, plainly dressed with greasy brown hair tucked behind her ears and tortoise-shell spectacles. She had an annoyingly shrill voice, but she certainly wasn't as strange as the librarian with the daughter Hattie Sherman had described. The library was soothingly ordinary. A place where you could read, think, and daydream, away from the cares of the everyday world.

"Looking for a good book?" Annie Tinker inquired while pulling a slim paperback out of her shoulder bag and putting it on the desk in front of where the librarian was filling out paperwork.

"First I need to get a library card," Liz answered. "I'm Liz Murphy," she said putting out her hand to shake Annie's. Nice scarf, she thought, admiring the way Annie had tied a wool paisley scarf with deep blue colors at the back of her neck rather than the front, positioning the large triangular section in the front. The colors and her partially opened, olive-green courdoroy jacket provided such a nice contrast with the warm colors of her hair and face. "We met at...."

"I know," said Annie, interrupting her. "Everyone in town knows who you are. And you just had lunch at Sally's Chowder Bowl. I saw you and your husband leaving just as we were finishing up. And I'm Annie Tinker."

Liz took note that Annie used her maiden name. Well, that was the style with artists. They kept their independence. She took a step away from the librarian's station. "Well, the lady behind the desk just asked me if I'm a resident, so I guess I'm not known by everyone," she told Annie in a quiet, conspiratorial tone.

"Oh, that's just Norma Heller. She lives in her own little world. Besides, maybe she thinks you're still commuting to Connecticut. That *is* where you used to live, right? Or maybe you found a house outside of town...Truro, perhaps? Everyone seems to be moving there."

"So what book were you going to recommend?" Liz was enjoying her conversation with this young woman who seemed to enjoy poking fun at everyone else.

"It really depends on what kind of books you like. Personally, I have very eclectic tastes, from E.M. Forster and George Sand to Jorge Amado and Marge Piercy, and then I always like a good mystery for some fast escapism. Say...I've been talking to my friend, Ellie, about starting a book club. You wouldn't be interested, would you? We're having a meeting tonight if you'd like to come."

"Oh, that would be wonderful. It would be a great way to get to know some other women in town, outside of the PTA. I've met a number of people, but I still feel like an outsider."

Annie smiled. "Yes, it's not easy to move to a new place and make friends. I was lucky. Coming here to work at the Fine Arts Work Center, I had an immediate network of colleagues. I got involved in various things going on in the community and friendships just followed."

"Your husband, Beau...he's a native, isn't he?"

"Born and educated here," replied Annie, "until he went away to the University of Massachusetts. Actually studied architecture, but he didn't bother to graduate. Dropped out after two years, he says because he'd figured out he could make more money building than designing and he didn't 'need no fancy degrees.' But the natives, they're a pretty close-knit community. They still think anyone not born here is an outsider. And the old-timers are pretty nasty about it, but they're dying out. One day, most of the old families will be gone.

"It's like the Yankees. This town used to be Yankee, not Portuguese, but most all of the Yankees moved away...went Up Cape or died off. The Portuguese originally came here to crew the fishing boats for the Yankee captains. They were considered the 'niggers.' But eventually they dominated the town and took over. Now the gay community has become a large influence. Interesting, isn't it?"

"Your card is all ready, dear," Norma Heller called out.

"We probably shouldn't be standing here talking, this being a library and all," commented Liz.

"Oh, don't worry too much about it," said Annie. "This is just the entry hall. The children's library is through those doors and the adult section is upstairs. I can't believe you haven't been here before. Anyway, I have to get going and do some real work. I'll give you a call later about when and where we're going to meet this evening."

"But you don't have my phone number."

"I'm sure it's listed...or maybe not. Your husband probably doesn't want people calling him at home. So what are your four digits?"

"5309," Liz answered, realizing that Annie only needed the last four digits because all Provincetown phone numbers began with the same first three numbers, 487.

Liz picked up her blue plastic library card at the desk and glanced over to see what book Annie had returned before Ms. Heller put it away. It was a book of poetry by T.S. Eliot. She certainly *does* have a wide range of tastes, thought Liz. Likes to read poetry, too, wondering if Annie ever reads it to her husband out loud.

Liz walked up the steps to the second floor, remembering the times she had read poetry out loud to John. It had been when they were courting. That was years ago before children and other pressing responsibilities. John was finishing up his MBA at Boston University and she was a receptionist/secretary at a law office and thinking about going to law school. That was a laugh. After one and a half years working in that law office, observing her bosses and how miserable most of them were, she'd begun considering teaching. But with getting pregnant right after their honeymoon, she had put her career plans on hold.

Children and family were more important, Liz had told herself... and they *were*. Being home had also given her time for volunteer work, helping out at the children's school, supporting political causes she believed in, and running an efficient household. She could cook nice dinners, plus do a little sewing and gardening.

Those women lawyers...always forgetting when their kids had a soccer game, sending a secretary out to buy a present for a birthday party they forgot their child was going to, picking up some pre-made, frozen casserole to serve for dinner on their way home from work. Of course, they all had au pairs, nannys, babysitters...whatever you wanted to call them. Or they had after-school, before-school care, or even both. That was another laugh, because she would hear them on the phone pleading with those babysitters to come back to work, or asking Liz to get some agency on the phone because they needed a new au pair. Too busy to put much time into finding the "right" childcare provider, they would often rely on agencies. They couldn't even spend the time to fill out the application forms. Many times, she was the one editing and typing up applications from their handwritten notes.

No, Liz was *not* going to be like them nor the male lawyers who talked about writing a novel on the side and quitting the practice or taking time off to sail around the world. One did actually go off to Hawaii to become a windsurfer, she recalled. All that time and education thrown away. If they were so bored with practicing law, why did they bother to become lawyers in the first place?

Law school was very expensive. Graduate school was very expensive. When the time came to get another degree, she was going to be certain it was what she wanted. So she'd waited...and was still waiting. Maybe now was the time....

Over in the Landons' living room, Sarah Carreiro was glad when Trooper O'Brien got up from his seat, shook her hand, and told her, "That's all the questions for now...and I'm so sorry for your loss. Let me know if you think of anything. You have my card, right?"

It was the first time she had felt happy all day. He's finally leaving, she told herself.

Most of the past two days had been a foggy blur. She kept grabbing at little things to help lift her spirits...the way her daughter, Stephanie, told her a story about a dog she had come across while taking a walk; the irony of the gossip Jo had shared with her the other night, after the children had gone to bed, about how the new town manager was having an affair with Roz Silva...and there they'd been, his wife, Liz, and Roz, sitting in the same room.

"Yes, I have your card right here in my pocket," Sarah had replied, eager to lead him to the front door.

Finally she could relax and not worry about choosing her words or what he might think. Not that he was a bad person. He was merely doing his job. Clean-cut...an attractive man, really. A little dimple on the left side of his chin, she had noticed that. Medium height, medium build.... Maybe they find people for these types of jobs who do look pleasing, she thought to herself. They have to look personable if they're going to be asking so many probing questions.

"Mrs. Carreiro...how shall I put this?" O'Brien had said. "Did you, at any time in your marriage, suspect that perhaps your husband was seeing someone?"

She had raised her eyebrows at the question. "Are you asking me if I think my husband was having an affair?"

O'Brien had nodded his head in assent.

"I left town almost seven months ago. We did come back Thanksgiving and Christmas. And Sonny came down for the girls' birthdays.... He might have started seeing someone after I left. He didn't mention it. He wanted to get back together. I was thinking about it. But in answer to your question, I don't know. It's possible. Sonny was a very complicated person."

"Well, did you two continue to be...intimate when you spent time together?"

"You're asking some very personal questions."

"You don't have to answer anything you don't want to answer. I'm just trying to picture his state of mind at the time of his death and who might have had a motive to kill him."

"We were still husband and wife," she had blurted out quickly, "if that's what you're driving at."

"That's all I wanted to know," he had replied sheepishly, looking almost embarrassed that he'd been so probing.

In some respects, O'Brien reminded her of a doctor invading parts of her body she wanted no one else to go. You let them look into your ears, palpate your breasts, listen to your heart, put their finger up your rectum, all under the assumption that it's for your own good, your protection. And maybe it was, but it was unpleasant nevertheless.

"When was the last time you saw your husband?" he had asked her.

"Christmas vacation. I came up with the girls over their winter break. Sonny was planning to come down over their spring break and take them to Bermuda. He said he had some big news to tell me, something to celebrate. He asked if I'd like to go to Bermuda, too. I said I'd think about it."

"Any idea what big news he was talking about?"

"Maybe he had pre-sold a lot of the units they're building. I really have no idea...."

What *was* the news Sonny had wanted tell her about, Sarah wondered. Maybe he left a note somewhere. Should she should go over to the house and take a look? No, it didn't seem that important now.

She turned her mind to other things. Now that O'Brien was gone, she could do whatever she wanted...at least for a short time. Tomorrow afternoon and evening was the wake at Sterling's Funeral Home. That was going to be a gruesome affair. She would have to sit pleasantly and act composed for what would probably seem like an eternity while she greeted assorted family and friends. Should the girls be there? They probably should; they were old enough.

Today they had gone out bicycle riding on the trails over the dunes and through the Beech Forest. It was a chance for them to have some fun in the midst of the tragedy that had occurred in their lives. Sarah's mother, Emma, hadn't been too pleased about them going.

"Maybe it would be more appropriate if they stayed here. Besides, there might be some derelict out there on those dunes, camping out."

"Mother, I don't think so...at least not this time of year. And it's part of the national seashore. Park rangers patrol that area."

"Well, I don't think it's a good idea. At least they ought to stay in the neighborhood, where we can see them."

"It will be fine. Don't worry about it."

Luckily, Jo had done something helpful for a change and had taken Emma with her to Hyannis to shop for paper plates, napkins, and beverages for the gathering after the funeral.

"I don't trust Frank Chambers' taste," Jo had told Sarah. "I'll pick up some paper plates myself, something elegant but heavy and sturdy," she had stated while buttoning up her wool jacket and smoothing the creases out of her short, plaid skirt. "I despise those paper plates that begin to fall apart as soon as you start loading them up with food. But Frank will be bringing his supply of stainless cutlery. There's nothing worse than plastic forks and knives that break on you all the time."

Sarah took note of the large diamond studs glittering in Jo's ears and her expensive designer watch. She certainly did spend a lot of money on clothes and jewelry, Sarah thought. But with no children, what else did Jo have to spend money on?

"A woman her age should be covering up her knees," Emma said to Sarah that very morning while brushing their teeth in the shared guest bathroom.

"She probably thinks her legs still look good," Sarah retorted. "She's in pretty good shape. Still spry from being out on the links playing golf."

"Have you ever played golf? They spend most of their time driving around in a cart. A lazy, rich person's sport, if you ask me!"

"Well, I think she also goes to one of the gyms and works out. And, yes, I have played golf once or twice...and you're right. It's much ado about nothing. Definitely a game that appeals to shallow people who have nothing better to do with their time. Hitting a ball with a metal stick around a manicured field, with slopes, valleys, ponds, sand traps, trying to get it into a small hole. It doesn't do anything for me, unless I'm in the mood to be silly. I think part of the appeal of golf is the outfits they wear and the people they're golfing with. It's a very social sport. Quite popular with business executive types."

"And social-climbing types," her mother added, "like your sister-in-law. Why did you let her take charge of the funeral? You should be handling the arrangements yourself."

"Easy for you to say, Mother. You don't know these people the way I do. They have a certain way of doing things. Besides, it's *their* town. You don't think I'm moving back *now*, do you? The only thing that kept me here was Sonny."

"You can say that again!" her mother harrumphed triumphantly.

Why did her mother have to keep rubbing salt in her wounds by reiterating facts that Sarah found so painful?

As she grabbed her jacket from a hanger in the hall closet and started putting it on, Sarah wondered why she had even brought her mother in the first place. She could be so annoying. Yes, but she *was* her mother and it was the right thing to do. And, after all, Emma was Sarah's ally when it came to the Carreiro clan. She was solely interested in what was best for her daughter and granddaughters, nobody else. She had no hidden agenda.

The wind was cold against Sarah's face when she stepped out the door. She should have brought a hat. She could always go back inside and borrow one. There were probably extras in the closet. Were the girls dressed warmly enough? Children...they were strong, resilient. It was amazing how they could go outdoors, bare-legged with short socks, in the middle of winter.

Sonny had been insistent about wearing hats in cold weather. "You do realize that you lose at least thirty percent of your body heat through your head when you go out without a head covering. If I don't wear a hat in the cold, I'll get sick," he would tell her.

So Sonny would always wear a hat. In the winter, it was to keep warm; and in the summertime, it was to keep the sun out of his eyes. He had several. There were Irish tweed wool caps, navy blue Greek fisherman's caps, heavy knitted stocking caps, baseball hats, safari and panama hats, even a cowboy hat. What was she going to do with his hat collection? The tears gathered and stung in her eyes.

It was too cold and windy to cry. She tried to hold back the tears. Luckily, there were some tissues in her pocket. Oh, Sonny...what a difficult man to love, you were. Hard. Tough as nails. And she didn't even get to say good-bye. The tears really began to stream down her face. But she refused to turn back.

Many of the houses in the neighborhood were empty, boarded up, silently waiting for their owners to return. Yes, they all had heat and were well insulated, but most belonged to seasonal visitors. Some of them might start coming up on weekends after Easter. Some of the houses remained vacant until the end of June. Others might be rented by the month or by the week to affluent families or groups of vacationers taking refuge from some hot, humid city in the South or a boring Midwestern suburb. Houses like these never really had a personality of their own. It was important that they remain generic so that they would appeal to a broad range of tastes. With the length of their actual owners' visits so brief and transitory, in Sarah's mind the houses seemed to be crying out for attention.

"I want people inside me, laughing," screamed one house, with gray, stained wooden siding.

"I want a nice big fire in my chimney, a nice big fire with folks cuddled in front and warming their hands," shouted another, with a driftwood sculpture in front by a long, curving driveway.

"I want dogs and children and people in love," another seemed to pine as the wind whistled by.

No one was out walking. A car was not to be seen; none driving by. The only companions around were the ones Sarah made up in her mind, the vacant houses.

And then she saw the delivery van coming up the road, the one with the lettering on the side: "The Little Flower Shoppe." It was heading towards the Landons' house and no one was home to answer the door. Should she walk back up the street to receive what probably was some sort of funereal bouquet?

"What? Flowers for me?" she might exclaim. They weren't for her, she reminded herself. They were for Sonny. They were for the Landon home. Maybe Jo even ordered them. No, she wouldn't have ordered them to arrive when she wasn't planning to be home.

"Sarah, could you please keep an eye out for the flowers? They're due to arrive some time this afternoon." No, Jo had said nothing like that to her before she left. It's not as if they needed any more in the house…a dozen white roses had already arrived from one of Jo and Bill's friends, and another, tightly constructed arrangement of various pastel spring flowers was sitting in the center of the dining room, sent by one of Jo's golfing partners.

What kind of flowers would Jo order? Probably gladiolas. Sarah could imagine Jo liking gladiolas or lilies, being symbolic of death.

"What kind of flowers would you like on the coffin?" Jo had asked.

"Something simple," Sarah had said. "Perhaps a spray of golden chrysanthemums...."

"Chrysanthemums?" repeated Jo with a dubious expression on her face. "I think of them as a fall flower, especially the golden ones. Are you sure?"

"It was the golden color I was thinking of...to bring to mind Sonny's personality, direct and simple. Fussy flowers just wouldn't be appropriate."

Sarah could tell that Jo was highly annoyed but backed into a corner. It was Sarah who was paying for the funeral expenses, although Jo had engineered most of the arrangements. On this one decision, Sarah had the upper hand, if only because Jo had actually involved her in the decision making. But the fact that the entire funeral service was Jo's idea was beyond Jo's comprehension because she couldn't imagine a funeral being done any other way.

For Jo, of course you had a Catholic mass at Saint Peter's of the Apostle, presided over by Father O'Malley. Of course, her brother would be buried in the family plot in the Catholic cemetery. And of course the reception afterwards would be at her home, which was, after all, much grander for entertaining than Sonny and Sarah's.

Sarah turned around to walk back towards the house. She might as well be there to accept whatever was inside the flower truck, waiting to be delivered; otherwise, the driver would have to make a second trip.

She began to daydream. Wouldn't it be nice if we could have a memorial service for Sonny in an open field, a field full of flowers, or on the beach or the sand dunes, out in the open with the sky as our roof.... But that wouldn't appeal to the older people in the community. It wouldn't be easy for them to get there and they'd want to sit down on chairs, not cross-legged on the ground. We could stand in a circle and everyone who had something to say about Sonny could step forward and speak, light a candle and put it in a big candelabra in the center of the circle. We'd all join hands. We'd sing and dance and pray to all our gods. We'd talk about living forever, through each other, and our memories, stories handed down, passed on from one to another. It would be so nice, so meaningful.

But that's wasn't going to happen, she told herself, snapping out of it and waving at the delivery man, who was just about to pull out of the driveway and leave.

"Mrs. Carreiro?" asked the driver, who appeared to be a gay man in his mid thirties.

"Yes," Sarah answered.

"I've got some flowers here for you." He opened the driver's side door, hopped down, and went around to open the rear doors of the vehicle. "It's a real terrible thing, the murder and all," he said, fumbling around with his keys. Dressed in greasy blue jeans and an old army jacket, hair pulled back in a pony tail, he crawled into the van and retrieved two flower arrangements. Written on one tag was: "To the Carreiro/Landon Families." The other said: "For Sarah Carreiro."

He handed her the smaller one, which consisted of daffodils, tulips, and narcissus in a clear, rose bowl. The large basket arrangement, with tall lilies, pompons, foxgloves, and roses, he carried to the door. Sarah pulled the keys out of her jacket pocket and opened the door.

"Just set that one down on the table here," she said, pointing to the side table below a tall, gilded mirror. She would need to move the silver-plated urn and candlesticks over to one side, to make it look symmetrical, but she could do that later. Besides, Jo would probably come home and move everything around again. The smaller arrangement she would take to her room. But, for the time being, she set it down on the coffee table in the living room.

"Did you need me to sign anything?" she asked.

"Yes. I almost forgot," answered the delivery man. She figured he probably wasn't just a driver but also helped out in the flower shop with the arrangements.

"They look very nice," she called to him as he walked out the door and back to his van.

Now, where had she left her purse, Sarah wondered while scouting about the room. She found it sitting on the floor next to the couch. She wanted to give him some kind of tip. Ten percent of what?…well, five dollars ought to do it, she decided.

The fellow seemed grateful when she handed him the bill. Probably a lot of people in this town don't even bother to tip, she was thinking.

"Thank you. Sorry, again, for your loss. I hope they catch the creep who did it," he said.

It seemed everybody must be talking about the murder, Sarah thought to herself, and that they also now knew who she was, if they hadn't already…and probably even a lot of details about her life. Like living in a fishbowl. But it was always like this. It's difficult to be anonymous when your husband owns lots of real estate in such a small town. Oh well…pretty soon she'd be gone, and in a year or two they most likely wouldn't remember her.

Sarah carried the rose bowl arrangement to her room and set it on her bureau. Pulling the taped envelope off its side and opening it, she sat down on her bed to read the card. The written sentiment was: "Thinking of you. Your friend, Fran."

She twisted the card back and forth in her hand, trying to dissect its meaning. Why had Fran chosen "Your friend" rather than "Sincerely" or "Love," two common salutations. "Thinking of you" was pretty straightforward and obvious. But if Fran was thinking of her, why hadn't she called? Maybe she was afraid. Maybe she was too busy, or just didn't want to get involved. Maybe all of those reasons.

At any rate, it was a sweet gesture, sweet and considerate. It wasn't what Sarah needed, but it seemed that she seldom got what she needed. What she needed was support, physical support, someone there to hold her, to wipe away her tears. But that was something Sonny would do, and he was gone. She had chosen to go off by herself and now she was alone. The pain in her stomach, inside the center of her being, like what she had first felt on learning of Sonny's death, returned with a vengeance. She crossed her arms and clutched them around her waist. For now, she would just have to live with the pain.

12

Late Tuesday Afternoon

WITH THIS WEEK'S NEWSPAPER put to bed, things were somewhat under control and Roz longed for an opportunity to unwind and relax. She hadn't been able to leave the office for lunch, only eating two slices of the pizza Elliot had ordered. Too much starch, she thought to herself. Maybe for dinner tonight she and Sally would just eat a nice salad. She could leave early...should leave early. Elliot had already left to go jogging on the beach, but Elliot was young, full of vim and vigor. A *walk* on the beach, though...Roz could definitely go for that.

Too bad she couldn't have a nice, romantic dinner with John. Too bad. Perhaps one weekend they could sneak away, some kind of brainstorming retreat on something critical to the town, like economic development, low-cost housing....

Who was she trying to kid? It was just the night before last that they had made love. Most likely they'd get a chance to meet tomorrow. Probably pushing my luck...or his, she thought to herself. Once or twice a week is probably fine. She mulled the consequences. How often could he be working at his office in the evening without arousing suspicion? During how many lunch hours could he disappear?

Roz realized there was no practical reason to keep thinking about something over which she had no control. Right now, a walk on the beach seemed the most practical alternative. She decided to drive her car home first and then walk over to Mitzi's Coffee Shop for a hot beverage to take with her. Certainly not coffee because she'd had too much already today and the caffeine was causing her brain to buzz a mile a minute. Maybe she could also do with a little snack to eat as she walked down on the sand.

She'd been acting like an adolescent, she told herself. A foolish adolescent, head over heels in love, thinking she's in control but really not. All these limits…the relationship really couldn't go anywhere. The best thing about seeing John was how he's managed to occupy her mind. And body. She couldn't forget about her body, she reasoned, laughing nervously to herself. After losing Gene, John had made Roz feel like a woman again.

"How's business?" she asked Mitzi, who was sitting in her usual place behind the counter. Wearing her usual bib-style white apron, soiled with drips of coffee and chocolate, wrapped around her broad middle as she stared vacantly out into space, Mitzi looked bored. It was that slow time of the day.

"Bus tour types," she said wearily. "They drive me crazy. Those senior citizens. They take so long to make up their minds. Everything has to be low calorie, fat free. *I use butter!* When I use something else, the baking just doesn't come out the same. And then they bitch about the prices, saying I charge too much for coffee.

"Out where I live, a cup of coffee costs 60 cents. You charge twice as much," says one.

"Well, maybe you live in a place where taxes, overhead costs, insurance, rent, and all are lower," I say.

"I know what coffee should cost," this man insists, "and you are charging too much."

"Fine. Then don't order any," I tell him.

"But I want a cup and you're the only place around that's open," he whines.

"So anyway, Roz, that's what my day has been like. How about yourself?" Mitzi asked.

"Oh, busy. Very busy." Roz looked down into the baked goods case. The pumpkin and raisin spice muffins looked yummy. *More* starch. Well, it was just one of those starch days, she resolved.

"How about one of the pumpkin muffins and a large cup of hot, spiced herbal tea," Roz requested.

Mitzi turned around and pulled a large plastic jug out of the commercial refrigerator and unscrewed the lid to inspect and smell the contents. "Good. It still smells fine. I've been having a problem with the apple juice turning," she explained.

"Ah! So I've uncovered one of your secret ingredients," said Roz. "Your spiced herbal tea contains apple juice. If only it was as easy to uncover clues about who murdered Sonny Carreiro."

"Maybe you should try and talk to Rusty Ogel's son," Mitzi said offhandedly.

"Son?" Roz asked incredulously.

"I take it then you know who Rusty Ogel was," Mitzi said while heating up the tea in the steam-heating section of the cappuccino maker, which created a slight sucking noise. She turned and placed the tall cardboard cup of tea on the counter in front of Roz.

"Yes. He's the bum who died in the fire at Cranberry Square some years back. I thought he had no living relatives."

"No living relatives they could find, I guess. This young man came in here a few months back and said he was Rusty's son. Said he'd come to town just to take a look around and see the last place his father had lived. Hadn't seen him in years...and had a different last name, too. Evidently, Rusty had gotten this kid's mother pregnant when she was still in high school, never married her, and she eventually married someone else. That's why the police didn't track down any son.

"But the mother kept track. Occasionally, he would send her money for the kid. She knew the last place he'd been living was Provincetown. So years later, when she's dying of cancer, this mother tells her son the truth and he goes looking for his real father. He comes to Provincetown."

Mitzi pulled a muffin from the case with a square of waxed paper lining her hand. "Did you want this on a plate or in a bag?"

" In a bag, please. How did you learn all this?" Roz asked.

"It's amazing what people will tell you over a cup of coffee. Especially when they're alone and they have no one else to talk to." She handed Roz a small, white bag with a muffin and napkin inside.

"Have you told any of this to the police?"

"You know, I haven't, because it didn't strike me till recently as being particularly important. The night Sonny was killed, I didn't even think about it. Everyone was talking about Beau being the likely suspect. But the other morning it came back to me, my conversation with the young man."

"So you haven't reported this to the police?" Roz asked again.

"I suppose I could, but I don't even think this fellow is still around. He visited several weeks ago, in February, during Presidents Day weekend."

"But did he ask you who was responsible for the fire? Did he ask who owned the building? Who collected the insurance money?"

"He was more interested in the town, in understanding why his dad had chosen here as his last place to live."

"So what was this fellow's name and where was he from?"

"Casey Long from Louisville, Kentucky."

"Damn. That's not exactly close to here."

"No, it isn't. But I suppose if I told the police, they could find him and ask him some questions if they wanted to."

"Do me a favor and wait until tomorrow to call the police."

"Well, the day is almost over as it is. Of course, I could use a little advertising discount."

Roz smiled. "I'll see what I can do."

She walked out the door and a few blocks to one of the town landings and turned down to the beach, trying to sip her tea as she walked. It was still hot, and it felt soothing on her tired, slightly scratchy throat.

Well, that was a pretty fruitful visit, Roz thought. Perhaps she could call long-distance Information and try to find a number for this Casey Long fellow. But what would he say to her...? "Yes, I killed Sonny Carreiro because I considered him to be responsible for my father's death." Or, "I paid someone to kill him," or "I tried to extort some money out of him and when he didn't produce, I sent a hit man."

Those were all pretty far-fetched scenarios, she admitted to herself. But maybe he knew something or precipitated something that caused the murder to take place. It was an interesting puzzle.

Roz pulled up the hood of her jacket to shield the wind from her head. Her ears started to ache from the inside when they got cold. The sun was nowhere to be seen, just clouds and a slight grayish tinge to the sky. It was getting chilly. In the distance, she could see Bob Sanderling, a well-known local writer, walking his two Weimaraners. They were beautiful dogs with grayish-lavender coats of fur and violet-colored eyes. Just like clockwork, she would see Bob walking his dogs, mid morning and late afternoon whenever she had time to sit vigil. He always ignored her.

Occasionally over the years, they would pass very close but he would never say "hello." She tried a few times but there was never any real acknowledgement. So she gave up. He wasn't entirely antisocial because sometimes she'd see him talking to other people, just not to her. Evidently, he didn't think her worth knowing, despite the fact they often shared the same walkways...and certainly shared the same town.

Back in her restaurant, Mitzi washed a few dishes and set them on the drain to dry. Oh, that Roz Silva thinks she really has one hot tip. It's amazing what people will believe, she chuckled to herself.

Steady, reliable, unassuming...all words that might have been used by some to describe Mitzi Jones. It was also known that on occasion she could become downright ornery, if sufficiently riled up, a regular bitch. But most of the time she projected the appearance of being a reasonable individual, a hard worker who had slowly and diligently developed a coffee bar and small bakery into a thriving business.

Fifty-two years old, married twice, and currently partial to women, Mitzi lived alone. She liked it that way. Years earlier, she realized that she really had neither the time nor inclination to work at relationships. It was enough to take care of her own needs, much less someone else's. She'd also learned that you didn't always need to tell the truth about everything. As long as you were generally honest, you could make up little lies and people would believe you.

People told small lies all the time, she reasoned. You lend a book to a friend and they lose it. Then they claim you never lent it to them; you must have confused them with someone else. Of course, you're never reimbursed for the book. Another friend forgets to RSVP to a party and then tells you they never received the invitation. Why shouldn't you believe them? A glass figurine is broken in a gift shop by a clumsy customer, who walks away and claims they didn't break it...that it was the shopkeeper's fault for placing it too close to the shelf's edge.

Then the lies get a little bigger. You back into a parked car and dent the fender. No one sees it happen, you *think*. But you pretend to place a note on the car's windshield, just in case someone is actually looking, and drive away. It never happened. As long as there are no witnesses, you get away with it. Another lie, only this time you've told a lie by your actions.

Late one fall your apartment is broken into, and when the police ask what's missing, you half jokingly tell them that you had just finished all your Christmas shopping and it's gone. They believe you. So when you file a claim on your renter's insurance, you list a lot of extra things. The company never bothers to check whether you'd really ever bought them or not. They assume you are telling the truth, because most people do.

People perceive the truth from what they observe and from what people tell them. What they're told is not always totally accurate, Mitzi reasoned, but if it sounds credible they will believe it. And her story about Rusty Ogel having a son sounded quite believable.

Nobody cared when he died. Roz just called him a bum. Rusty was really a harmless soul. He was someone who had been devalued because he had no home, no regular job. He kept himself busy collecting cans and bottles for recycling. Most of the year, he wore no shoes, until the temperature went down into the thirties. Then he'd don an old pair of army combat boots someone had given him. He kept his stash of possessions under an old, abandoned boat near the wharf.

Mitzi had operated her first coffee bar at Cranberry Square. It was cheap rent because Sonny had been desperate for tenants. It was she who had shown Rusty a way to sneak into the building so he'd have shelter during rain and snow. Perhaps, indirectly, she'd been responsible for his death. When the police asked her about the fire, she had told them she knew nothing. And she hadn't known anything about how the fire began. She merely had her suspicions.

Sonny got plenty of money for his loss, but not Mitzi. She had lost her fixtures, her lease, and then had to scramble for a new place to locate her business. She considered the fire to be suspicious, but couldn't prove anything. With Sonny's murder, perhaps the case should be reopened. She reasoned it wouldn't hurt...at least for Rusty to be remembered.

Mitzi's thoughts again returned to Roz Silva...she thinks she's going to solve that murder in a flash and sell a lot of newspapers. The arrogant bitch! It's a lot more complicated, thought Mitzi. Let that Roz spin her wheels a little bit on a wild-goose chase. Mitzi had never forgotten Roz's friend, Janet Olivera, being on the Board of Appeals and trying to bar her from serving people outdoors. Special permits and all that crap... the newspaper coverage.

Her business had now been at its present location for five and a half years. She'd bought the fixtures from the previous tenant, Nate Cowan, who had attempted to operate a New York-style deli there. His prices were too high and it scared customers away.

"You just can't get good deli meats on Cape Cod," Nate had told her. "I've got to drive over to Boston. Rye bread and decent bagels are scarce. So many people are vegetarians. No one these days seems to appreciate a hot pastrami sandwich or some nice, lean corned beef."

"Too bad Cranberry Square burnt down, but this is one of the few places for rent right now where you can serve food on a small scale," Polly Smithfield had told her. "Yes, there's a number of storefronts, for T-shirt shops and the like, and there are some large restaurant locations, but that's not what you're looking for. This is it, dear. This is it. You're not going to find anything better, so I'd grab it if I were you... or someone else will."

So Mitzi had signed a five-year lease, and recently renewed it, but she felt like all her money was going towards the rent. Very little was left for herself.

I work very hard, six days a week, she would think to herself, and that bastard who owns the building, Walter Campbell, collects his big, fat rent check. He probably doesn't even know what hard work is, living off all that rent money. He owns several buildings and spends half the year in Florida. It's just not fair.

Over the years, Mitzi had developed a growing resentment towards those in town who owned considerable property. Recently, with the drop in interest rates, she had scraped together enough money to buy a one-bedroom condo, but she remembered all those years of renting apartments and paying ridiculously high prices...apartments with worn-out carpeting and dingy curtains that real estate agents told her she should be happy to find.

The up-front money was always painful. First and last month's rent, plus a security deposit, before you'd even gotten your previous security deposit back, *if* you got it back at all. Try to get something repaired and they gave you all kinds of excuses. If you paid for it out of your own pocket, who knew whether the landlord would see fit to reimburse you. You could withhold the amount from your rent payment, but then they wouldn't want to renew your lease. And you also might get a bad reputation as a tenant with the real estate agents. Since there were more prospective tenants than apartments, a year-round apartment was very hard to find. Better to grin and bear it, Mitzi had always figured. But inside she longed to get even.

In Mitzi's mind, Roz was a landowner, one of the "haves" in a town with plenty of "have-nots." So Mitzi felt perfectly justified in having made up the entire story about this supposed son of Rusty Ogel named Casey Long. It was one of her small lies.

The tea had quickly gotten cold as the cup in Roz's hand grew lighter and lighter. It was time to start walking. Should she turn right or left? To the left, the town would become more and more residential. She'd start seeing a combination of winter tenants in luxury condos and summer houses that had been boarded up for the winter. Fran lived in one of those luxury condo units, up on the second or third floor, with her girlfriend, Shauna. Perhaps if Roz walked in an easterly direction, she would see the two of them sipping afternoon cocktails out on their deck.

If she walked in the other direction, towards downtown, there was more clutter and congestion, even on the beach. Decks jutted out further, where restaurants provided outside service and apartments were clustered together, trying to take advantage of every available bit of space. No longer could you build so close to the water. But preexisting buildings remained, their porches and decks now frequently enclosed, making these buildings even larger.

Did waterfront property owners own their beach to the high-tide mark or the low-tide mark? Roz could never remember. She knew it was different for the far East End than the more commercial area of town. The state of Massachusetts also had their beachfront jurisdiction. There were plenty of rules and regulations to protect the fragile coastline environment, but to Roz it seemed like too little too late.

If she walked towards the center of town, there was also the remote possibility she'd run into John. Sometimes after work he walked across towards Lopes Square and down onto the beach. She'd met him there once when their relationship had just begun.

Wasn't it always so uncanny when you accidentally ran into people just when they were on your mind? The town was small, but there were some people she seldom saw because their routines and the places they worked and walked were such that their paths rarely crossed. Others kept popping up in front of her, like the writer walking his dogs, Frank Chambers at the A&P, and regulars at the post office.

John...wouldn't it be nice to see him. He was back in her mind again. She could try calling him at his office on her cell phone, which was safely tucked inside the canvas bag swung over her shoulder, but that would be cheating. She turned to the right and started walking west.

The day was getting late. Cassie knew it was time to head home or her mother would be worried, but the bike trails that threaded through the Beech Forest were so beautiful she hated to leave. It was like being in the woods of a fairy tale, just the quiet sounds of leaves rustling in the wind and birds cawing to each other. Perhaps she and her younger sister would be lucky and see a fox. Cassie had once spotted a fox walking down a trail towards the outer shore when she'd been there with her father.

"Quiet," he whispered. "You must be very quiet when you walk in the woods so you don't scare any animals away. Pretend you're an Indian wearing soft, leather moccasins that barely make a sound." Sometimes they'd seen garter and ribbon snakes. Other times, they would select toadstools and mushrooms for spore prints. During the summer months, they'd gather small toads and bring them back to the house to watch them hopping around in the garden. Her father always had his camera hanging from a strap around his neck, eager to take pictures. Perhaps his ghost was in the forest now, taking photographs of the nature scenes he'd loved so much. It wasn't fair that someone could just take a gun, shoot him, and end his life. It happened all the time on television and in movies, but those weren't real people. This was real. Her dad was dead.

"You know what really stinks?" Stephanie was saying while struggling on her bicycle to catch up with Cassie. "We barely got to spend any time with him lately. Why'd they have to start talking about getting a divorce?"

"Who said that?" Cassie asked.

"Why else do you separate unless you're planning to file divorce papers? That's what Emily Milburn told me."

"Emily Milburn doesn't know what she's talking about."

"Her parents got divorced two years ago and her mom is getting remarried. She knows all about that stuff. Do you think Mom will get married again?" Stephanie asked her older sister.

"I don't know," Cassie replied. "She says she likes being by herself, but I don't think that's really true. I see her crying a lot, even at the most silly things...."

"You mean like the time we were watching *The Wizard of Oz* and Dorothy was saying, "There's no place like home. There's no place like home?""

"Yeah," Cassie said while getting off her bike and laying it down. Stephanie then did the same. "I think Mom left because she couldn't stand living in Provincetown anymore. She was trying to convince Dad to move. Don't you like the schools better in Virginia? And there's so much more to do there...."

"Who do you think murdered Dad?" Stephanie asked.

"Maybe it was Aunt Jo, so she could get all of Grandmother's money...or maybe Beau did it, so he could run their building business all by himself," Cassie said in a spooky-sounding voice.

"I like Uncle Beau," Stephanie said indignantly. "He always used to give us the best presents at Christmas: packages of pastels, big drawing pads, modeling clay, and giant chocolate bars."

"Maybe he was just trying to bribe us. But don't you remember...? He didn't give us any presents *last* Christmas."

"That's because Dad and he were barely speaking to each other, and he probably spends all his money now on his wife, Annie."

"Jealous? Were you were hoping to be the future Mrs. Costa?" Cassie asked while playfully pinching her sister's cheek.

"Oh, he's way too old for me. Maybe if he had a younger brother...."

"Even a younger brother would probably be too old. Perhaps he and Annie will have a son, and then you can marry him!"

"Remember when we used to gather toads?"

"I was just thinking about that. It's too early in the season. They probably are still pollywogs, if they're even that."

"There's a small pond up ahead. Let's go see if we can find anything living inside."

"We didn't bring a jar to put anything in," Cassie told her. "But we can scout around a bit now, and then maybe come back tomorrow."

"If they'll let us out tomorrow. We've got that thing at the funeral home in the afternoon and we have to get all dressed up for it. Aunt Jo was even talking about getting everyone's hair done."

"She *would*. She's always worrying about her appearance, primping in front of the mirror. The only way she could look better is to get herself a facelift."

Stephanie grabbed a large stick she found at the edge of the trail. "This is my magic wand," she chanted, "my divining rod." She ran forward and started swishing it around in the water. The color was a deep green and the surface was dotted with dead leaves and lily pads.

Cassie looked around for a stick of her own, and found a tall one leaned up against a broad tree. She stepped to the edge of the pond until her toes almost touched the water. If she stood there long enough, the water would probably seep inside and get her shoes all wet, she thought to herself. But she decided to live life dangerously.

Moving her stick through the water in broad strokes, Cassie tried to see if any life moved underneath the surface...a fish, a turtle, some tadpoles. There were plenty of buzzing insects. And then her stick hit something hard. The pond was shallow, only about two feet deep because it hadn't rained much that winter. She positioned the stick to try and pull the object to the pond's edge.

"Stephanie, I think I've found something that someone must have thrown into the pond. Bring your stick over here," she called to her sister. "Maybe together we can slide it out."

"What do you think it is?" asked Stephanie.

"I don't know, but it's something kind of heavy," said Cassie, whose stick had found a hole inside the object to help drag it along.

Between Cassie's dragging the object and Stephanie's stick pushing from behind, a minute later they had managed to get the object over to the water's edge. It was a gun.

"Don't touch it," Stephanie called out. "It might go off."

"I think you have to pull the trigger first," Cassie said sarcastically. "Besides, being in the water like that, I don't think it would fire at all. But I agree...we shouldn't touch it with our hands. Fingerprints."

"Do you think it's the murder weapon?" Stephanie asked excitedly. "This is awesome!"

"Well, why would anyone throw a gun in a pond unless it was used in some kind of crime?"

"Why didn't they just throw it in the ocean or bay?"

"Maybe they were worried the tide would go out and then someone would find it, or maybe the tide was already out when they wanted to get rid of the gun, and this pond was just closer."

"Hey, we shouldn't be walking around here. They could come and search for footprints...."

"I think we better turn it over to the police."

"What should we pick it up with?"

"I guess I'll use my jacket." Cassie quickly took off her jacket and tried to not think about being cold. She carefully picked up the revolver, with the barrel facing away from herself and her sister, and carried it back to their bikes. After placing it in the front basket, they both started walking their bikes back down the trail towards the highway and the route back to Aunt Jo's home.

"Maybe we should go directly to the police station," Stephanie suggested.

"No, we can call them from the house. Otherwise, Mom is going to get so worried," Cassie told her sister solemnly while thinking about the uncanny likelihood that they had found the actual murder weapon, which might help link the murderer to her father's death. What was the probability that the murder weapon was ever going to be found? And especially by the victim's own children! They'd be famous...but that still wouldn't bring their father back. The murderer would pay, and she hoped it would be with his or her life. Did Massachusetts have capital punishment? She'd have to check on it.

It had already been a long day for Trooper Marc O'Brien, and this would be his third interview in one long afternoon. Perhaps this one would be the most promising. It was definitely the most profitable. He was clocking into overtime. Bill Landon had insisted, in no uncertain terms, that the interview occur after four o'clock because he had important clients to see, as if his time was more important than anyone else's.

"I've got to cover the office," he had said. "My customer service gal is out sick, and with Sonny gone it seems like everyone and their uncle wants to check on their policies to make sure they still have them. And this time of year, there's a lot of new business to write policies for, with new stores just about to open."

Business, business," O'Brien thought while entering through the heavy, green-painted door of the Carreiro Insurance and Real Estate offices.

"I just don't understand it," an elderly lady was saying. "Why do I have insurance if you're telling me the insurance doesn't cover it?"

"I didn't say the insurance didn't cover it," the man, evidently Bill Landon, dressed in a dark gray suit with a navy and red striped tie, replied to the woman, who was shaking an accusatory finger at him. "I said it will count against you and your rates will go up if you file this claim. You've already had two claims this year. They may just decide to cancel you altogether," he said, raising his voice ever so slightly.

"What difference does it make how many claims I have. I paid for the insurance. I can make as many claims as I want."

Appearing to be in her seventies, with steel-gray hair pulled back into a stylish bun, tortoise shell designer glasses, and a coordinated ensemble of wide slacks, sweater, and tunic, Mr. Landon's client was not about to be convinced she couldn't file just one more claim on her insurance.

"The windstorm last week knocked those shingles off my roof, and they have to be replaced or my roof will leak."

"Why are you the only person coming in here and claiming damage from that windstorm. Perhaps, due to normal wear and tear, you need a new roof."

"Put in the claim, Mr. Landon, or I'll be reporting you to the insurance commissioner, which I have a good mind to do anyway. It took me two months to get the check for my stolen pearls."

Bill Landon turned his attention to O'Brien. "Marc O'Brien, I presume. So sorry to keep you waiting. Mrs. Albertson, we'll have to continue this another time."

"There is nothing to continue. Put in the claim, and meanwhile I'm going to find myself another insurance agent," Mrs. Albertson said while shaking her head. She picked up her large purse, which was sitting on the front reception desk, and started searching for her keys. O'Brien held the door open for her and inquired, "Ma'am, do you need any help getting to your car?"

"I may be old," she retorted, "but I'm not feeble. Thank you for the thought, though." The door slammed behind her.

"That woman is a piece of work," Bill grumbled. "Bangs up her car every other year and always claims it's some other person's fault. Lucky, in this state we have no-fault auto insurance. Then she puts in all kinds of small claims for vandalism, robbery, storm damage. Let's see...there was also the water damage from a broken hose to her washing machine. She decided to start some laundry right before going Up Cape to Hyannis to do some shopping. Gone for over five hours, and her kitchen and dining room were filled with water. I put that claim in for her...over fifteen hundred dollars in damage to replace the linoleum and carpeting. She also put in a vandalism claim about some windows getting broken in her garage. It didn't meet the deductible, thank goodness, but she was furious about that.... Mind if I take a seat? Or perhaps we should step into my office."

"Wherever you prefer. I'm fine right here," said O'Brien, pulling up a chair from the waiting area of the room, which had been positioned in front of a coffee table that held several magazines, and facing it towards the reception desk.

Bill sat down in the large swivel chair behind the desk and continued his tirade. "Her policy only costs six hundred dollars a year, but so far the company has already paid out eight thousand. They're not going to put up with this much longer, and what she doesn't realize is that no other company is going to take her with that kind of record. I try to explain to people that they should save claims for the really major losses. Don't nickel-and-dime your insurance to death...you'll only lose in the end. They think it's a game, and since the company must be making lots of money, being a big corporation and all, they're going to cash in.

"And then there's all the time I spend processing these claims," continued Landon. "Technically, I don't do the paperwork, but I oversee everything. If my customers don't like the claims adjusters or they don't get paid fast enough, it's me they call. And it's not as though this kind of business pays a lot of money...ten to fifteen percent on most homeowner and auto policies, depending on the company. Not a lot to cover all the overhead and labor costs."

"Right. But you do make a lot on life insurance sales, don't you?" reasoned O'Brien, waiting for Bill Landon's reaction.

"Someone in your family sell life insurance?" Bill asked, readjusting his wire-framed glasses on his nose.

"Yes, I have an uncle who sold life insurance for a while. He sold a policy to just about everyone in the family. Tried to get me interested in insurance sales while I was attending college. Told me all about the fifty-percent commissions you guys make the first year a policy is sold."

"That big commission is only for whole life. Term insurance and life products linked to variable annuities pay twenty and thirty-five percent. Most people buy term. It's true...if I sold you a whole life policy with a thousand-dollar premium, I'd receive a five-hundred-dollar commission, which is good money. However, there's a lot of time and legwork involved in selling any kind of life insurance policy: medical exams, lab reports, investment analysis for the prospective policyholder. A lot of the time, a policy that we think has been sold doesn't get booked. Plus, people will sometimes take out a policy, keep it for six months or a year, and then let it lapse. Well, then we don't get paid that fat commission you were talking about. In fact, we get charge-backs. The company takes back the commission they paid us in the first place."

"So, who got the commissions from the life insurance written on Sonny?"

"He did, if he wrote it."

"Isn't that unethical?"

"Are you kidding? Agents write policies on themselves and their families all the time in order to make sales quotas. You ought to know that from your uncle. I suppose on the one he wrote between himself and Beau, it was a little unfair. They split the cost of the policy, and then Sonny got twenty percent of it back off the top as a commission. But hey, Beau is the one collecting."

"You don't seem upset at all about Sonny's death."

"Of course, I'm upset. A member of my family. My wife's brother. But I'm a man who served in the military. I don't wear my emotions on my sleeve."

"In the Navy, right?"

"How'd you know?"

"Sarah told me."

O'Brien was beginning to find Mr. Landon annoying. He was the first annoying suspect he'd interviewed all day. He wondered to himself whether Mr. Landon was aware that he was a suspect. But, then again, he supposed *he* could be just as annoying by putting Mr. Landon in the "hot seat" a little. Besides, it was a long drive back to Harwich, and though he was the officer in charge of murder investigations, he was starting to fade.

"So tell me, Mr. Landon…or may I call you Bill?"

"By all means, do."

"Where were you on Sunday night at the time of the murder?"

"Home or at the office. It depends on what time you're talking about. When did the murder occur?"

"At approximately eight thirty."

"I might have been here. You see, I just got back into town on Sunday evening. I was at an insurance seminar in Reading, Pennsylvania, over the weekend. It began on Thursday night. And I was here checking up on messages and paperwork from when I was away."

"Anyone here in the office with you?"

"No. It's not easy to get good help nowadays. Someone who comes in and works at night? I don't think so."

"Did you make any phone calls that could establish your time and place?"

"I had the computer on part of the time, transmitting data to one of the companies I work with. Does that count?"

"You could have turned on the computer and left, couldn't you?" asked O'Brien.

"Are you accusing me of committing the murder?" Bill retorted.

"Until I solve this case, everyone who knew Sonny Carreiro is a suspect."

"That's just about everyone in town."

"Lucky for me, it's a small town," O'Brien said, smiling conspiratorially. "So tell me about Sarah. Was she seeing anyone?"

"I don't think so, but I try to stay out of other people's personal business, even my family's. She may have been dating someone down in Virginia. Who knows?"

The telephone rang and Bill picked it up. "Carreiro Insurance and Real Estate," he answered in a deep, personable voice.

O'Brien noticed that Mr. Landon's face appeared to slightly redden as he listened to what was evidently a tirade on the other end of the line.

"Now, Mr. Evans," he said, adding a smoother tone to his voice, "there's no reason to get ugly. A lawyer is just not going to expedite the situation. The company is processing the claim as quickly as possible."

"You did what?" Bill asked in a raised tone of voice and then intentionally lowering it with his next sentence. "That really wasn't necessary. This kind of thing happens all the time. Some of these companies lose paperwork once in a while. Just let me handle it. Don't worry. You'll get your money. You have my guarantee. I'll give you a call at the beginning of next week." Bill took a handkerchief out of his pocket and wiped off the top of his brow after hanging up the phone.

"Some customers," he said to O'Brien, shaking his head, "just get so impatient. They file a claim and expect to have their check the next morning. I suppose you have the same problems in your line of work... people expect you to instantly solve a case. But usually it takes days, weeks, even months, doesn't it? Nothing is taken care of instantly."

"You can say that again," O'Brien agreed while looking down at his pad of notes. "Was there some big sale or deal Sonny was working on?"

"Big sale?" Bill repeated quizzically.

"Yeah, some big something he was soon going to tell Sarah. I figured sharing the same office, working together and all, you might know something."

"Nothing comes to mind."

"Well, if you do think of something, be sure and let me know. What time does your secretary come in?"

"Secretary?"

"Receptionist, assistant, whatever you want to call her."

"Oh! Susan. I call her our customer service rep. As soon as she passes the exam for licensing, she'll earn the title of Associate Agent. I've given her a few days off."

"Well, I'd like to ask her a few questions. Perhaps you can give me her home number."

"Be happy to." Bill fished around in the top drawer of the large, dark, cherry, front-office desk and pulled out a business card that had "Susan Stafford, Customer Service Representative, Carreiro Insurance Agency" embossed on the front. He wrote a phone number on the face of the card with a ballpoint pen.

"Been with you long?" O'Brien inquired.

"About six months. She started after Labor Day. Had one of those high-pressure jobs selling time-share condominiums. Didn't want to leave town so I gave her a job. Sonny approved. Has good potential."

"So tell me about Sonny. Was he involved with drugs? Another woman, perhaps? Was he working regular hours? Anything you can think of?"

"Sonny was a morning person. Came in early, seven o'clock, and was out by noon. Midday he was off to the bank, visiting clients, and doing errands. Occasionally, he came back to the office later in the day, but he liked to play, take walks on the dunes, take pictures...not the ones for our homeowner policies but as a hobby. That's one of his photos over there," Bill said, pointing to a stark, black-and-white photo of shadows and beach grass on a sand dune that was hanging on the front, left-hand wall. "Did his own developing...had a lab in what should have been the laundry room of his house. He was a nice guy."

"So, no hanky-panky?"

"Didn't I say I don't nose around in other people's private lives? For one thing, the 'private lives' in this town are too weird. I keep to myself."

"Well, thank you for your time. You've been very helpful," said O'Brien, slowly rising from his chair. "I may be calling on you again. At any rate, maybe I'll see you at the funeral home tomorrow afternoon. What time did you say the visitation begins?"

"I didn't say. But we will be receiving friends and family from three to five and again from seven to nine at Sterling's. You're welcome to come by."

"I thought it would be a good opportunity for me...see who shows up, reactions and all. Of course, I won't be in uniform."

"I would expect not, although sometimes I'm tempted to wear my old one for formal occasions. But, no, I only wear it in parades."

"Veteran?"

"Yes," said Bill while showing O'Brien to the door. "As an officer, I served in Vietnam. Did my time."

"Thanks again," said O'Brien as he stepped outside, noticing the air had turned brisk. He could clearly see his breath as a white mist, evidence the temperature had gone down to below forty degrees.

A hot dinner was going to taste mighty good when he got home in less than an hour. At this time of year, the roads were fairly empty and he could make good time on the four-lane and two-lane highways of Route 6 over to Route 28. What did Jill say she was cooking? Roast chicken? That's what he seemed to remember her saying.

No choir rehearsal or building development meeting tonight, thank goodness. Jill, O'Brien's wife of two years, was a court reporter and also very involved with their church, United Methodist. On the evenings she had activities to attend, dinner was hastily thrown together. But the other nights, she cooked a good meal, did the laundry, kept the house pretty much together. Soon, he hoped, she'd get pregnant. Maybe that was something they could work on this evening.... Perhaps he should stop at the liquor store and buy her a bottle of wine or some flowers to get her in the mood, something romantic. Women...they were so funny. All his friends had warned him...once you get married, the sex stops. True, she wasn't as eager now as when they were dating. The best times had been during their engagement and on their honeymoon. Now, she often talked about being too tired, about how he should wait until the weekend. He really had to coax her. Perhaps if he offered to do the dishes....

O'Brien pulled his car onto the road as a call came in over the radio. It was from the Provincetown Police Department. "You're probably on your way home by now, but if you haven't left town yet, you need to come by here. I think we've got the murder weapon," said the voice on the other end of the line.

13

Tuesday Evening

BRUNO PULLED HIS CASSEROLE out of the oven. It looked delicious, but would the others think it tasted as delicious as it looked? Everyone always brought pasta dishes to potlucks because the costs of the ingredients were minimal. Once you set your dish on the table, the maker was anonymous. Bruno was thinking that people should put their name on their dish, in big block letters, at potlucks. Then maybe folks would take a little more pride in what they brought. Of course, being that this was a potluck dinner/meeting of the Italian-American Club, there was bound to be lots of pasta, because that's what Italians like to eat, along with some good salads, veal, chicken, fish, steak, and crusty bread. Bruno laughed softly to himself, patting his broad stomach.

Bruno, himself, was bringing pasta, but he considered manicotti to be in a class by itself. Although he hadn't prepared the pasta from scratch, he had put together the filling of ricotta cheese, egg, parsley, garlic, and fresh basil and had carefully stuffed it inside the large, still-warm manicotti tubes. And he'd also made the sauce, using browned ground veal, beef, onions, and mushrooms, mixed with two large cans of generic tomato sauce, herbs, and wine. No, he was not the cook Frank Chambers was. Frank would have made his sauce using fresh Roma tomatoes or maybe sun-dried ones.

But Frank was not a member of the Italian-American Club. Your heritage had to be at least twenty-five percent Italian, not that anyone was really going to check. It was just a good excuse to have a social club, a group of people who could meet, talk, eat, and reminisce about all things Italian. They talked a lot about the Catholic church, about their grandmothers, forgotten expressions, and traditions. Once a month they met, sometimes at a restaurant and other times at someone's home. Anywhere from six to a dozen people might show up.

Bruno wondered whether he should talk about the magazine. There might be someone there who had an interest in advertising. Perhaps Fred Boccacio, the plumber...not that plumbers around here needed to drum up any business. And there's Mary Antionini, who does acupuncture. But the big ads, the bigger-paying ads, needed to be the restaurants, real estate agents, banks, guesthouses.... Bruno stopped himself at the thought of other guesthouses advertising in the *Province Town Crier*.

Frank had called him earlier in the day to tell him about the name idea. "What do you think of it? Isn't it a cool idea, double entendre and all?"

Frank had sounded like a little kid, and Bruno imagined him jumping up and down with glee while holding the telephone to his ear. Well, the creation of a magazine did feel something like the joy you would feel after being given a new toy.

Bruno thought back to his own childhood, the way he had always pleaded to stay in the toy department while his mother went to other departments in the store to shop. That was in the old days, before people were so concerned about children being grabbed and kidnapped. He would admire all the shiny toys in their brightly colored, cardboard and cellophane packages, trying to decide what he would ask Santa to bring him for Christmas. And just like he did with his imaginary games of playing the stock market, he would fantasize about what he would buy if he suddenly won lots of money.

However, the joy of pretending was often more exciting than the actual toy itself. The G.I. Joe figures never seemed as valiant and strong marching across the carpet in his bedroom as they did in action, being advertised on TV between Saturday morning cartoon shows. The magical sword that glowed, and made crashing sounds when you moved it to slay imaginary dragons, was never as thrilling as what he would visualize while watching a young boy in a television ad use the sword to fight off the evil Black Knight.

Should he blame it all on television, or was it the thought of always looking forward to something that was so intriguing? Don't wish for anything too hard, he had told himself as a child, because then you'll only be disappointed. His older brothers, Paul and Vince, told him to pray if he wanted something special. "Prayer is powerful," his mother would say. But, oh, how he had prayed and prayed for a new bicycle and he still didn't get one, just the hand-me-down that Paul had outgrown.

It's better not to pray, not to wish too hard, because then you feel badly if you don't get what you want, Bruno had reasoned. It is better to expect less and be pleasantly surprised if you get more.

So what was he expecting from the *Province Town Crier*? He had to be realistic, Bruno told himself, because this magazine may only be the size of two standard-size pieces of paper put together, six interior pages. It may go bust after only one or two issues. Maybe it should only come out every other week or once a month. Better to have quality than quantity, he reasoned.

Other guesthouses advertising? Well, competition was always a good thing. If Provincetown had a reputation for being a place with quality guesthouses, more tourists would come. Yes, Bruno wanted his Willows Guest House to be the first one sporting a "No Vacancy" sign, but quantity and variety were important criteria for attracting the tourist trade. The Provincetown Business Guild, Chamber of Commerce…they knew that. Naturally, he'd demand the best placement for his ad. Being in on the ground floor of the magazine's inception, it was only fair.

And his article? Well, it should definitely be the cover story with a big picture of Willows Guest House on the front of the magazine. Why not? But Frank would probably want something more to do with cooking, a picture of a restaurant, *his* restaurant. Bruno would just have to wait and see.

He pulled out a box of tin foil from the top drawer to the right of the kitchen sink and tore out enough to cover the manicotti dish and keep it warm. He neatly folded the edges down to seal the heat inside. Satisfied that his cooking work was done, he headed to the dining room to reread his article one more time.

Initially, he had written the text in longhand. Using a blue ballpoint pen and a notebook of lined paper, he had written down everything that came to mind pertaining to running a guesthouse: the creativity of decorating unique, comfortable rooms; meeting people from all over the country, sometimes from all over the world; feeling satisfaction in helping to create a memorable experience and vacation; along with the grueling work of cleaning up other people's messes, listening to petty complaints, and juggling the horrors of last-minute cancellations and bounced checks.

Bruno didn't dare write about the disgust at having to scrub down a bathroom at three o'clock in the morning because one of the guests had thrown up from drinking too much. He didn't write about finding used condoms under the beds while he cleaned, pecker tracks on the sheets, cum spots on the carpeting. Thank goodness he had someone else doing the cleaning most of the time, professional houseboys or chambermaids. Bruno only had to pinch-hit when the regulars didn't show up or something unforeseen happened in the middle of the night. That was the problem with shared bathrooms...you had to be more meticulous because it wasn't fair to the other guests. Fresh flowers and scented soap, he used those to try and distract from the unpleasant smells. Did he put the part about fresh flowers and scented soap in his article?

He picked up the six printed pages of paper, clipped together, and scanned for his description of the accommodations. After jotting down his thoughts, done an outline, and written the article in longhand, he had typed it into his computer, printed it out, and edited it again. "Editing is very important," he had always told his English students. "Scrutinize every sentence you write. Is it accurate? Does it have a purpose? Does it make sense?"

During his years of teaching, Bruno had found that the tendency of most kids was to write flowery prose in run-on sentences. They wanted to use a lot of big words and sound important. But when he made them read their papers out loud, they made little sense. "Write like you talk. Write like you think. Don't try to sound like somebody else. Be yourself," he would instruct.

He tried to follow his own advice. He wanted to be honest...but he couldn't be too honest in a lighthearted magazine piece. Readers don't want to know about your hopes and fears; they want to know how you run your guesthouse.

And what were Bruno's fears? That one year business would be so bad that he wouldn't be able to make his mortgage payments. That one day his septic system would fail and he'd have to forfeit both his building and business because he didn't have the money to fix it. That he'd go for his yearly checkup and his blood work would reveal he'd contracted HIV. Those were worries Bruno Marchessi had put into the back of his mind.

His dreams? A booming business. Reliable, honest employees. A steady lover...did he *really* want a steady lover? It could be nice. Such comforts seemed to make other people happy. But maybe it was better to remain independent. This was a moot question, though, at least until the "right" somebody came along.

Sonny Carreiro...he seemed to have it all: a successful business, wife, children. And look what had happened to him. Should he ask the Holy Order of Saint Luke to say a novena for him? Perhaps nine days of prayer would get him out of purgatory. At the very least, he should buy a perpetual mass card for the poor guy. Sonny's family was Catholic...not Sarah, but the rest. It was easier than buying flowers, and they would probably appreciate it.

It had been a while since Bruno had stepped foot inside a church. He had attended church at least once a week when growing up, plus every day during Lent one year when his mother was praying for her father's recovery from cancer. Sometimes it was early-morning mass; sometimes it was in the evening. Saturday nights, early, for a while he would attend. It beat getting up in the morning on Sundays.

The music, the sense of grandeur, the beautiful stained-glass windows, robes, vestments, chalice...it was all very comforting. All very comforting *until* you heard that all-to-familiar: "Forgive me, Father, for I have sinned."

Bruno knew his sins would never be forgiven unless he chose, in his old age or on his deathbed, to renounce his "lifestyle." They might be forgiven if he served enough penances, did enough good acts of Christian kindness...it all depended on whether he thought of God, the Son, and the Holy Ghost as being forgiving, as opposed to being a powerful tyrant who had set up a host of rules by which to live.

Priests, bishops, the Pope…they'd have you believe that the rules were the most important thing to follow. Bruno didn't think it was the rules; rather, it was the intent. It was the hope, the aspiration to be a good and kind person. How could God possibly condemn someone who had led a life, basically good, to an eternity in hell? How could he be so unforgiving as to damn the unbaptized, the nonbeliever, the Moslems, the Hindus, the Jews, the Protestants?

Part of Bruno wanted to believe that Catholicism was the *only* way; that he was part of the "private club," and that at the end of his life a priest would come to him and he would confess: "Forgive me, Father, for I have sinned." After a time assigned to purgatory, he would sail up to heaven and join his relatives, his parents. Another part of him believed only in the present and refused to think about an afterlife. The day after tomorrow, Bruno would be attending Sonny's funeral mass, and he *would* take communion. No questions would be asked.

Jo Landon smoothed back her hair, patted her hands on her knees, and smiled. It had been a productive afternoon. Emma had not been bad company, plus she had been able to take the wheel, so to speak, and drive the Lincoln Continental home from their shopping trip, allowing Jo to partake in a few drinks with their mid-afternoon lunch.

"Oh, you need it…" Emma had assured her, "…losing your brother and all. Don't worry about the drive home. I know the way. It's just a straight shot back up Route 6!"

Those Chinese restaurants did know how to make the best drinks, sweet and tangy, with a cherry and a nice slice of orange skewered on one of those plastic toothpicks with the ridiculous little paper umbrella attached to the top.

"I used to save those for the girls," Emma had told her. "They used to put them in their little dollhouses and such. Actually, it was Sarah who liked them. Cassie and Stephanie…well, you know kids nowadays. They grow up so fast. They stop playing with dolls by the time they're nine or ten years old and start worrying about boys and being a teenager. I've caught Cassie wearing makeup already, more than once, and I've talked to Sarah about it. Told her it's not right and she shouldn't let her daughter look that way. But do you think it does any good? I'm only their grandmother...."

Jo had nodded her head in assent, but in reality she was only half listening to Emma. She was too busy thinking how grand her house was going to look on Thursday with the linen tablecloths, opulent spread of food, large quantity of flower arrangements, and well-dressed guests. The Navy Grog she was discreetly sipping, while pretending to be attentively listening, was quickly taking effect. Jo had been so thirsty, downright parched when they first arrived, that it had been difficult not to appear as if she was guzzling down her drink. She'd take a handful of crunchy noodles and chew them up very fine, take a drink of ice water, and then take as many sips as she dared of her Navy Grog before putting it down.

By the time their luncheon platters had arrived, the restaurant, the waiters, the food, and the conversation all seemed pleasantly fuzzy around the edges. The egg roll was nice and crisp, and she had slathered it with duck sauce. But on taking her first bite, the inside was a disappointment...too many chewy vegetables. The fried rice and moo goo gai pan, with white chicken in a mild, creamy sauce and green, crispy bean pods, had been dependably good, though.

"You'd be surprised how many oriental restaurants we have in the Arlington area," Emma was telling her. "Thai, Japanese, Korean, Vietnamese. Not just your traditional Chinese/Polynesian type of fare like they have here. But then you've traveled a lot, haven't you? Surely you've tasted a lot of different oriental dishes. It's very healthy, all the fresh vegetables. But not the fried stuff," she asserted, setting her untouched egg roll aside and onto a small appetizer plate. "I guess Cape Cod just doesn't have the clientele for that kind of cooking."

"Oh, we have lots of exotic restaurants," Jo had responded, feeling that Emma was being a bit condescending. "But Bill says that most oriental restaurants are owned and operated by entire families, like many of those Greek and Italian places. They bring over relatives from back home as cheap labor but then they have to keep them busy all year round. It's a seasonal economy on the Cape, remember, so the concept doesn't usually work here."

"Yes, a seasonal economy," agreed Emma. "And that's the problem with this place. It doesn't seem as bad down here in Hyannis. Things look pretty normal. There's mall, plenty of active businesses. But those small towns at the end of the Cape become like ghost towns in the winter. If you're older and have the means to travel, I suppose it's fine. But to raise a family in such a skewed environment...."

"I beg your pardon!" Jo had countered back. "Sonny and I grew up in Provincetown, graduated from the high school, went on to college. There are plenty of things going on in the off-season, just not a lot of businesses open. Of course, it has become somewhat overgrown, what with the gays and all, but so has the rest of the world. The town has been our bread and butter. Provided my father and mother, and their parents, with a good living. A good living for my husband and me, as well. Don't think for even a minute that your daughter and grandchildren haven't reaped the benefits...."

Jo had stopped herself from saying anything more right there, realizing she had raised her voice and risked the possibility of making a scene. Next week, her houseguests would be gone, so there was no reason for her not to remain civil and hold her tongue. As she knew already, out-of-towners usually were such snobs, and Emma Green was no exception. Quickly changing the subject, Jo had suggested they order dessert...ice cream with pineapple and coconut syrup.

The paper goods had been easy to find at the specialty shop in Hyannis Mall that sold only party goods. She hadn't been able to purchase her first-choice pattern...not enough of the nine-and-a-half-inch dinner plates in stock. But her second choice was almost as nice, a cream-color background with a deep blue border and swirls of yellow. The colors and pattern matched her dining room wallpaper, Jo had thought, feeling pleased with herself, and would look very distinguished and elegant. She'd need to call Frank Chambers first thing in the morning to make certain he hadn't gone ahead and ordered the paper goods himself. If he had, he could send it all back but at least he'd bring extra cutlery from the restaurant when he arrived with the food.

When the two talked about Sarah during the drive, Jo had learned Sarah was making good money, was about to buy a new car, not dating...in fact, hadn't dated anyone during the separation.

"Just stays at home and reads most nights," Emma told her, "and watches videos. She does stuff with the girls, of course. Takes them roller blading, to the movies, fairs, cultural events. And then there are sports. The girls have been playing on a lot of different teams, soccer in the fall, basketball, and now lacrosse, so she does a lot of chauffeuring.

I try to help her when I can, but watching all those games, standing out in the cold and wind, is just not for me.

"The only way Sarah could possibly meet any men would be if one of the sports coaches or fathers, unmarried or divorced certainly, took an interest. Perhaps she could meet a fellow at work, but nowadays fraternizing among employees is considered a form of sexual harassment. Anyway, she really hasn't seemed interested in dating...still in love with her husband. It's a shame. If he were still alive, they might have been back together by summer," Emma had reasoned.

So any theorizing about Sonny being killed by a jealous boyfriend of Sarah's would go nowhere. And at least there would be no scandalous gossip about Sarah playing around.

The day's surprise had been the discovery of that gun, possibly the murder weapon, by Stephanie and Cassie. The girls had been so excited, thinking they might be helping to solve the case. It seemed to take their minds off their father's death alone and give them a sense of actually having a role in solving his murder.

The full impact of their loss probably hadn't hit them yet, Jo assured herself, believing the girls were most likely still in shock. Jo was thirty-two when her and Sonny's father had died, and still it seemed like a dream. For months afterwards, she had kept thinking that if she just went to the house and knocked on the door, he'd still be there to answer it. After spending Christmas without him was when it finally sank in that he was gone. When he wasn't at the head of the table to carve the turkey and harass her about why she hadn't borne him any grandchildren...that's when Jo knew her father had permanently left this earth to join the Lord.

"Sorry, Papa," Jo now told her father, whispering aloud to herself, "but it was not in God's plan for me to have children. You *do* have grandchildren, Cassie and Stephanie. Girls, it's true. But no one to carry on the family name. Surely, though, one of them will bear a son and the Carreiro line will live on...if not by name, then at least by blood." With that last whispered word, Jo snapped out of it.

Blood...figuratively, blood was fine when talking about family connections. But actual blood, Jo found it repulsive, just like she did all other fluids that had to do with bodily functions. What a relief it was when she had finally stopped menstruating, and luckily at the relatively early age of forty-four. She still took estrogen pills to look young but had convinced Bill that their days of marital, "required" sex were pretty much over.

Occasionally she'd let him climb on top of her, stick his thing inside, huff and puff until he made a grunting noise, seemed satisfied, and fell asleep. The ordeal had become slightly less of a chore after she'd read in a magazine about using lubricating cream. At least the process didn't hurt as much. But pleasure? Sex didn't bring her any pleasure. It was strictly a man's business.

Kissing, caressing, hugging...all had seemed pleasurable when Jo had been younger. But the intermixing of "private" body parts had mostly left her unmoved. She didn't want to touch herself on her breasts or down below, so why would she want her husband to touch her there? And the very thought of touching *him*...! Bill had tried in the beginning to induce her to play with his "Tommy Tucker." She could never say the real word, the "p" word. Too embarrassing. She had tried, in the interests of being a good wife, when they were first married. But she'd found the whole thing disgusting. The fact that she had been so modest was initially exciting to Bill. He had called her his "little virgin," his "chaste nun." Men! What went on inside their heads?

Kind words, holding hands, going places together...this is what love and romance were all about. It had nothing to do with sex.

Bill would be down soon, having gone upstairs to change into more comfortable clothes after getting home from the office. What was she going to serve him and the others for dinner? Jo wasn't particularly hungry herself.

She got up from the living room couch, where she'd been sitting to rest and think for a bit. Emma had gone directly upstairs "to use the facilities and freshen up," or so she said. Jo hoped Emma wasn't too upset or angry at what she might have perceived as Jo's intolerance of her criticisms about Cape Cod. She didn't want any unpleasantness while Emma, Sarah, and the girls were under her roof. They'd be leaving soon enough. And other than maybe an occasional visit, she'd then only have to worry about sending them cards and presents on holidays and a periodic phone call.

"And how was your day, my dear?" asked Bill while entering the living room in corduroys and a sweater, taking Jo somewhat by surprise as she'd been deep in her own thoughts. "Are you all set and organized for tomorrow?"

"Tomorrow?" Jo replied quizzically. "It's Thursday I'm worried about."

"But there's the visitation at Sterling's tomorrow afternoon and evening."

"Oh, that.... I just need to get my hair done. Sterling's will take care of the coffee, tea, and a few platters of cookies and such."

"Everything going okay in the household?" Bill inquired. "I know having a lot of houseguests can be stressful."

"Oh, they're all right. I can handle it," said Jo. "I was just going back to the kitchen to see what I can put on the table for dinner tonight."

"Sarah told me your friend, Peggy Noonan, dropped some food off, roast chicken and other things, for us to eat. So, I think you're all set. How about if I help you put the stuff out."

"Well, this is quite a change! I can't remember the last time you helped me set the table."

"Now, I didn't say I'd set the table. That's women's work. What I said was that I'd help you bring out the food."

"Well, excuse me...any kind of help would be nice. Did that state trooper stop by your office to ask you some questions? He was supposedly coming here this afternoon to talk to Sarah. What was his name...O'Malley?"

"O'Brien," Bill corrected her. "Marc O'Brien. A bit cocky, I would say, but maybe he hasn't had much experience on the job. Yes, he asked me a bunch of questions, and I think he wants to talk to Susan next. You should probably expect to see him tomorrow at Sterling's."

"Quite unexpected, the girls finding the murder weapon, don't you think?" Jo asked her husband, having mentioned the latest development in the investigation to him as soon as he'd arrived home and was heading up the stairs.

"A gun in the woods...doesn't necessarily mean it's the murder weapon," reasoned Bill as they walked to the kitchen and began taking the wrapped-up chicken, potato salad, fruit salad, and bread out of the large box of food that had been left sitting on the kitchen table. "Sarah should have put some of this stuff in the refrigerator," he complained. "The potato salad looks like it has mayonnaise in it. Do you think it's okay to eat?"

"Her mind is preoccupied. And it's not exactly hot outside...how long has this been here? Oh, probably just an hour or so," said Jo, answering her own question. "See if it smells all right."

Bill pulled the plastic wrap off the top of the bowl and positioned his nose an inch above the mixture of chopped potato, celery, egg, and mayonnaise. "Smells okay to me. Should I taste it?"

"You're just hungry," Jo said teasingly. "Why don't you see if you can get the others to come downstairs and sit around the table."

"First," said Bill, "why don't I pour myself a drink."

Elliot walked into Napi's Restaurant, having decided tonight he would treat himself and eat out, rather than scrounging around in his kitchen for something to eat. Not that he was going to find much of anything in his cupboards or refrigerator, and it was too late to swing by the A&P. Perhaps he should sit at the bar...maybe there would be someone interesting to pick up.

Perhaps Leslie Martin had gotten back early from Key West, where she was managing a clothing store over the winter. The season was probably about over down there, wasn't it? A lot of students go to Florida for their various spring breaks, but after that she'd be heading north. And she'd only sublet her apartment.

Eventually she would return, and then he'd try to be a little more aggressive than before and actually ask her out. Not that Elliot was ever shy, but he didn't like to be turned down so he usually waited until he felt a woman had sent him a sign that she liked him before he made any move. Leslie had sent mixed messages. Then she'd started spending time with Rick Westin, a young lawyer in town, so Elliot decided to wait. Leslie and Rick had broken up in September, but then Leslie left for Key West.

Located at the corner of Winslow and Bradford Streets, Napi's was known for its warm, inviting environment with plenty of colorful stained-glass windows, plants, and wooden surfaces. Offering a mix of native specialties and vegetarian dishes, works by local artists were often featured on the walls and in the upstairs gallery while various musicians performed at the bar.

Elliot positioned himself in the bar area and looked around. Leslie had gray eyes and long blonde hair...she might even be a natural blonde...if there was such a thing, he'd always thought. But tonight, no blondes that he could see. Just brownettes, brunettes, and redheads. One head of hair looked familiar, though; in fact, it *was* familiar, someone he saw at the office almost every day. It was Sky, sitting with two girlfriends. He walked over to say hello.

"Out for a night on the town, I see," he said as a way of making an introduction.

"Bud went Up Cape on some errands and I don't expect him back until later this evening," said Sky. "So I thought, hey, why stay home when maybe I can go out with some friends. Elliot, this is Margie Adams and Antonia Henrique, in case you haven't met before."

"I believe I've met Antonia, being that Manuel was a co-chairman of the Blessing of the Fleet Committee last year. Margie...I don't think we've met, have we?"

"My husband, Matt, co-manages the gas station in the center of town, on the left hand side as you drive in. In the summertime, I'm in there working behind the counter."

So...Sky's hanging out with two other married women, Elliot thought to himself. These were not likely pickup candidates, besides which Margie was considerably overweight. But they might be fun to flirt with. Antonia, although large-boned, was very attractive with dark, thick hair and heavily sculpted eyebrows. As a rule, Elliot stayed away from married women...too dangerous. Even though other men did it, the concept was not for him...too much sneaking around. Besides, he liked to think that, just maybe, one of his relationships might lead to real love.

One summer, while performing with a theater group in Amherst when he was still in college, he had fallen head over heels in love with a married woman. Elliot's infatuation had come about quite by accident, and he had forced himself to quit the group as soon as the play, *The Importance of Being Ernest*, was over. She was the director and he played the role of Ernest.

Elliot had been attracted to her immediately, and she seemed to be flirting with him. To add to the confusion, she wasn't wearing a wedding ring. Slender and petite with long dark hair, but not classically attractive, she had a vibrancy about her that he'd found appealing.

They went out a few times for coffee after rehearsals to discuss the play. And then she had casually mentioned her husband, who was an assistant professor at Mount Holyoke. But it was too late...Elliot had already fallen for her.

Now he had to figure out how to extricate himself. He tried avoiding her, but she kept wanting to talk. Perhaps she just wanted his friendship. Perhaps she wanted more. It was fun to fantasize about honest conversations, where he'd ask her whether she was still in love with her husband and why she put so much energy into the theater when she could be spending time with her family at home. She had two stepchildren from her husband's previous marriage. Perhaps she didn't like them. Or maybe her husband ignored her.

Elliot never bothered to find out. As soon as the play's run was over, he moved on to something else. He asked for some evening hours and got promoted to waiter by August. To occupy his spare time, he signed up for a yoga class and a workshop on outdoor photography.

One day, he ran into her at the local grocery store. "What happened to your interest in theater?" she had asked. "You have so much talent. It's a shame to let it go to waste."

"Just too busy," he'd told her, and was not about to say anything else.

"Elliot, pull up a seat and join us," said Antonia, bringing him back to the present.

He quickly surveyed the room one last time. There was no one else around who looked appealing to consort with, so he might as well park himself for a while with these chicks, he reasoned. If things got too boring, he could always leave.

Sky was drinking a glass of white wine. Antonia and Margie were each drinking a Vodka Collins. Elliot ordered a beer. "How can you drink that stuff?" he asked them. It's so sickeningly sweet."

"It depends on the mix," said Margie. "If they're made right, they taste like a refreshing glass of lemonade...with a little kick."

"Care for my cherry?" teased Antonia, dangling the cherry from her drink in front of Elliot's nose. It was obvious that she was on her second or third drink. "I got here first," she explained, "so I had to get the party started for everyone else."

"Pay no attention to her," said Sky. "She's just a cheap drunk."

"I think you ladies need to get something to eat," Elliot suggested.

"We asked for some munchies a while ago," said Margie, "but no one seems to be able to bring anything over here. I suppose they want us to order appetizers."

"Do you want to eat here or at a regular table in the dining area?" Sky asked the others.

"Oh, let's move to a big table," said Margie, "so we can spread out."

At this point, Elliot was thinking that now was his opportunity to make either a swift exit or, at the very minimum, extricate himself from the group.

"Come on, Elliot," said Antonia, beckoning him to follow them. "You can't eat alone."

It was Mexican night, so everyone ordered tacos, burritos, or enchiladas, served on a platter with black beans and rice. The portions were plentiful and the salsa pungent, with plenty of fresh tomatoes, chilies, onions, and cilantro. Sky ordered a vegetarian dish that included a cheese enchilada and a bean and rice burrito with guacamole; Antonia, Margie, and Elliot munched on the combination platter, which included a taco filled with ground turkey and a chicken enchilada.

"It's going to be difficult walking home after this meal," Sky lamented. "Maybe Bud will be home and I can call him to pick me up."

"You should. Otherwise, the whole way walking home you'll be going 'toot toot,'" giggled Antonia.

Sky elbowed Antonia and shook her head. "You've eaten as many beans as I have, Miss Smarty Pants."

Margie and Elliot both raised their glasses and toasted, "To friends and farting!"

This certainly is the gross bunch, Sky thought to herself, remembering the days she would try to avoid eating beans on dates, precisely for that reason. She even knew a guy, one of the fellows helping Bud out on the boat the previous summer, who talked about buying that enzyme stuff, Beano, and pouring it all over his food when he went out on a date. She'd wondered what his date must have thought when she saw him sprinkle that stuff on his food. Or maybe he did it when she wasn't looking. What was his name?...Fred. A slimy guy. Stole some of the cash receipts. Luckily, Bud got rid of him. It took all kinds....

"So, Elliot, what's the inside scoop on the murder?" Margie asked. "Sky won't tell us anything."

"There's nothing to tell," Sky interjected. "They don't have a real suspect or much in the way of clues to work with."

"Sky's just jealous," Elliot nudged, "because she doesn't work on the hard-core investigative stuff. She's more oriented towards features. You have to understand, ladies, a murder investigation is complicated. Witnesses need to be interviewed. Evidence must be gathered carefully before any arrests are made. And so far, the police haven't been able to draw any definite conclusions. But there are some possibilities...."

"In other words, you have nothing," Antonia stated point blank, her brown eyes staring straight into his and raising her eyebrows knowingly.

"Well, maybe *I* can tell you something interesting, which may or may not have any bearing on the case," Margie said.

"What?" the other three said in unison, instinctively lowering their voices and leaning forward as if to hear a secret.

"I see a lot of things when I'm working at the gas station. People drive in to get gas. They use the restroom. They run in to buy cigarettes and candy."

"Go on," said Elliot, hoping what she was about to reveal would be as good as her build-up.

"Most locals don't even use our gas station. Let's face it...they get their gas Up Cape, where the prices are cheaper."

"And...?" said Elliot.

"And anyway, one day, who do I see, stopping to top off his gas tank and buy a pack of cigarettes, but Bill Landon...."

"Bill doesn't smoke, does he?" asked Elliot.

"That's right. He doesn't. He's always been something of a health nut, goes jogging and all. But, you see, Bill was not alone. There was someone else in the car...Susan Stafford."

"So?" Sky sarcastically questioned Margie. "She's his employee. He was probably giving her a ride home."

"So...why didn't she get out of the car and buy her own cigarettes?"

"He was just being polite. No big deal," Sky reasoned.

"There's more," said Margie. "I swear I saw him squeeze her thigh when he got back in his car...*and* give her a big smile, as if he was getting laid."

"Maybe he is," Antonia interjected. "His wife is a dried-up old bitch!"

"I always thought of Jo Landon as being somewhat attractive for a woman her age," Sky said. "She's over fifty."

"A lot of glamorous women are over fifty," said Antonia, "and what I have against *her* is not her looks but her attitude. She just rubs me the wrong way. Very snobby."

"Getting back to what you were saying," Elliot chimed in, "what you're suggesting, Margie, is that based on your observations you think Bill Landon and Susan Stafford were, and may still be, having an affair. But that's no motive for murder."

"Maybe Sonny found out and was going to tell his sister, so they killed him to shut him up."

Sky laughed. "You've been reading too many murder mysteries!"

"Wait a minute," said Elliot. "Maybe this is a valid theory, because if the Landons were to get divorced...the insurance business belongs to the Carreiros, so Bill's interest really belongs to his wife."

"Come come now, Mr. Brilliant Detective," said Sky. "Wouldn't it make more sense for them to kill Jo rather than Sonny? Then Bill would inherit her share."

"Maybe she's next," said Antonia ominously, in a pseudo scary voice.

"You realize this is how rumors get started around here," cautioned Sky. "Somebody thinks they saw something, and the next thing you know it's all over the place...so and so is getting a divorce, this one and that one are having an affair, Joe Schmo is leaving town...."

"I'm just telling you what I saw and what it looked like to me," Margie insisted.

"Well, I think it's all very interesting," said Elliot. "Whether we can use it or not, I don't know. But you might want to share this with the police, or that state trooper doing the investigation, if they haven't figured it out already."

"I don't know if I want to get that involved. They might call on me to testify about something."

"You could always leave them an anonymous tip," Elliot suggested. "Write them a note."

"But don't leave any fingerprints," advised Sky teasingly. "Elliot, should we tell her about the reward money?"

"What reward money?" Margie and Antonia simultaneously asked.

"Fifteen hundred dollars," Sky told them, "for information leading to the murderer's arrest. Maybe you don't want to be anonymous after all...?"

After paying the bill, the four left the restaurant together. Antonia and Margie headed up towards Bradford Street to where Antonia's husband Manuel's small pickup truck was parked.

"Come on," Antonia gestured to Sky. "We can squeeze you in if you'd like a ride." There had been no answer when Sky called from Napi's earlier to see if Bud had gotten home. "We'll just be a little squished in, that's all."

Sky hesitated for a moment and then thought about being pressed in between the wide bulk of Margie and the large elbows of Antonia, her stomach filled with Mexican food.

"I think it'll be better if I just walk home," she said. "I need the fresh air."

"You seem to forget that we're practically neighbors," Elliot joked. "I can walk you home...if you think I'm trustworthy."

Sky looked him up and down with mock scrutiny. "I think you'll do okay. If not, I'll set the dogs on you if you dare try anything."

Sky lived on Franklin Street, while Elliot's small rental cottage was on Pleasant. The two streets ran parallel to each other with a few small courts and lanes in between, both connecting Commercial and Bradford, the two main thoroughfares, and then going on beyond to intersect with Race Road.

"My dogs will be waiting for me," she continued. Sky and Bud owned two dogs, a Labrador mix and an English setter. "They're very protective. Particularly when they're hungry...and they haven't had their dinner yet," she said, widening her eyes, "because from work I never went home."

"I think you're all taken care of, Sky," Margie called out, waving from the open window of the pickup truck as she and Antonia drove by. "See you around."

"How many glasses of wine did you have?" Elliot inquired as they walked up Freeman to Commercial Street. They passed the library on their right as they turned and headed towards the center of town. If anything was open at this time of year, it was here in the thick of the business district, between Standish and Ryder. If you kept walking towards the bay, you'd soon be out over the water and onto the wharf.

At one time, railroad tracks had run all the way down Standish Street, onto the wharf, and directly to the docks so that the freshly caught fish on ice could be rushed back by train to the profitable markets in New York. But that was long ago. Now large factory boats directly processed the fish they caught at sea, selling their wares around the world. Former fishing colonies like Provincetown saw their fleets grow smaller as the bay's natural resources became more and more depleted.

"Oh, I only had three glasses," Sky replied. "I'm just tired...and I like giving you a hard time."

"And why is that?" Elliot asked, feeling more relaxed and carefree, having downed three bottles of beer himself.

"You think I'm a lightweight. That's why. A real fluff writer. And, meanwhile, you think you're always working on the heavy stuff."

"What do you mean by that?"

"You know what I mean. Don't play dumb, Elliot. Who writes the news stories, deals with political issues, et cetera? You, of course. And you're so into it that you've forgotten why you're even here."

"And why is that?"

"To have a good time. To learn something.... Hey, Elliot, this is Provincetown, Massachusetts. It's not Washington, D.C. Nothing political going on here is *that* important. It's just a game. Somebody's going to win and somebody's going to lose. Whether it's an election or a change in the zoning laws, it's just about money."

"Exactly, Sky. It is just about money. And the same goes on in Washington. If they decide whether or not to fund a needle-exchange program to help slow the spread of AIDS, it's all about money and power, not about caring if someone ultimately lives or dies. But, hey... guess what? We have a real live-or-die case in town now. Someone has committed a murder. Someone has decided to play God and take another person's life. Is it about money? Maybe. But it could just as easily be about power or jealousy, for that matter."

"I'd say it's about someone so frustrated they could no longer play by the rules."

"The rules?"

"Yes. They simply couldn't outmaneuver their opponent, Sonny. So they put a bullet in his head. Look, there are people who get in my way and those who get in yours. We have to outsmart them. We may *wish* they were dead, but we work out a way to get around them. The murderer evidently decided the only way to stop Sonny was to kill him."

"Stop him from doing what?" asked Elliot.

"That's what we have to find out," Sky answered smugly. They had now passed Ryder Street and were walking in front of the meat rack, which at ten o'clock on a chilly Wednesday night was very much deserted. Only one lone older man with a long beard and wearing a large double-knit cap sat on one of the inside benches that head up towards the town hall, while a pair of teenagers sat on an outside corner bench along the sidewalk, smoking cigarettes.

"Did it ever occur to you that the killer might be insane, at the very least mentally unbalanced, and merely felt committing murder was the only way out?"

"Insane, confused...they still would have left clues. But this crime was too neat."

"Perhaps just beginner's luck. Don't get me wrong. I am looking for a motive. I see plenty. That's part of the problem...too many people with possible motives but nothing that clearly stands out."

By the time they arrived at Sky's house, Elliot had grown tired of the conversation. Maybe he was just tired. All he knew was he needed to get home and get a good night's sleep so he could have a fresh start in the morning.

Bud's jeep was in the driveway. The dogs were barking eagerly on hearing their approach, and the smaller one had jumped up on the couch and was poking his head through the curtains, pressing against the window to greet his mistress.

"Get down from there!" Sky scolded, as if the dogs could hear her. She turned to face Elliot. "I guess this is where we part. Thank you for the escort service."

"No problem," Elliot grinned. "See you in the morning."

Even without going inside, he could easily imagine the interior of Sky and Bud's house. The brightly painted windmill on the lawn, which turned in the breeze when the little man lowered down his ax to cut wood, and the wooden cutout of "Mary, Quite Contrary" watering her garden, gave Elliot a good indication that their home was filled with clutter and bric-a-brac.

It was a common Provincetown disease…collecting things. Maybe it had started with beachcombing, picking up odds and ends that washed ashore. During the era of pirates and clipper ships, before radar and satellite tracking and diesel engines, Cape Codders thrived on shipwrecks. They picked up all sorts of things…from wood, nails, and canned goods, to barrels of rum, rope, fabric, and tools. While artists looked for unusual pieces of driftwood, pieces of sandblasted glass and shells, those of a more practical nature looked for useful pieces of boating equipment, such as oars, life preservers, a fishing rod.

Yard sales, thrift shops, and the local dump were filled with the discards of summer visitors who used something for a month or a season and couldn't be bothered to pack it up or transport it home. For those with little money and limited means of transportation, secondhand items were a godsend. It was hard to say "no" to just one more thing when it was free or almost free.

Elliot was certain the shelves in Sky's home were filled with secondhand paperback books, china and glass figurines, and vases filled with dried money plant and cattails. On the walls probably hung amateur paintings by aspiring summer artists who had left them behind. He was right…Sky was indeed a clutter bug, whereas he furnished his cottage like a hermit.

What was in Elliot's two-room cottage was there when he rented it: one rickety, pine kitchen table covered with oil cloth, two odd rung-back wooden chairs painted pale yellow, a heavy maple easy chair with vinyl-covered cushions, and a two-tiered side table made of nondescript wood that had been covered with dark blue contact paper. A wrought-iron floor lamp with its torn paper shade, and two converted kerosene lamps along with some antiquated overhead fixtures, provided light in the front room, which was used for cooking, eating, and relaxing.

The few new acquisitions he had indulged himself with were in the bedroom: a queen-size bed atop a platform he had built, since he couldn't bring himself to sleep in one of the two maple twin beds that were already in the cottage, a pair of side table/bookshelves constructed of old wooden fruit crates, and a powerful chrome floor lamp for reading. The old bedroom furniture, the two beds and a pair of white, plastic stacking tables, he'd put in Mrs. Medeiros' garage.

It had been a long day. Elliot turned on the hot water in the shower stall and looked at the shower floor in disgust. The coating of enamel, fiberglass, paint, or whatever, was flaking away. He walked back to the kitchen and grabbed paper towels to pick some of it up as it became saturated with water. Besides a new refrigerator, he definitely needed a new shower, he thought to himself. But the likelihood of getting one was not great. One day, he'd have to start making some real money so he could afford to live in a nice place. In a year or two, maybe he'd think about moving on...maybe getting that law degree or doing something that would pull him up out of the lowest tax bracket.

14

Wednesday Morning

FRAN ROLLED OUT OF BED with the sudden urge to smoke a cigarette. True, officially she had given up smoking. It was bad for you…led to emphysema, lung cancer, heart disease, all that stuff that had to do with rotting lung tissue. But hey, she was still relatively young, not quite thirty. There was still plenty of time to mend her ways, mend her body, when she started sinking into middle age, if she lived that long.

It would be a terrible thing, so Fran thought, to lead a holier-than-thou life, follow all the rules about taking care of your body, and then find out you had some kind of potentially terminal disease anyway, like leukemia or breast cancer.

But it did happen. It had happened to her high school friend, Bobby, dead at age twenty-five from leukemia. A bone marrow transplant and numerous blood transfusions didn't do the trick. "Guess I just have the wrong kind," he had told her. "Aren't you sorry now you didn't let me boink you that night after the Homecoming Dance?" That was typical Bobby…always had a sense of humor and never lost it even while dying. It was a good thing her mother had insisted she go visit him in the hospital. Continuously nagging Fran until she finally made the trip…a short bus ride and a two-block walk. Otherwise, she would never have gone.

There was no mother here to nag her into doing the right thing, though. Fran had to listen to the small voice in her head, the one people referred to as one's conscience, the voice that supposedly told you right from wrong. "Go to the visitation," the voice had been telling her. "You need to offer your condolences to Sarah in person. Don't wait until the day of the funeral. It will be too hectic."

"Okay, okay already. I hear you," Fran whispered to herself as she got up, pulled on her soft terry robe with large pockets and rummaged around in the top drawer of her bureau for the cigarettes and matches. Placing them in her pocket, she walked into the kitchen/dining area of the condo to the sliding glass door that opened out onto the deck. First she needed to pull out the piece of wood that prevented the slider from being opened on the outside by intruders. Next she flicked the lever that kept the slider locked in place and moved the door a few inches to the left. Shauna was still asleep, so Fran tried to be as quiet as she could as she cracked the door just enough to blow her smoke outside into the morning air.

She placed the tip of a cigarette between her lips and fumbled around with striking a match along the edge of the matchbook once it was closed. "F.J.'s Bistro" was printed on the matchbook cover. Now, that was a place she hadn't been to in a while…pretty stained-glass windows, delicious grilled fish. Fran wondered how long ago she'd picked the book of matches up, trying to recall the last time she'd been to Boston.

She deeply inhaled the blend of nicotine and tobacco. It tasted nothing like that delicious grilled fish she'd remembered…or the buttered English muffin she was thinking about having for breakfast. But the effect was exhilarating. She now felt alert and focused. Maybe she should do this more often. She took a few more drags and placed the cigarette inside a large clamshell she'd grabbed from the collection of seashells arranged in the center of the dining room table. Then she set the clamshell and half-smoked cigarette on the deck next to the slightly ajar slider.

"No, you shouldn't," countered that small voice in her head. "Smoking is bad for you."

Imagine what it must be like for those poor people who talk about hearing several voices in their head, giving all kinds of advice, Fran pondered as she opened the refrigerator door and reached for a carton of orange juice to pour herself a glass. Which voice did they listen to, anyway...and is that why they go crazy?

Setting the carton down on the pale blue Formica counter, she reached up to open a cabinet and selected a glass, settling on a medium-size glass of heavy weight, avoiding the light, plastic ones and cheap, crackle-glass tumblers that primarily occupied the shelves inside the kitchen cabinets.

The condo was equipped with everything from a television to pots, pans, and dishes. Fran had very little in the way of housewares, anyway. She'd put her few boxes, along with Shauna's, Up Cape in storage. All they needed here were their sheets and linens. A rustic summer cottage in the woods of Truro would not be as luxurious. Even if it was supposedly fully equipped, they'd still need some decent cooking pots and a few nice matching dishes.

Many voices...Fran went back to stand beside the sliding glass door and finish her cigarette, still wondering about those people who hear many voices. Perhaps some people would think her strange, the way she'd have these conversations with herself in her head. She asked herself what other people think about when they're alone...and did they have imaginary conversations with themselves, too?

What scared Fran was when someone talked about outside forces telling them, whispering to them, to do things they shouldn't or wouldn't normally do. Now, *that* is crazy, she reasoned. Schizophrenia...that's what they call it. The inability to distinguish fantasy from reality. Many people associate it with multiple personalities, but that's a relatively rare occurrence.

Fran remembered Shauna saying her brother was schizophrenic, takes special medication. Fran had never met the guy. Talked to him on the phone once and he seemed perfectly normal. They say mental illness has a tendency to run in families. She certainly hoped Shauna was okay.

The phone started ringing. Fran looked up at the clock on the wall. It was awfully early, only eight o'clock. Most businesses didn't open until ten. But Shauna needed to get over to the bank in another half an hour. Fran needed to wake her up. First she picked up the phone.

"Fran? This is Polly. Sorry to call you so early but I thought I'd try and have a chat with you before you went to work."

"Polly, can you hold the line for a minute?"

Fran put down the receiver and walked over to the bedroom. "Shauna...sweetie pie. I let you sleep in. You need to get to work, pronto," she said, leaning over Shauna's sleeping figure and whispering into her ear.

Shauna turned over and looked at the time on the alarm clock. "How could you let me sleep so late? And why didn't this alarm go off?" She jumped out of bed and ran towards the bathroom to shower.

Fran walked back to the kitchen, picked up the phone receiver, and put it to her ear. "Sorry to keep you waiting, Polly. You were saying...."

"I was saying, dear, that I'd like to get together with you this morning before you go over to the newspaper office. I have a business proposition."

"Don't tell me you want me to go after my real estate license. I don't have time to take a class and study for some bullshit exam when I can make money right now selling advertising accounts and still have time for design work."

"Listen," said Polly. "I'd rather talk to you in person. You know I'm no good on an empty stomach. Doesn't a buttery croissant or a piece of cream cheese Danish sound good?"

"Sounds like you're talking about meeting at Café Edwige," said Fran, trying to suppress a chuckle. She knew Polly Smithfield well enough to know that food occupied at least half her waking hours and that her fascination with eating had created the huge bulk of flab she carried on her mid-size frame. Talk about unhealthy habits...her own secret love affair with cigarettes was nothing compared to Polly's addiction to anything rich and fattening, Fran thought to herself.

"Why don't we meet in about twenty minutes," Polly proposed.

"Let's make it thirty," replied Fran.

Café Edwige was across the street from the library. Unlike most businesses on the ground level or slightly below, here there was a second-floor location that was reached by ascending a narrow, steep staircase. Bright and airy, with local artwork hung on the wall and a small outside porch for dining during the summer season, Café Edwige was known among the breakfast crowd for its bountiful omelets featuring various fresh vegetable combinations along with warm baked pastries, just out of the oven.

Fran had decided it was a good day to wear green. She walked through the door wearing a bright green, fuzzy lamb's wool sweater and form-fitting electric green pants, with a green and blue silk scarf tied around her neck, underneath her black and red ski parka.

Sitting at a table in the center of the room, Polly was already eating an avocado, mushroom, and cheese omelet with a double order of home fries. "Sorry," she said. "I just couldn't wait. I get so hungry in the morning."

The woman was hungry all the time. Fran just smiled and said, "So do I. So do I. Where's the waitress so I can order something, too?"

She looked at Polly, dressed in a pair of khaki pants, brown work boots, and what must have been a triple-large black sweatshirt. When you're big, you don't want to stand out...you want to blend in, Fran reasoned, while taking off her jacket and draping it over the back of her chair.

"Very nice, Fran...very nice. Are you re-celebrating Saint Paddy's Day?" Polly asked her wryly as a way of commenting on Fran's attire. The girl was certainly flamboyant, Polly had often remarked to herself, the kind of gal that could sell ice to the Eskimos if she wanted to. How long did that kind of supercharged charm last? "So, how's business over at the newspaper?"

"Couldn't be better," Fran said. "Lots going on and it's that time of year when things are gearing up, but the staff is still small. Anything special you'd like to add to your regular listings for next week? With all the interest in the murder investigation, sales are certain to increase significantly with our Up Cape readers over the next month."

Fran hailed the waitress, who was busy pouring coffee for patrons at a booth against the wall. She looked vaguely familiar, perhaps someone she had met dancing one night...or wasn't she the woman she always saw trying things on at the thrift shop, Ruthie's Boutique? Yes, she was one of the regulars, a thrift shop junkie who stopped in at least once a week to check out the new donations that had arrived. Kind of pretty. Fluffy, pale yellow-blonde hair, full lips, and hazel eyes. Fran gave her a big smile. "Could I please have a cup of coffee, and a cream cheese and poppy seed Danish...oh, and a bowl of fresh fruit?"

The waitress smiled back. "Sure. I think there's one piece of Danish left. I'll go check."

Damn. I should have ordered a Danish earlier, Polly thought to herself. Aloud she said, "So how much is Roz paying you?"

"I get a commission of twenty percent plus comprehensive health insurance coverage and a retirement plan."

"What if I offered you twenty-five percent?"

"Twenty-five percent of what?"

"Sales commissions on a new weekly magazine."

"What kind of circulation?"

"I don't know for certain...ten, maybe fifteen thousand to start, I guess."

"And what will be your advertising rates?"

"Lower than the *Observer*'s."

"The lower the rates, the lower my commission checks."

"Well, not real low. Just low enough to attract advertisers and make them think it's a good value."

"If people don't read it, it's not a good value."

"Oh, they'll read it, for sure. It's going to be free. Why wouldn't they want to pick it up and take it home?"

"You're forgetting about the subscribers, all the people who receive the *Observer* in the mail. They're part of our circulation, and that impresses the advertising folks." Fran had been leaning forward, with her elbows on the table, but now pulled her arms down and placed them neatly in her lap as her breakfast was being placed on the table. Steam was rising from the white coffee mug. The strawberries, orange slices, and honeydew melon were brightly colored and looked succulent and fresh. And, as usual, the Danish looked delicious. She noticed Polly gluttonously eyeing it but wasn't about to offer her a piece.

"Will you be needing anything else?" asked their waitress. "My name's Sofie, by the way. I should have introduced myself sooner," she said while looking more directly at Fran than at Polly.

"Thank you, Sofie," said Polly. "I think we're all set."

As soon as she walked away, Polly told Fran conspiratorially, "I think she's flirting with you."

"Oh, she's just doing her job. Besides, it's too early in the morning for flirting."

"So, tell me about the subscribers," said Polly, forcing herself to focus on business rather than on food or romantic dalliances. "How much business do advertisers get from those out-of-town subscribers?"

"They're the ones looking for summer rentals and that future summer or retirement home, aren't they?" Fran replied.

Polly had to think for a minute. She'd only eaten half the food on her plate but her stomach felt a little pained, perhaps from eating too fast. Maybe this magazine wasn't such a good idea...at least from a real estate point of view, unless it was so attractive that it was something people wanted to keep around and periodically thumb through.

"Listen, Polly. We'll be doing another magazine insert on spring real estate next month. How many pages would you like? We've got some real good articles on home improvement and gardening. How about a full-page photo of some luxury home you've listed. It's sure to get a lot of notice."

"Let me think about it, dear," Polly answered before taking another sip of coffee. "So, you're not interested in a career move at this time, even with the potential to work for me part-time and get into real estate?"

"I like to make money as well as the next person," answered Fran. "But I also have to think about long-term priorities. I'm really a graphic artist, and I'd prefer to be doing more of that kind of work. I'm only doing this advertising gig to put food on the table. As soon as I've built up a large enough client base, I'll quit the paper. If you'd really like to help my career, then why don't you let me do a nice color brochure for your real estate office to match a new logo and a new sign out front."

Polly smiled politely while thinking to herself that she didn't need to be wasting money on fancy artwork. She just wanted sales, lots of sales, and to be making a lot of money selling. And this gal was just wasting her time with all this artistic image crap.

Out loud, Polly said, "Fran, I had my sign repainted just a little over a year ago, and I like it. But if I hear of anyone who needs a graphic artist, I'll be sure to recommend you."

Things weren't going the way Polly had hoped. Maybe that's what she got for sticking her neck out and trying to help someone else on some project that had nothing to do directly with herself. Well, yes, it did...ultimately, she did want to see another newspaper or some other type of publication besides the *Observer*. But was this a good time to move on? Was this the right time for a challenge? The problem with selling advertising, which was crucial for financing, was that you had to pay the ad rep a lot of money to get ads placed...twenty percent.

In real estate, you only got six, or once in a while up to ten percent, and most of the time that was split in half. Unless the others...Bruno, Frank...were willing to sell direct, soliciting ads themselves....

Polly looked at her partially eaten omelet and home fries. She might as well finish her breakfast, even though it was getting cold. Maybe the pain in her side would go away if she ate some more and downed her coffee. First she reached for her glass of ice water.

Fran started seriously diving into her bowl of fruit. She needed to finish eating and get over to the newspaper. Should she warn Roz about what was going on? Apparently, some kind of new magazine would be trying to take away some of the *Observer*'s longtime clients. Polly was keeping the backers' names to herself, although it was obvious she was one of them.

On the one hand, Fran felt honored that Polly was trying to enlist her help as well as offer her more money. But if this new publication flopped, where would she be then? Fran knew it was important to choose one's friends wisely. She didn't want to do anything rash, anything that would piss Polly or any other established businesspeople off because one never knew the way the tide would turn. On the other hand, forewarned was forearmed. If Roz was aware that another publication was in the works, she'd at least be prepared.

"The murder weapon has been found," Elliot called out triumphantly to anyone who might be listening. "A .38-caliber handgun. No fingerprints, and the serial numbers were filed off."

"What was that you said?" Roz stuck her head out of her office.

"Ballistic tests have proven conclusively that a .38-caliber automatic handgun found Wednesday afternoon on the edge of Great Pond in the Beech Forest area of the national seashore bicycle trail by ten-year-old Stephanie Carreiro, daughter of the victim, is the murder weapon," Elliot said, reciting what he planned to type into his computer. "However, the removal of the serial numbers and lack of fingerprints mean that it does not provide any substantial evidence in solving the murder of Sonny Carreiro."

"It does tell us something," Roz maintained. It tells us that the murderer has to be a local. If the murderer was some paid assassin from out of town, he would have taken the gun with him. This person had reason to believe that perhaps they might be a suspect and their home searched. So they had to get rid of the gun and they filed the serial numbers off first so it couldn't be traced.

"Elliot, we need to get a list from the county of all the registered gun owners in Provincetown. I bet that gun legitimately belonged to someone and now it's missing. Only a local is going to throw the gun in a pond on the bike trails."

"I was wondering why they didn't just throw the gun in the ocean or the bay." replied Elliot.

"Don't you see? They didn't have time. From Snob Hill, they got onto Harry Kemp Way or Route 6 and drove west to Conwell Street out to the bike trails, parked in the lot by the Beech Forest, and then probably followed Beach Highway back around to Route 6 and ultimately went home, to a bar, or wherever."

"Interesting theory, Roz. So you're saying they carefully planned the murder, filed the numbers off the gun in advance, and then disposed of the gun right away...."

"Yes, and they would have been more likely to be seen on the bay side if they'd decided to throw the gun in the bay. Plus, if they headed out of town, they risked the police having immediately set up a roadblock or at least taking note of anyone leaving."

"Let's get serious! There's no way the police would have had time to put up a roadblock before someone drove off and into Truro. They didn't even know a murder had taken place until they got on the scene."

"You're right, Elliot. But suppose a cop was stationed at the edge of town looking for speeders, as there often is...the murderer might have been spotted and was playing it safe."

"So you think we're looking for someone careful and meticulous?"

"Yes, I do."

"Well, that only slightly narrows down the field."

Fran walked into the office to see Elliot and Roz engaged in a heated discussion on possible murder suspects.

"Beau could have weaved his way back on Route 6, east to Howland, and then gone Howland to Bradford to Atkins Mayo Road. He even could have snuck back along the old railroad bed from Howland to Atkins Mayo," Roz was saying.

Meanwhile, at her desk, Sky was going over what appeared to be astrological charts and thumbing through what she called ephemerides, which had tables of which planet was where at what time of the day. She seemed to take her astrology forecasting very seriously, Fran mused to herself.

Jenny, the production editor, was busy opening mail and putting news releases and information in various stacks to distribute or type into the system, while Ron, fellow advertising sales rep and layout person, was sorting through and filing old ads. Sky, Ron, Jenny, and Fran's assistant, Betty, seemed wrapped up in their own worlds with no apparent interest in Roz and Elliot's conversation. Perhaps they had heard so much speculative talk on the Sonny Carreiro murder, they were bored with the topic.

"With Jupiter rising that night, the emphasis was on material goods and money," Sky called out.

"What? Are you doing a chart of the heavens for last Sunday evening?" retorted Elliot. "What a bunch of horse shit!"

"I told her to," said Roz. "I thought it would be an interesting little feature item for next week's paper."

Elliot rolled his eyes.

"Got to take care of those cosmic-consciousness readers," Fran called out to announce her presence. "They do buy newspapers."

"Fran, can you come into my office for a minute?" Roz requested almost hesitantly.

Must have something to do with money, Fran thought, because the only time Roz ever acted unsure of herself was when she had to talk about money.

"Sure thing," Fran said. "Just let me hang up my jacket and put my stuff away. I'll be right there."

If she wanted to be really cruel, Fran knew she could move slowly while Roz fidgeted in her office waiting for her...maybe get a cup of coffee, make a phone call. She was probably late on her paycheck again, or maybe someone was wiggling out of paying their bill. Too bad she couldn't just get her commission checks as soon as she made the sale.

Fran got paid when the newspaper got paid. Sometimes she was even the one who phoned advertisers to find out why they were late on their bills. She sold hard on the "pay up front and get a two percent discount," because that money was a sure thing. The only incentive to

get advertisers to pay within a reasonable time was the threat of pulling their ads. If there was another local publication, as far as paying
bills, businesspeople could play one against the other. When their credit
ran out at the *Observer*, they could place an ad in that new magazine,
whatever they were planning to call it. That wouldn't be good...maybe
they should be aggressively stopped. Fran considered the possibility
and headed into Roz's office.

Her desk was disheveled, a usual sight, and the trash can was overflowing. Even the leather couch against the wall looked rumpled and
the pillows flattened down. Fran wondered if that was where Roz and
John fucked some nights, as her eyes focused in on a large spot on the
couch's far left corner. "Such a dirty mind," said that other voice, the
one in her head that she presumed to be her conscience.

"Fran," said Roz, "I have to be honest with you. I got a fifteen-
hundred-dollar check from Mason's Hardware and Marine, but I need
to wait a week or so to pay your commission...until the bank comes
through with refinancing. You aren't hurting for money or anything,
I hope...?"

"This time of year..." Fran rolled her eyes. "Everything is cool until we have to come up with the money to move into a summer place.
Even a ramshackle cottage in Truro isn't cheap, and they want a third
of the rent up front plus one month's security deposit. But that's not
until the end of May."

The small summer rental cottage Fran was talking about was not to
be confused with the palatial Truro houses that had views of the bay or
ocean and rented for as much as several thousand dollars a week. With
no insulation, heat, or modern kitchen, the cottage Fran and Shauna had
reserved was what once had been referred to as a tourist cottage in the
early 1900s. In a wooded setting with squeaky, metal-frame beds, and
shabby but sturdy maple furniture, it sure fit the definition of "roughing
it" for the summer. If a property owner didn't want to provide towels
and linens for weekly rentals to bargain-hunting vacationers, they sometimes chose instead to rent their places by the season to locals.

"That's good to hear, because I really do appreciate the hard work
you've been doing for the paper and I'm hoping we'll have another
great summer season."

"Speaking of the summer season," said Fran, "I think you should
know there's talk of another local publication."

"There's always talk about someone starting up another newspaper or something...."

"This is different," Fran interjected. "I think it may actually happen...a magazine. Not direct competition, but still...."

"Magazine, huh...what type of focus?" Roz started tapping her fingers on her desk. "The arts? Theater? Social stuff like where's a good place to get picked up? What happens after the bars close down on our pleasant back streets? How to find the lesbian of your dreams? Sorry, Fran. I didn't mean to say...."

"Yes, you did...but it's no big deal. Some people are interested in reading that type of stuff, for sure. But I haven't seen a dummy copy of whatever it is. The only reason I even know about it is because they tried to offer me a job."

"Who tried to offer you a job?"

"I'd rather not say. It will only piss you off. I'm only telling you this because forewarned is forearmed. Besides, I have an idea."

"What kind of idea?" Roz asked curiously.

"I think you should expand more Up Cape, with a special edition just for Wellfleet. It will prevent the Wellfleet people from buying those weekly newspapers published out of Orleans. Right now, their choice is either a paper out of Orleans or a paper out of Provincetown, with some news about the towns in between, including Wellfleet. But if you published *The Wellfleet Observer*...."

"That would mean I'd need one or two more reporters, more money for production costs...."

"Think about it. It could be good," reasoned Fran. If those others were smart, they'd start their magazine out of Wellfleet, not to be in direct competition, but they won't."

"Primarily gay businesspeople behind this, huh?"

"You might conclude something like that."

"Well, thanks for the info," Roz said. "I'll take it under advisement."

Roz was relieved when Fran left her office, because she could now try to put the thought of a competing magazine out of her mind. If only she hadn't told me, Roz lamented to herself. Her morning had steadily been going downhill, and this information is just the icing on the cake. Roz felt she always had to worry about the wolves nipping at her heels. The people she thought were friends were really enemies. It was always *something*....

Thinking back, it had started out a glorious morning. She had literally gotten up with the sunrise, looked out the window to greet the coming day, eager to get to work and try and track down the tip about Casey Long in Louisville. But increasingly, with the flow of events, she'd grown more and more frustrated and depressed.

The first order of business had been to jump into the shower, lather up with sandalwood-scented soap, and indulge herself in washing her hair a second day in a row...just to get the residue and thought of the previous day's meeting with bank president Ernie Martin completely removed from her body and mind. A deal had been struck. She would move forward. Yes, she was in debt, deeply in debt, but for now the bills would continue to be paid. And great stories were coming along, soon to be printed in the *Observer*...wonderful, exciting stories that everyone would want to read.

The world would take notice of her small but vibrant newspaper, which dug out the best, and spiciest, stories. Roz's greatest triumph would be when locals rushed to the newsstands tomorrow morning for a copy of the paper, *her* paper, not even waiting until they got it with their afternoon mail delivery. That's what happened when she had a really hot story to print.

She had dressed to be comfortable, casual, and aggressive. Tight jeans, a red cotton turtleneck, blue bandanna tied around her neck, and a forest green fleece vest. As soon as her hair was dry, she had pulled the front part back away from her face and gathered it in a barrette, leaving a few stray pieces to curl around her cheeks. A pair of diamond studs in her ears and her gold-toned bracelet watch on her left wrist, and she'd been ready to face the world.

Eating a banana while the coffee was brewing, Roz had considered going for a morning walk before making breakfast. Sally was still asleep. Nothing much would be open. Stepping outside to get her morning paper, she'd wondered what time it was in Louisville. Was it in the same time zone? She looked at the chart in the phone book. No luck last night finding a Casey, but there were plenty of Longs. No direct number to call. And then she hadn't been sure whether to just call anyone with the last name of Long...and what kind of name would evolve into the nickname of Casey? Without a Louisville phone book, she knew the task wouldn't be easy. Roz had thought that perhaps she should go back to Mitzi and ask her a few more questions.

Charles? Keith? Maybe he had a sissy name like Francis or Emerson and he adopted Casey as a nickname.

"Do you have a listing for a Francis Long?" she'd asked the Directory Assistance operator in Louisville.

There actually was such a listing...but why, oh why, had she persisted in dialing that number?

"Casey? You're looking for someone with the nickname of Casey?" asked a gruff voice that sounded like it belonged to someone over sixty-five. "How about the train engineer in that song, 'Casey Jones going over the track'...?" followed by a loud guffaw. "Ain't no one here by that name, lady. Where did you say you were calling from?"

Her phone calls were followed by a walk back to Mitzi's. She could have driven to the coffee shop on her way to the office. This time of year, this early in the morning, it was easy to find parking on the street. But Roz had decided the walk would do her good. A little exercise... clear the cobwebs out of her brain, she'd rationalized.

"Good morning," Mitzi had greeted Roz. "Come for another muffin? Cup of tea?"

"Actually, I'd prefer some coffee and a little more information about what we were talking about yesterday afternoon. You told me about a fellow named Casey Long, Rusty Ogel's son...."

"Oh, yes," said Mitzi with a wry smile. "I told you everything I know...what he told me." She handed Roz a styrofoam cup to fill from one of the tall coffee thermoses on the front counter.

"Did he give you his real name?" Roz asked while filling her cup from the thermos labeled "Breakfast Blend" and then snapping a white plastic lid on the top.

"Well, I didn't ask to see his driver's license. Tried to find him in the phone book?"

"Unfortunately, I don't have a phone book for Louisville, but I did call Information. No one listed by that name."

"It could be a nickname."

"That's what I thought, too, so I called several people with the last name of Long, hoping perhaps they might be related. No one has heard of him."

"Sorry, Roz. Think I should still tell the police?"

"Well, it wouldn't hurt. Maybe they can find him."

"I'll talk to one of my friends on the force. Here, have a blueberry muffin. Fresh out of the oven. It's on me."

Mitzi took a pair of tongs, grabbed a muffin from the corner of the tray where they were cooling on the counter behind her, and slid it into a white paper bag.

"Too hot to touch," she cautioned. "Give it another five minutes and it will melt in your mouth."

Roz put a dollar on the counter to pay for her coffee.

"Oh, don't worry about it. The coffee's on the house, too."

Roz left the dollar anyway, grabbing the coffee in one hand and the warm bag in the other. She needed to open the front door without letting the coffee spill, lid or no lid. It wasn't usual for Mitzi to give food away for free, especially when it was fresh, plus coffee...? She must be hiding something, Roz thought.

"What do you think about the likelihood that the drunk, Rusty Ogel, had an illegitimate son who came to town to learn the circumstances of his father's death, held Sonny Carreiro accountable, and either murdered him or arranged for his murder?" Roz had asked Elliot as soon as she got to the office.

Also dressed in jeans, though considerably more faded than hers, with a pale blue, button-down shirt and gray V-neck sweater, Elliot almost looked like the preppy college student he once was. Too bad he wasn't wearing penny loafers, Roz mused, instead of the grubby athletic shoes with broken, tied-together shoelaces that he had on.

Elliot ran his fingers through his hair and scrunched up his mouth to give the appearance he was thinking hard. "I'd say that would be quite a long-shot of a theory. What would the son gain? Not much. If he was angry at anyone, it should be at his father for leaving him in the first place and ending up a drunken bum.... On another note, I have an interesting tidbit for you, which may or may not be true. According to someone I talked to last night, Bill Landon could be having an affair with his employee, Susan Stafford."

"That bimbo!" Roz exclaimed. "She's certainly a switch from that high and mighty Jo. So, who told you this, anyway?"

"Margie Adams, who helps out in the summer at the gas station on Bradford in the center of town. I ran into her last night at Napi's.

She was there with Sky and Antonia Henrique. Sky can tell you about it."

"So we have a love triangle. Wouldn't they want to kill Jo instead of Sonny, so the two could have the house, money...?"

"But think a minute, Roz. Suppose Sonny was also sleeping with Susan. Maybe *that* was the love triangle and Bill got jealous of Sonny."

"Gee, I would have thought Sonny had better taste. She's nothing like Sarah.

"Vive la différence!" replied Elliot.

"Oh, come on. I thought he went for more sophisticated, intelligent women. Do you know any of Susan's neighbors? Maybe we can ask who they might have seen her with lately," Roz suggested.

Susan Stafford lived in a year-round apartment on Center Street. Once an elegant, grand home, built in the late 1800s, it had been divided into four various-size apartments. Susan had the one-bedroom unit. Small in actual square footage, it seemed spacious due to its high ceilings and bay windows. The hardwood floors, hard-edged black-and-white photographs on the walls, abundance of plants, and large computer setup in the corner of the living room gave Trooper Marc O'Brien the feeling he had just stepped into an apartment in downtown Boston.

One look at Susan Stafford had O'Brien thinking that perhaps he was instead in Miami or Hollywood. His eyes immediately gravitated down. Her large breasts, strapped tightly into a workhorse of a bra that managed to push them up and out of the low-cut, blue knit pullover she was wearing, seemed to have taken on a life of their own. It was hard not to stare. Then he noticed her hair...full, thick, wavy, and dyed a shade of reddish gold. It hung halfway down her back.

Even-featured with a skillful application of makeup that highlighted her mouth, cheekbones, and eyes, O'Brien theorized that fifteen pounds lighter she'd be considered quite a looker by men who went for her type. Not tall enough to be a model, she looked like a sixties movie starlet. Had she been caught in a time warp? As for himself, he preferred women with a more natural look. So, what was she doing in Provincetown? She didn't seem to fit in...on the other hand, maybe she did since she was the epitome of what every drag queen spent hours trying to emulate.

"Bayonne, New Jersey," Susan told O'Brien. "That's where I'm from originally. They call it 'the armpit of New York City.' My father owned a bar there.... Hey, have a seat. Stay a while. Can I get you a cup of coffee, juice, something else?"

O'Brien was reluctant to take her up on the offer, despite his rule of accepting an informant's hospitality. Dishes were piled so high in the sink of the kitchen area, easily visible from where he was standing, he doubted whether she'd even be able to find a clean coffee mug. He noticed dried food, possibly old spaghetti and tomato sauce, clung to the plates that were stacked amidst an assortment of glasses, mugs, cutlery, pots, and pans. The garbage can was overflowing with what looked like those aluminum tins that TV dinners came in. As lovely as this Susan Stafford appeared, he couldn't help thinking that her apartment was just the opposite. If she only spent half as much time cleaning up as she obviously did on her makeup, hair, and nails....

"Please excuse the mess around here," she said apologetically, gesturing to the stacks of papers, books, and binders strewn across her dining table, as well as to the dirty dishes overflowing from the sink, as if she'd been reading his mind. "I've been studying for the exam to get my P&C, property and casualty license, so I'll be able to sell insurance in Massachusetts. You have to memorize a lot of stuff, but I'm determined to pass.... I do have some clean cups in the cupboard, and the coffee was just made."

"I take mine black," he said with a grin while sinking into a faded tweed couch, only to find he had accidentally sat on what felt like either a pen or pencil. O'Brien shifted his weight to one side, reached down, picked the pencil up, and checked to see whether it had broken before putting it on the table in front of him. "Malgam and Sons Insurance" was printed in gold on a royal blue background. Malgam and Sons... maybe her previous employer in Florida?

"So, how did you end up in Provincetown? Did you come here straight from New Jersey?" he inquired as she handed him a white china cup filled to the brim with hot coffee.

"Hang on. I'll get you a coaster," she called, going back to the kitchen area to find one amidst all the clutter. Unsuccessful, she returned with a few napkins. "Here. Just put these on the table underneath your cup so you don't leave a mark on the wood. This isn't my furniture. I'm borrowing it from a friend so I try to be careful."

Susan went into the kitchen area again to pour herself a cup of coffee, as well, to which she added a couple large spoonfuls of sugar and some milk. Bringing more napkins and mug in hand, she sat down on the couch next to O'Brien.

"I wanted to get out and see the world," she explained. "Been married once. Lived in Philadelphia, on the north side. Moved to Florida after the divorce and worked at an insurance office in Key Largo. Some friends in Key West told me about Provincetown, so I visited during an extended summer vacation, even sold time-share condos for a week. Then I saw an ad in the newspaper. I interviewed and got the position. I was getting pretty sick of my boss down in Key Largo, so I went back, quit that job, and moved here...just this past September."

"Found a nice place right away, I see."

"It was pure dumb luck. I used to be a cosmetologist and was helping out part-time at Hair and There during that August visit...pinch hitting, so to speak. You know the place over on Commercial Street?" She looked for O'Brien to nod his head in assent but continued talking anyway. "Well, I was doing some boys' makeup for a drag show and a fellow named Bobby and I really hit it off. He told me he was moving back to Key West after the season was over and turned me on to this apartment. In exchange, I shared it with him for the next few weeks, even though I'd already signed and taken over the lease. I let him sleep on the couch when he needed to. That was cool. Most of this furniture belongs to him."

"Will he want it when he comes back?" asked O'Brien. "And the furniture, too?"

"I'm hoping he finds a sugar daddy. I signed a year-round lease, but I guess if he wants his furniture...I try not to think about it too much. Besides, I've saved some money so I can probably get some furniture of my own."

"Didn't you own stuff down in Florida?"

"Sure. But it's so expensive to move. I just sold it all. It's not as if I had anything that great."

So he'd been partly right, O'Brien crowed proudly to himself. The drag queen connection, her friend Bobby.... But why had she decided to take the job here? Were the benefits that good?

"So, you've been working for Mr. Landon for approximately six months. How did he get along with his brother-in-law?"

"They got long fine, as far as I could tell. Mr. Carreiro didn't spend that much time in the office."

"Any big deals he was working on that you were aware of?"

"Big deals.... He has all that real estate."

"No, this was something else," O'Brien said. "Something to do with the insurance agency...something he mentioned to his wife, Sarah."

"You've got me stumped," she replied. "Like I said, he was hardly in the office. He seemed to be preoccupied with other things."

"Ever witness any arguments? Any dissatisfied customers?"

"No." Susan shook her head.

"So tell me, what you were doing the night of the murder, this past Sunday evening?"

"I was with Mr. Landon, catching up on some work. He'd been out of town."

"That's not what he told me. He said he was working alone."

"Maybe he forgot I was in the office. He seemed pretty tired. Those weekend insurance seminars can be grueling."

"Well, he specifically said that you were not there. Even mentioned it was difficult to get employees to work during the evening. One of you must be lying."

Susan got up and paced back and forth. "Do you mind if I smoke?" she asked solicitously.

"It's your apartment. I don't smoke, but I can tolerate it as long as you don't blow it in my direction."

"Bill doesn't let me smoke in the office. He makes me go outside, which is pretty tough in the dead of winter. He keeps telling me I need to quit, but I'm addicted to the nicotine, I guess." Susan walked over to the dining table and reached for her purse, which was sitting on top of some papers. Out of it she pulled a pack of cigarettes and matches, lit a cigarette, looked around for an ashtray, and finally just grabbed a saucer from the kitchen. "Maybe I should try those nicotine patches or the gum. Know anyone who's actually been successful at quitting that way?"

"One of the dispatch clerks used the patches and totally quit in about six weeks." O'Brien thought of telling her more about Jan Seward's experiences when trying to quit smoking, but caught himself in time. She was obviously trying to change the subject, and succeeding, he told himself.

"Ms. Stafford," he said, darkening the tone of his voice, "back to what we were talking about. Where were you on Sunday night?"

"I told you. I was with Bill, Mr. Landon, at the office. If he said I wasn't there, he was just trying to protect me...protect us from people getting the wrong impression about our relationship."

"And what exactly is your relationship?"

There was a long pause. "Let me ask you something, Officer. If I tell you something, can it be off the record?"

"Well, you can ask me to hold something back in confidence. You may or may not be subpoenaed to testify if the case goes to court. But right now, *someone* isn't telling me the truth. What I don't understand is why Mr. Landon would insist he was working alone, when you're now telling me you'd be able to verify his alibi. It doesn't make sense."

Susan took a deep breath. "Yes, it makes sense...Bill and I are lovers," she blurted out. "We started seeing each other back in October. He doesn't want his wife to find out. Please don't tell his wife...especially now, when she's mourning her brother's death."

15

Later Wednesday Morning

FRANK CARRIED the last of the boxes into the restaurant. Filled with giant cans of tuna fish, triple packs of dinner rolls, large containers of mixed fruit, and various staples such as rice, butter, and olive oil, their weight strained his arm muscles.

There had to be a better way, he'd often thought. He should just have everything delivered by the wholesalers. But prices on certain things were always much better at the large discount food warehouses, and staples like sugar and eggs were even cheaper at regular supermarkets when they have their false leaders to bring in customers. That's why turkey around Thanksgiving was always so cheap. If you buy a turkey, they figure you'll buy all the fixings too, at full price. What they didn't bank on were people like him coming in and just buying the false leaders and nothing else. They lose money then.

The produce Frank needed was being delivered in the afternoon. As soon as the parsley and celery arrived, he could mix up the tuna salad, egg salad, and the fruit salads. Jo had nixed the luncheon loaf idea. So instead of various salads stuffed inside hollowed-out loaves of white bread, he was just arranging the standard bowls and platters of things to place on her dining room table, with plenty of lavish garnishes. At least he'd convinced her to try one platter of nibbles, just to have something a little different...skewers of marinated roast beef and mushrooms along with skewers of prosciutto and melon.

In the meantime, he decided to focus on his Friday through Sunday menu at the restaurant. During high season, when he was also open on Wednesdays and Thursdays, his offerings those two evenings were limited to three prix fixe dinners. But on weekends, he presented a more varied selection of choices.

He decided to let the boxes just stay on the floor, near the worktable, rather than bothering to put things away since he'd be using many of the items soon. He put a kettle of water on the stove to make some tea, and sat down on a stool behind the worktable to think.

On Frank's mind were the several phone calls earlier about the magazine. One had been Polly Smithfield lamenting the fact that she had been unable to convince the *Observer*'s crackerjack advertising saleswoman, Fran, into switching horses and working for their new publication.

"Do you know anyone who can go out there and sell advertising?" Polly had asked.

"I'll see on who I can come up with," he'd replied.

No sooner had he hung up the phone than Sean Gilligan had called, asking him to stop by the Cowboy Club at eleven thirty so they could talk.

He decided it was easier to just think about cooking and his plans for food preparation than the magazine. For chopping, for mixing, for assembling, Frank used his worktable. A long table made of pine, with three drawers for his utensils, it was his favorite work surface in the kitchen. He also had the side counters next to the stainless steel, six-burner stove and his twenty-four-inch grill. But the counters were Formica, cheap Formica, and he liked so much better the warm feel of wood. Above the worktable hung a multitude of pots.

Linquicia quiche might be a good appetizer if the weather stayed cool, he considered. He hadn't prepared that for a while. Bacon, Swiss cheese, cheddar cheese, and, of course, linquicia, along with some light cream, eggs, butter, and onion were the necessary ingredients. Yes, he had everything on hand. That would have been a good hot dish to serve at the Landons', but Jo didn't want anything hot. Too much money and fuss, she had said.

Ah well. What else for the restaurant? Curried chicken breasts with a yogurt-based sauce, garnished with kiwi fruit. A little chutney on the side, basmati rice, and a few sprigs of mint. Good thing he had a flourishing herb garden, Frank proudly boasted to himself.

Now, for something unexpected...he thought and thought and thought. Ginestra, egg-Marsala soup! Easy to make, too. Just chicken broth, egg yolks, dry Marsala, cinnamon, butter, and nutmeg. But it tasted so good and the preparation time was short.

Now the ideas were flowing. He wrote them down in a blue-lined spiral notebook. Veal pizzaiola, a traditional Italian sautéed veal dish with mushroom, onion, white wine, and marinara sauce to which he would add olives and artichoke hearts. A fish/seafood stew was always well received, depending on what the boats brought in. It was always important to have seafood along with a fish-of-the-day offering, perhaps this week with lemon and capers.

The ringing of the telephone broke Frank's concentration.

"Guess who this is?" said a deep, booming voice on the other end of the line.

"Tom? Dick? Harry?..." responded Frank, trying to play the caller's bluff. "Or maybe all three?"

"It's Mike, Mike Hammil from Boston. I used to come to your restaurant on the Hill all the time. Do you remember?"

"Yes, Mike..." Frank said, recalling a handsome, muscular man with close-cropped, sandy-colored hair and a bushy mustache. "I remember."

"Well, guess what? I'm now a fellow townie. I'm staying with some friends, waiting for some housing to come through, and I heard through the grapevine about your new magazine. Thought I'd give you a call and see if I can get in on the ground floor because that's the kind of work I like to do."

"Heard about my magazine?" replied Frank in disbelief.

"Yeah. Sean Gilligan over at the Cowboy Club was talking about it. Said you were going to take the town by storm."

"That's an exaggeration if I ever heard one," said Frank, now amused. "You used to do PR for one of the colleges, didn't you?"

"Right. I got laid off. Sued them for discrimination, being HIV-positive and all, and now I'm on disability so I don't need to earn a lot of money. I just like to keep busy, keep my hand in things. You understand."

"I understand.... So tell me, do you still eat up at F.J.'s?" Frank asked, curious to hear news of his old restaurant and the old crowd.

"Occasionally. The food wasn't as good after you left, but the panache was still there. And now they have this new chef, Manuel, and they're serving Cuban cuisine, which is different. I hear Jake is on the outs with his honey, but I think the business partnership is still going. Rumor has it that Jake is making it with Manuel. But I kind of lost track."

"What about Jake's health? I heard a rumor...."

"Jake is healthy as a horse, as a matter of fact.... One thing my friend, Keith, told me was how he was in the bar late one night and in comes Jake, bragging about how his tests came back negative for HIV and he was giving everyone drinks on the house, which I think was in very poor taste. Such a selfish son of a bitch. I remember how he dumped you behind your back. But you're doing well, aren't you? Sean was telling me how the Indigo Inn is *the* place to eat."

Frank's head was spinning. So Jake hadn't given him the virus. Jake was clean. Not honest, but also not spreading the disease. So where had Frank gotten it, then? Park Drive near the Fenway, that time he'd been so depressed? It was New Year's, right after he knew it was over with Jake....

"So, Mike...," he said to keep the conversation going, although he longed to hang up the phone and just think. "I have no doubt you're a good writer. My question is, would you be willing to sell some ads? We need to get some money together."

"I could try. I've never really been a salesman before, but it might be a good way to meet some people in town, get my bearings in the community."

"Great. We'll have to get together and talk about this some more after I get through the funeral I'm catering tomorrow...for Sonny Carreiro. You've heard about the murder and all?"

"Oh, yes. I've heard all the stories. Wealthy native gets shot in the head. Estranged wife, feuding business partner...I've heard all about it."

"So how are you feeling?" asked Frank, realizing the world did not center on *his* problems and that he should be a little more solicitous. "You sound in good spirits."

"Well, I take a lot of pills, a lot of those different combinations. I have alarms that go off on my wristwatch to remind me it's time to take some pill or other. So far, so good. Some people have gone into complete remission. I can only hope and pray that happens to me. The support group helps a lot. I go to meetings a few times a week, and it helps to know I'm not alone."

"How about giving me a call after the weekend, then. Oh, what's your number?"

"6708," Mike replied.

"Great. We'll talk then," said Frank, hanging up the phone.

What a relief, Mike thought to himself. He now had something else to do besides go to those damn meetings and filling out forms, something to take his mind off of himself. If he could only keep busy, maybe he wouldn't be thinking all the time about dying."

Frank hated the fact that he obsessed some days about where he had picked up the virus. It wasn't as though it mattered, he'd always tell himself. Once you've got it, you've got it. What difference does it make other than if he knew who the person was, he could try to stop that person from infecting someone else. But it was probably no one he really knew...just a faceless someone in a dark car on a desperate night, someone as seduced by the idea of anonymity and risk as Frank was at the time. Power...it's really all about power. The power to attract. The power to create desire. The power to give joy and satisfaction to somebody else. Even if it did only last a few moments.

Now those days were over. Even when he played with himself in the shower, even when he reached orgasm, he couldn't wait for his semen to be washed away, down the drain under the pressure of the hot water beating on his thighs, because he felt it was unclean. It was a part of himself, nothing to be ashamed of, but now it had been contaminated... the bearer of death and disease.

So it was better to be pure, to think of other things, to concentrate on the spiritual side of himself. And some days, Frank liked to think of this as a blessing. He could force himself to try and be a better person through his actions, to make each day count and to savor each moment. Some days he even forgot. But now, after his conversation with Mike, he was remembering....

Annie looked at herself in the mirror as she brushed her hair. It was a little flyaway, too much static electricity. Maybe she should have used more conditioner.... And she looked tired. The partial circles beneath her eyes were more pronounced today than usual. She opened a tube of moisturizing cream and dabbed some on her face. What day of the month was it? She knew it was Wednesday, but what was the date? Had it been more than four weeks since her last period? She went to the calendar on the kitchen wall and checked the previous month for the date she had marked as the beginning of her cycle. She counted out twenty-eight days. She was now four days late.

It had been intentional, not to have written down the day she was due, just so she wouldn't be waiting and worrying. Wasn't it just yesterday or the day before that she'd been bemoaning the fact that it was taking so long to conceive a baby, and now.... She'd wait one more day and do a pregnancy test.

Beau would be so excited. Annie couldn't wait to tell him. No, she wouldn't tell him until she was certain. Why raise false hopes? Several times into the third week of her cycle she'd been sure this was it, and then the following week her period came. What a disappointment. But this time she was actually late. This could be it. "Hang on, baby," she told the potential life inside her and smiled. Annie had her own private secret, a spark of life, a spark of love. This shared life, this shared love would make their marriage different. Maybe Beau would now learn to curb his short temper. She did love him...short temper, inflated ego, and all.

So far, her morning had been productive. A new form was taking shape on her worktable, a reclining woman that Annie imagined to be staring up at the stars. Perhaps she should construct a mobile hanging above with stars hanging down? But that would be tacky, wouldn't it? It would have to be done right. First things first, though. She needed to complete the woman and then see. That's what she liked about creating...the act of deciding, of judging, of experimenting, until just the right balance was achieved.

She rinsed her hands in the sink one more time. Looking down at them, she noticed a tiny bit of clay was still embedded around her nails.

She got out her nailbrush and scrubbed with some soap until satisfied she'd done the best she could. Then it was time for the hand lotion.

Hope I didn't get any clay on my face, Annie thought to herself. That's what came from worrying about dark circles and wrinkles around her eyes before making sure her hands were really clean. Served her right, she supposed. Why did she have to be so vain?

Annie was always chastising herself for spending too much time on her appearance when time was so precious. It amazed her that some women could spend hours on beauty treatments...manicuring their nails, setting their hair, shaving their legs, and applying makeup. She used her hands in her work. She burrowed them in clay. She cooked and cleaned. Certainly she couldn't spend time worrying about chipping her polish or breaking a nail. How did all those other women do it? Her only indulgences were taking care of her hair and skin, and choosing and wearing clothes that had flattering colors and textures.

What should she fix herself to eat? Would Beau be coming home for lunch? She tried to remember what he had told her early in the morning, while she was still half asleep, after they'd made love. Five thirty in the morning, when it was still dark, he had been all over her, warm and passionate. She liked that feeling, the feeling of drifting in and out of sleep while being caressed and stimulated to orgasm. That's when he had entered her, just as she had hit her peak, causing her to climax over and over again. And then she'd ridden his wave, accompanied him on his journey, until he had reached his apex and filled her with his sperm. A few wipes with some tissue and she had quickly fallen back into a deep sleep, while Beau had bounced out of bed and gotten into a hot shower.

What was it he had whispered when she was starting to fall back asleep? Oh, something about not seeing her until the afternoon, when they would stop by the funeral home. It wasn't enough that she had agreed to attend the service at Saint Peter's; he was also going to drag her to the visitation. She'd have to say something to Sonny's family. But what? "I'm sorry for your loss"...that's what they always said on TV shows. It sounded innocuous enough, but what did it really mean?

"I'm so sorry," Annie had wanted to say at the post office when she noticed Tanya Phillips, whose teenage daughter had just died in a car accident. "My heart goes out...." But she hadn't been able to get the words out, and instead merely stood there and stared at Tanya as she fumbled with her keys to open her box. She was sure that Tanya could feel her stare. She turned to face her for a moment, their eyes met, and still she couldn't walk towards her or say anything. Instead, she had quickly turned and walked away, pretending to herself that she had never intended to say anything at all.

It wasn't as if she really knew Tanya. She'd only met her in passing at a couple of gallery openings. She and her husband operated a framing shop and small gallery in the West End. And it wasn't as though she even knew what their daughter looked like, except from the blurry photo in the newspaper. "I'm sorry for your loss...." The words just sounded cold and empty.

And the words were totally inappropriate when it came to talking to Sarah. Hadn't she left Sonny? Was she planning to ever return? Annie wondered if Sarah felt a sense of loss or a sense of relief. Now there was no reason to return.

What had people said to her when her mother died? Annie remembered them speaking about what a wonderful person her mother was and how they would miss her. And they talked about her volunteer work in the community and for the church. Former students came to the wake and talked about how she had made a difference in their lives. The stories had made her both laugh and cry.

What funny stories could she tell about Sonny? He was one of the first people in town to buy one of her sculptures. He bargained down the price, though. "Don't you want your piece to be part of the Sonny Carreiro collection? One day my collection will be famous and I'll give it to a museum," he had boasted. She had only half believed him. Still, she needed the money. It was her first winter in town. She had wanted to buy a new coat and purchase more art supplies, plus buy a plane ticket to visit her family in Ohio.

A twenty-percent discount...no, she had offered him twenty-five percent off but he'd gotten forty percent. That's what a gallery would take if they were to sell the piece. Nowadays, some even want fifty percent. But she'd been satisfied with forty.

Sonny had paid in cash. Where had he gotten so much cash? From one of his tenants or from some kind of kickback? He probably didn't report the money to the IRS. Most likely, he'd just gone out and spent it. But had she and Beau always reported every cent they made?

He loved good food. Sonny was always happy to be invited to dinner, and he was crazy about her lasagna. And there were those martinis he used to drink. Vodka martinis, straight up, and extra dry with plenty of olives. At his house, he made martinis using a vintage chrome shaker with a strainer, and he always drank them out of deep cobalt blue martini glasses. "Wouldn't you like one, Annie?" he would offer whenever she and Beau visited his home. Sometimes Beau would indulge, but Annie preferred white wine, dry and crisp.

"I've got something nice for you, Annie," Sonny had told her the last time they had been to his house. It was towards the end of summer, before their final blowup fight and before Sarah had left. "An estate-bottled chardonnay from the south of France, highly recommended."

It was an excellent wine, perfectly chilled, and it had been thought-ful of him to think of her when shopping at the liquor store. Sometimes Sonny did surprise her. Sometimes he wasn't such a selfish oaf. Although, at the time, she was sure he'd made the purchase as more of a bribe… to get her to take his side rather than Beau's when they talked about building plans for the new project. Yes, Sonny was a complicated fellow. Not totally bad. No one was totally bad. Just a thorn in Annie's side.

In fact, Sarah had once told her about how, every December, Sonny would go out and buy a few bundles of Christmas trees at the wholesaler in Hyannis, and then deliver them to senior citizens who weren't able to get out to buy their own and to families too poor to spend money on superfluous decorations.

"He's crazy about Christmas," Sarah would explain. "He wants everyone to celebrate. Some years, he dresses up as Santa and goes to the hospital to distribute gifts to the children who are too sick to be home with their families. He likes practicing that 'Ho ho ho.' He uses two pillows, one in the front and one in the back."

Next year, where would those nice Christmas trees come from? Maybe she could say something good to Sarah about Sonny after all. As much as Annie's relationship with Sonny had developed into a slow-burning hatred, she had to admit that he wasn't totally bad. He was a human being, with positives and negatives.

But it was in their business relationship that the negatives had outweighed everything else, because Sonny always had to get his way. He'd been ruthless. A real pain in the ass. Yet other people saw a different side. Sarah had obviously seen a different side when she fell in love with him.

Annie could try to be nice to Sarah. She must be devastated, with so much unfinished business, and she probably feels guilty about leaving town. Who was she seeing? Annie was sure Sarah was seeing someone. Call it a woman's intuition. Anyway, funerals were for the living, not the dead. So she would try to be kind to the living.

She certainly was not going to wear somber black. Black was just too depressing by itself, although everyone told her she looked good in black. Contrasted nicely with her skin and hair. But when you wore black, you needed accessories: pearls, gold, a scarf. She did have a very nice black wool skirt, short and tailored, which she usually wore with black ribbed panty hose. If she put it together with a white silk blouse or a nice pullover sweater....

Annie walked over to her bedroom and opened the louvered, bifold doors of her closet. The silk blouse was hung all the way in the back. She pulled it out to examine it, laying it out on the bed. One side of the collar had a bend in it from being pressed up against the wall by all the other clothes on hangers. That, she could iron out. But there were also two stains on the right cuff. Why hadn't she noticed them before? Spaghetti sauce, maybe? When was the last time she'd worn this blouse?

Such a slob, she lamented to herself. And it was the type of silk that needed to be dry-cleaned. Well, that ruled out this blouse. Maybe she should just get rid of it...high maintenance. Better to just own stuff you can throw in the washing machine.

She pulled a cream-colored, ribbed sweater out of her bureau drawer. Fine, she thought...and she even had some black onyx beads to wear with it, plus earrings to match.

The beads had been a gift from Garrett...Annie paused to wonder what he was doing now. It had been a long time since their paths had crossed. Wouldn't he be surprised in a year when he saw her with her new baby. *If he ever saw her.* The last time had been in Bradlees, in Orleans, of all places. She was looking at sheets. They said an abrupt "hello" to one another and then moved on. It had been a surprise, seeing him there and then. And what was she going to say, anyway? "Sometimes I miss you...?" "Sometimes I miss your silence...?" Very odd. Better to express it in a poem, or a drawing that might evolve into a sculpture. Two people together, but separate, following their own creative paths. Not easy to depict.

Did *they* ever talk about having children? Did they ever even talk about getting married? Seeing her pregnant, or with a child, it probably wouldn't matter much to Garrett. If she had really mattered, he would have reached out harder to pull her closer and make the relationship work. They had fallen into a routine, a comfortable routine, and she was still growing, still searching.

Life now was exciting, unpredictable, and often challenging. No, Beau was not perfect. No one was perfect. She had to accept him as he was, with all his imperfections, and hope that just maybe she could smooth out a few of his rough edges.

⊱━━━⊰

Today was the day she would have to meet everyone in public, at the funeral home, Sarah bemoaned. And Jo was getting really annoying. They'd all be there this afternoon: all the relatives, friends, and nosy acquaintances. And they would all come around to hold her hand and show concern. But how many of them truly cared about her? Most of them would be Jo's friends.

Sarah could hear Jo on the phone talking to her friends, acquaintances, whatever, and making arrangements, as though she were planning some festive party.

"Do you have any idea how devastating it is to lose your brother, *your younger brother?*" she would emphasize. "It gives you a sense of your own mortality," she would add, as though she was saying something truly deep. Sarah, the grieving widow, was just a minor character in the play that Jo was writing.

"Oh, that would be lovely if you brought a platter of bread and cheese, Millie."

"We loved the flowers, Betty. It was so thoughtful of you."

"Yes, if you could just help us out by serving the tea and coffee, we'd really appreciate it. My friends from the bridge club are sending a big platter of donuts and cookies. Isn't that nice of them?"

The chatter went on and on. Fortunately, Jo was then gone from the house for a while, over at the hairdresser's making sure she looked perfect for today's late-afternoon and tomorrow's events. Sarah was surprised her mother, Emma, hadn't gone with her. The involvement in gossip and preparations seemed to be contagious, and Emma had gotten right into the spirit, worrying about where people were going to sit when they came back to the house from tomorrow's funeral services and what she was going to wear.

It was like a dream, one long unfortunate dream that had no ending. Only the children seemed to be acting somewhat normal. They continued to bicker with one another and scheme about when they could go off roaming on their bicycles or shopping downtown or having a bite to eat at some restaurant.

Sarah had continually reminded them that this wasn't summertime and many of their favorite stores were closed, but that didn't stop the girls.

"We know Marine Specialties is open," Cassie kept insisting. "Remember the time we got those neat army capes and the emergency rations? I know they're open year-round, Mom. We did used to live here all year, you know, and I promised my friend, Sheri, I would bring back something neat."

"Mom, I'm getting so tired of Aunt Jo's cooking. She uses too many spices or something. And all those casseroles people have brought us are getting boring. Can't we go out for a hamburger? Can't we go to Sally's Chowder Bowl?" Stephanie started nagging. "While we're here, we have to have some real New England clam chowder, and you know how I love to look at that giant stuffed lobster they have on the wall."

For now, the girls were upstairs playing Monopoly, which they'd retrieved from their former house. It would have been impractical to drag all their possessions to Virginia, so Sarah had left some things behind. They rarely played much Monopoly except during snowstorms or when they went on family skiing trips, but this morning they seemed to be absorbed in the game.

Sarah had not wanted to go back inside their old home. She'd put it off for as long as possible, but finally forced herself because it was something she had to do sooner or later. She needed to sort through all the closets one more time, evaluate what paintings, furniture, and housewares to keep, and then maybe, just maybe, an auction house would come and haul it away and get it sold in one fell swoop. There were a fair amount of antiques, so maybe one of the major Up Cape auction houses would be interested; if not, there were so-so ones that

sold "not so great" things. Some way or other, she was going to liqui-
date and start all over again.

Bill was right. Sarah had no intention of being involved in any of
Sonny's business. His real estate, his insurance agency, that was all part
of Sonny's world. They were enterprises that existed long before she
had come into his life.

"So what are you going to wear?" Emma asked, disturbing Sarah
from her reverie. "Did you want to go out, get something to eat, and
then get dressed? It looks to me like you need to get out of the house and
get away from the Carreiro sphere of influence for a short while."

Her mother's voice had surprised her, because she had not so much
as heard her creep down the stairs in her chunky, raised-heel shoes,
which usually made so much noise. Perhaps the carpeting on the staircase had muffled the sound, Sarah reasoned. Plus, she obviously had
been absorbed in her thoughts.

"Where do you think we're going to go?" she asked her mother.
"It's already pushing towards eleven o'clock."

"Isn't something open in Truro? This town gets awfully claustro-
phobic after a while."

"Tell me about it. And we've only been here a few days. That's just
the way it is. If you want a change of scenery, you head up to Orleans
or Hyannis...and, as I recall, didn't you do that yesterday?"

"It's a shame you didn't come with us, then."

"And be cooped up in a car with Jo for a good portion of the afternoon? No, thank you."

"Oh, she's not so bad once you get used to her, and she *is* being a
good hostess."

"Yes, she knows how to arrange things. That, she's good at. But
still she gets on my nerves, as I'm sure I do on hers."

"The thing you have to keep remembering is that it will all be over
soon," said Emma, "and then we'll all be going home."

"Home? *Home* is where the heart is," Sarah said, with her voice
starting to crack. "I've got no heart. There's a big numb place where
my heart used to be. And now I'm cold, so cold that I ache. I never
should have left. Poor Sonny, here in this town all by himself, without
his wife and girls. He died alone."

"He died so fast," Emma corrected her. "He didn't know what hit him. The medical examiner said he died instantly. He felt no pain. He didn't suffer."

"Of course he suffered. He suffered all those months we were gone. You didn't see him. You didn't see his face when we came back over Christmas. The way he looked when we packed up again to leave...."

"But that's why you left, isn't it? To get him to change or perhaps make some kind of change in yourself? You wanted your marriage to be something better. You told me so. You told me if it couldn't grow, and you couldn't develop into more of an independent person, you wanted out. Maybe that would have happened over time. Maybe things would have worked out. But it's not your fault. You can't blame yourself. Blame the murderer. Blame fate. But it has nothing to do with you."

"I should have seen it coming. I should have known his life was in danger."

"Now you're talking nonsense, unless there's something he told you that you didn't tell me or the police."

"No, he certainly did not tell me anyone was stalking him, planning to kill him."

"Well, there you have it then. It was nothing anyone could predict. It's just something that happened in this crazy, mixed-up world of ours, and maybe one day you'll look back on it all and decide it happened for the best."

"Excuse me. No one's death is for the best."

"That's not what I meant, and you know it," Emma retorted.

"Well, I don't even want to know what you did mean then. Why don't you go back upstairs, fix your hair, and I'll call you when I'm ready to go out, if and when I think of a place," Sarah told her defiantly, deciding it was time she started bossing her mother around and treating her like a child, rather than the other way around. How could her mother be so insightful one moment and so insensitive the next?

Sure, that's what they did in some novels, kill off the hero or the heroine before the protagonist had a chance to make a choice. The device was particularly effective in love triangles. But this was not a love triangle. This was real life. There was no third person...that she was aware of. Her other lover, her brief affair with Fran, didn't count. Fran had only been an agent of change. If Sonny had made love to anyone in her absence, it made no difference. The bond, the commitment, had been between the two of them: "For better and for worse, in sickness and in health, till death do us part" had still been there.

What would she say to Sonny if he were still alive to hear her? "My darling, I've come back. Somehow we'll work things out...." No, she wouldn't say that. She didn't want to move back to Provincetown. She wanted him to move away, to make a new life somewhere else, to break the bonds that tied him here, to move beyond the realm of this one small town and into a larger world.

Emma moved slowly back up the stairs to brush her teeth. Her bones seemed to creak a bit. Maybe she was getting too fat, needed to lose some weight, she told herself, and then she'd get some spring back into her step. No, it was just the by-product of growing old...less flexibility. She should probably sign up for one of those senior citizens' aerobics classes, maybe do some exercises over at the swimming pool. She didn't care so much about looking young...just to feel confident instead of worrying about whether she'd trip, fall, and break her neck. Millie Sanderson...why, she broke her ankle just walking down the stairs. Twisted it the wrong way or something and had to wear a cast for weeks, or had it been months? It had to have been brittle bones. That's why it was so important to take her calcium. Emma reminded herself that she needed to take another calcium pill when she got up the stairs and into the bathroom, that and her multiple vitamin....

She was now determined to think of other things rather than anything more pertaining to Sarah and Sonny. It was too disturbing, too painful. She didn't like to see her daughter hurt, in emotional distress. It made her relive her own husband's death, even though his death had been quite different. Prostate cancer...long and slow and painful. But the years it took to fight death, and finally lose, had given them plenty of time to say whatever it was that a longtime married couple wanted to say to each other.

They'd had thirty-eight years together. That was quite a long time. He had been thirty-four and she twenty-five when they first married. He was handsome then, with a full head of hair, and quite thin. She was thinner then herself. But they'd grown older together. One child, only one, but two grandchildren. It would be five years next month since his death. Five years sounded like a long time, but when you're sixty-eight years old, five years is like yesterday.

Jo was not the only one at her favorite beauty parlor, Rags to Riches, which was tucked away in the back half of a condominium complex on Commercial Street, a bit west of the center of town.

It was a shame, she thought to herself, that chubby, uppity girl, Margie Adams, just *had* to be here at the same time, getting one of those putrid, smelly perms."

The smell of ammonia was overpowering, but at least the person getting the perm, Margie Adams, didn't travel in the same circle and wouldn't be paying much attention to the kind of color Jo was having applied to her roots. Not that she cared if people saw her, with the strips of aluminum foil and glop, getting highlights. But she hated for people to see the amount of gray that was growing in amongst the hairs on her head. So she tried to cover as much as she could, asking her stylist, Mona, to just leave a stray gray hair out here and there to make it appear natural.

"I don't know, Jo," Mona had said discouragingly at her last appointment. "The gray in your hair is getting more and more difficult to cover. Have you ever thought about backlighting? We could pull some of it through a cap and let the rest go natural."

"Nonsense," Jo had told her. "It looks fine. Just keep doing what you're doing. Why don't I come in every other week instead of every three weeks."

"It's fine with me, although we may want to go with a shorter cut. You don't want dried-out ends," Mona had advised. "You could also choose a lighter shade so the roots aren't so obvious. Dark brunettes always have to color their hair more often than blondes, because of the roots."

"No way do I want to go blonde," Jo decisively replied. "Then I'd look cheap and flighty, trying to be something I'm not."

Mona had smiled politely. The customer is always right, she told herself. The customer is always right. It was her mantra. It was the code she lived by while at work. Give them what they want. Tell them they look beautiful. They certainly don't want to hear anything else.

Mona, a straight woman, was a rarity in a town crawling with male beauticians. Her clientele was primarily the locals, particularly the senior-citizen crowd, which provided her with a steady customer base. There was no shortage of beauty parlors, which offered every-thing from pedicures, waxings, facials, and massages, to highlighting, permanents, and buzz cuts. Senior citizens always got a discount. They were the lifeblood of the beauty industry during the off-season because they had their hair done every week.

Jo tipped well when she was pleased with the results. She tipped well when she got more individualized service. Mona had tried not to schedule Margie at quite the same time, but business was business. Both a perm as well as a coloring required reaction time, and she needed to keep her part-time assistant busy when she was in the shop, sweeping and shampooing.

Man, that Jo Landon is a big pain in the ass, but she's also a consis-tent customer, Mona thought to herself as she recalled stories her mother had told her about Jo when they were in high school together. "Always stuck up; always thought she was better than everyone else. But she did have her loyal circle of friends and never had a problem getting a date for a dance. Some people lead a charmed life," her mother had said. "Born into money, those Carreiros, but the father worked hard."

"I think I'm done," Margie called from the other side of the room. She had already pulled apart one of the narrow, pink rubber rollers lined with paper that had been set up in neat rows all over her head. Mona longed to tell her to keep her hands away from her head and leave the hairdressing to her, but she bit her tongue instead.

"Let's see," she said, walking over to personally inspect a lock of Margie's mousy brown hair.

Losing fifteen or twenty pounds would probably do much more for her appearance than a frame of curly locks around her head, Mona was thinking. But her customers weren't paying for advice. Besides, they wanted instant gratification. A new hairstyle was so much easier than going on a diet or exercising.

"Matt's thinking of buying a new car," Margie called over to Jo. "Is anyone in the office these days to give a quote or have you closed down for a while in respect for Sonny?"

"I believe the insurance office is open this morning," Jo replied, annoyed at being interrupted from the article on window treatments she was reading in *Better Homes and Gardens*. Maybe it was time to redecorate some portion of the house. The new see-through drapes with an overlay of heavier fabric at the top looked inviting.

"But it will be closed this afternoon and tomorrow," Jo continued coldly, thinking the oafish Margie Adams didn't even have the courtesy to first offer her condolences before worrying about herself. Didn't her mother teach her proper etiquette? In all likelihood, no. Margie's mother, Sally Goodrich, always was quite casual. Not too bright, either. Always got bad grades in school. No wonder she married a grease monkey. And her daughter was no better…married yet another grease monkey who pumped gas and co-managed a gas station.

"So how's that girl working out…Susan? Think she'll stay in town?" Margie continued.

"As far as I know," Jo responded. "I try not to get too involved in the insurance business. I've got other things on my mind," she stated, attempting to end the chitchat and get back to her magazine.

"Isn't Susan a trained beautician?" Margie asked Mona, who was busy taking all the rollers and papers out of her hair. "She's quite a looker, don't you think?" she continued, waiting for Mona's response while knowing very well that Jo could hear.

"Yes," Mona replied. "She helped out some over at Hair and There, making up the drag queens. I think it was towards the end of last summer. She's into the 'glamour look'…for herself, too." Mona didn't mind gossip, but she preferred not talking about the competition, the other hair salons in town. She knew it was bad business to say anything nasty; but, on the other hand, she certainly didn't want to give any other hairdresser a glowing recommendation.

"Pretty stacked, too," Margie chattered away. "I wonder if her boobs are real. She must have an awful lot of boyfriends, don't you think? Men chasing after her…?"

Margie looked out of the corner of her eyes to catch Jo's reaction. Not a clue, she thought to herself. She really has no idea her husband is playing around. But wasn't that the way with all wives…they didn't want to see clearly what was really going on?

Margie thought about her own husband, Matt. She'd put a frying pan to his head if she ever caught him screwing someone else. But he knew better. They had two kids he was crazy about. The wife always gets custody. No, Matt wouldn't jeopardize that, she reasoned.

"I think we're just about ready to comb this out," Mona told Margie. "But first let me check on Jo and see if it's time for her wash and rinse."

The door opened and slammed shut behind April, Mona's assistant, who had just returned from the Portuguese bakery with a bag of *malassados* (fried Portuguese bread dough rolled in sugar and cinnamon), milk, and the morning's newspaper.

"Should I make a fresh pot of coffee?" she asked while setting the bag on the front desk where the telephone and appointment book were kept.

"Sure. What's left in the pot is pretty old by now," Mona told her. "But could you first wash out Mrs. Landon's hair. Use the Longee conditioner and leave it on for five minutes."

Margie glanced over at today's *Boston Globe* that April bought. Maybe it had something about the murder investigation. "Do you mind if I take a look at the paper?" she asked. "We get the *Cape Cod Times* delivered in the afternoon, but maybe the *Globe* has something different." She didn't bother to say more, figuring everyone in the room knew what she was interested in reading about.

"Hey, that's why we bought it," replied Mona, "to give customers something to read. How about a *malassado*, Margie, once we get some fresh coffee made? Jo, would you like one, too?"

"None for me. It's getting too close to lunchtime. Besides, I have to watch my girlish figure," Jo said half jokingly but with a certain amount of pride.

Margie said nothing. She wanted one of the pieces of sweet fried dough, and would probably have one...but of all the women in the room, she knew she was the one who needed it the least. It was so hard, after having her two children, getting back her figure. And was it really worth it? But she needed energy, so she grabbed a cookie, donut, or bowl of ice cream here and there. She also had a habit of finishing the food on the children's plates, whatever they had refused to eat. It was easier than throwing it away, plus she hated to see anything wasted, she rationalized.

Maybe tomorrow, or next week, she would go on a diet, one of those high-protein diets she'd read about in *Family Circle*. That type of diet didn't sound too depriving. But in the meantime, she would eat as she pleased. Matt had always said that he liked a woman with "meat on her bones." And he didn't seem dissatisfied with her weight.

Margie opened the newspaper and turned to the local and regional news pages. Sure enough, there was a story, even though just a short

piece, which quoted the state trooper who was working on the investigation, as well as the Provincetown police chief, saying they were still
gathering evidence and conducting interviews about the case. "I feel
we've made some progress in our investigation, and I'm confident that
in the next few weeks we will be able to make an arrest," read the quote
attributed to Trooper Marc O'Brien.

"A couple of weeks!" Margie exclaimed. "There's a murderer loose
and the police don't have enough evidence yet to arrest him? It's all
pretty pathetic, I think."

"Well, they don't want to arrest the wrong man...or woman, for
that matter," Jo said matter-of-factly while her head was pulled back
into the sink and slathered with conditioner. Leaning back this way was
really uncomfortable, she thought to herself while longing to get the
kink out of her neck, which was jammed up against the cold, porcelain
sink. Her neck and head were starting to feel chilled. The shop was a
little drafty. When the coffee was ready and she was sitting up again,
perhaps she'd have a cup while her hair was being dried and styled.

"Well, they need to arrest somebody," Margie said decisively.

16

Midday Wednesday

SEAN GILLIGAN TAPPED his foot impatiently. He had asked Frank Chambers to drop by the club for a meeting, and he still hadn't arrived. Frank was not one to be late. If they were going ahead with this magazine idea, they needed to move full force now before the start of the summer season and take the *Observer* by surprise. Instead, these others, Frank, Bruno, and Polly Smithfield, seemed to be futzing around, looking for sales reps and checking out printing prices.

So what if Fran Harrington had no interest in heading up the advertising department, as Polly had hoped. Those dammed dykes were always sticking together, trying to take over things. He would just as soon keep Polly out of it, but they needed her money. The old cow had lots of cash, and everyone knew it.

Sean, on the other hand, lived close to the edge. He took in a lot of money, but he also spent a lot of money. Maybe it was on drugs, getting high. Maybe it was on expensive dinners, or trips to Boston, New York, New Orleans, or San Francisco to play. But Sean felt perfectly justified in having no savings. Live for the moment, he always said. You can't take it with you, so spend it now.

The Cowboy Club had been a gold mine, a great concept: waiters dressed in tight chinos, vests, and cowboy hats; tea dances, where all the fellows swirled around in couples doing the two-step; and those hokey early-evening line dance lessons. Silly, but it worked.

The club became *the* place, not only for casual pickups but a place where you could take your fantasies over the edge. Upstairs were rooms where, after hours, guys could be tied up and whipped, tortured, and titillated if they so desired. In other rooms, young boys, with down still growing on their faces, could be had for the right price. Of course, drugs were easy to come by. That happened everywhere. Drugs and sex were good partners. Sean had made some profitable deals with his drug connections. If you were at the right place and time, all kinds of money could be made.

"Sorry I'm late," said Frank, walking into the bar. The door was open so I came on in. "That old restaurant patron of mine from Boston, Mike Hammil, I guess you've been talking to him or talking in general about the magazine.... Well, he called me a little while ago about doing some writing. I think I've convinced him to be our advertising rep."

"Very good," Sean said. "Would you like some coffee? I need a couple of gallons of it to get going in the morning."

Frank grinned, looking at Sean's handsome but haggard face. What was the term his father always used? "Looks like someone who's been ridden hard and put away wet." Yeah, that described Sean to a T. "Sure, I'll have a cup," Frank replied. "A little bit of poison in my veins won't be so bad. It'll give me the jolt I need to get all my cooking and catering duties taken care of. Usually I drink decaf, but I could use a little bit of caffeine."

"Sweetheart, you don't know what poison is," Sean told him boastfully. "I can tell you've lived a pretty clean and sheltered life."

"I don't know about sheltered, but us Midwestern boys like to stay pretty wholesome."

"Oh, I didn't know you were from the Midwest. Where from? "

"Des Moines, Iowa."

"No kidding. What goes on out there?"

"Nothing much. That's why I came east. Went to the University of Iowa for a year and decided to see the rest of the world. I went to a fancy culinary school in New York for six months and then moved on. The tuition was too expensive and it was too hoity-toity. I headed for Boston and got a job as a chef; told them I had lots of experience. They didn't bother to check my references."

"Hey, the proof is in what you produce. As long as you cook delicious food and the customers are happy, there's no reason to complain."

"So why did you want me to come by?" Frank asked. "Certainly not to hear my curriculum vitae."

"I just wanted to hear directly from you how the magazine is coming along because I have a feeling some cash will be coming my way and I wanted to consider whether now is the time to invest."

"Now is as good a time as any. We need some seed money to get started and we'll give you a really nice spot for your ad. The whole inside back page if you want, or the outside back cover."

"I suppose Polly will take the other spot, the one I reject, for her real estate ad."

"Actually, she's talking about having a four-page pullout section with photos of all her listings. There's no glossy, color real estate magazine here on the Lower Cape like they have in the other communities, so she's thinking her own section in the *Province Town Crier* would be a good investment. I don't believe she's worried about getting a placement on the back outside or inside cover."

"That's what I like to hear. That's what I like to hear," Sean repeated. "It gives me the confidence to go ahead with my own plans."

Although the day had been getting steadily worse, Roz knew there was one thing she might possibly look forward to: a lunchtime rendezvous with John. She usually took Wednesday afternoons off, with the paper coming out Thursday. If John was able to clear his schedule, they met during his lunch hour.

John would always take a circuitous route to Roz's house, just in case anyone was following him. He'd park his car somewhere along Brewster Street, a distance away, and would walk the rest of the way.

Sally, Roz's daughter, was still at school this time of day. But as a precaution, in case Sally decided to cut a class or came home because she didn't feel well, they'd put the chain across the front door and wedge a chair underneath the knob of the back door. The chain would prevent the front door from being opened, and the chair would either jam the back door or crash to the floor if anyone tried to enter. They wanted a warning so they wouldn't be found in a totally compromising situation.

"If she finds us here just talking," Roz would tell John, "that could easily be explained by my saying I'm doing research for an in-depth article on town government and you didn't want anyone at town hall to know about our conversation."

"It's too bad there's no moderately priced motel we could go to," John had said the first time Roz suggested they meet at her home after his family had arrived in town. "I hate to put you in a risky position."

"I don't have a jealous husband to worry about," said Roz. "Besides, there's no such thing as cheap motel around here. And in a small town like this, even if we were to go to Truro, word would spread in no time at all…we aren't exactly anonymous around here. And we're not going to drive all the way to Hyannis. So it's either here or some remote place on the sand dunes. Frankly, my dear, when the weather gets cold I'd rather meet indoors."

Roz had always thought people were being careless and stupid when they conducted cheating love affairs in their own beds. Now she could understand. Where were you going to go? Renting a motel room involved witnesses and receipts. The alternatives? In a car? Behind the locked doors of an office? Well, Roz *had* used her office, and it had worked out. But not during a work day.

The question right now was, should she give John a call or wait for him to call her? Was it better to call from here or from home? No, if John wasn't able to meet her today, maybe she wouldn't go back to the house just now. It would just be too depressing, imagining he was going to come and then being disappointed.

There was a rap on her office door. "Yes?"

The knob turned and Sky entered.

"What is it?"

"I'm usually on desk duty Wednesday afternoon, but do you mind if I leave early today? I'm feeling a little under the weather and I'd like to stop by Sterling's later."

Roz rapped her fingers impatiently on her desk. Should she exhibit some soft-heartedness today? Why not let the woman go home? Why not let everyone take a half day off, for that matter? They had all been working hard, and Sky and Elliot had both put in plenty of overtime. On the other hand, there were principles involved. Never let your employees think you're a soft touch. Never let them think you'd give anything away that they might be willing to work for. Always make them think you're watching their every move so they don't take advantage of your generosity. You gave them a job. You pay them for the work they do. They owe you.

"Okay, Sky. Just this once. I don't like to leave the office short-staffed, especially when late-breaking news may come in…and hardly anyone's going to be here tomorrow morning because of the funeral. But I realize this has been a tense week, so go ahead. I'll either see you at Sterling's later on or at the services in the morning."

The phone rang as Sky was leaving.

"Yes?" Roz said breathlessly. "Hello"…she didn't dare say "John" when Sky might still be within earshot.

"Can you get away?" John's voice on the other end of the line asked matter-of-factly.

"But of course. What time?"

"At one o'clock?"

"See you then."

Roz longed to say more, but not when her employees might over-hear something.

The important thing was that he had called and would be at her house in less than thirty minutes. She needed to get going. Was there anything in the refrigerator to eat if there was any time left? She knew there were eggs, so she could always whip up a couple of omelets. She was still on her period, but most of the flow had subsided, and she could take care of that.... How did her face look? She got out her compact. Not bad, she thought. Just a little blush, powder, and lipstick would do. She powdered her nose so it wouldn't look so shiny and brushed some pink blush powder on her cheekbones. The stick of wine-colored lipstick had fallen out of its case, but she managed to find it in the bottom corner of her purse.

Filled with small slips of paper, notes to herself, and receipts, her purse was full to the point of overflowing. Quickly, Roz pulled out a handful of papers and stuffed them in a blank envelope to be sorted later. If there was too much in her purse, she was liable to lose something when she opened it…a batch of odds and ends might just fly out and end up on the ground. It had happened before. But she didn't want to throw anything important away so she put some things back in her purse, at least temporarily. Those bits of paper she'd put in an envelope would join the piles already on her desk. Most of it was probably going in the circular file, she told herself, but not before going through it first.

Pulling on her jacket and scarf, she walked out into the main room and addressed Elliot, speaking loudly enough for the others to hear, as well. "I'm heading out to grab some lunch. I may or may not check back in before going to the visitation later to pay my respects to the Carreiros and Landons. If anything comes up, you can beep me on my pager."

"Okay, boss," he replied. "Have a good one."

Sky had already left, so Elliot couldn't give her a conspiratorial wink. He had a pretty good idea where Roz was going and who she was meeting. The spark to her step, the expectant glow in her face...why couldn't the whole world be in love all the time? Why couldn't Roz act like she was in love all the time? She was so compartmentalized, and ever since Gene's death she showed a slight paranoid fear that the world was trying to take advantage of her. In her mind, it probably was.

Roz didn't need to take backroads to get home. She drove the most direct route. Her radio was tuned to the local station, WOMR, and she turned up the volume to hear a rendition of "Babe I'm going to leave you, you know I'm going to leave you, leave you when ole summer, summer comes a rolling, leave you when ole summer, summer comes along," sung in plaintive soprano tones by a female vocalist accompanied by guitar and banjo.

She hadn't heard that song in years, Roz thought to herself. Was it Joan Baez or Judy Collins?

Strangely, though the message of "moving on" was sad, it wasn't depressing to her. Many songs had moved her to tears, more than once. Was it the words or was it the cadence of the melody that would strike her in a certain way? Whatever...Roz was determined that no one would see her cry. After Gene's death, she'd often found herself crying at the oddest moments. Luckily, most of those times she had been alone or with no one else nearby. Walking or driving, whenever there was the slightest hint of sunlight, she wore sunglasses. That way, even if just the hint of a tear appeared in her eyes, no one was likely to notice.

Roz pulled into her gravel driveway, brusquely slammed the car door, and nearly ran up the steps to open her front door. Too bad she hadn't remembered to buy fresh flowers this week for her bedroom.

There had been too much going on, she told herself, to deal with little details like that.

The sheets were clean. She had just changed them, in hopeful anticipation of a rendezvous with John. No, this was not some fancy hotel, but at least her room could look nice. She had recently bought new sheets, pure white with lacy edges, and another set in a solid, azure blue with embroidered white flowers on the edges. She needed something new, something crisp, for a fresh start at love. She had bought them at Filene's, the same department store where she'd gotten her silk pajamas. Not that she ever wore bedclothes with John, but still she thought about him when lying in bed at night.

Gene had hated women wearing pajamas to bed. "Too dammed inconvenient," he'd say. But now it didn't matter. She bought a bright red pair. They felt luxurious and comfortable and rather mischievous.

Schoolbooks were scattered across the bottom stairs. "Sally!" Roz muttered aloud to herself. Too lazy to carry her books up to her room. After hanging up her coat, rather than draping it over the banister or on the back of a chair, she scooped up the books in her arms and carried them up to Sally's room.

Roz wondered when all this clutter would stop. Probably the day she died, she figured. Because even with less children at home now, the clutter was still a problem. Realistically, though, much of the clutter was her own.

She took a peek in her bedroom and then straightened the cover on the bed. Opening the top drawer of her bureau where she kept her underwear, she pulled out a small, cotton drawstring bag, which contained her diaphragm and contraceptive jelly. It was an old trick she had used during her college days. A diaphragm could hold several hours' worth of menstrual flow.

Before returning downstairs, she checked her bedroom one more time. An empty glass and a stack of magazines she'd already read were on the nightstand. She took them downstairs.

The kitchen trash was overflowing, so she decided to take the bag outside. Some animal had knocked over the garbage can, leaving a mess to clean up.

Bending over is good exercise, Roz kept telling herself as she picked up pieces of tin foil, empty cans, and ice cream wrappers, noting that

Sally had eaten all the ice cream sandwiches *again*! Probably by the time she was finished, John would arrive.

She quickly washed her hands to remove the putrid smell of garbage. As she rubbed some scented lotion on her hands, there was a faint knock on the front door.

Face flushed and her hair in disarray, in John Murphy's eyes Roz looked simply stunning. He'd been thinking about her since mid morning...the feel of her skin, how his hands felt in her hair. Roz was so much more interesting to think about than preparing a quarterly analysis of the town's budget or reviewing the recently updated Facility Managers Report, which was an assessment of the condition, maintenance, and repairs for all town-owned facilities.

John's head ached from all the cash flow problems at the Cape End Manor. It was so difficult in a small town to project with any accuracy the number of patients who would be served in any given month, or their specific needs, in order to provide the correct staffing ratio. Those kinds of statistics were necessary for getting all the mandatory paperwork done and submitted to receive timely federal and state reimbursements.

Finding and retaining a top-notch nursing home director, who had the right qualifications, and the needed visionary skills and managerial experience, also seemed to be a constant problem. Was it the pay scale or the environment? What was the town doing running a nursing home, anyway?

What had he gotten himself into when he had taken this job? He'd opened up a can of worms, in so many ways, by moving here...the politics, this love affair.... But how could he compare Roz to a worm? Maybe the town politicians were all worms, but *not* Roz Silva.

The feel of her pressed up close against him, her scent, her aggressive kisses so different from Liz's...whatever the risks, they were worth taking.

"You weren't waiting for me long?" he asked with a smile.

"Time passes quickly when you have a household to run," said Roz enigmatically.

"I've missed you," he said, taking her hand as though they had been separated for months.

"Me, too," said Roz. Each knew that "missed you" had to do with how long it had been since they'd last made love. Always limited in their intimate time together, they considered their lovemaking opportunities precious.

"We've been seeing each other for over a year now," she told him as they climbed the stairs holding hands.

"That long? It seems like just yesterday that we met," he replied. Love was so fiery, so sweet, when it first began, John thought to himself, only to become a comfortable, slightly boring routine after being married for fifteen, twenty years.

"You have to use your imagination," a friend had told him. "Think of sexy things when you're doing it, to hold your concentration and build your pleasure, or get a little something on the side. A little something on the side never hurt."

"All I want to think about when we're together is you, and when I'm not with you I start thinking about when we'll be together again," John told Roz.

"Why you sweet-talking hypocrite...I'm sure you think of plenty of other things besides me," Roz replied coyly. Like your wife and children, she thought to herself silently, not wanting to spoil the mood.

And if, by some strange accident, John Murphy's wife, son, and daughter should suddenly disappear, would she be happy completely sharing her life with him? Was this really what she wanted? She wasn't sure. What she did know was that it felt good...oh, he felt damned good nuzzling against her neck and putting his hands up underneath her turtleneck to unclasp the back of her brassiere.

"I think she knows," said John, lying next to Roz in bed afterwards.

"Knows?" Roz questioned with a slight quaver in her voice.

"Knows about us," John continued. "I think Liz knows I'm having an affair with you."

"Has she said anything?"

"No, she hasn't said anything. But she was at some meeting last night with a group of women who are starting a book group, and I think someone may have told her something because she was looking at me very strangely when she came home. It's just a feeling I have. She seemed cold and distant."

"Maybe she was just thinking about her evening, the books she's going to read and the women she met," said Roz hopefully, "and just wasn't her usual bubbly self."

"I wish that was the case, but I don't think it is."

"So, why did you come today? Maybe she's following you. Maybe she's having you followed and a detective with a camera is going to burst into the room at any moment," said Roz, half teasing but on the verge of feeling annoyed. "Did you want to cool it for a while?"

"Well, maybe if she believes the affair is no longer going on, just some misstep I made in the past, perhaps she'll never confront me about it. After a while, when it's no longer foremost in her mind, we can start seeing each other again."

"Are you trying to dump me or put me in cold storage for a while?"

"I don't know what I'm trying to do. I don't want to stop seeing you. I love you. But I also don't want to lose my family."

"Sounds like you're stuck between a rock and a hard place." Roz could feel her heart beating faster than normal. She gently ran her fingers through John's hair and tried to make her voice sound as calm as possible. "You realize this is all very subjective," she said reassuringly. "You have absolutely no evidence she knows...but from what you're telling me, you seem to believe everyone else in town knows."

"What I know is that one of the women in this book club group is Annie Tinker, Beau Costa's wife. She's the one who invited Liz to the meeting. She's also the one who commented to me last May at a Fine Arts Work Center opening, "I see you've made yourself right at home." It was before Liz and the kids had moved up here. You were there that evening, and Annie looked suggestively over to you when she made the comment, as if she knew there was something between us. Remember now?...that night, we talked about it."

"Anything is possible. We were bound to get caught sooner or later. Everyone gets caught, don't they? Of course, the ones who never do get caught we never hear about. They're not part of the statistical equation. If a tree falls in the forest, does it make a sound?"

John fidgeted restlessly on the bed. "Ever read *The Once and Future King*...you know, the story of King Arthur?"

"Hasn't everyone? It was one of my favorite books when I was growing up," Roz replied.

"Well, what did you think of Guinevere? Was she right or wrong to carry on an affair with Lancelot?"

"She was in love. No children were involved. But an entire kingdom was destroyed. It was the fatal flaw."

"I have a confession to make. Sometimes I think I'm a male version of Guinevere."

"Well, don't let yourself get burned at the stake because I'm not going to be able to come and save you."

❦━━⚒━━❦

The lunch dishes had all been cleared away at the Cape End Manor, and Jo Landon was with her mother, Mary Rose Carreiro, in the recreation room attempting to engage her in a normal conversation.

"I don wanna go. I'll watch de mass on television," Mary Rose told Jo firmly while shaking her trembling head up and down and strongly clenching her right fist.

"Calm down, Mother. Calm down," Jo instructed in the deepest, most commanding voice she could. She was trying to sound like Sonny. Jo was trying to act like the ruling family patriarch. Certainly, she had held the family together since her mother's health had failed, doing the most important things: Thanksgiving dinner, the Easter feast, giving to all the right causes from the coffers of the Carreiro family business....

Wasn't there a plaque at the Heritage Museum with the Carreiro name on it? Why was her brother always considered so much more important? They'd favored him because he was the male, of course. He had the name, the family name, and he was carrying on the family line.

"*Eu nao me sinto bem.*"

"Don't talk to me in Portuguese, Mother. I can't understand you."

"You should understand Portuguese. It's our native tongue."

There was no use arguing. Jo wanted to continue discussing the basic reason why she had come. While gathering her thoughts, she looked around at her surroundings. In the center of the room was a large television, tuned in to a soap opera...and no one but the staff was watching. Facing the TV was a lumpy, dark brown couch with two matching chairs, a scratched-up coffee table covered with magazines, and three patients seated in wheelchairs. There was only one word to describe it: *depressing!*

"When I get too old to take care of myself," Jo would often pray, "please, God, let me die in my sleep." To be warehoused with all these other old and sickly people, all being fed the same food, being led through the same routine day after day.... Jo likened it to being in prison.

Yet Mary Rose seemed reasonably happy. She liked being with her friends. Her old classmate, Catherine DeSousa, was in the room next door, crippled with arthritis and half blind from glaucoma. On good days, when Mary Rose felt like talking, Catherine would listen. Those two would giggle like schoolgirls. John Milard, president of their high school senior class, was down the hall recovering from his second heart attack but dying of prostate cancer.

"It's a regular class reunion," Mary Rose and Catherine would repeat to one another. "A regular reunion."

On other days, the nurses had told Jo, Mary Rose would be quite unsociable, totally disagreeable, and stubbornly refuse to eat, drink, or take her medication. No wonder she looked so pale and skinny.

The alternative for Jo was to bring her mother home. No, she couldn't do that...too much trouble, too much aggravation, and too much work, even with the help of a visiting nurse. Her mother now needed help doing everything from reaching for a glass of water to going to the bathroom. It wasn't as though she had a few months left to live and Jo would be bringing her home to die. No...despite the stroke and senility, the woman refused to let go of life. She might live for five or even ten more years.

"There is no mass on television, Mother, on Thursday mornings," Jo repeated.

"Holy Thursday. Holy Thursday."

"Tomorrow is not Holy Thursday, Mother."

"Who killed my Sonny? Did that *bruxo* kill my Sonny?"

"What *bruxo*? Who are you talking about?"

"That Jewish woman pretending to be his wife."

Jo shook her head, convinced at this point that she was wasting her time. This was not a good day. But she had to make the effort. She had to at least try. She looked down at her pink polished nails; fortunately, none were chipped. They still looked pretty good, as did her hands... unlike her mother's. Mary Rose's hands were brown, wrinkled, and heavily veined. And she never did bother with polish.

Jo *could* hire one of the nurses, maybe Ellen Macara, to help transport Mary Rose and look after her during the funeral mass. But seeing as how things were, it was probably better to just leave her mother where she was. She would only embarrass everyone with her rantings and ravings, anyway.

"Did you walk Lucky today?" asked Mary Rose, breaking Jo's concentration. "He needs his exercise."

"Lucky died ten years ago, Mother. He was a good dog, but he's dead."

"He's a good dog. You need to take care of him. He'll protect us from strangers."

"Mother, I'm going to go now. I have things to do. I'll try to come back tomorrow, maybe in the late afternoon."

"You get going, then. I've got my own things to take care of."

With her good hand, Mary Rose pulled her rosary from the pocket of her faded, navy blue knit dress and started saying some "Hail Marys." The dress hung loosely on her form, emphasizing her thin, bony figure, but she didn't care. Others could wear slacks, but not Mary Rose... she was a *lady*, and only dresses would do. Soon it would be time for their afternoon snack: juice, tea, pudding, and cookies. If she moved the right side of her jaw just right, cookies weren't a problem to eat. Perhaps today they would be chocolate ones.

No, she didn't want to go to no funeral. No, she didn't want to go out anywhere. Too much bother. Yes, Lucky was a good dog, if only to annoy the hell out of Jo. That girl never liked dogs, didn't like animals... too much of a selfish creature herself.

17

Mid Wednesday Afternoon

DRESSED IN A NAVY BLUE KNIT, empire-waist dress, which barely covered her knees, Susan Stafford was one of the first dozen guests to arrive at Sterling's Funeral Home for the afternoon visitation. The dress had been custom-made by Amy Stevens, a friend of Susan's when she lived in Key Largo, to accommodate Susan's large bust. "It has to be well tucked-in underneath the chest," Amy had explained. "Otherwise, it will make you look fat. An empire waist is great device for camouflaging, you know, when your belly sticks out a little bit."

"How about when your belly sticks out a lot?" Susan had jokingly asked.

"Just don't get pregnant," Amy had advised.

"What kind of fool do you think I am?" Susan had countered. Sure, one day she'd like to have a few kids. But it would be good if she had a decent husband first, if she could ever find one, and definitely not someone like her ex-husband.

The funeral director, Arnold Sterling, greeted her at the door with a big smile. Susan wondered how he could possibly be smiling at a time like this, and then it dawned on her the hefty sum of money he made each time he provided funeral arrangements. Of course he was smiling! Death was a profitable business. He then ushered her into the visitation room with a practiced look of grave concern. "The family and friends are in here," he told her.

Susan glanced around the room and regretted she hadn't smoked a cigarette before going inside. Maybe she could quietly turn around, go back outside, have a smoke, and then walk back in.

Sky Johnson, one of the reporters from the newspaper, looked in Susan's direction and waved hello. Sky was standing with Sarah and holding her hand. How touching, Susan thought. Isn't she the one who writes the astrology column, one of the few things worth reading in that paper…along with the classifieds, movie schedule, and tide chart? Susan could do without the political bickering back and forth that was always printed in the *Observer*. Week after week, it all started sounding the same. She wondered if they were aware of that.

Her eyes surveyed the room. She needed to see where they had placed the coffin so that she could be certain to avoid it. There it was…in its own little alcove on the far side of the room. Now, that was tasteful on the part of whoever designed the building. It was always so miserable to attend a visitation, out of a sense of duty, and be confronted with a corpse as soon as you entered the room. She had no intention of looking in an open coffin ever again.

Once, when she was sixteen years old, she had looked. It was her Uncle Henry. And once was enough. Her poor cousins…the figure in the coffin was a wax mannequin…not the cheerful, friendly uncle she'd known. Aunt Betty had actually made them kiss it…kiss that freakish-looking imposter dressed up in her late uncle's clothes. Oh, it was awful!

In order to get her mind off such unpleasant thoughts, Susan focused her attention once again on the person standing with Sarah. A friendly girl…Sky. That's her name, she now remembered. Sky…she must have had hippie types for parents to give her a name like that. Very mousy, and definitely should lose the glasses and shapeless dress, Susan thought as she waved back before turning around and heading outside for some fresh air. No, she wasn't quite ready to go have a "good cry" with Sarah and the rest of the family.

Sky put the hand she had waved with back inside one of the pockets of her paisley print dress and turned her attention again to Sarah.

Sky was wearing one of her favorite dresses, although she probably should have touched it up with an iron. She always felt graceful in it.

The long skirt that flared out at the bottom...that's what did the trick. But she should have worn heels. Instead, she was wearing practical, lace-up flats. Her husband, Bud, called them Buster Browns. "Why can't women wear pretty shoes anymore," he would complain, "instead of those homely, heavy things?"

What did men know, Sky had always reasoned. At least these were dressier than tennis shoes. And it wasn't as though she'd be sitting down. No, she would be standing. They never had enough chairs at these kinds of things. She should be comfortable.

Physically, maybe Sky was comfortable, but emotionally she was barely holding together. Perhaps that's why she couldn't bring herself to move from where she was standing, holding Sarah's hand. They had hugged. They had cried. Now she couldn't quite bring herself to let go, perhaps knowing that the connection between her and Sarah was fragile indeed. They were not close friends...hadn't really been friends at all, just acquaintances. Yet Sky felt that now she knew Sarah fairly well, if only because she had written Sonny's obituary. Besides, how many friends did Sarah have?

Sky cast a glance in Bud's direction. She'd had her doubts about dragging him along. How well did he know Sonny, anyway? Well, one time Sonny did hire out their charter fishing boat, *Blue Moon*, and he had recommended it to some clients, folks he'd sold real estate to...the Benningtons, who lived a few doors down from the Landons. The husband was a CEO in one of those software companies, and they'd been regulars, chartering the boat for tuna fishing several times last season when their important customers or business associates came to town.

So, no, Bud didn't mind coming along. "What else do I have to do this time of year except maintenance work on the boat or the house, and it's good to take a break," he'd said. He seemed totally oblivious of the coffin, the tears, and the large urns filled with flowers. There he was, chatting it up with Charlie Sousa, or Captain Charlie as everyone called him, owner of one of the few remaining commercial fishing boats, the *Captiva*. He'd been an old friend of Sonny and his father.

"Docking fees these days," she could hear Charlie saying, "are highway robbery. They take our money, but what do they do for the fishermen? One of these days, the town is going to have to spend some major money on capital improvements, like fixing up the wharf before it falls apart."

"So, you like living in Virginia?" Sky was asking Sarah after having half listened to her talking about how well Stephanie and Cassie were doing in school. Why was it that people who had children, especially women, had a tendency to talk mostly about their children's sports, school, and musical activities whenever they made small talk at gatherings? Is that all they had on their minds? It was a frightening thought. In this case, however, Sky considered Sarah's talk about her girls to be somewhat of a diversion; after all, she needed something positive to dwell on, something to make her life worth living. And that's what children were for. To many people, children added value to their lives.

With no children of her own, Sky wasn't particularly interested in hearing about the new method they had for teaching geometry or about the wonderful community soccer leagues in Sarah's new community. It didn't apply to her. One day maybe, but she was in no big hurry to add children to her life. Things were fine the way they were.

And children needed stability. You never knew what was going to happen in a parent's life. They might just get frustrated and start hitting people, like her father had done to her mother. They might start hurting members of their own family. And when you tried to stop them by walking out the door, they might feel so devastated that, like her father, they'd put a gun to their head. Maybe it was better to just leave the job of rearing children to somebody else.

"In the long run, I'm not sure where I'd like to live," Sarah told Sky. "Living with my mother has been convenient, as far as her watching the girls, but it's temporary. I'll have to see how the job market develops."

Standing to the left of Sarah was Henry Westin, the older half of the Westin and Son team, most likely the Carreiros' lawyer, waiting to say a few words to the grieving widow. Tall and broad, with a flushed face and full head of wispy, white hair, he was dressed in a white shirt and dark suit.

"My dear Sarah," he said, edging his way between Sky and Sarah. "I want you to know how sorry I am. Of course, you'll have to come to the office in a few days for a talk. I'm sure Rick would like to express his concerns, as well," he said, gesturing in the direction of Rick Westin, who was on the other side of the room talking to Peggy Noonan's attractive daughter, home from college. "But in the meantime, if there's anything I can do," he murmured in a confidential tone, "you know we're here for you."

Sarah gave him a superficial smile. One had to be nice to their lawyer, but she strongly suspected that any time he spent assisting her would be followed by a bill. There were, of course, some legal matters he could help her with, the paperwork for the estate and all, but that could wait.

Moving towards them was Ernie Martin, president of the Cape and Islands Savings Bank, with his wife, Rachel. "So sorry for your loss," said Ernie, holding out his hand. "He was a good man. This is a tremendous loss to the community."

"I remember when Sonny was just a little boy," said Rachel, nervously smiling in her black-and-white print dress and dark pumps, evidently searching for something to say. "He was in my younger sister's class. Always very polite and a good student...."

"Help yourself to some refreshments," Sarah offered, deciding to play the hostess. "In the little room to the side over there, you'll find tea, coffee, and cookies."

Ernie had already stuck his head in the adjacent room and caught sight of the cookies. There appeared to be some chocolate chip cookies, the large, chewy kind, lined up on a tray along with oatmeal cookies and shortbread. It had been a few hours since lunch, and this type of gathering always made him edgy and hungry.

What a mess this condo project of Sonny and Beau's had turned out to be, but he knew they had insurance and everything would be taken care of eventually, as long as the thing got completed on schedule. The bank would get its money, monthly payments at the high commercial rate.

Ernie Martin's duty had been done...he'd made an appearance and offered his condolences. Now he'd go eat a few of those cookies and wash them down with a cup of coffee. Then he'd see if there was anyone he wanted to briefly talk to before going on his way.

Betty Townsend was behind the table laying out napkins and Styrofoam cups, trying to look useful and important. "In Jo's bridge club, aren't you?" asked Ernie, trying to make light conversation before piling up a napkin with cookies.

"Oh, yes. Jo is a wicked bridge player," Betty replied.

"Maybe you'd like to try one of these," offered Millie Oliviera, arriving behind the table carrying a tray of donuts. "These were just baked fresh at The Donut Place. They smell delicious, don't they?"

Which did he want? Ernie debated whether donuts were a good idea, and decided to have one anyway because they tasted so good with coffee. Jo Landon rushed over to the table and tapped Millie on the shoulder. "Maybe you shouldn't put all those out at once," she quietly suggested.

"Oh, I don't think it makes any difference, dear. Now you just leave this to us. Relax and talk to your friends. We'll worry about the refreshments," Millie told her.

"Why, Ernie!" greeted Jo, realizing he was standing on the other side of the table. "We appreciate your coming. Is Rachel here with you?"

Ernie, who had a big bite of cookie in his mouth, pointed to his wife, who was on the other side of the room talking to Henry Westin's wife, Irma.

"I wanted to find out if she was still playing golf...whether she'd like to join in with our little group next month."

"Gee, I don't know," Ernie mumbled, having quickly managed to finish chewing and swallowing most of the cookie piece. "You'd have to ask her." Grabbing for a cup, he filled it with coffee, added cream and sugar, and started sipping the hot stuff in hopes that he wouldn't start coughing from the scratchy cookie pieces still at the back of his mouth.

Jo smiled and went to find Rachel Martin. Looking around, she was pleased with the number of people who had already turned out. She almost collided head-on with Fred Boccacio, one of the town's three plumbers, as she was making her way across the room. *"Por Deus!"* she exclaimed, half angry he almost smeared her makeup. "I didn't see you."

Fred looked at Jo Landon, in her navy blue, tailored suit, accented by a gold circle pin and heavy gold earrings. He suddenly felt underdressed in his khaki pants, plaid shirt, and corduroy sports jacket. However, he was a working stiff, and in another thirty or forty minutes he'd be heading back to a job.

"So sorry, Jo," he said, trying to sound as concerned for her well-being as possible. "Are you okay?"

"Yes, I'm fine," Jo replied, while putting her hands to her head to ascertain that her hairdo was still in place.

"So sorry for your loss," Fred continued.

"Thank you for your concern," she said curtly. "Sarah's right over there if you'd like to talk to her." She pointed to Sarah, who was talking with Sky and Henry Westin. Fred Boccacio was not the plumber Jo and Bill used. They preferred Tom Veara, who had followed his father into the plumbing trade. Fred had a reputation for being more interested in the big building projects rather than taking care of people's small maintenance jobs.

Sonny and Beau had probably been using him for their condo project. That was why he was here. But as far as Jo was concerned, she needn't waste her time talking to him. "There's someone I need to speak with," Jo told Fred. "Thank you for coming," she seemed to say as an afterthought.

Henry Westin appeared to be taking his leave as Fred Boccacio made his way towards Sarah. Sky Johnson was still standing there and perhaps she would remind him that he needed to come by and fix the leaky faucet in their kitchen. On the other hand, maybe Bud had already taken care of it. He'd have to take his chances.

"Sarah," he said, shaking his head. "I'm so sorry. If there's anything you need done," he told her, "plumbing or whatever, just give me a call. I'll look out for the house for you."

Sarah nodded her head in thanks. "I think everything is okay. I've set the temperature to fifty-eight degrees. And I don't think the pipes are going to freeze now that winter's over."

"Well, I'll keep an eye out. I have a key if anything needs to be done," said Fred, sensing this was not a subject Sarah cared to talk about. Standing behind him were Gil and Margaret Hanover, waiting their turn to speak with Sarah.

"Of course, being neighbors," Gil chimed in, "we'll look after the house for you, Sarah, when we're in town. Planning to sell it, are you?"

Gil's wife gave him a slight nudge on the arm, as if to say this was not the proper time to talk about such things. "Sarah," said Margaret, "such a terrible loss. Such a fine young man."

Fred's beeper went off. "I better see who this is," he said, adopting a professional tone and pulling his beeper off of his belt to check the phone number it displayed. Maybe now was a good time to make his exit.

"Do you know if there's a phone here that I can use?" he asked.

"I believe I noticed one in the hallway as I came in," suggested Sky.

"Sonny always had a love-hate relationship with plumbers," Sarah told Sky and the Hanovers as soon as Fred left. "He was always complaining about how much they charge for the work they do. But when you need a good plumber, and you need one fast, reliability is important. And I must say that Fred *is* reliable."

"Well, I guess he's pretty good on emergencies, but on little projects...he'll put them off a long time. You need to keep bugging him. Can I get you something?" Sky asked Sarah. "How about a cup of coffee or tea?"

"A cup of tea would be great," said Sarah, feeling a little chilled. Even though she was wearing her charcoal-colored, wool knit dress, which she'd bought at an after-Christmas sale at one of the upscale stores at the mall near her mother's house, she still felt cold. Perhaps it was her legs in their sheer stockings. Underneath their covering of sheer nylon, she had the sense they were covered with goose bumps. The room seemed a bit drafty, as institutional places usually were, though in a place like this they tried to make it as warm and homey as possible. Sarah glanced behind her towards Sonny's coffin. Not as many people had been walking over to say "good-bye" as she had imagined.

She had been against the idea of a visitation at first. Jo had maintained it was a family tradition. But that was not why she changed her mind. Tradition or no tradition, Sarah needed to confirm that Sonny was really dead. Part of her preferred to cling to the memory of Sonny alive and smiling. Perhaps if she had been with him up to the time of his murder, she wouldn't have needed an open casket. But the reality was, she needed some closure...and she supposed many other people in town did, as well.

The carpet had felt thick and springy as she gingerly walked up to the casket, twenty minutes earlier, in advance of any guests, to lay her hands on the top and say her own personal prayer. He looked as though he was sleeping. But she knew he was not about to wake up. He was too pale. And when she looked closely, she could see where the bullet had entered the side of his head and where they had opened the skull and re-stitched him up. Oh, morticians were skillful. And Sonny still had his full head of black hair…but they couldn't restore breath to the dead.

Cassie and Stephanie had followed, half running after her. "I don't want to look," Stephanie had said while burying her face in the crook of her mother's arm. "But Cassie dared me to."

"You don't have to look if you don't want to," she told them firmly. "If you prefer remembering him as he was, it's okay. I just don't want you to feel I didn't give you the opportunity to see him one last time."

They had looked at each other and shrugged. "Aunt Jo said it was important," Cassie told her. "Aunt Jo said she saw him yesterday and he looked just like he was sleeping. She kissed him on the cheek and put his Saint Christopher's medal in his pocket. That's what she said she did."

"Your Aunt Jo can do as she likes," retorted Sarah, too weary to get angry. "You live on in your spirit, not through your body. Your body is not important, so you don't have to see a corpse."

She could sense Stephanie glancing towards the coffin briefly as she clutched her other hand around her mother's waist. She quickly turned her head inward and started to sob. Cassie boldly went close to the coffin, looked inside, took a deep breath, and turned to walk back to the other side of the room where Emma and Jo were standing. When Sarah turned to walk away, her arm still around Stephanie, she saw Cassie being embraced by her grandmother, but heard no sounds of crying. She must be keeping it all bottled up inside, thought Sarah.

It was too bad the girls had to be exposed to the grief and sadness surrounding their father's death. But he was their father and she couldn't shield them from it and pretend it didn't happen. They were old enough to understand. Life was not always going to be easy. You have to take the good with the bad.

They had eaten a pleasant enough lunch less than two hours earlier at the Provincetown Inn. She had forgotten about the Inn, about how few locals ever patronized the restaurants or bars there, despite the reasonable prices and lovely view. They had played tourist…she, her mother, and the girls. The Inn, situated at the far western tip of town, was almost empty. They lingered in the hallway and looked at the hand-painted murals, which depicted how Provincetown used to look a hundred years earlier.

"See, there's the town hall and the bakery," she had pointed out. "They didn't have streets and sidewalks then. It was a dirt road and a wooden boardwalk. Many people got around by boat because it was faster."

Susan was just finishing up her cigarette when Bill Landon arrived. "Aren't you a little late?" she inquired. "Shouldn't you have been here from the very start?"

"The less time I spend inside a funeral home, the better. I guess I just lost track of the time. Got here as soon as I could, Susan." He gave her a knowing smile, the kind you give to someone you know very well... intimately, the way a man could know a woman.

The reason for the delay had been his shoes. He had stopped to polish his shoes, make them look nice. They had certainly gotten scuffed up, and at a funeral, wake, visitation, whatever, it was important to look nice. With the polish, they now looked presentable but he was aware the soles were worn. He was so hard on his shoes that they always wore down quickly.

"Is Jo inside?"

"I think I saw her."

"Well, I'll go ahead in," said Bill, not wanting to spend any more time talking with Susan where people might see them. He needed to be standing by his wife, commiserating with the well-wishers who would be coming by this afternoon. It was an unpleasant business, these types of gatherings. What could you say? What can you say? Peggy Noonan greeted him as soon as he walked in the room. She had evidently just signed her name in the guestbook. "Oh, Bill," she said, giving him a hug. "I'm so sorry. What a young man. What a waste."

"Yes," he said solemnly, "I know. Thank you for coming." He clutched her hand briefly as a gesture of gratitude and looked around the room. There was Jo, Sarah, Cassie, Stephanie, and Sarah's mother, Emma. The adults were standing. The two girls were sitting. Cassie's face was buried in a paperback book and Stephanie appeared to be sketching something on a pad. Well, what else did they have to do? There were no other kids to talk to.

Over in the corner was that fat, obnoxious real estate agent, Polly Smithfield, chattering away to an attractive young man in a dark suit who looked vaguely familiar. It was Trooper O'Brien, out of uniform.

O'Brien had mentioned at the interview that he'd be stopping by. Snooping around for clues, Bill thought to himself.

Frank Chambers liked to get to events, such as visitations, early, before they got too crowded. You can't really express your feelings to someone who has suffered a tremendous loss when they're surrounded by a pressing throng of people, he felt. It was probably better to write a note, send a card. Well, he could do that, too.

By the time he'd laid out his clothes, took a shower, fumbled with the collar buttons of his shirt after completing the knot on a navy and light blue paisley tie, he looked at his watch and saw it was already past three o'clock.

Ah well. He would get there when he got there. No one in Provincetown ever got anywhere on time, he reasoned to himself while walking to his old Toyota sedan, which was parked behind his apartment complex.

The room was pretty full by the time Roz Silva arrived, just as Beau and Annie had walked in. She had seen them parking their old BMW in the parking lot. Annie was wearing a striking green woven cape over her dark clothes. As she and Beau were hanging up their wraps on the coat rack before they entered the visitation room, she could hear them talking in subdued tones. "Don't worry about it," Beau was saying. "I told you not to worry about it."

Susan Stafford was writing some kind of long-winded statement in the guestbook. Roz decided to write something in the book later. She looked around the room to see if she could catch a glimpse of Bill Landon, at the same time wondering if this would be a good time to talk.

Just as she was stepping out of the shower, after John had left to return to his office, the phone had rang. It had been Laura Evans, one her friends, perhaps the only female friend she tried to maintain a relationship with, and Roz had thought she was probably calling to ask about getting together for lunch. Laura, a marine biologist who studied whales over at the Center for Coastal Studies, had a ten-year-old daughter and a schedule almost as hectic as Roz's.

"Hey Roz," said Laura's warm, friendly voice on the other end of the line, "how's it going?"

"Well," answered Roz, "I just jumped out of the shower. I'm soaking wet and I've got a towel around my waist. I'm getting ready for Sonny Carreiro's visitation."

"Oh yes. I forgot about that. It's today, isn't it...I wonder if Jonathon and I should go. Stephanie and Katie used to be friends at school. I suppose I should offer my condolences to Sarah. But that's not why I called, and I promise not to keep you too long. Do you want to go put a robe on?" she asked solicitously. "You haven't caught that little flu bug that's been going around? No, you never get sick."

"It's okay, Laura," said Roz a little impatiently. "Just go ahead and tell me why you called."

"Remember when my house was broken into, right before Christmas, and our new computer was stolen, along with a bunch of my good jewelry, camera equipment, and Katie's piggy bank?"

"Yes, I remember," said Roz. "I think we ran the story on page five, no picture. Yes. And...?"

"Well, I filed a claim with my insurance agent, Bill Landon...I'm with Bowswell Insurance. Bill said he'd take care of everything. Several months have passed...and we're talking about approximately forty thousand dollars. I had some nice pieces of jewelry, family heirlooms, and they were all separately itemized on the policy. I started getting impatient, wondering what's going on here, so I called Bowswell directly and gave them the policy number. Guess what? They said the policy number was bogus; that the number sequence for a homeowners policy was incorrect and that I must be mistaken. Jonathon called Bill Landon, and Bill said that kind of paperwork confusion happens all the time. I don't know. What do you think? Jonathon is thinking of hiring a lawyer. I was thinking you might want to dig around for a news story."

"That does sound mighty suspicious," Roz told her friend while marveling at the fact that Bill Landon always seemed so proper and aboveboard. Maybe he was selling bogus insurance. Perhaps the illusion of propriety was created from the fact he was married to Jo. If you combined shady business dealings with a love affair on the side, those might just be the ingredients for murder. It was certainly an angle worth pursuing. Regardless, a crooked local insurance agent was always a good news story. It was something Elliot would probably like to work on, but perhaps she'd do a little groundwork of her own first.

"I think you should hire a lawyer," she told Laura. "But I'll see what we can dig up, as well. Putting the situation into the public eye usually yields fast results."

"That's what I thought," replied Laura. "I'll let you get dressed. Maybe I'll see you at Sterling's...no, I'll probably go this evening after dinner, and it sounds like you're heading over there soon."

"I like to get these kinds of things out of the way," Roz said.

"Well, say hi to 'lover boy' for me if you see him."

"You keep your mouth shut," insisted Roz, questioning her judgment in trusting Laura as a confidante. Well, she'd needed to tell someone about John Murphy. She couldn't keep it all to herself.

Regardless of her desires to ferret out another news story, Roz knew she should walk by the coffin and get the viewing over with first. She had only looked inside a coffin once before, a long time ago. A friend of her mother's had died and she had gone with her to the visitation for moral support. Roz supposed she had looked more out of morbid curiosity than because she was really interested in saying good-bye. It had all been so strange, so surreal.

Her mother's friend had been relatively young, just turned fifty, a victim of pulmonary embolism. Gail Bellflower...that was her name. Roz remembered looking down at her, smartly dressed in a crisp white blouse and suit. That was what had looked so strange, someone sleeping in neatly pressed, formal clothes. Roz's mother was proud of having picked out the suit...dark blue, her favorite color. She had wanted to ask her mother why she hadn't picked out a pretty nightgown or a lounging outfit, something the woman would be comfortable in.

But the ritual of laying out a corpse for burial was not practical. There was the pretense of dressing someone for a journey, which is why Gene had been cremated. Roz had scattered some his ashes over the dunes and the rest into the bay.

She looked down into the coffin. Sonny's sleeping face looked free of all cares. You can't take it with you, she thought to herself. All the money he had tried to make. All the wheeling and dealing. She was almost jealous at how peaceful he looked. It was the same sense of jealousy she had felt towards Gene when he died and left her with all the responsibilities of the newspaper and the girls weighing heavily on her shoulders.

"I thought I'd find you here." Elliot's voice startled Roz out of her self-pitying thoughts.

"Yes. Here I am." She turned to face Elliot, who looked fresh out of the shower, with still-damp hair, wearing a pair of dark brown khakis and a tan plaid jacket.

"Is that as dressy as you can get?" she asked, wanting to tease him.

"This is Provincetown. I've never found it necessary to buy a dark suit. That's why I live here. And if I were you, I wouldn't be so critical. Those stockings you're wearing have a run in them."

"Oh shit!" Roz exclaimed before stopping herself from making any further exclamations. "This is the first time I've worn them. They must have gotten a snag on my fingernail."

Elliot laughed. "The dress is very becoming. Dark purple suits you."

"I bought this out of a mail-order catalog about ten years ago. It goes with just about everything. To think I went to all that trouble shaving my legs, just to have a run. Typical!"

"So tell me, Roz. Who is that fellow in the nicely tailored suit over there talking to Sarah?"

"I don't know. I've never seen him before. Maybe he's the state trooper assigned to the case."

"No, that would be Trooper O'Brien. He's over there talking to Sarah's mother, Mrs. Green."

"Then I'll just have to walk over there, offer my condolences, and find out," Roz told Elliot emphatically.

John Murphy gallantly hung up his wife's coat while Liz took a peek inside the room. They were all there, she observed, many of the town's major players. How many of them knew? How many snickered secretly to themselves when they saw her walking down the street, well aware that their town manager was getting a little something extra on the side. And not just with some anonymous bimbo. No, he had to pick someone important, someone with power…the publisher and editor of the newspaper.

Maybe her power was what he found so attractive. Maybe Liz had been playing the docile, supportive wife for way too long…?

She had thought about confronting him. She had considered bringing it all out into the open after Annie Tinker let on to her suspicions the previous night about John and Roz being an item as she and Annie were cleaning up the scattered coffee cups and dessert plates following the book club meeting.

It would have been easy to rant and rave, to look wounded and act hurt. Instead, Liz was shocked and numb. This affair *had* to be the reason for all those nights he'd claimed to be working at the office and her feeling that he'd become inaccessible. And there *were* clues that she'd refused to recognize.

No wonder John seemed distracted some evenings when she had called him...as though someone else was in the room...? Well, someone *had indeed been* in the room. No wonder he'd never immediately jumped on her bones all those nights after they had been apart, all those nights he'd been supposedly working late at the office. He'd been getting laid by the fascinating Roz Silva, so what did he need with his wife?

If she confronted him, would he deny it or confess the truth and ask to be forgiven? And could she bring herself to selflessly forgive him? Was it possible that he had been working up the courage to ask for a divorce? But there were no signs of him wanting to end their marriage. He was always very affable. And he'd done nothing to displease her, except act slightly detached and less amorous.

Liz wondered what she should do. She still loved him and still wanted to be married. However, in some ways she wanted him punished. But pushing the issue could drive him away. If she demanded he make a choice, Roz or herself, he might just choose Roz. If she confronted him, perhaps he would walk out the door. She didn't want that to happen. No, she needed to think things through and plan a strategy. Perhaps the best punishment would be for her to give John no excuse to leave her....

Liz's thoughts about how to preserve her marriage were interrupted by Jo. "Why Liz, how sweet of you to come. Your lasagna was delicious. Please don't forget to sign the guestbook."

Before she could say a word in response, John came up behind her and put his arm around her shoulder.

"We thought it was important to be here, Jo. I've only been in town a short time, but I know that Sonny's death is a terrible loss to the community, and especially to his family."

"Yes, it's been a tremendous shock," Jo said in a trembling voice while pulling a tissue from the pocket of her suit and dabbing a tear from the corner of her eye, "to lose my younger brother at this time in his life...."

"I understand," John told her, putting his hand on top of Jo's.

What did he understand? Liz's eyes began to swell with tears. She was suddenly overcome by a feeling of helplessness and sadness. Looking over at Sonny's two daughters, sitting on the other side of the room and knowing that someone had intentionally ended their father's life, made Liz angry. It wasn't fair.

It also wasn't fair that Roz Silva had the audacity to sleep with someone else's husband. No, life wasn't fair at all. The tears started running down her cheeks and she quickly opened her handbag to search for tissues or a handkerchief.

Fran looked up from the guestbook she was writing in, just underneath Susan Stafford's entry, only to see Liz Murphy, standing with John Murphy and Jo Carreiro Landon just a few feet away, with tears streaming down her face. Some people just have to cry at funerals was Fran's immediate thought. Liz couldn't have known Sonny well. Maybe he had sold her some insurance. Maybe he was trying to sell the Murphys a house...."

Fran didn't want to look too hard at Liz's tears. She certainly didn't want to start crying herself. A lump in the throat was okay, but tears were messy. They smeared your eye makeup.

And the idea of laying someone out in a coffin was pretty morbid, as far as Fran was concerned, but she couldn't voice that opinion out loud. She might offend someone. Evidently, Sarah needed to do this, needed to see her husband one last time.

She looked around the room to find Sarah, and saw her standing in the corner talking to a middle-aged man in a suit who Fran did not recognize. Roz was standing with them.

That Roz was always in the thick of everything, Fran thought to herself. Just like her to be monopolizing the grieving widow's time.

Bruno Marchessi tapped her on the shoulder. "I'm very disappointed in you, Fran. I thought you'd want to come aboard on our little project."

"You know, Bruno," Fran replied, "ultimately, I really don't even want to sell advertising. I want to open my own design firm, so I really don't want to get in the middle of politics around here."

"This has nothing to do with politics. This has to do with freedom of the press, the chance for other voices to be heard."

"Whatever. I wish you well." Fran turned to move on.

Fran didn't think this was either the time or place to discuss business. Since Sarah appeared to be preoccupied, she decided to offer her condolences to Bill Landon. He seemed to have just finished a conversation with Henry Westin and looked fidgety, as if he didn't know what to do with himself.

"Bill, we've met before. I'm Fran Harrington."

Bill met her eyes briefly and nodded his head. He glanced over to where Sarah was standing and then back at Fran.

"I'm so sorry for your loss."

"Thank you very much. I appreciate your concern," he replied. "Please excuse me." He started walking towards the corner where the stranger in the suit was talking to Roz. Changing his mind, he stopped, turned around, and began walking towards Susan Stafford.

"Did I overhear you telling Sarah you were in the insurance business?" Roz asked the suited gentleman who had been so interested in talking to Sarah.

"Yes," he replied while extending his hand to shake hers. "Jerry Malgam of Malgam and Sons Insurance. We have offices in Boston and we're looking to expand to the Cape. That's why I'm here today. It was such shocking news to learn of Mr. Carreiro's murder. I had to offer my condolences to his family. We were just about to sign the final papers to buy his insurance agency."

Roz's eyes nearly popped out of her head. "But he didn't totally own the agency," she blurted out.

"Well, he and his mother were the primary shareholders, and he was her guardian...."

His words were suddenly interrupted by the blast of the fire station's siren. It went off every day to inform everyone it was twelve o'clock, but noon had already come and gone. Otherwise, it was a signal for the local volunteer firemen to man their stations.

The town was divided into five pumper stations, and the number of blasts signaled the section of town where there was a fire. The siren had now gone off one, two, three times, so it was somewhere in the center of town. The *Observer* building, constructed of wood like so many of Provincetown's buildings, was in the center of town and could go up in flames easily and spread quickly. Whenever Roz heard three sirens, she kept her fingers crossed.

Fred Boccacio ran into the room waving his hands over his head. "It's the *Observer*. The *Observer* building is on fire."

Roz felt a knot in the pit of her stomach and her face turned pale. "I need to go and see if they can save my building," she told Mr. Malgam. "Maybe we can continue this conversation later."

Because of its construction, Roz was afraid the building would burn down fast. But then she remembered she'd installed that new smoke and fire alarm system last year, at the same time she had upgraded her computers, in order to get a reduction on her insurance premiums.

"How could a fire have started?" she nervously whispered to herself. It couldn't be faulty wiring...she'd just had the wiring updated, too. And smoking in the building was no longer permitted. But she hadn't been there that afternoon. Maybe someone *had* been smoking when she wasn't around and threw their still-burning cigarette butt in a trashcan, thinking they'd put it out completely. Several of her employees were smokers.

※───ﾊﾊﾊ───※

Officer Jean Cook, who was directing traffic away from the building, told Roz, "You're pretty lucky. At the first sign of smoke, your alarm went off. There's probably a whole lot of smoke damage and soggy desks and papers, but the fellows said your building was pretty much saved."

"What a mess!" was all Roz could say. "I suppose I ought to get my photographer over here to take pictures, if she's not here already. Fortunately, this week's paper has been put to bed and it's at the printer's."

She looked over the crowd of people that had gathered and were watching the big yellow fire trucks and volunteer firemen in tall rubber boots, hats, and jackets walk around, checking the building. She recognized Kathy and Manny Jason who ran the Seashell Guest Cottages, standing along with Peggy and Bob Noonan. How did the Noonans manage to get here from the funeral home so quickly? And then there was Jesse Cronin, owner of the Windsor Gallery, along with Mitzi Jones, Aida Clementine, and Aida's friend…whatever her name was. Amongst the volunteer firemen, she recognized Matt Adams and Manuel Henrique, who were reloading the hoses back on the truck.

Officer John Rose approached her. "Roz, we need to talk to you down at the station. Have you received any threats at the newspaper lately?" he asked in a very low voice. "It looks like this fire was intentional."

Frank Chambers never made it to the funeral home. He'd caught sight of smoke coming from the side window of the *Observer* building, heard the sirens, and parked his car in the lot at the foot of Standish Street just before the fire engines arrived. The newspaper building was located on Bradford Street, between Standish and Center Streets. At first, he thought it an amazingly good stroke of luck that Roz's building had gone up in flames. It was cosmic justice that she, who seemed to have everything, fail. If she were put out of business for a while, it would give the *Province Town Crier* a head start.

Then Frank started thinking that it was all too neat. Suppose it wasn't just the fickle finger of fate that was causing the building to burn. Suppose it's arson. Who would have a motive and the opportunity? A disgruntled employee? A partner or potential investor in his new magazine?

He watched as the fire trucks parked in front of the building. The street became filled with onlookers. A barricade was set up to prevent non-fire personnel from getting too close. The crowd moved back to the parking lot. The sun would soon be setting and the air was becoming chilly. Frank reached inside his car for his winter jacket.

"It looks like the fire is pretty much under control," he could hear Norma Heller, the librarian, say to Tanya Phillips.

"It's not that I go around watching fires," Tanya was explaining, "but I was walking my dog and heard all this commotion."

"I understand," said Norma. "I was just closing the library, and, of course, I'm so close by."

Tanya bent down to stroke the head and ears of her old basset hound. "Luckily, no one got hurt. I don't see any ambulances. Come on, Lulu," she instructed her dog. "Let's go." She headed down Bradford Street in a westerly direction.

"Since when do the fire trucks get here so fast? Damn!" It was Sean Gilligan, standing there shaking his head.

"Sean, I didn't see you," said Frank. "How long have you been watching?"

Sean shrugged his shoulders. "I wonder how much damage...? I suppose we can read about it in the *Cape Cod Times* tomorrow." He reached inside his pocket, pulled out a cigarette and lighter, turned away from the wind to light it, and inhaled deeply. "C'est la guerre."

"How do you think the fire started?" Frank asked.

"Who knows?" replied Sean. "It could be something electrical or...maybe Roz set it. Maybe she wanted to collect some insurance money."

"That doesn't make much sense at this time of year, just when the summer season is around the corner."

"Maybe a disgruntled employee."

"That's what I was thinking."

"Or one of her many enemies...she must have plenty. Maybe Liz Murphy decided she'd had just about enough of her husband's fooling around with the bitch and decided to get even."

"And how would Liz Murphy know how to set a fire without anyone finding out?"

"Oh, there are ways. There are ways...," Sean replied knowingly. "For a long-term result, there's the old 'put the candle in a closet and when it burns down some nearby papers ignite.' Or you can tie a small burning candle or rag to a rodent's tail. The little critter runs around spreading the fire. It's not easy to trace."

"The poor mouse!" Frank exclaimed.

"You set mousetraps, don't you?"

"Yeah."

"Personally, I prefer the live traps. You never know when you might need a mouse."

Frank gave Sean a startled look, and Sean smiled enigmatically. "Did I tell you I keep a boa constrictor in my basement?" Sean offered. "They like live prey." His cigarette now finished, he threw it on the asphalt and stepped down on it hard. "See you around." With his hands in his pockets, Sean strode off in the direction of his club, on the west side of town.

Frank watched as Sean walked away. Strange guy...a little unsettling, he thought to himself.

Most of the crowd had dispersed and only one fire truck was left, standing by in case sparks reignited, so Frank decided to take a walk around the building and see for himself the amount of damage that had been done. As soon as he crossed the street, he caught sight of Lefty Geiger, one of the Cowboy Club regulars who at one time had dated Sean.

"Hey Lefty," he hailed. "I know this sounds like a strange question in the midst of everything going on.... But does Sean have a pet snake?"

Lefty scowled at Frank and ran his fingers through his artificially enhanced, short red hair. "Sweetheart, the only pet snake Sean has is the one in his pants," he responded with a giggle, gesturing at his own crotch.

Frank shifted his weight nervously from one foot to the other. Maybe he should have put on a hat...the air was getting more chilly. He was beginning to get a sinking feeling in his stomach that Sean Gilligan had something to do with the fire.

"Are you sure he doesn't keep a snake at his place?"

"Hey, what is this with you and snakes?"

Elliot was walking past the two, after interviewing some of the firemen on the scene, and overheard the tail-end of their conversation. "What's this about a snake?"

"Damned if I know," said Lefty. "Hey, aren't you one of those nosy reporters?"

"I consider myself to be more of a thoughtful reporter. Actually, I'm the news editor," said Elliot, holding out his hand. "Elliot Chance. You might have noticed my by-line in the paper."

"Probably. I don't pay much attention to who writes the stories, just the theater reviews. I do a lot of theater in town. You don't write any of the theater reviews, do you?"

"No, that's not my department."

"What about restaurant reviews?" Frank chimed in.

"I'm just interested in the facts, the hard facts," Elliot reiterated. "Do either of you have any idea about who might have started this fire? I overheard the police and fire chief talking, and I heard the word 'arson.'"

"I might know something," Frank blurted out. "But why should I help you with your story? I'm not exactly fond of the *Observer*. Maybe I should just talk directly to the police."

"Be my guest. If it leads to something, they're going to tell us anyway. Of course, maybe if you tell me first, I can help you figure out if it's an important lead or whether you'd just be wasting the police department's time."

Frank studied Elliot's face. He seemed like a likeable enough fellow. He reminded him a little of his friend from culinary school. It would be nice to unburden his suspicions to someone, in an unofficial capacity, because if he was wrong and pointed a finger at Sean Gilligan and he turned out to be blameless, Sean would never trust him again...and he'd definitely pull his financial backing from the magazine. Frank thought hard about what he should do. "Would you like to buy me a cup of coffee?"

Adam's Pharmacy was nearby on Commercial Street. Nothing fancy, but the coffee was good and hot. Elliot and Frank sat at the counter. It was the time of day when business was slow. In another thirty minutes, the manager would lock the doors for the evening. The girl behind the counter was vigorously washing down the kitchen equipment, having just returned from a quick jaunt down the block to Bradford Street and three blocks over to check out the fire damage. She wanted to make sure the manager didn't think she was shirking on the job, since he had allowed her to leave her post for fifteen minutes on an unscheduled break. She had given him a full report. "A lot of smoke but not a lot of fire. No one hurt."

"Thank goodness!" was his response. "I still remember the fire at Cranberry Square, just up the street. It was terrible. You were just a child then. Fire can be a terrible thing, and especially in this town where so many buildings are constructed of wood."

"You were saying?" Elliot was trying to prompt the conversation.

"Well, where should I begin?" Frank pondered aloud, uncertain as to where to start. "I'm going to be publishing a magazine. Actually, it's not really my money. I have some financial backers in town. But I guess you could call me the publisher since it was my idea. Potentially, it could steal some of the *Observer*'s advertising revenue, since they've held a virtual monopoly for so long as the only other truly local publication.

"One of my investors is Sean Gilligan. As you probably already know, he's a little off the wall sometimes, lives life hard and fast, but definitely successful with his bar and everything."

Frank continued, "I talked to him earlier today and he seemed concerned about whether our magazine would really get off the ground... because he'd decided to invest a good sum of money. Then I saw him at the fire and got the impression that he was disappointed at the lack of damage. Also, he seemed pretty knowledgeable when it came to fires being intentionally started. He even mentioned something about tying a small candle or rag...I know this sounds ridiculous, but tying it to the tail of a mouse, and how he always trapped his mice and kept them alive in case he needed one."

After taking a good swig of his coffee, Frank went on with the story. "When I did a double take on catching live mice, he then said he had a pet snake, inferring he caught mice for his snake. That's why you heard me talking about snakes to Lefty. Lefty is one of Sean's good friends and swears that Sean doesn't have a snake. That's what got me suspicious. Why would he lie unless he was covering up something? I mean, sure, he probably doesn't like Roz or her newspaper, and he may very well know about setting fires, but why lie about Sean owning a snake?"

Elliot brushed his front locks of black hair, which were once again falling forward and over his eyes, away from his face. The story sounded pretty far-fetched, unless Sean got kicks from setting fires. Arson was serious business. Were there any other reasons Sean might have it in for the *Observer* other than trying to wipe out the competition? Could Sean be connected to any other fires, fires that had maybe taken place in the last few years?

"Wait a minute," said Elliot with a start. "Didn't Sean have a business in Cranberry Square before he opened the Cowboy Club? Didn't he own a porno shop of sorts where he sold all kinds of S&M gear... magazines, toys...? And I seem to recall he even got busted a few times for selling explicitly sexual material to minors. Yes...I read about that when I was researching Sonny's business enterprises in back issues of the newspaper. Sean's was the only other business in that mall fully stocked with merchandise during the fire, other than Sonny's antiques shop. I recall the articles. Sean told the insurance adjusters he did a large mail-order business. He had plenty of merchandise to fill his orders and all his records had been destroyed. He said he suffered a huge loss. I bet the insurance people paid him a lot of money. And what did he do with it? A year later, he opened the Cowboy Club."

Elliot rambled on, talking more to himself than to Frank Chambers. "Maybe he killed Sonny because Sonny had figured out it was arson and was going to tell the police about it."

"How long is the statute of limitations on arson charges?" Frank inquired. "Hasn't it been longer than ten years? I know it took place before I moved to town."

"Let's go to the police station and talk to them," said Elliot. "Want to take a ride with me?"

Frank smiled. "Might as well. This is getting to be pretty exciting... and I thought I was on my way to a visitation. You never know how your day will turn out," he joked.

"By the way," Elliot said as he pushed open the heavy glass and metal door of Adam's Pharmacy and walked out onto the sidewalk, "I like your restaurant, even if Roz doesn't."

Inside one of the interview rooms at the police station, Roz tried to make herself comfortable. "Is the detective on the Sonny Carreiro murder case anywhere around?" she asked Officer Rose. "I believe I saw him over at Sterling's a while ago."

"We can page him," said Officer Rose.

"Well, why don't you...I need to talk with him. I think I've solved the murder case."

A few minutes later, Detectives Carl Duarte and Eddie Lema entered the interview room, along with Trooper Marc O'Brien.

"I hear you think you've solved the Carreiro case," said Duarte as he pulled a package of gum from his breast pocket, unwrapped one stick, and bent the piece in half before putting it in his mouth. "I'm trying to quit smoking," he explained to Roz and O'Brien, knowing that Lema had heard his story about giving up cigarettes many times. "Would you like a piece?"

"No, thank you," replied Roz. O'Brien shook his head.

Detectives Duarte, Lema, and Trooper O'Brien all began taking seats around the small rectangular table as Officer Rose stuck his head in the room to rejoin them. "This looks like a regular party. Maybe we should move into a larger room," he suggested.

"Mrs. Silva," Marc O'Brien said, holding out his hand to shake Roz's, "I'm State Trooper Marc O'Brien. Feel free to call me O'Brien... everyone else does. Large room. Small room. Makes no difference. I'd just like to hear what you have to say. "

"You realize," said Lema, settling his broad backside into a plastic and metal chair, "she's merely interested in being the first newspaper to print the story. Mrs. Silva is publisher and editor-in-chief of the *Provincetown Observer*," he informed O'Brien, just in case O'Brien was not aware of her identity.

"Well, that's not going to happen, is it?" Roz bitterly retorted while staring into his dark brown, almost-black, eyes. She wondered when the last time he shaved was, thinking to herself that his beard must be the epitome of what was referred to as a five o'clock shadow. The dark black stubble emphasized the dark olive tones of his skin. Now I know why I never liked this Eddie Lema guy, one of Gene's former classmates, Roz thought to herself...he came across as a regular pain in the ass.

Aloud she said, "I can't exactly publish my newspaper next week with all the computers fucked up by all that water! Oops! Excuse my 'French,' but you know what I mean. This week's paper is already at the printer's, thank goodness, and will be distributed in the morning. But I'm still interested in solving the case. If I put a few stories on a disk on my home computer, I suppose I could get a smaller, special edition of the paper put together off-site...hmm." Roz realized she was rambling and had gotten off her original subject. She looked at O'Brien, only to see he was sporting a large grin.

"You were saying...?" he prompted her.

"I was saying, I think I know who killed Sonny. And it wasn't so much about money as it was about maintaining a way of life, Bill Landon's way of life.

"Just briefly, before I was pulled away from the funeral home due to the fire, I met Jerry Malgam, owner of Malgam and Sons Insurance. He told me that just before Sonny's murder, they were about to sign the final papers to purchase the Carreiro Insurance Agency and expand their Boston-based operations to the Cape.

"Sonny, along with his and Jo's mother, Mary Rose, were the primary shareholders with controlling interest in Carreiro Insurance, and

Sonny was Mary Rose's legal guardian. He controlled her financial affairs. So if he wanted to sell the business, he had the controlling votes to do so. But there was one problem: Bill Landon. Bill didn't want the business sold, even if the new owners were going to give him a job, because before the sale was consummated they were going to have to examine the books. And what were they going to find? They'd find that Bill Landon was on the take.

"Suppose you sell someone an insurance policy, take their money, but fail to actually purchase any insurance. At first, maybe it happens by accident. You bind coverage over the phone, your customer mails you a check, and you deposit that money into your business account… but you neglect to mail a check to the insurance company right away. You discover your mistake two months later…but instead of back-dating the coverage, since you know there are no claims you start it on the date you actually mail the check. Your client has then paid for two months of insurance that you hadn't yet purchased. Who keeps the extra money? You do, of course.

"Then you start getting cocky, purchasing coverage later and later, months after customers believe their policy is already in effect. Oh, you can't play this game on renewals since they're billed directly by the insurance company. But new customers are fair game. And if you transfer an old customer to another carrier, you can do the same thing."

"Isn't there a paper trail?" asked Officer Rose.

"A lot of customers pay with cash. The agent pockets the cash and deposits the checks. Who knows what money is for what policy unless you do a complete audit? Handling all that money can be very tempting, which is why insurance agents are licensed. If they're caught doing anything questionable, such as mixing their customers' money with their own, they lose their license and they're out of a job. Most companies do a background check on insurance agents who sell their product. If an agent has a poor credit rating, doesn't pay their bills on time, lacks financial stability, it could mean trouble. It's common knowledge that people who are desperate for money steal."

"How do you know so much about the insurance business, Roz?" asked Duarte. The younger of the Duarte/Lema detective team, Carl Duarte had fine, closely cut, sandy hair and hazel eyes. Even-featured with a pink, finely grained complexion, in Roz's opinion he was too young and naive-looking to be a cop.

"My uncle was an insurance broker. I grew up in Franklin, and back when I was in high school I remember there was this big fraud case. One of my uncle's colleagues went to prison for insurance fraud, caught doing just this sort of thing. He'd gotten himself financially overextended. His wife had lost her job. He had a large family and they lived beyond their means: new car, fancy vacations, and a lot of credit card debt. So, out of desperation, he started borrowing money from his business account, only he never paid it back...and he kept delaying on mailing in premiums.

"As long as you have no claims, no one is the wiser. No one realizes they're not insured until they file a claim. Let's say they get into a car accident. People are injured, the car is totaled...and, surprise, the insurance they believed they had doesn't exist."

"What tipped you off?" asked O'Brien.

"I got a phone call from a friend, Laura Evans. She had put in a claim, through Bill Landon, for a forty-thousand-dollar loss a few months ago and he was giving her the runaround. She and her husband were getting suspicious. When I met Jerry Malgam and he told me about the pending sale, that's when I put it all together, because I didn't think fraud alone was a motive for murder, especially when Bill has always struck me as being so calm and level-headed."

"That's not what I've heard," O'Brien said with a laugh. "You see, someone else beat you to the punch. While you were checking out the fire, Susan Stafford hightailed it over to me to give her version of what happened. With Mr. Malgam there at the visitation, she could see that Bill Landon was starting to lose it and she didn't want to be charged as an accessory to his crimes."

"You better go talk to her right away before she gives an exclusive interview to the *Boston Globe*," Lema chimed in.

"I don't think she's going to be giving any interviews just yet," O'Brien told the others. "She made her statement in the presence of her attorney, Rick Westin, and he made it very clear to her that she shouldn't say anything regarding the case without him present."

"Since when is Rick Westin a criminal attorney?" asked Officer Rose. "I thought he handled mostly real estate and family law."

"Hey," said Duarte, "you know how Rick likes big-titted women. He'll study up on the criminal defense...."

All the men started laughing and then guiltily looked in Roz's direction. "We didn't mean to offend you," said Officer Rose.

"That's quite all right. I'm a big girl," Roz told them. "I guess if the *Observer* wants the scoop on Susan Stafford and her knowledge of the murder, we'll just have to send a big-breasted woman reporter to interview Rick."

"All kidding aside," O'Brien stated, "I think Mr. Westin was at Sterling's when Ms. Stafford started getting nervous, and he was the first available lawyer around."

"Whatever," said Roz. "I think the most important thing is that you've caught the murderer and he's not going to harm anyone else."

"Yes, we're in the process of issuing an arrest warrant for Mrs. Landon right now."

"*Mrs.* Landon!" Roz said incredulously.

"Yes. Well, she's the one who actually fired the gun, to protect her husband. You see, it was Mrs. Landon who was actually spending all the money, leaving Mr. Landon with no choice but to commit fraud. The woman is a compulsive shopper. She watches that Home Shopping Network program late at night and evidently orders just about everything and anything she sees," O'Brien told Roz and his colleagues. "Just go down into the Landons' basement and you'll find it filled with unopened boxes of merchandise. The woman has a weakness for diamonds, designer clothes, overpriced Beanie Babies...."

"She killed her own brother!" Roz exclaimed.

"It does happen in some families," O'Brien told her.

By the time Elliot and Frank arrived, Roz was walking out the front door of the police station.

"What are you doing here?" she asked. "Oh, hello Frank.... What's up?"

"I think we know who set the fire," Elliot said. "Frank and I were going to discuss it with the police."

"Really.... This has been quite a day." Roz longed to reveal to her news editor the murderer's identity but thought it best to keep it a secret until she got out some kind of publication. If she said anything in front of Frank, the news would quickly be all over town.

"Actually, Elliot, tired as I am, I'm glad to see you. Somehow we've got to put out another newspaper. I'm going to give some of my off-Cape newspaper friends a call. As soon as you're done here, drop by my house. I'll be working on my home computer with the phone modem on."

"Hey, Roz. Don't you want to know who the arsonist is?"

"Yes. So tell me...who is it?"

"Sean Gilligan. Cowboy Club...."

"Well, I guess he's not going to be running for Selectman any time soon," Roz said smugly. "So, Frank, are you thinking of taking out nomination papers?"

"Not me. I have a restaurant to run and a magazine to put out. I suppose you've heard about it."

"Yes...the kind that always gives their advertisers good reviews."

18

Saturday Morning

"THAT WAS QUITE AN INTERESTING FUNERAL," Fran commented to Sarah as the wind whipped her short, burgundy-colored hair high above her head. "I couldn't quite tell if people were there to see if any of the guilty parties were going to be present or to observe firsthand what state of mind you were in."

"I wish I could have postponed the whole thing," said Sarah, shoving her hands into her jeans pockets. She had forgotten how cold it could get on the beach with the wind coming off of the water. Low tide or no low tide, it was chilly. "Jo made almost all the arrangements," she told Fran, her friend and former lover. "And I wish I could send her the bill." It was easier for Sarah to think of Fran as a close friend. The sexual bond between them was in the past, but it was comforting to feel Fran's arm around her shoulder.

"Frank Chambers was very sweet," Sarah continued. "He and his catering staff helped me clean up the house and remove a few layers of dust before the guests arrived. We certainly couldn't gather over at the Landon house. I don't think I'll ever step foot in there again, bought with ill-gotten money.... All that greed! When everyone duped out of their insurance coverage files their lawsuits, the Landons will probably have to sell the house to pay the bills."

"Too bad you couldn't have held the gathering after the services at a restaurant."

"The Indigo Inn is too small and there's no place to park. I couldn't just set something up someplace else. Frank had already ordered and prepared all the food. And I'd just as soon not had the mass at the Catholic church, but what could I do? Father O'Malley had prepared his sermon...I just had to go with the flow, as Sonny would say."

"Well, it was all pretty funny...your neighbor, Gil Hanover, out there directing traffic."

"It made him feel important."

"So where did Jo get the gun?" asked Fran.

"It was Bill's old military pistol. He filed off the serial numbers and disposed of it, after the fact."

"But how did she learn how to shoot it?"

"Jo was somewhat of a tomboy when she was growing up, even though she always tried to maintain the appearance of doing the 'proper thing.' She used to go hunting with her father. Sonny hated hunting. He told me how once he had shot a rabbit and, when he went to pick it up, discovered she was a nursing mother. There was milk dripping from her breast. It turned his stomach away from shooting anything again. Jo always called him a sissy because of it." Sarah felt a lump well up inside her throat. The tears starting to form in her eyes were making it difficult to see the beachfront ahead.

Fran heard Sarah's voice becoming choked with emotion. "Why don't you come over and have dinner with me and Shauna this evening," she suggested. "Shauna's a great cook, and I promise she won't serve rabbit."

"Can I take a rain check?" Sarah turned her thoughts back to practical matters...the tears would stop if she didn't think about Sonny right now. "Maybe Monday or Tuesday night when the kids are gone. I'm going to stick around to settle some things over the next week, but Cassie and Stephanie are flying home tomorrow with my mom. I promised to take them out tonight to the restaurant of their choice, and it will probably be...." Fran's voice chimed in to join her own. "Sally's Chowder Bowl."

"How did you know?"

"Because you were always telling me how much they like Sally's fried clams and the chowdah," said Fran, imitating a heavy New England accent.

Sarah shook her head. "You have a good memory. You know that? A knack with people and places, young lady. Maybe you should go into advertising," she said jokingly.

"I think I already have, and I'd like to get out of it. Ah well...maybe one more season. Are you coming back this summer?"

"The girls have mentioned they'd like to, if they can invite their friends."

"You have a big enough house."

"I know, but how many parents would be willing to pay the airfare from D.C. to Boston to the Cape? And I've already made arrangements to send them both to camp for a few weeks, Cassie as a counselor-in-training. But for my state of mind, it would probably be good for me to spend one more summer here, partially alone, to sort some things out."

Up ahead, sitting on a blanket, a couple looked out on the view of exposed sandbars, rivulets of water trickling like small streams, seaweed, shells, moorings, exposed logs, and beached boats. From the profile of the man's Roman nose and the woman's long, auburn-colored hair, Fran could tell who they were, even from several hundred yards away: Annie and Beau. Instinctively, she pulled herself slightly away from Sarah, lest they get the wrong idea if they were to turn their heads in their direction. But Beau and Annie were too busy talking, cuddling, and trying to stay warm, while admiring the panoramic view that stretched as far as the eye could see, to pay attention to who happened to be walking on the beach.

"I'm just not sure I like 'Zachary' as a boy's name," Annie was telling her husband. "They'll call him 'Zach' for short, and that sounds kind of zany."

"So he'll be 'Zany Zach,'" Beau joked. "Nice alliteration."

"What about Derek?"

"It sounds too close to 'derelict.'"

"Picky, picky. But we both agree on 'Emily' if the baby's a girl, after my mother?"

"Absolutely," said Beau, kissing the top of Annie's head.

"Beau...," said Annie, gathering up her courage, "...now that the case is solved and you no longer need an alibi, won't you tell me where you were last Sunday night?"

"You really want to know?"

"Yes, I do," Annie told him sternly.

"I was with a couple of guys from Wellfleet who were pumping out that old cesspool over at the rental property on Court Street, clearing away some of the sludge and putting some gravel on the bottom."

"On a Sunday evening?" Annie questioned.

"It was the only time I could get them to come when the neighbors were away...Tim and Lou were returning from their cruise at the end of the week. Early morning is certainly better because you can see what you're doing, but these guys have regular day jobs and I had to get them when I could. They needed me to set up some lights."

"Don't you need some kind of permit?"

"That's the point. No way is the Board of Health going to grant permits to repair old septic systems. You have to construct new ones, according to their regulations."

"So you didn't want to tell the police because that would get you into trouble with the town. But why didn't you just tell me that?"

"Well, I was a little angry at you because I thought you were over-reacting about the dish I broke, so I thought you might also overreact to my not observing the Board of Health's rules. Besides, there's an old saying: 'What you don't know won't hurt you.'"

Almost directly in front of them were Fran and Sarah, walking down by the edge of the tidemark where the bottom trough became lower and the sand wet.

"Hey." Annie waved, trying to flash a warm smile.

Fran and Sarah waved back, being cordial, but kept walking.

Try as she might, Annie knew she was never going to get close to Sarah. They had never really been friends and weren't going to become friends now, perhaps because she was jealous of Sarah. Beau would always speak of Sarah in glowing terms, talking about her cooking and how well she was raising her girls. Perhaps it was because she found Sarah disappointing, someone who could be so much more than just an accomplished homemaker. Well, now she was on her own, working and making a new life that Annie knew nothing about. Whatever the reason, there were other things Annie wanted to focus on...her sculpture, the new baby....

"How about we head home," said Beau, pushing Annie up and off of his lap, kneeling forward, and rising to a standing position. "Man!

My legs were falling asleep," he said while massaging them. "I'll make you a nice brunch. How about some Eggs Benedict?"

"Hmm," said Annie, pushing her hands down into the sand and bending her knees forward to stand. "I'm starting to feel creaky already. They say that happens when you're pregnant. Guess I'll have to start doing some stretching exercises. Eggs Benedict? That sounds great."

A Week Later

"I love the typeface you picked out," Bruno was telling Frank. "It's going to look great!" They were sitting at the dining room table at the Willows Guest House. The morning sun coming through the piece of colored, leaded glass hanging in the front window enhanced everything that was spread out on the long, mahogany table, including the cover design for the *Province Town Crier* and all the pages of proofs lying beside it.

"It does look pretty slick," Frank responded. "But I *am* worried about the money. It's not easy to shell out seven thousand dollars right now, before the tourist season begins, and I especially don't like taking the majority of it from Polly."

"We've got to strike while the iron is hot," Bruno told him. "With the *Observer* office temporarily located in Wellfleet until their building here is repaired from all the fire and water damage, we're in a good position to sell the advertising we need."

"Hey, all Roz has to do is send Fran back to town with a few other salespeople and she's still got the town covered. Plus, now she's building a power base in Wellfleet so she can sell them a separate edition of her paper."

"Frank, don't be such a wimp. This magazine was your idea in the first place.... How's Mike Hammil doing with ad sales?" Bruno asked, deciding the best course of action was to change the subject.

"He's doing great. And he's really a nice guy."

"Oh really!" declared Bruno. "Are you two becoming an item?"

Frank cleared his throat in embarrassment. He didn't particularly want to talk about his romantic life, but how could he smoothly change the subject? Since he felt trapped, he decided to just get it out.... Carefully choosing his words, Frank told Bruno, "I like Mike a lot, but he's made it no secret that he's HIV-positive. He's already had full-blown AIDS, although now it's apparently gone into remission. We're talking about dangerous stuff. I have to be very careful, safe sex to the max, so we're just going to take it nice and slow," Frank stated obliquely. He wondered if it was cowardly for him to talk that way. It wasn't as though he didn't have a trace of the virus himself, running through his own bloodstream. But there were different strains. He'd do the best he could. It would also be nice to have someone to love, for a change.

Charlene's was just a little hole-in-the-wall of a restaurant on the west end of town. Primarily a bar, it had a limited menu of sandwiches, stuffed clams, soup, plus breakfast was served on weekends. Charlene… in actuality, Charlene's daughter…knew how to make a mean omelet, stuffed with buttery sautéed vegetables, not raw like in some restaurants, and juicy tomatoes, chunks of ham, and melted Vermont cheddar cheese. It was "Charlene's Omelet Special," and both Roz and Laura Evans were chowing down, dipping their toasted Portuguese bread into the melted cheese and butter that was oozing from their omelets.

"I don't know how you do it, Roz…," Laura was saying while pulling her shoulder-length, blonde-streaked hair away from her face, "…eating the way you do and keeping so trim."

"It's all my running around," Roz told her. She glanced at Laura, observing that she was not particularly overweight, merely big-boned and full-figured, but nicely proportioned. All women didn't have to be skinny. Roz thought she ought to tell her she was looking good but didn't have time to get the words out before Laura intervened....

"Really…!" said Laura. "Running around with whom?"

"Not *him*," said Roz, shaking her head. "John's been keeping his distance, scared of his wife. Besides, I'm so busy right now. Do I really have the time?" she rationalized, taking a sip of coffee from the white china mug that had been sitting to the right of her plate. "I'm not super-woman. True, I could probably make the time, but with commuting back and forth.... I should probably just let him go. Oh, I don't know what to do, so I'll probably do nothing and just see how it all plays out."

"So tell me, is Susan Stafford going to jail?" Laura asked.

"Hell no. She's not even going to lose her license, because she didn't have a license...yet. Rumor has it that Malgam and Sons Insurance is going to hire her to stay on once their acquisition is complete and all the bookkeeping is straightened out. Something about personnel continuity."

"And here I thought she was going to have to go back to being a hairdresser," Laura said cattily.

"The word is 'beautician,' my dear," said Roz, not be outdone. "People with real talent for dealing with hair are hard to find. But looking at the way she wears hers, I think she should stick with the insurance business and liven up all those dull men in white shirts and dark suits."

"Why, Roz...you certainly are being sarcastic this morning," Laura remarked.

"Yes, I suppose I am being a bit mean. Appearances shouldn't count as much as they do. Susan's not a bad person, just a dim-witted opportunist who happened to get mixed up with the wrong guy." Roz took another sip of coffee and cleared her throat. "I think what I'm really irked about is that Jo may actually get off scot-free with merely a slap on the wrist."

"What!" exclaimed Laura in the midst of swallowing a big bite of her omelet. She started to choke, grabbed a glass of water to swig down a few gulps, and then took a few sips of warm coffee. Her coughing subsided.

"Are you okay?"

"I think it went down the wrong pipe. I'm fine now. What's this about Jo getting away with murder?"

"Well, she's at the 'funny farm' now," Roz said. "Her lawyer's strategy is to plea insanity. They're making all kinds of claims that she was abused as a child, that she's psychotic, unable to distinguish right from wrong, and suffers from some new disease with a fancy name that translates into some sort of compulsive shopping disorder. Meanwhile, her husband, lover boy Bill, is out on bail. Who knows where he got the money to post the bond...probably had an extra bank account stashed away somewhere, plus there's that house. Real estate values keep going up. Anyway, that's justice for you."

"Well," said Laura, "I did read somewhere that when wealthy, educated people commit a crime, even one as serious as murder, they're rarely ever sentenced to the amount of time a poor person is."

"That's our society for you. The degree of guilt in our society is determined by the amount you're able to spend on hiring the best lawyer money can buy. Sean Gilligan will probably lose his liquor license, though. He's another one out on bail. But what's likely to happen is he'll end up selling the club and transferring the license to someone else. I bet he'll serve at least some time in prison, and I don't think he's going to like it there. But he should have considered the consequences before he started setting fires."

"Surely you must have gotten some mileage out of your newspaper story, didn't you?" Laura asked.

"In a backhanded way I did. The forced move to Wellfleet, with the extra edition, has gotten me a lot more readership Up Cape, and that means more advertisers. The one who really scored is Elliot. The *Globe* was so impressed by his articles, his research, and in-depth interviews, they've offered him a job. I think he's going to take it."

"Well, that's a loss. Who's going to be your news editor? Sky?"

"No, I don't think she can handle the responsibility. I'm trying out some new staff writers, and I'll just have to see who has the potential."

"So, how do you like working in Wellfleet?"

"It's not a bad town. A little stodgy. Some people say it's the way Provincetown used to be before it became so commercialized. A lot of refugees have moved to Wellfleet from P-town, you know."

"Meet anyone interesting on your lunch hour, my dear?" Laura asked teasingly.

"Listen, I'm just about chained to my desk. You think I have time to go out for lunch? But there is one interesting man...."

"Yes? Go on...."

"Well, their new shellfish warden is awfully cute."

Made in the USA
Charleston, SC
17 May 2013